Wizard's Holiday

**Diane Duane's
Young Wizards Series**

DIANE DUANE

Wizard's Holiday

Harcourt, Inc.

Orlando Austin New York San Diego
Toronto London

Requests for permission to make copies of any part
of the work should be mailed to the following address:
Permissions Department, Harcourt, Inc.,
6277 Sea Harbor Drive, Orlando, Florida 32887-6777.

www.HarcourtBooks.com

Library of Congress Cataloging-in-Publication Data
Duane, Diane.
Wizard's holiday/Diane Duane.
p.   cm.—(The young wizards series; 7)
Sequel to: A wizard alone.
Summary: While Nita's sister and her dad host three young alien
wizards, teenage wizards Nita and Kit travel halfway across the
galaxy as part of an exchange program and find themselves again
caught up in the dark doings of their nemesis, the Lone Power.
[1. Wizards—Fiction.   2. Extraterrestrial beings—Fiction.
3. Life on other planets—Fiction.   4. Fantasy.]   I. Title.
PZ7.D84915Wm   2003
[Fic]—dc22   2003013263
ISBN 0-15-204771-9

Text set in Stempel Garamond
Design by Trina Stahl

First edition
A C E G H F D B

Printed in the United States of America

For Virginia Heinlein

Contents

Unending stairs reach up the mountain above you,
And you keep climbing, while the welcoming voices
Cheer you along. They make the long climb easier,
Though the gift you're bringing may to you seem small.
Don't worry, it's what they need: For all the cheering,
See how empty the streets are? Take your time.
Make your way upward steadily toward what waits,
Through day's blind radiance to the city's pinnacle,
And fall up the last few steps into empty sky....
    —*hexagram 46, Sheng*
    "Onward and Upward"

"With me, a change of trouble is as good as a vacation."
    —*David Lloyd George (1863–1945)*

What, can the Devil speak true?
    —*William Shakespeare,*
    Macbeth, *I, iii*

*Wizard's
Holiday*

That Getaway Urge

IT WAS THE FRIDAY AFTERNOON before the start of spring break. The weather was nothing like spring. It was cold and gray outside; the wind hissed unrepentantly through the still-bare limbs of the maple trees that lined the street, and in that wind the rain was blowing horizontally from west to east, seemingly right into the face of the girl, in parka and jeans, running down the sidewalk toward her driveway. Except for her, the street was empty, and no one looking out the window of any nearby house was close enough to notice that the rain wasn't getting the young girl wet. Even if someone *had* noticed, probably nothing would have come of it; human beings generally don't recognize wizardry even when it's being done right under their noses.

Nita Callahan jogged up her driveway, unlocked the back door of her house, and plunged through it into the warmth of the kitchen. The back door blew back and slammed against the stairwell wall behind her in a sudden gust of wind, but she didn't care. She pushed the door shut again, then struggled briefly to get her backpack off, flinging it onto the kitchen counter.

"Freedom!" she said to no one in particular as she pulled off her jacket and tossed it through the kitchen door onto the back of one of the dining room chairs. "Freedom! *Free at last!*" And she actually did a small impromptu dance in the middle of the kitchen at the sheer pleasure of the concept of two weeks off from school...though the dancing lasted only until her stomach suddenly growled.

"Freedom and *food*," Nita said then, and opened the refrigerator and stuck her head into it to see what was there to eat.

There was precious little. Half a quart of milk and half a stick of butter; some small, unidentifiable pieces of cheese bundled up in plastic wrap, at least a couple of them turning green or blue because of the presence of other life-forms; way back in a corner, a plastic-bagged head of lettuce that had seen better days, probably several weeks ago; and a last slice of frozen pizza that someone, probably her sister, Dairine, had left in the fridge on a plate without wrapping it, and which was now desiccated enough to curl up at the edges.

"Make that freedom and *starvation*," Nita said under her breath, and shut the refrigerator door. It was the end of the week, and in her family, shopping was something that happened after her dad got home on

Fridays. Nita went over to the bread box on the counter, thinking that at least she could make a sandwich—but inside the bread box was only a crumpled-up bread wrapper, which, she saw when she opened it, contained one rather stale slice of bread between two heel pieces.

"I hate those," Nita muttered, wrapping up the bread again. She opened a cupboard over the counter, pulled down a peanut butter jar, and saw that the jar had been scraped almost clear inside. She rummaged around among various nondescript canned goods, but there was no soup or ravioli or any of the faster foods she favored—just beans and other canned vegetables, things that would need a lot of work to make them edible.

Nita glanced at the clock. It was at least half an hour before the time her dad usually shut his florist's shop on Fridays and came home to pick up whoever wanted to go along to help do the shopping. "I will *die* of hunger before then," Nita said to herself. "Die horribly."

Then she glanced at the refrigerator again. *Aha,* Nita thought. She went to the wall by the doorway into the dining room and picked up the receiver of the kitchen phone.

She dialed. The phone at the other end rang, and after a couple of rings someone picked up. "Rodriguez residence..."

Behind the voice was a noise that sounded rather like a jackhammer, if jackhammers could sing. "Kit? How'd you beat me home?"

"My last-period study hall was optional today...I was finished with my homework so I went home early. What's up?"

"I was going to ask you that," Nita said, raising her voice over the racket. "Is your dad redoing the kitchen or something?"

She heard Kit let out an exasperated breath. "It's the TV."

"It's acting up again?" Nita said. Kit's last attempt to use wizardry to repair his family's new home entertainment system had produced some peculiar side effects, such as the TV showing other planets' cable channels without warning.

"Neets," Kit said, "it's worse than just acting up now. I think the TV's trying to evolve into an intelligent life-form."

Nita's eyebrows went up. "*That* could be an improvement..."

"Yeah, but evolution can have a lot of dead ends," Kit said. "And I'm getting really tempted to end this one with a hammer. The TV says it's meditating...but most things get *quieter* when they meditate."

She snickered. "Knowing *your* electronics, you may need that hammer. Meanwhile, I don't want to talk about your TV. I want to talk about your refrigerator."

"*Uh*-oh," Kit said.

"*Uh*-oh," something inside Nita's house also said, like an echo. She glanced around her but couldn't figure out what had said it. *Weird...* "Kit," Nita said, "I'm dying here. *You* saw what lunch was like today.

Nothing human could have eaten it. Mystery meat in secret sauce again."

"Fridays are always bad in that cafeteria," Kit said. "That's why I eat at home so much."

"Don't torture me. What's in your fridge?"

There was a pause while Kit walked into his kitchen, and Nita heard his refrigerator door open. "Milk, eggs, some of Carmela's yogurt drinks, beer, some of that lemon soda, mineral water, half a chocolate cake, roast chicken—"

"You mean cold cuts?"

"No, I mean half a chicken. Mama made it last night. You've had this recipe before. She rubs it with this hot-smoked paprika she gets from the gourmet store, and then she stuffs it with smoked garlic, and then she—"

Nita's mouth had started to water. "You're doing this on purpose," she said. "Let me raid your fridge."

"Hey, I don't know, Neets, that chicken breast would be pretty good in a sandwich with some mayo, and I don't know if there's enough for—"

"*Kit!*"

He snorted with laughter. "You really need to get your dad to buy more food when he shops," Kit said. "You keep running out on Friday. If he'd just—"

"*KIT!!*"

Kit laughed harder. "Okay, look, there's plenty of chicken. Don't bust your gnaester. You coming over later?"

"Yeah, after we shop."

"Bring a spare hammer," Kit said. "This job I'm doing might need two."

"Yeah, thanks. Keep everybody out of the fridge for five minutes. See you later, bye!"

Nita hung up, then stood for a moment and considered her own refrigerator. "You know what I've got in mind," she said to it in the Speech.

And you keep having to do it, the refrigerator "said." Being inanimate, it wasn't actually talking, of course, but it still managed to produce a "sound" and sensation that came across as grumpy. —

"It's not your fault you're not as full as you should be, come the end of the week," Nita said. "I'll talk to my dad. Do you mind, though?"

It's my job to feed you, the refrigerator said, sounding less grumpy but still a little unhappy. *But in a more usual way. Talk to him, will you?*

"First thing. And, in the meantime, think how broadening it is for you to swap insides with a colleague every now and then!"

Well, I guess you've got a point, the refrigerator said, sounding more interested. *Yeah, go ahead...*

Nita whistled for her wizard's manual. Her book bag wriggled and jumped around on the counter as if something alive were struggling to get out. Nita glanced over and just had time to realize that only one of the two flap-fasteners was undone when the manual worked its way out from under the flap and shot across the kitchen into her hand.

"Sorry about that," she said to the manual. "Casual wizardries, home utilities, fridge routine, please..."

The manual flipped open in her hand, laying itself out to a page about half covered with the graceful curly cursive of the wizardly Speech. "Right," Nita said, and began to read.

The spell went as spells usually did—the workaday sounds of the wind and the occasional passing traffic outside, the soft hum of the fridge motor and other kitchen noises inside, all gradually muting down and down as that concentrating silence, the universe listening to what Nita was saying in the Speech, came into ever greater force and began to assert its authority over merely physical things. The wizardry itself was a straightforward temporospatial translocation, or exchange of one volume of local space for another, though even a spell like that wasn't necessarily simple when you considered that each of the volumes in question was corkscrewing its way through space-time in a slightly different direction, because of their differing locations on the Earth's surface. As Nita read from the manual, an iridescent fog of light surrounded her while the words in the Speech wove and wrapped themselves through physical reality, coaxing it for just a little while into a slightly different shape. She said the spell's last word, the verbal expression of the wizard's knot, the completion that would turn it loose to work—

The spell activated with a crash of silent thunder, enacting the change. Silence ebbed; sound came back— the wind still whistling outside, the splash and hiss of a car going by. Completed, the spell extracted its price, a small but significant portion of the energy presently available to Nita. She stood there breathing hard, sweat standing out on her brow, as she reached out and opened the refrigerator door.

The fridge wasn't empty now. The shelves looked different from the ones that were usually there, and on one of those shelves was that lemon soda Kit had mentioned, a few plastic bottles of it. Nita reached in and pulled one of those out first, opened it, and had a long swig, smiling slightly: It was her favorite brand, which Kit's mom had taken to buying for her. Then Nita looked over Kit's refrigerator's other contents and weighed the possibilities. She had a brief flirtation with the idea of one of those yogurt drinks, but this was not a yogurt moment; anyway, those were Carmela's special thing. However, there was that chicken, sitting there wrapped in plastic on a plate. About half of it was gone, but the breast on the other side was intact and golden brown, gorgeous.

"Okay, you," Nita said, "come here and have a starring role in a sandwich." She reached in, took out the roast chicken, put it on a clean plate, and then unwrapped it. Nita pulled the sharpest knife off the magnetic knife rack by the sink and carved a couple of slices off the breast.

She contemplated a third slice, then paused, not wanting to make too much of a pig of herself.

"*Uh*-oh," something said again.

Nita looked around her, but couldn't see anything. *Something in the dining room?* she thought. "Hello?" she said.

Instead of a reply, there came a clunking noise, like a door being pulled open. "Kit," said a female voice, "what's wrong with the fridge? All the food's gone. No, wait, though, there's a really ugly alien in here disguised as a leaky lettuce. Hey, I guess I shouldn't be rude to it; it's a visitor. *Welcome to our planet, Mr. Alien!*"

This was followed by some muffled remark that Nita couldn't make out, possibly something Kit was saying. A moment later, Kit's sister Carmela's voice came out of Nita's refrigerator again. "*Hola,* Nita, are your phone bills getting too big? This is a weird way to deal with it..."

Nita snickered. "No, 'Mela," she said into the fridge, "I'm just dying of hunger here. I'll trade you a roast chicken from the store later on."

"It won't be as good as my mama's," Carmela said. "But you're welcome to some of this one. We can't have you starving. Hey, come on over later. We can shop."

Nita had to grin at that, and at the wicked twist Carmela put on the last word. "I'll be over," she said.

Clunk! went the door of Kit's refrigerator, a block and a half away. Or three feet away, depending on how you looked at it. Nita smiled slightly, put the chicken back in the fridge, and closed the door. She'd left a verbal "tag" hanging out of the wizardry she'd worked, like a single strand of yarn hanging off the hem of a sweater. Nita said the word, and the spell unraveled itself to nothing.

She went back to the bread box, got those two heel pieces of bread, which no longer looked so repulsive now that the chicken was here, and started constructing her sandwich, smiling in slight bemusement. "Welcome to our planet, Mr. Alien," Carmela had said. Nita absolutely approved of the sentiment. What was unusual was that Carmela had used the Speech to express it.

Nita shook her head. Things were getting increasingly strange over at Kit's house lately, and it wasn't just the electronics—his family, even his *dog*, seemed to be experiencing the effects of his wizardry more and more plainly all the time, and no one was sure why. *Though Carmela's always been good with languages,* Nita thought. *I guess I should have expected her to pick up the Speech eventually, once she started to be exposed to it. After all, lots of people who aren't wizards use it— on other planets, anyway. And at least the lettuce didn't answer her back...* Of course, the fact that it *hadn't* suggested that it should have been in the compost heap several days ago. Nita got up, opened the fridge again, and fished the lettuce out in a gingerly manner. Carmela was right: It was leaking. Nita put the poor soggy thing in the sink to drain—it would have to be unwrapped before it went into the compost—rinsed and dried her hands, and went back to her sandwich.

"*Uh*-oh," said that small voice again.

Wait a minute, I know who that is... Nita stood in the doorway between the kitchen and the dining room, with half the sandwich in her hand, looking around. "Spot," she said, looking around. "Where are you?"

"*Uh*-oh," Spot said.

She couldn't quite locate the sound. *Is he invisible or something?* "It's okay, Spot," Nita said. "It's me."

No answer came back. Nita glanced around the dining room for a moment or so, looking on the seats of the chairs, and briefly under them, but she still couldn't see anything. After a moment she shook her head. Spot was an unusually personal kind of personal computer—he would speak to her and her father occasionally, but never at any length. Probably, Nita thought, this had to do with the fact that he was in some kind of symbiotic relationship with Dairine—part wizard's manual, part pet, part... Nita shook her head and went back to her sandwich. Spot was difficult to describe accurately; he had been through a great deal in his short life. The part of this that Nita knew about—Spot's participation in the creation of a whole species of sentient computers—would have been enough to account for the weird way he sometimes behaved. But he had been constant companion to Dairine on all her errantry after that, and for all Nita knew, Spot had since been involved in stranger things.

There were no further utterances from Spot. "Okay," Nita said, straightening up. "You stay where you are, then... She'll be back in a while."

She sat down at the table and called her manual to her again. *Two weeks of my own,* she thought. *Yeah!* There were a hundred things to think about over the school holiday: projects she was working on with Kit, and things she was doing for her own enjoyment that she would finally have some time to really get into.

She opened the manual to the area where she kept wizardries-in-progress and paged through it idly, pausing as she came to a page that was about half full of the graceful characters of the Speech. But the last line was blinking on and off to remind her that the entry was incomplete. *Oh yeah,* she thought. *I'd better finish this while the material's still fresh.*

Nita sat back and eyed the page, munching on her sandwich. Since she'd first become a wizard, she tended to dream things that later turned out to be useful—not strictly predictions of the future, but scenes from her life, or sometimes other people's lives, fragments of future history. The saying went that those who forgot history were doomed to repeat it; and since Nita hated repeating herself, she'd started looking for ways to make better use of the information from her dreams, rather than just be suddenly reminded of them when the events actually happened.

Her local Advisory Wizard had given her some hints on how to use "lucid" dreaming to her advantage, and had finally suggested that Nita keep a log of her dreams to refer to later. Nita had started doing this and had discovered that the dreams were getting easier to remember. Now she glanced down at the page and had a look at this morning's notes.

Reading them brought the images and impressions up fresh in her mind again. Last night's dream had started with the sound of laughter, with kind of an edge to it. At first Nita had thought that the source of the laughter was her old adversary, the Lone Power, but the voice had been different. There was an edge of malice to this laughter, all right, but it was far less menacing than the Lone One had ever sounded in Nita's dealings with it, and far more ambivalent. And the voice was a woman's.

Then a man's voice, very clear: "I've been waiting for you for a long time," he says. His voice is friendly. The timbre of the voice is young, but there's something behind it that sounds really old somehow. Nita closed her eyes, tried to remember something more about that moment than the voice. *Light!* There was a sense of radiance all around, and a big, vague murmuring at the edge of things, as if some kind of crowd scene was going on just out of Nita's range of vision.

And there was barking, absolutely deafening barking. Nita had to smile at that, because she knew that bark extremely well. It was Kit's dog, Ponch, barking excitedly about something, which wasn't at all strange. What *was* strange was the absolute hugeness of the sound, in the darkness.

The darkness, Nita thought, and shivered once as the image, which hadn't been clear this morning, suddenly presented itself.

"Record," she said to the manual, and sat back with her eyes closed.

Space, with stars in it. Well, you would expect space to be dark. But slowly, slowly, some of the stars seemed to go faint, as if something filmy was getting between her and them, like a cloud, a creeping fog. . . .

Slowly the dark fog had crept across Nita's field of vision. It swallowed the stars. Now that she was awake, the image gave her the creeps. Yet in the dream, somehow this hadn't been the case. She saw it happening; she was somehow not even surprised by it. In the dream, she knew what it meant, and its only effect on Nita had been to make her incredibly angry.

She opened her eyes now, feeling a little flushed with the memory of the anger. Nita looked down at the manual, where the last line of the Speech, recording her last impression, was blinking quietly on and off, waiting for her to add anything further.

She searched her memory, then shook her head. Nothing new was coming up for now. "Close the entry," she said to the manual, and that last line stopped blinking.

Nita shut the manual and reached out to pick up her sandwich and have another bite. It was frustrating to get these bits and pieces and not understand what they meant; but, eventually, when she got enough of them together, they would start to make some kind of sense. *I just hope that it happens in time to be of some use. For sure, something's going to start happening shortly.* The darkness had not "felt" very far away in time. *I'll mention it to Tom when I have a chance.*

Meanwhile, there were plenty of other things to think about. *That Martian project, for example,* she thought as she finished her sandwich. She got up to go into the kitchen and get rid of the plate. *Now that's going to be a whole lot of fun—*

From outside the house came a splash and hiss as someone drove through the puddle that always collected at the end of the driveway in rainy weather. Nita glanced out the kitchen window and saw the car coming up the driveway. *Daddy's a little early,* she thought. *It must have been quiet in the store this afternoon. But where is Dairine? I thought she'd be back by now ...*

Nita ran some cold water from the tap into a measuring cup, filled up the water reservoir of the coffeemaker by the sink, put one of the premeasured coffee filters her dad favored into the top of the machine, and hit the ON switch. The coffeemaker started making the usual wheeze-and-gurgle noises. Outside, the car door slammed; a few moments later, shaking the rain out of his hair, Nita's dad came in—a tall man, silver-haired, big-shouldered, and getting a little thick around the waist; he'd been putting on a little weight these past few months. He was splattered with rain about the shoulders, and he was carrying a long paper package in his arms. "Hi, sweetie."

"Hi, Daddy." Nita sniffed the air. "Mums?" she said. She recognized that slightly musty scent before she saw the rust- and gold-colored flowers sticking out of the wide end of the package.

Her dad nodded. "We had a few left over this afternoon...No point leaving them in the store. I'll find a vase for them." He put the flowers down on the drain board, then peered into the sink. "Good lord, what's that?"

"Lettuce," Nita said. "Previously."

"I see what you mean," Nita's dad said. "Well, that's my fault. I meant to make some salad last weekend, but it never happened. That shouldn't have gone bad so fast, though..."

"You have to put the vegetables in the crisper, Daddy. It's too dry in the main part of the fridge, and probably too cold." Nita sighed. "Speaking of which, I was talking to the fridge a little while ago..."

Her father gave her a cockeyed look. Nita had to laugh at the expression.

"You're going to tell me that the refrigerator has a problem of some kind? Not a mechanical one, I take it."

"Uh, no."

Her dad leaned against the counter, rubbing his face a little wearily. "I still have trouble with this idea of inanimate objects being able to think and have emotions."

"Not emotions the way we have them," Nita said. "Ways they want things to be...and a reaction when they're not. And as for inanimate...They're just not alive the way *we* are." She shrugged. "Just call this 'life not as we know it,' if it helps."

"But it *is* life as *you* know it."

"I just have better equipment to detect it with," Nita said. "I talk to it and it talks back. It'd be rude not to answer, after that. Anyway, Daddy, it's weird to hear *you* say you have a problem with this! You talk to your plants all the time. In the shop *and* here. You should hear yourself out in the garden."

At that, her dad looked nonplussed. "But even the scientists say it's good to talk to plants. It's the frequency of the sound waves or something."

"That's like saying that telling someone you love them is good just because of the sound waves," Nita said. "If you were from Mars and you didn't know how important knowing people loved you was, you might think it was the sound waves, too. Don't you feel how the plants like it when you talk to them?"

"They do grow better," her dad said after a moment.

"*Liking*... I don't know. Give me a while to get used to the idea. What's the fridge's problem?"

"It hates being empty. A fridge's nature is to have things in it for people to eat! But there's hardly anything in it half the week, and that makes it sad." Nita gave her dad a stern look. "Not to mention that it makes *me* sad, when I get home from school. We need to get more stuff on Fridays!"

"Well, okay. But at least—"

"*Uh*-oh," said a little voice.

Nita's dad glanced up, and both of them looked around. "What?" he said.

"It's Spot," said Nita.

"What's the matter with him?"

"I don't know," Nita said. "He's been doing that every now and then since I got home."

"Where is he?"

"I don't know. I looked for him before, but I couldn't see him. Dairine can probably tell us when she gets back. So, Daddy, about the shopping..."

"Okay," her father said. "Your mom was such an expert at judging what we needed right down to Friday afternoon. Maybe I didn't pay enough attention. You probably did, though."

"Uh, no," Nita said, "but I saw her do it often enough that I can imitate what she did until I start understanding the rules myself."

"Fine," her dad said. "That's your job now, then. Let me get out of my work clothes and we'll go out as soon as Dairine gets back."

"Uh-oh," said that small voice again. "Uh-oh. *Uh*-oh!"

"What *is* it with him?" Nita's father said, looking around in confusion. "He sounds like he's having a guilt attack. Wherever he is..."

The *uh-oh*-ing stopped short.

Nita's dad looked into the dining room and spied something. "Hey, wait, I see where he is," he said, and went to the corner behind the dining room table. There was a little cupboard and pantry area there, set into the wall, and one of the lower cupboard's doors was partly open. Nita's dad looked into it. "What's the matter with you, fella?"

"*Uh-oh,*" said Spot's voice, much smaller still.

"Come on," Nita's dad said, "let's have a look at you." He reached down into the bottom of the cupboard, in among the unpolished silver and the big serving plates, and brought out the little laptop computer. It had been undergoing some changes recently, what Dairine referred to as an "upgrade." In this case, upgrading seemed to involve getting smaller and cooler looking, so that a computer that had once been fairly big and heavy was now not much bigger than a large paperback book in a dark silvery case.

Spot, however, had equipment that no other laptop had, as far as Nita knew—not just sentience but (at least sometimes) legs. These—all ten of them, silvery and with two ball-and-socket joints each—now popped out and wiggled and rowed and made helpless circles in the air while Nita's dad held Spot up, blowing a little dislodged cupboard dust off the top of him.

"Some of that stuff in there needs to be polished," her dad said. "It's all brown. Never mind. You got a problem, big guy?"

It was surprising how much expression a closed computer case could seem to have, at least as far as Spot was concerned. He managed to look not only nervous but embarrassed. "Not me," Spot said.

"Well, who then?"

"*Uh*-oh," Spot said again.

Nita could immediately think of one reason why Spot might not want to go into detail. She was reluctant to say anything: It wasn't her style to go out of her way to get her little sister into trouble. *Besides, since when does she need* my *help for that?*

"All right," Nita's father said, sounding resigned. "What's Dairine done now?"

Despite her best intentions, Nita had to grin, though she turned away a little so that it wouldn't be too obvious.

"Come on, buddy," Nita's father said. "You know we're on her side. Give."

Spot's little legs revolved faster and faster in their ball-and-socket joints, as if he were trying to rev up to takeoff speed. "Spot," her dad said, "come on, it's all right. Don't get all—"

With a *pop!* and a little implosion of air that made the dining room window curtains swing inward, Spot vanished.

Nita's dad looked at his empty hands, then looked over at Nita and dusted his palms. "Now where'd he go?"

Nita shook her head. "No idea."

"I haven't seen him do that before."

"Usually I don't see him coming or going, either," Nita said. "But he can do that kind of stuff if he wants to. He's got a lot of the manual in him; wizardry is his operating system, and Spot can probably use it for function calls I've never even thought about." She went into the kitchen and got her backpack off the counter, bringing it into the dining room and dropping it on the table. "He and Dairine aren't usually far apart for long, though. When she comes back, he will, too."

"Did she have a late day today?" Nita's dad said.

"Choir practice, I think," Nita said. "No, wait, that was yesterday. She should be home any minute."

Nita's dad nodded. "Any coffee left from this morning?"

"I threw it out when I left for school," Nita said. "You know what it tastes like when you leave it all day. I just made you some fresh."

"Thanks."

Her dad headed into the kitchen. As he did, the front doorbell rang. "It's probably the newspaper guy," Nita's dad said. "He collects around now. Get that, will you, honey?"

"Sure, Daddy." Nita went to the front door and opened it.

Instead of the *Newsday* guy, Nita found Tom Swale standing there—a tall man in his mid-thirties, dark-haired, good-looking, and one of the Senior Wizards for the New York metropolitan area. He was bundled up in a bright red ski parka and dripping slightly from the rain. "Hi, Nita. I saw the car in the driveway. Is your dad around?"

"Uh, yeah, come on in."

"You need money, Nita?" said her dad from the kitchen.

"Not for Tom, Daddy," Nita said. "He's free." She led Tom into the dining room and took his coat as he slipped out of it, hanging it over the back of one of the chairs. Her dad looked around the kitchen door, slightly surprised.

"Harry," Tom said, "I'm sorry to turn up unannounced like this. Is Dairine around?"

"Uh, not at the moment." Nita's dad suddenly looked a little pale—and Nita wondered whether her dad was thinking back to the last time the local Senior Wizard had turned up on their doorstep asking for Dairine. "It's whatever Dairine's done, isn't it?"

Tom's rueful expression suggested that he understood what was going through Nita's dad's head. "Well, yes. I wouldn't say it was on the scale of previous transgressions. But there's something she needs to take some correction on."

At that, Nita's dad looked somewhat relieved. "A daily occurrence," he said, "if not hourly. Tom, come on in, have a cup of something, and tell me about it."

"Thanks."

They headed past Nita into the kitchen. "By the way, you any good with vanishing computers?" Nita's dad said.

"Please. I have enough trouble with them when

they're visible," Tom said, giving Nita a wink in passing. Nita took this as a signal that she was meant to be elsewhere, so she went into the living room, picked up the extension phone, and dialed.

When Kit picked up the phone this time, the noise in the background was more muted. "Talked to the TV, huh?" Nita said.

"At length," Kit said. "It seems to have worked for the moment."

"Yeah," Nita said, "I had to sweet-talk the fridge a little myself just now."

"You're getting good at that," Kit said. "Used to be you had more trouble with machines."

Nita shrugged. "Experience?" she said. "Maybe I'm changing specialties. Or maybe yours is rubbing off. Look, don't ask me." She lowered her voice. "I was going to say that if the noise is still too much for you over there, maybe you want to find an excuse to come over here for a while. It may not be any quieter, but it's gonna be more interesting."

"Why? What's happening?"

"I don't know, but—" Nita heard something then: a voice, higher than hers, younger than hers, coming up the driveway and singing, more or less to the tune of the chorus of "My Bonnie Lies Over the Ocean," "Two *weeks*! Two *weeks*! I *get* two weeks *off* now, hurray, hurray—"

"Oh, boy," Nita said. "Here it comes!"

The back door opened. "Two *weeks*! Two— *Uh*." There was a soft *bang!* as something materialized in the kitchen without being too careful about air displacement. "*Uh-oh,*" Spot's voice said, sounding panic-stricken.

"Both of you stay right where you are," Nita's dad said.

Nita choked down her laughter. "Can't miss this, gotta go!" she whispered, and hung up.

Dealing with Unforeseen Circumstances

CAREFULLY, INTENDING TO SEEM neither too sneaky nor too enthusiastic about it, Nita made her way into the dining room and sat down very quietly at the end of the dining room table, where she could just see into the kitchen.

Her dad and Tom were leaning against the kitchen counter, coffee cups in hand, looking at a suddenly very subdued Dairine. "I'll give you three guesses," Tom said, "why I'm here."

Dairine leaned against the opposite counter and brushed her red bangs out of her eyes in a way that was meant to look casual, but to Nita's practiced eye, the act was failing miserably. Dairine was freaked.

"And Spot knows, too, I'll bet," Tom said, "which is why he's so skittish all of a sudden. Dairine, you know that as a responsible wizard you have an obligation to tell the people who're still helping you manage your life about what's going on with you...and when you're intending to embark on some course of action that is going to affect them."

"Uh, yeah, well, I was about to—"

"In some cases that information should really reach your family *before* you embark on the course of action, wouldn't you say? Assuming that you want to stay in a good relationship with the Powers That Be. Which right now seems increasingly unlikely."

Nita saw Dairine go so pale that her freckles looked about four shades darker than usual.

Tom put out his hand, and as if from the empty air, his wizard's manual fell into it. It was a manual larger than Nita's, nearly the size of a phone book—but as one of the supervisory wizards for this part of the East Coast, he had a lot more people, places, and things to look after in the course of his practice than Nita did. "Let me read you my copy of a message that doubtless will have reached you via Spot not too long ago," Tom said, looking over his manual at Dairine as he opened the book and paged through it. "And which is doubtless why poor Spot is having a crisis of the nerves. 'To: D. Callahan, T. Swale, C. Romeo: We confirm availability for two of your species in the sponsored noninterventional excursus program at this time. However, your applicant supervisee-wizard's proposal for an excursus is rejected for the following reasons: Durational impropriety. Evasion of local issues. Attempt to circumvent local dirigent authority...'" Tom paused, looking down the page with an expression of annoyed bemusement.

"Actually," he said, "despite the fact that the Powers That Be have listed about twelve other reasons here, those three are probably sufficient for the moment."

"Okay, Tom," Nita's dad said. "For the wizardly challenged among us, this means … ?"

"Dairine," Tom said, taking another drink of his coffee with his free hand, "has signed herself and Nita up for a cultural outreach program."

What? Nita thought, her eyes going wide. She pushed herself very quietly back out of sight of the kitchen, flushing hot in one instant and cold in the next. Then, ever so carefully, she leaned forward again to see what her dad's expression looked like.

He had raised his eyebrows, that was all. "Well, that doesn't sound so bad…"

"Probably not, until you consider that it would have involved them spending ten to fourteen days halfway across the galaxy," Tom said. "Or sometimes somewhere further off… though these young-practitioner exchanges usually stay within a radius of a hundred thousand light-years, for administrative reasons."

Nita watched her dad's expression shift from bemused to slightly concerned. "You mean," he said, "this is like a student-exchange program here on Earth."

"There are similarities," Tom said. "But the similarities also mean that while Dairine and Nita were gone, *you* would have had other wizards staying here with you."

Dairine's father slowly turned his head and trained a look on Dairine that was so blank it was scary.

"I was going to tell you, Daddy," Dairine said in a much smaller voice than previously. "It was just that—"

"You were going to *tell* me, huh?" Nita's father said, in a flat, unrevealing voice that matched his expression. "Not *ask* me?"

Nita swallowed.

"I just thought if I got everything arranged," Dairine said, in a smaller voice yet, "got it all set up, then I could talk to you and we could—"

Dairine's dad looked at her severely. "What?" he said. "You were thinking you'd just present this thing to me as a fait accompli? Bad move."

"Daddy, we've all been—" Dairine stopped. "Some time off would have been really—"

"Uh-huh," Nita's dad said, absolutely without inflection. Out of his view, Nita covered her face with her hands. "Did Nita know anything about this?"

"No." Now Dairine was starting to sound a little sullen. "It was going to be a surprise."

"The message confirms that," Tom said. "It wasn't Nita who was being sanctioned, Harry."

Nita's dad's expression broke enough for him to frown at Dairine. "Well, it didn't sound like Nita's style. But for *your* part, consider yourself lucky that I don't ground you."

"I, however, don't have that much leeway," Tom said. "The message the Powers That Be dropped on *my* head, *after* this one, requires me to restrict you to Sol System for the next two weeks, as a corrective. So consider it done."

"Aww, *Tom!*"

Tom snapped his manual closed and tossed it into the air. It vanished. "Next time," Tom said, "think it through."

Nita's dad gave Dairine that terrible level look again. "Dairine, I think you should go take some private time to consider what you've been up to," he said. "Forget leaving the solar system: For the time being, I don't want you to leave the house. By *any* means, so no doing transport spells in your room, young lady. In fact, I don't think I want to lay eyes on you again till Nita and I get back from doing the shopping. So go on now."

"I really am sorry," Dairine said, very, very low. Nita listened to the words, judging the tone critically, and gave Dairine about a six on a scale of ten for penitence. As Dairine hurried through the dining room past her, Nita kept her face carefully straight, but the glance that Dairine threw at her, knowing their dad couldn't see it, made Nita revise the score about half a point upward. Dairine was angry, but also genuinely sorry.

Dairine vanished through the living room and up the stairs to her bedroom. "And since *you*'ve been sitting there taking all this in..." Tom said through the kitchen doorway. Nita blushed. Tom gave Nita a look that wasn't half as severe as it might have been.

"She really didn't give you any idea that she was up to this?" Nita's dad said, coming into the dining room.

Nita shook her head as Tom and her dad sat down at the table with her. "It was news to me," Nita said. "She doesn't tell me everything she does, not by a long shot. And I can't always guess. Which may be a good thing, since if I'd known about this, I'd have—" *Reamed her out,* Nita was about to say, and then she stopped, because she didn't know if it was strictly true.

She looked over at Tom. "I've seen the section in the manual about this exchange thing," Nita said, "but when I read it, it never occurred to me that you could just sign yourself up for one. I thought someone had to nominate you."

"Oh, not always," Tom said. "You can sign up for it yourself, if you have the spare time and think the circumstances warrant it."

"Which plainly Dairine did," Nita's dad said.

"Harry," Tom said, "I think all we have here is a case of Dairine doing what she usually does: pushing the envelope. Testing. It's not that unusual for an early-latency wizard. You come into your power in a big way, then it drops off in a big way, and afterward you're likely to spend a while plunging around trying to re-define yourself as more than a wonder child. There's always the fear, 'Was that all I had? Was the way I was when I started out as good as I'm ever going to get?' It takes a while to put that to bed."

Nita's dad sighed, leaned back in his chair and drank some coffee, then made a face: It had gone cold. "This hasn't made trouble for you, has it? If it has, I'm sorry."

Tom shook his head. "It's nothing major," he said. "Not compared with some of the sanctioning I have to deal with. The adult wizards are worse than the kids, in some ways: As you get older, there's an unfortunate tendency to start to lose the innate hunger for rules that you have when you're young. Some of us start trying to bend them in ways that aren't always innocuous..."

Nita's dad abruptly burst out laughing. "Whoa, you lost me. *Kids* have an innate hunger for rules?"

Tom looked wry. "Played hopscotch lately?" he said. "One toe over that chalk line and you are *dead*. But let me extend the metaphor more toward adult experience, because one of the places where the rule-hunger does persist is sports. You're a soccer fan, Harry; I see you up at the high school refereeing on weekends. About this weird and complex regulation called the offside rule—"

"I can explain that," Nita's dad said.

"And what's more, you'll *enjoy* explaining it," Tom said. "Possibly as much as you enjoy enforcing it on the would-be violators."

Nita's dad opened his mouth and then shut it again, grinning. "You might be able to convince me about this eventually," he said.

Tom just smiled. "Anyway, this isn't anything that I don't deal with more remotely, twenty or thirty times a week. It just happens that we live around the corner, so I have an excuse to exert my influence personally... and to drink your coffee, which is better than Carl's: He thinks any coffee that doesn't eat the pot is a waste." Tom sighed and leaned back in his chair. "As far as this particular problem goes, it's no big deal. Since we've had the energy authorized for an excursus, I need to think about what to do with it. But that's the least of my worries at the moment."

He ran one hand through his hair as he spoke. Nita looked at it in slight shock; she saw something she'd never noticed before. All of a sudden there was some silver showing there, above the ears, and sprinkled in salt-and-pepper fashion through the rest of Tom's hair. *When did* that *start? Is he okay?*

"Interesting times?" Nita's dad said.

Tom nodded. "Interesting times. The world isn't quite what it used to be, lately ..."

"Most of us have noticed," Nita's dad said. "Come on, let me give you another cup of that; we'll stick it in the microwave. I can't believe how fast this stuff seems to get cold. More milk?"

Her dad and Tom went back into the kitchen. Nita got up and headed upstairs.

Her sister was sitting at her desk, her arms folded, her head down on them. Nita stood there in the doorway, looking at her.

"Are you okay?" she said.

"Oh, yeah," Dairine said, not lifting her head. "See how okay I am. Thanks for asking."

Nita had been practicing ignoring her sister's sarcasm for years and by now was expert at the art. "What was the *matter* with you?" Nita said, though not nearly as loudly as she'd have liked.

There was a long silence before Dairine said anything. "I needed to get away," she said at last. "Just for a while. I needed ... I don't know. Not a vacation. I needed to do something else, somewhere else. Millman said a change would be a good idea if I could swing it.

And for you, too." She gave Nita a look that was almost fierce.

Millman was the school psychologist who had been counseling them both, on and off, since their mom died. "I'll bet he didn't tell you to do anything like *this*," Nita said, annoyed. "You know how it has to look to Dad! He's going to think you don't think he's being a good enough dad or something."

"But it's not like we were going to be away all the time, Neets!" Dairine said. "It's easy to come home at nights if you want to. There's a protocol all set up—the Powers give you an expanded worldgating allowance and everything: You don't have to worry about blowing huge amounts of energy on transport to come back from your host world if you get homesick, or if you need to deal with something else back here. You can be back anytime you need to be, no problem—and the rest of the time, you can concentrate on being where you are."

Nita let out a long breath. "That," she said, "kind of looks like the last thing you were doing, Dair."

Dairine rubbed her eyes with her hands. It was their dad's gesture, helpless and pained, and Nita's insides seized up when she saw it.

"I didn't think it through," Dairine said after a little while. "Tom got that right."

She was quiet for another long time, almost too long, but there was no break in the tension. After a moment, Nita sat down on Dairine's bed. It creaked when she did so.

Dairine threw her a look, though not the one Nita was expecting. "You've been toughing it out all the time," Dairine said, and went back to staring at her desk, all cluttered with diskettes and blank CDs and artwork and paperwork, with the flat-screen monitor of her main computer, and also now with Spot, his legs all retracted, looking as muted and unhappy as Dairine did. "You think I don't see?" Dairine said, reaching out to trace some aimless design on Spot's upper case with one finger. "And when Dad and I can't connect, you're the one who winds up talking sense to him, and to me, and getting us all going in the same direction. But who's there to make things easier for *you*?... You're getting worn out with it. You need a change of pace, something besides worrying about whether we're okay. We're tougher than you think we are. But you..."

Dairine fell silent, possibly unwilling to say what she was thinking. Nita looked at her and felt equally unwilling to force the issue, for she was afraid their thoughts were running in tandem. *How many times have I had this idea myself in the past couple of months?* Nita thought. *How many times have I thought, I wish I were out of here. I wish that just for a few days a week, I was somewhere I didn't have to deal with helping to put everything back together in some new shape, one that doesn't have Mom in it?...*

"Look," Nita said to Dairine after a moment. "You *meant* well. You just have to take these things past the meaning sometimes! Especially when it's Dad. You know what a disciplinarian he is... or thinks he is.

Now that Mom's not here, he thinks he has to be twice as much of one. Have you given any thought to trying to be, you know, *good* for a while?"

Dairine didn't look up, but she snickered, a supremely cynical sound.

It was what Nita had been hoping to hear. "Yeah," Nita said. "Well, think about that, too. You could throw him seriously off balance if you kept at it long enough."

"Yeah," Dairine said after a moment or so. "That might be worth seeing..."

"Do what you can," Nita said. "Give him some relief."

"What about you?" Dairine said.

"What about me *what*?" Nita said, and then abruptly heard in her head what her present English teacher would say to her if she uttered such a sentence in class. Mr. Neary was fiercer about correct grammar than some people were about the eternal battle between Good and Evil.

"*You* could still go," Dairine said.

Nita stared at her sister.

"And you could still take someone else. Say, Kit..."

After a moment, Nita shook her head. "You're crazy," she said. "This thing with Dad is going to take some patching up. There's no way he'd go for it right now..."

But Nita was somehow finding it hard to be as energetic about the refusal as she thought she should have been. Dairine just looked at her, straight-faced, for a moment or two. Finally Nita shook her head once more and got up. The bed creaked again.

"That thing's never recovered from being down that crevasse on Pluto," Dairine said. "Its springs are shot. You owe me a new one."

Nita threw a look back at the desk, at Spot. How a featureless silvery-dark metal case could look less depressed than it had five minutes ago, Nita didn't know, but Spot's did. This reassured her, too, for Spot was a good reflection of Dairine's genuine moods—Dairine might successfully fake what was going on with her, but Spot had no such talent.

"It was *not* down any crevasse," Nita said. "I left it in the middle of a plain of perfectly good frozen nitrogen, high and dry. But who knows, I might read up on the crystal-reconstruction spells in the metals section of the manual over the next day or so, and talk the steel back the way it used to be. I'm getting good with metal, I'm told."

This airy and overconfident statement elicited another snicker, even more cynical than the last one. Nita grinned. She had been a talk-to-the-trees type in the beginning of her wizardry, a specialist in work with organic life-forms, but everything changed eventually.

"You sit here and think about stuff," Nita said. "Be real contrite in case Dad comes in. And when we're gone, if Dad hasn't done it already, make a little effort to get on his good side by taking that poor lettuce out of the sink and sticking it in the compost heap. It's time it got recycled into something alive to make up for what happened to it in the fridge."

"Sure."

Nita went softly down the stairs and headed toward

the dining room. Voices were speaking there. She stopped not far from the stairs, out of sight.

"I'm parenting for two here, Tom," Nita heard her dad say.

"I know," Tom said quietly. "It can't be easy."

"I don't want to be hard on her. But at the same time, I have to try to keep some semblance of normalcy around here…keep some structures in place that the kids know they can depend on." There was one of those pauses in which Nita could practically hear her father rubbing his face.

"You're doing the right thing," Tom said, getting up. "You know you are. In the meantime, Harry, any time you need a friendly ear, you know our number. One or the other of us is almost always around. Wizardry isn't all about errantry. Mostly it's just talking."

"I know," her dad said. "I see that here a lot—"

There was a knock at the back door. Nita heard her dad's chair scrape back as he went to answer it. "Oh, hi, Kit," her dad said. "Come on in. I can't get used to it, the times when you walk over: I keep expecting you to just appear out of nothing in the living room, as usual." Her dad laughed then. "'As usual…'"

"Uh, hi, Mr. Callahan. No, I didn't want to, be-cause…"

Tom got up as Nita put her head around the living room door into the dining room. "News travels fast, huh?" Tom said to her as the back door shut behind Kit.

"Uh, yeah," Nita said. She picked up Tom's jacket,

which was still wet, and shook it off before handing it to him. Residual water went everywhere. "Why didn't you keep the rain off you when you came over?" she said.

"I don't always do wizardry just because I can," Tom said, smiling slightly and shrugging into the parka. "An attitude toward errantry that you'll understand a lot better when you're my age. Besides, I like the rain. By the way, how's the reading coming?"

When Tom asked Nita this, she knew it didn't have anything to do with fiction. Nita had been spending a lot of time with the manual over the past months, starting to explore for herself the kind of "research" wizardry that Tom did. In particular, she had been studying the Speech more closely, mostly for its own sake—there was always something new to find out about the language in which the Universe had been written—but also with an eye to finding other ways to deal with the Lone Power than just brute force. "I've been doing some more research on the Enactive and pre-Enactive modes," Nita said. "Ancillary Oaths and bindings."

"Oh ho," Tom said. "That'll keep you busy for the next couple of years...There's a lot of finicky material there. A lot of memory work, too. Hit the Binding Oath yet?"

"Some references to it," Nita said. "But I haven't seen the Oath itself."

"It's worth a look," Tom said. "Our own Oath is based on it. Or maybe I should say closely related. It's worth studying, even if its uses are limited. Meanwhile, we've got more immediate problems than research." He glanced back toward the stairs. "Talk to her, will you?"

"I did."

"Good. See you later. See you, Kit."

Tom went out the front door and closed it behind him.

"Honey," Nita's dad said, "I need to change out of my work clothes. Give me a few minutes."

"It's such a pleasure to get out of the house," Kit said. "The phone hasn't stopped ringing all afternoon."

"Why?"

"Carmela. Every five minutes it's yet another of her slavering horde of boyfriends."

"I didn't think she'd gotten up to the 'horde' level," Nita said. "She told me she was just planning to test the wonderful world of dating."

"*Test?*" Kit said. "It's more like she's holding auditions. There's a new one on the phone every ten minutes. And I really don't want to be around when she narrows them down to the 'short list.' Being here is a relief...even just for a little while. So are you coming over for dinner?"

Nita sat down and reached across the table for a pen and a pad of sticky notes, pulling off the top note and starting to jot down a list of needed groceries. "We have to go shop first. I'll come over when we get back. We've really got to talk about the next couple of weeks."

"That business on Mars," Kit said as he sat down

across from her. "We need to get that taken care of before it gets out of hand. Those depth charges in Great South Bay...It's time to get together with S'reee and the rest of the deep-side team to deal with those before they get any more unstable. And then there's that gate-relocation thing in the city..."

Kit paused, glancing toward the back of the house as he heard the bedroom door close. "It was Dairine, yeah?" Kit whispered.

"Yeah."

"What did she *do*? What did Tom do?"

"He grounded her. She can't leave the system."

Kit whistled softly. "What about your dad?"

"I thought he was going to lose it completely," Nita said, under her breath. "He sent her to her room. I can't even *remember* the last time he did that."

"What did she *do*?" Kit said.

Nita finished with the sticky note, then put the pen down and told him. Kit's eyes slowly went wide.

"Wow," Kit said. "Halfway across the galaxy, he said?"

"Yeah," said Nita.

"That'd really be something. You don't get to do a transit like that every day, and this would be a *sponsored* one! Think of being able to go that far and not have to pay for the energy."

Nita had been thinking of it, in an idle way. "Halfway across the galaxy" was forty-five thousand light-years or so. If you independently constructed a spell to do that kind of distance, it would really take it out of you.

And doing such a transit using a previously set-up world-gate had its costs, too—you needed a good reason to do it, such as being formally "on errantry."

"It's a shame you couldn't go, anyway," Kit said.

"Oh, come on," Nita said. "I couldn't go now."

"Why not? It's spring break. We've got two whole weeks off!"

Nita frowned, shook her head. "It wouldn't be right somehow. My dad—"

"Your dad wouldn't mind," Kit said. And then his expression went very amused. "Come to think of it, *my* dad wouldn't mind."

Nita looked at Kit in confusion. "What?"

"You haven't been over in the past couple of days," Kit said. "Between Carmela and Ponch—"

"Oh no," Nita said. "What's Ponch doing now?"

"Wait till you come over," Kit said, looking rather resigned. "It'll be easier for you to see than for me to explain. But when I told my pop that we were going to have to go to Mars, he said, 'Don't let me keep you.'"

Nita stared at Kit in surprise. "I bet your mama didn't say that, though."

Kit's grin had a slight edge to it. "No. My mama suggested I go take a look at Neptune while I was at it, and not hurry home."

Nita snickered. "Seriously," Kit said. "This would be really neat. If we went to see Tom…"

They heard the door to Nita's dad's bedroom open. "Look," Nita said, "let's talk about it later. But I don't think—"

Nita's dad came in from the living room. "You ready?" he said to her.

"Yeah," Nita said, getting up. "Daddy, can I have dinner at Kit's?"

"Sure," her dad said. "Kit, she'll see you later. Neets, let's get this shopping done."

Fifteen minutes later, Nita and her dad walked in the sliding doors of the grocery store. The way things had gone in the old days, on occasions when the whole family went to the store together, it had been Nita's dad's job to push the cart and make helpful suggestions: Her mom had done the choosing. Nita now sighed a little as her dad went for the cart, and she consciously took on the choosing role for the first time. When shopping before, she had been rather halfhearted about it, which possibly had been the cause of some of the trouble. *I guess I owe the fridge a little apology,* she thought, and got out the sticky-pad page on which she'd made her list.

They went down the vegetable aisle and got potatoes, celery, tomatoes, and a head of lettuce, which Nita very pointedly handed to her dad. "The crisper this time," she said. "He's counting on you."

" 'He'?" Nita's dad said, turning the lettuce over several times in his hands and looking at it closely. "How can you tell?"

"If you're a wizard, you can look at the gender equivalent of the word *lettuce* in the Speech," Nita said. "Or, on the other hand, you can just *ask* him."

"I'd probably prefer to pass on that second option," Nita's dad said as they came to the cold cuts and prepackaged meats. "I don't know if I'd want to talk to something I might eat."

"Daddy, this might sound weird to you," Nita said, looking for her preferred brand of bologna, "but some things are less upset about being eaten than they are about being wasted."

"Ouch."

Nita looked at her dad in sudden shock. "Daddy, I'm sorry, I didn't mean it that way."

Her dad smiled slightly as they turned into the next aisle. "I didn't think you did. But sometimes 'ouch' is a healthy reaction. Or so I hear."

"You've been talking to Tom again," Nita said.

"No, Millman. Never mind. We need some pizzas." Her father paused in front of a freezer case.

"Yeah." Nita picked a pizza from the freezer compartment. The front of it was full of images of ancient stone ovens. Nita turned it over and started reading the ingredients. "This is disgusting," Nita said. "Look at all the junk they put in this!"

"That's probably why they call it junk food."

"Used to be that just meant the empty calories," Nita said. "These days..." Not even this year's unit on organic chemistry had prepared her to cope with some of the ingredient names on that label. Nita made a face and put the package back. "I'm not sure I want to be eating so many things I can't pronounce."

"Home cooking means a lot more work..."

"I know," Nita said. "I'm beginning to see why

Mom was so intense about it. I guess I'm just going to have to learn."

They turned into the paper-towels-and-toilet-paper aisle, and Nita's dad put a couple of the giant economy-size bundles of toilet paper in the cart. "It has been tough, hasn't it?" her dad said.

Nita sighed and nodded. "It hurts sometimes," she said after a moment. "Hurts pretty bad." Then, having a sudden thought, she added, "But not so much that I need to leave the planet for extended periods."

Her father looked thoughtful. "You sure about that?" he said.

Nita looked at him, uncertain what was going through his mind.

"What are other kids at school doing over spring break?" he said.

Nita shrugged. "Some of them are going away," she said. Among a few of her friends there had been excited talk of family vacations, trips to Florida or even, in one or two cases, to Europe. These by themselves had left Nita unimpressed, for travel by itself was no problem for a wizard. You could be planets or star-systems away from home in a matter of minutes or hours, depending on whether you used private or public transport. But the idea of being able to get away with the family, even for just a few days, had an entirely different attraction. Unfortunately, this was the busy time of year for Nita's dad. Even though the craziness of Valentine's Day was over, it would be Easter soon, and no florist in his right mind took a vacation right now.

"It doesn't matter, Daddy," Nita said. "Kit and I

have a lot of stuff we've been planning to do. We might need to travel, but not far. No farther than Mars, anyway. It'll be nice to just kind of take it easy for a while. Don't worry about it."

"I'm not worrying," said her dad. But there was a strangely neutral sound to his voice, and Nita didn't know quite what to make of it.

"Daddy," Nita said, "are you okay?"

"Sure, honey," he said.

Nita wasn't so sure, but she didn't say anything. She and her dad went to the checkout, paid for the groceries, bagged them up, and carted everything out to the car. Then they headed for home.

They were only a few minutes away from the supermarket when Nita's dad said, "There were going to be aliens in the house?"

Nita's thoughts had been occupied with the weather on Mars this time of year, and the question took her by surprise. "Uh, yeah," she said. "It *is* an exchange program."

"Not incredibly strange aliens, I take it."

"Well, they'd have to be able to handle the basic environment," Nita said. "Our atmosphere, our gravity. That doesn't mean they'd be humanoid; there's a lot of variation in body structures among the kinds of carbon-based life that breathe oxygen. Anyway, whoever these guys were supposed to be, they might *look* pretty weird. But that wouldn't matter. If they're wizards, we'd have the most important stuff in common."

Her dad looked thoughtful. "They wouldn't be, you

know, saving the world or anything while they were here?"

Nita wondered what he was getting at. "I don't think so," she said. "The manual says it's supposed to be a chance to see what the practice of wizardry looks like in some place really different, so that you get some new ideas about how to handle it at home. You're never formally sent out on errantry when you're on one of these, or so the manual says. If something minor comes up in passing, sure, you handle it. Otherwise..." She shrugged. "Pretty much you take it easy."

Her dad nodded, stopped the car at a traffic light. "We did get the milk, didn't we?"

"Plenty."

"I keep having this feeling that I've forgotten something."

Nita pulled out her Post-it note and once again compared it against the list in her head. "No," she said. "I don't think so..."

Her dad brooded briefly. "This is going to drive me crazy until I remember what it is I think I forgot," he said. "Never mind. Nita, why don't you go?"

"Where, to Mars?"

"No. On this exchange."

Nita stared at him.

He glanced back at her. Then the traffic light changed to green, and her dad turned his attention back to his driving.

"Are you *kidding*?" Nita said.

"No," said her dad, turning the corner off Nassau Road onto their street.

At first Nita didn't know what to say. "Uh, I don't know if I can," she said at last. "Tom may already have used the energy for something else."

"Somehow I doubt that," her father said.

"Did you talk to him about this?" Nita said, still very confused.

"In generalities, yes," her dad said. "I doubt you would have heard it, as you were occupied. I could hear you sneaking up the stairs."

"Uh, yeah," Nita said, "okay..."

"Well?"

Nita was flummoxed. "But, Daddy," she said at last, "what about the aliens?"

"They're wizards, you said."

"Yeah, but—"

"And they'll be able to disguise themselves, so the neighbors won't get into a panic and call the cops or the FBI or anything like that?"

"Daddy, I think you've been watching too much TV. I don't think the FBI really does aliens."

"So these other wizards can cover up for themselves?"

"Well, sure, that would be part of it, lots of times you have to do that when you're on another planet, but—"

"And Dairine will be here. From what you've told me, Dairine doesn't have any trouble with aliens."

Nita thought about that. Dairine's response to aliens could range from partying with them to blowing them up, but so far she didn't seem to have misjudged how to handle any given situation involving sentient beings who *weren't* human. It was her own species she seemed to have trouble with. "No, she does okay."

"I hear another 'but' coming," her father said, as they paused at the last traffic light before their block.

"I don't know if this is a good time to go away and leave you alone," Nita said at last.

"If Dairine's here, I won't be alone," her dad said.

"I mean—"

"Sweetie," said her dad, "I think maybe a break would be a smart thing for you right now. Dairine and I would be capable of coping here. And among other things, it'll give me a chance to practice talking to her *without* a mediator. Possibly a useful life skill."

Nita smiled half a smile. "You really have been talking to Millman," she said.

"About this? No. Some things I can figure out for myself. I *am* forty-one, you know."

"Uh, yeah," Nita said, and then was quiet for a moment.

"You need time to think about this?" her dad said. "Maybe the thought of going so far away scares you a little?"

"Daddy!" Nita said. "I've been a lot farther away than this."

"On 'business,' yes," her dad said. "But this is different. Honey, you ought to be a little kinder to yourself. Go on, goof off a little! You deserve it. And maybe I could use a little controlled weirdness. Sounds like that's what we'd be in for." And he threw Nita a sly look. "Also, it's a way to give Dairine a little something on the sly to make up for me, and your friends the Powers That Be, slapping her down so hard. Yeah?"

You are such a softie, Nita thought, with a sudden great rush of love for her dad. "Okay," Nita said. "Thanks, Daddy!"

"One thing," her dad said. "I really would be happier if Kit was with you. You two've been pretty good backup for each other in the past, and he's worked hard, too. I don't think a break from routine would hurt him, either. Obviously it's going to be up to his folks, but when you go over there, see what they think."

Without knowing how she knew, Nita was already certain of what they'd think. "You talked to them about me going already!" Nita said. "When you didn't even know what I was going to say!"

Her dad shot her another amused look. "We have many mysterious modes of communication," he said as he signaled the turn into their driveway. "Aided by the fact that not even children who are wizards can keep an eye on their parents *every* minute of the day."

Nita had to grin as the car splashed through the puddle at the bottom of the driveway. "Let's get this stuff unpacked," her dad said. "Then you'd better go talk to Kit and make plans."

Planning Your Trip

KIT WAS SITTING IN HIS room, riffling through his wizard's manual, frowning in concentration and trying not to be distracted by the sound of his dog's snoring, when his sister stuck her head in through the open doorway. "You busy?" Carmela said.

Kit sighed, pushed back from the desk. "No. What is it?"

"You *are* busy," his sister said, walking carefully around Ponch, who had stretched his big black self right across the rug in the middle of the floor and was lying there with his paws in the air, taking up most of the spare floor space in the room. "Good, I'll hang around and make you crazy." She leaned over his shoulder, so far over that her single long dark braid hung down in front of Kit's face. "What's that little red glowing thing in the air there?"

"Just a wizardry. I'm playing with the speed of light."

"I thought that was supposed to be a law," Carmela said. "You shouldn't break laws."

"I'm not. I'm not even bending this one," Kit said. "Just bending space."

"For the *fun* of it," his sister said in wonder. "You make my brains bleed sometimes, you know that?"

"Not half as much as I wish I did," Kit said. "'Mela, what *is* it?"

She turned away, sat down on Kit's bed, and grinned. "I wanted to know what you thought of Mark."

Endless possible answers spun through Kit's mind, all of them true, but none of them particularly kind. He settled for one of the less injurious ones. "He looks like a dork," Kit said.

"How cruel!" Carmela cried. Then she smiled, and the smile was wicked. "True, but cruel."

"It's the backward baseball cap," Kit said. "I'm sorry, but that's getting pretty ancient. Plus his cap's too small for him, and the pop-fasteners in it always leave these marks like little rivets on his forehead—" Kit stopped himself. *I'm seriously discussing my sister's would-be boyfriends,* he thought. *This is* not *something I want her to get used to.* "Listen," Kit said, "there's something more important than this that we need to discuss. You've been having a lot of fun with the TV ..."

"Since you fixed it so it shows alien cable," his sister said, "I've revised my opinion of you way upward."

"That concerns me so deeply," Kit said. The "fix" hadn't been intended to add that particular feature to the new entertainment system, but when Kit had later tried to remove the alien content, the TV and DVD player had gone on strike. Kit had been forced to re-store the system, and had had to admit privately that his sister's demands that it be put back the way it'd been after the "fix" were even more annoying than the system's refusal to function normally.

"So what's your problem?" his sister said.

"We need to talk about that first thing you ordered off the Mizarthu shopping channel."

"Which thing?"

"The laser dissociator."

"Oh, that! It's in my bedroom somewhere."

Kit sighed. It sometimes seemed that the contents of whole planets could be accurately described as "in Carmela's bedroom somewhere." "Where, exactly?"

"I don't know. I'll look for it later; I'm busy right now. What's the matter with it?"

"I need to make it safe."

"From what?"

Kit rolled his eyes. "Not from," he said, "*for*. As in, safe for being on the same planet with."

"Oh, come on, Kit. There haven't been any prob-lems since we figured out where the safety switch was."

There haven't been any problems, Kit thought, his eyes nearly crossing with frustration. Repairing the tile and the plastering in the bathroom had been a week's work, at a time when he had much better things to do—and his pop had insisted Kit do it the "old-fashioned way," meaning by hand and not by wiz-ardry. "There was nearly a problem," Kit said, "when you thought you had it set for 'hot curler' and it was set for 'low disintegrate.'"

"I got that sorted out," Carmela said. "You always have to harp on the small stuff! I thought that wasn't good for a wizard."

I will not kill her, Kit thought. *It would speed up entropy.*

But only a little...

Kit let out a long breath. "Just find it for me in the next day or so, okay?" he said. "You can still use it on your hair, but I want to make sure that nobody else, like one of your friends when they're over, can find it accidentally, go off with it, and blow up their bathrooms. Or more valuable real estate, like the insides of their heads."

An odd look grew on Carmela's face. "Like the inside of *my* head isn't valuable?"

Kit gave her a dry look. His sister opened her mouth.

"Left yourself open for that one," Kit said. "And another thing. These alien chat rooms you've been using..."

"You're just jealous because I'm getting good at the Speech," Carmela said, producing a pouting expression resembling that of a cranky supermodel.

Kit rolled his eyes. "No, I'm not jealous. I just think you should be careful about who you talk to!" he said. "It's like any other kind of Net chat. What they show you and what they sound like may not have anything to do with who or what they really are."

"I know that!"

"I don't think you know how much you *don't* know

that! I don't want you thinking you're having harmless clothes-and-hair-and-pop-star talk with some alien girloid, and then have Earth get invaded because it turns out you were actually talking to some twelve-legged, methane-breathing centipede prince who's decided to turn up with a battle fleet and demand your hand in marriage!"

Carmela's face wrinkled up. "*Euuuuuu,*" she said. "Centipedes. You just said the unmagic word."

Kit kept his face straight. His sister was not wild about bugs of any kind, and he knew it. "So don't give people in alien chat rooms your real name or address or anything, okay?" he said.

"Okay," Carmela said with a long-suffering sigh. Then she looked curious. "What *is* the Earth's address, by the way?"

"I'm not telling you," Kit said.

"You don't trust me!"

"No. And, anyway, it's complicated, and you don't have the technical vocabulary to say it."

"Yet," Carmela said. "I don't think it's going to take me that long. And once I'm really good at the Speech, maybe I should look into becoming a wizard, too."

"It doesn't work that way," Kit said, feeling incredibly relieved that it didn't. Yet the very idea still freaked him out somewhat. *Just what I need. My very own version of Dairine . . . ! Oh, please, no.* "You can't be a wizard unless the Powers invite you," Kit said. "And you're too old." *Oh, please, let her be too old!* "Besides, it's a lot of hard work."

"I'm not sure I believe that," Carmela said. "*Nita* makes it look easy. She just reads out of her book, or waves that little white wooden wand of hers, and things happen."

"It is *not* that easy," Kit said, starting to get irritated, possibly by the insinuation that wizardry was easier for Nita than it was for him. "It's like saying that someone just sits down at their computer and fiddles with the keys and things happen. Wands are just hardware. At the end of the day, it's the software that does the job . . . and you have to write it yourself."

Carmela gave Kit a not-entirely-convinced look. "Well," she said, getting up, "I'll go get the thingy for you."

Downstairs, the phone rang. "In a while," Carmela said as she ran out, pounding down the hall. "And when you're playing around with it," she added from halfway down the stairs, "*make sure you don't void the warranty!*"

Kit felt like banging his head against the wall. "The warranty," he said to no one in particular. "Why should she care about the warranty?"

He looked down at Ponch and heaved a sigh. Ponch opened one eye.

"You weren't asleep," Kit said.

Not the whole time, Ponch said silently.

"What am I going to do with her?"

Ponch looked after her. *Ignore her. She's just saying things like that to make you chase your tail; I can hear it in her voice. She thinks it's fun.*

Kit shook his head. "The problem with sisters is that

you can never tell what they're going to pull next. And she's been getting...*unusual* lately."

Then Kit wondered if he should have chosen another word. Ponch, too, had been getting unusual lately. This by itself wasn't a surprise—wizards' pets often start to acquire strange abilities or behaviors as their companions use their wizardry more, but in Ponch's case, the level of unusual had become very high indeed. Here was a dog who recently had developed the ability to create a new universe and take Kit for a walk through it. *And you have to wonder,* Kit thought, *is someone who can do that really a dog anymore?*

Ponch rolled to his feet, got up, stretched fore and aft, and then came over to Kit and put his nose on Kit's knee. *Dinner?* Ponch said.

Kit laughed. Whatever his own concerns, there were still some things about Ponch that were entirely doggy. "Yeah," he said. "Come on."

The two of them went downstairs together. Kit's mama was slumped on the dining room sofa reading a newspaper, dressed in one of her pink nurse's uniforms; she was just back from the day shift at the local hospital and hadn't yet bothered to change. In the living room, Carmela was on the phone, talking rapidly about some new CD to what Kit assumed was yet another of the crowd of guys who were chasing her around. "Mama," Kit said, "when's dinner ready?"

"About an hour. Nita coming?"

"She said so, yeah."

"Okay. You feed the monster there?"

"I'm doing that now."

"You looked outside yet?"

"Not yet," Kit said, with dread. He was sure he knew what he was going to see.

As they went into the kitchen together, Ponch started alternating between dancing around and spinning in circles on the same spot. *Dinner!*

"Yeah," Kit said, "and you know what it is?"

What?

"It's dog food!"

Oh, hurray! Dog food again! Ponch said, and jumped up and down some more; but Kit caught the amused glint in his eye.

Kit got a can of dog food out of the cupboard where the canned goods were kept. "You making fun of me?" Kit said.

His eyes on the can, Ponch sat down, very proper, with his front feet placed so that the white tips on his forefeet came right together, making him look extremely composed and serious. *Never,* Ponch said. *At least, not at dinnertime.*

Kit opened the can and dumped it into Ponch's dish, filled the dry food dish, and checked to make sure that there was plenty of water in the bowl beside it. Ponch jumped up again, turned around in excited circles a few times more, and then went over to the dish and started to gobble his food.

Kit shook his head and rinsed out the can at the sink before throwing it out. In the living room it had gone quieter as Carmela got off the phone and went back to talking to the TV, or rather to someone the Powers That Be only knew how many light-years away. From the sound of it, she was translating a subtitled display rather than listening to live Speech, but at the moment, this didn't seem to be helping her much. "What?" Kit heard her say. "Do I what? Do I *grenfelz*? Uh, I don't think so. No, I am *not* shy! Okay then, show me an image—"

There was a moment's silence, after which Carmela dissolved into uncontrollable laughter. Kit was incredibly tempted to go see what she was looking at. *I won't do it,* he thought. *She'll get the idea I'm trying to chaperone her, and she'll give me all kinds of grief.*

And I would *be trying to chaperone her*—

Kit went to look out the kitchen window again. He'd done this earlier, when he'd just come back from Nita's and Ponch had still been asleep. Then, the sidewalk outside their house had been empty. Now, though, it was full of dogs.

There were at least ten of them. Most were neighborhood dogs: various multicolored and multisized mutts, the big blue-merle collie from the Winchesters' place down the block, a pair of bulldogs from two streets over, and even the dysfunctional little terrier from three houses down, Tinkerbell—the one who normally threatened, in unusually fluent dog-language, that if he ever got out of his yard, he'd rip Kit's throat out. Yet there he was, sitting peacefully on the sidewalk and gazing at the Rodriguez house as intently as all the other dogs were. The big silvery Great Dane from down Nita's street, sitting next to Tinkerbell and as intent on the house as he was, shifted position slightly and put one huge foot on Tinkerbell's rear end, nearly squashing him flat. Tinkerbell just wriggled out from under, shook himself, sat down again, and resumed staring at the house.

Kit let out an annoyed breath.

"Are they still out there?" Kit's mama said from the dining room couch, turning a page of the paper.

"Yeah," Kit said.

"Remember our little talk the other day?" Kit's mama said, her voice just slightly edgy.

"Yeah, Mama. I'm working on it."

"Well, work harder."

Kit turned away from the window, annoyed. He had spent some weeks in consultation with Tom Swale on the question of what was causing the increasing weirdness around his house. The best explanation Tom had been able to come up with was "hypermantic contagion syndrome," an irritatingly vague suite of symptoms usually more casually described as "wizardry leakage." Days of perusing his manual had left Kit completely in the dark as to exactly what kind of wizardry, or whose, was leaking, from where, into what...and until he figured those things out, there was no stopping the leak.

Kit looked out at the dogs and sighed. At least they were quiet at the moment. But they tended not to stay that way. And when they started making noise and drawing the attention of the whole neighborhood, his folks got tense. It wasn't that they'd started giving him trouble about his wizardry as such. But the Rodriguez house used to be a fairly quiet and peaceful place, before the past month or so. Before the dogs, that is. Before the TV began evolving. Before Carmela became a boy magnet. The noise wasn't his fault, and Kit had pointed out more than once that there was nothing he could do about the amount of noise Carmela made— the number of times the phone rang in a given day was hardly anything to do with wizardry. But any time Kit said this, his mom would just glance first at the TV, which *did* have something to do with it... and then she'd look out the window to where half the dogs in the neighborhood were sitting, gazing at their house as if it were full of top sirloin, or something even more important. And then the howling would start—

Kit turned away from the kitchen window. "Ponch," he said softly to his dog, "they're all out there again."

I keep telling them they shouldn't do that, Ponch said silently, concentrating on licking his bowl clean. *And for a while, they don't. But then they forget.*

"But *why* are they doing it?"

I don't know. I keep asking them, but they don't understand it, either. They're not so good at figuring things out. Ponch looked up, licking his chops. He sounded faintly aggrieved. *I'll let you know when I figure out what's on their minds.*

"Well, hurry up and do what you have to do to find out," Kit said. "And when you go out there, tell them no howling!"

They like to sing, Ponch said, sounding a little injured. *I like it, too. Even Carmela likes to sing. What's the matter with it?*

Kit closed his eyes briefly. His sister's singing voice was, to put it kindly, untrained. "Just tell them, okay?" Kit said.

Okay . . .

Ponch turned his attention back to the bowls, starting a long, noisy, sloppy drink of water. From the living room, Kit heard Carmela start laughing again. Grenfelzing, Kit thought. *Should I be worried that my sister is being invited to* grenfelz? *I just hope this isn't something that's going to rot her morals somehow . . .*

From down the street, Kit could faintly hear the sound of a familiar car engine coming toward the house: his dad, coming back from the printing plant three towns over where one of the bigger suburban New York newspapers was produced. The station wagon pulled in and parked. A few minutes later, Kit's father came in the back door, pulled his jacket off his burly self, and chucked it at the new coat tree by the back door, which Kit's mama had bought a few weeks before. The coat tree swayed threateningly, but for once it didn't fall over—Kit's pop was getting the hang of the maneuver. "Son, they're out there again," he said as he came through the kitchen.

"I know, Pop," Kit said. "Ponch is working on it. Aren't you?"

There was no reply. Kit looked over at Ponch, who had left the water bowl and turned his attention to the neighboring bowl of dry, crunchy dog food. He was now steadily eating his way through it with an air of total concentration.

Kit's pop sighed as he came into the dining room, leaned over Kit's mama (now sprawled out on the sofa) to smooch her, and took the newspaper from her, straightening up to glance out the window of the dining room. "It's like being in a Hitchcock movie," Kit's pop said, "except I don't think he would have gotten the same effect if he'd covered someone's front yard with sheepdogs and Great Danes. Whose sheepdog *is* that? I've never seen it before."

"I don't know, Pop. I could go ask it."

"Look, son," Kit's dad said. "Don't bother. Just ask Ponch to have another word with them, okay? Otherwise we're going to have the neighbors over here again, in a group, like last time... and I have a feeling this time they might think about bringing torches and pitchforks."

"I asked him, Pop. He'll go out when he's finished his dinner."

"Right. When's ours, honey?"

"Three-quarters of an hour."

"Then I'm going to go sit down and read this awful rag," Kit's pop said, "and see if I can figure out what's wrong with the world." He walked into the living room, leaving Kit wondering yet again why his dad was so unfailingly rude about the newspaper he worked for as a pressman. "Carmela, what are they doing there?"

"*Grenfelzing.*"

"Really. What's the fire hose for?"

"I don't think it's a fire hose, Popi..."

"Oh, my *lord*—" Kit's pop said.

The phone rang again. Halfway to the living room, Kit dived back into the kitchen for the wireless phone on the counter, and managed to pick it up and hit the

TALK button before Carmela could pick up the extension in the living room. "Rodriguez residence."

"It's me," Nita said.

"Oh, good. Thanks for not being yet another of the thundering herd."

Click. "I heard that!"

"Get off, 'Mela. It's for me."

"Wow, I'll call the media." *Click.*

"She giving you a hard time?"

"Always." Kit let out a harassed-sounding breath. "Please, please, *please,* come on over and give me something to do besides keep my sister off the phone. That chicken's gonna be ready soon, anyway."

"I'll be over in a few. But you need to hear about this first. My dad wants me to go away on this exchange thing!"

"You gonna go?" Kit immediately began to itch with something that felt embarrassingly like envy.

"Yeah. And when we got back from shopping, my manual was about half an inch thicker than when we'd left, and a whole bunch of sealed claudication packages were sitting on my desk."

"Hey, super," Kit said, and was instantly annoyed at himself for not sounding as enthusiastic as he thought he should have. "This is going to be really great for you! You should get out there and have a good time—"

"What do you mean, *I* should go?" And Nita burst out laughing. "You're so pitiful when you're trying to be a good loser. I was *going* to tell you that my dad doesn't want me to go alone. Tom still has an opening, and he's holding it for you!"

"*Wow,*" Kit said. The envy instantly dissolved, first in delight, then in mild outrage. "Hey, and you let me stew for a whole, I don't know, five *seconds,* thinking I was going to have to sit here while you were gone!"

"That's to get you back for the chicken thing," Nita said, and started imitating Kit. "'Oh, I don't know. I might want it myself...'" She broke up laughing again.

"Cut it out!" But Kit had to laugh, too. "Okay," he said. "I have to figure out how to handle this. Where're we supposed to be going?"

"The manual says it's some planet called Alaalu."

"Never heard of it," Kit said. He put out a hand and felt around for something only he would be able to feel, the tag of a wizardly "zipper" in the air, which controlled entry to the personal otherspace pocket that followed him around. Kit found the tag, pulled it down, and pushed his hand into the opening so that it appeared to vanish while he felt around for his manual. "Alaalu...Is it in this galaxy?"

"Yeah," Nita said, and Kit heard manual pages rustling again at her end. "Outer Arm Four, around radian one-sixty."

Kit thought about that for a moment as he felt around and found his manual, then pulled it out of the claudication into local space. "That's the Scutum Arm, right? Straight across the Bar from us."

"Yeah," Nita said as Kit zipped the pocket up again. "The mirror of the arm we're in. The system's a little more than sixty thousand light-years from here."

Kit put his manual down on the counter and started flipping through it to the galaxography section. "Alaalu,

Alaalu," he muttered, paging through to the section dealing with the Scutum Arm. Kit ran one finger down the long column of planet names and coordinates on the index page and found Alaalu there.

"Got it," Kit said, and riffled along to the page in question, which had an image of the planet's star system. Apparently there was only one inhabited planet in the system, an exception to the usual rule. The star around which Alaalu IV circled was about the same size as Earth's Sun, and in the same general class, a little golden G0. "Not exactly next door," Kit said, studying the star's position about three-quarters of the way down the long arm on the other side of the galaxy's spiral. He tapped on the image of the star system to zoom in on the planet. "Who lives there?"

"Well, people. Who else? Humanoids, anyway: real tall people, all kind of a tan color." Nita said. "Check page..." She glanced at her own manual. "I have it on page nine-sixty-two."

"Right," Kit said. For the moment his attention was on the image of the planet, banded blindingly around its equator with a white, two-way highway of swirling weather systems. The view was in real time, and the very slightest shift was visible as Alaalu turned in the amber light of its sun. The planet's seas were as blue as Earth's, and huge; there were only three landmasses, none of them large enough to be considered a continent. One was a big, rough-edged crescent, about a third of the way up from the equator toward Alaalu's north pole—a three-quarter circle with the open end pointing more or less north. Kit wondered if he was looking at a remnant of some gigantic, ancient meteor strike—the rest of the "splash" rim damaged in some recent earthquake or plate movement. The other two landmasses were halfway around the planet from the crescent island—they were irregularly shaped blobs, long and narrow, with great chains of islands large and small strung out from them at either end, and each chain straddling Alaalu's equator. One island chain ran almost vertically, pointing at the poles; the other crossed the equator more diagonally, like a sword stuck in the planet's equatorial belt.

At first, Kit thought these were relatively short island chains, but then he got a look at the scale indicator plotted against the planet's globe. "Neets," he said, "those island chains are nine *thousand* miles long!"

"I know," Nita said. "I had to look twice, too. Check the main stats for the planet. Thirty-six thousand miles in diameter..."

"Wow," Kit said. He put the manual aside for the moment. There was a ton of technical detail there to digest.

"It's a nice place, anyway. A peaceful planet, no recent wars, not a lot of intraspecies hostility of any kind. Warm climate at the equator, but not too hot."

"One of those places where life really *is* a beach," Kit said, starting to smile in anticipation. "Could this actually be a vacation for a change?"

"Looks that way. Oh, there'd be some cultural stuff. We'd have to travel around on their planet, find out what it's like living in one of their families. That kind of thing."

"Sounds boring. In a good way."

"I don't know about you," Nita said, sounding a little sharp, "but I could *use* some good boring about now."

"No argument there," Kit said. Recent months had featured too many excitements by half.

"But you know what's really weird about this place?"

"What, besides that it's peaceful?"

"Yeah. Know how many wizards it has?"

"How many?"

"*One.*"

Kit blinked.

"One?" he said. "For the whole planet?"

"Yup."

"And *how* many people live there?"

"It says a billion and a half."

Kit stared at the manual, not knowing what to make of this. "They haven't had a big catastrophe or something that's wiped out all their wizards?"

"Nope. The manual says one wizard is all they need."

Kit shook his head. "Wow," he said again. He had trouble even imagining any world so peaceful and orderly that one wizard was enough to keep things running smoothly.

"So go ask your folks! Wouldn't they like to get rid of you for a couple of weeks?"

Kit fell silent, listening to his home. The TV was now shouting with a cacophony of alien voices, the audio expression of yet another chat room, and his sister was alternately shouting at the screen in the Speech and talking into her cell phone.

"Come on over and we'll find out," Kit said. "I think this'll go all right."

Outside, without warning, the howling started . . . in chorus.

"*Kit!*" his father said.

"Just hurry up," Kit said. "I need some moral support!"

To Kit, it seemed to take hours for Nita to arrive: His brain was buzzing with plans and possibilities that couldn't start getting handled until he'd settled things with his folks. But it was really only about ten minutes before Nita bounced in the back door, grinning. "Here," she said, and handed Kit a chicken, wrapped in plastic wrap on a little cardboard tray.

"Thanks," Kit said, and stowed it in the fridge.

"What's that noise? Opera?"

Beyond, in the living room, the entertainment system was making a sound like a fire siren bewailing its lot. "No," Kit said, "just 'Mela's chat application again. Come on."

"By the way, the K-9 Corps is out there again," Nita said as she and Kit headed through the dining room. "Hi, Mrs. Rodriguez."

"Hi, Nita," Kit's mama said from the sofa, where she was still lying with her feet up on the arm and her eyes closed. "Dinner in half an hour."

"Thanks!"

"At least they're just sitting there now," Kit said softly. "They were howling before."

"I missed that. Where's Ponch?"

"Out back somewhere. He got them to be quiet, and after that he took off. For some reason he's never real social after he has to go talk to them."

They went into the living room. There, Carmela was sitting cross-legged on the rug in front of the TV, a cell phone on the floor nearby but, miraculously, not in use. "Hi, 'Mela," Nita said. She peered at the screen. "'Multispecies General Discussion,'" she read off the channel-indicator band at the bottom. "What's it like?"

"Interesting, mostly."

"What're you talking about?"

"*Grenfelzing*. Which for some reason Kit doesn't want me to get involved with. He thinks it'll stunt my growth."

"Anything that would keep you from needing to buy new clothes every other week would be welcome," said Kit's pop from behind the paper. "If *grenfelzing* has that effect, bring it on."

Kit looked at the screen, which Nita was studying with interest. It was divided into three main parts: a status bar along the bottom; a constantly scrolling column down one side; and the main part of the screen, subdivided into eight squares, each of which featured a live image, or what looked like one. The scrolling column was full of words in the Speech, moving very fast indeed, and the audio was screeching or blatting or warbling or hooting with any number of alien-sounding voices, all talking (it seemed) at once.

"Which one is supposed to be you?" Nita said, looking at the screen.

"That one." Carmela pointed at what appeared to be a portrait of a pink octopus. "I picked it off a screenful of sample cover faces."

"'Mela," Nita said, "you know what would be better? Go off-line and pick something more humanoid. Otherwise, if Pink Octopus Guy turns up at school someday and wants to sit next to you, the explanation you're going to find yourself making is going to sound like something out of a lame sitcom."

"Oh," Carmela said. "Okay." She tossed the remote to Kit. "But do aliens really turn up on Earth just like that?"

"There's no other possible way to explain *you*," Kit said.

"*Ooooooooo,*" Carmela said, standing up without uncrossing her legs. "I feel unloved now. Nita, come see my catalogs!"

"I'll come up in a while," Nita said. "Thanks."

Carmela wandered upstairs.

Kit glanced at his pop. "Uh, Popi," Kit said, "uh, is it okay if I go halfway across the galaxy for a couple of weeks?"

"Sure," Kit's father said from behind the paper. "Is Nita going with you?"

"Uh, yeah, Pop."

"Her dad said it's okay?"

"Yeah."

"Fine. Dress warm," Kit's father said, and turned to the comics section.

Kit and Nita exchanged a glance. Finally, Kit turned toward the kitchen.

"You'll want to fill Mama in on the details," Kit's father said, in a tone of voice suggesting complete un-concern.

Kit couldn't bear it anymore. He looked over his shoulder and saw his father just peering over the top of the newspaper at him, waiting for his reaction. His father bent the paper down just enough to let Kit see his grin, then let the paper pop up again and went on with his reading.

"I've been had," Kit muttered to Nita as they went back into the kitchen.

Kit's mama was up off the couch now, and looked up as she poured herself some coffee. "In case you were wondering," she said, "Tom was on the phone a while ago."

"Oh," Kit said.

"He gave us the basics," Kit's mama said, leaning against the counter. "I gather that this isn't going to be at all dangerous, and that you'll be able to come home at night if you want to, or if we want you to."

"Uh, yeah," Kit said.

"Well, let's think about this," his mother said. "Your grades have been okay..." Kit was already beginning to grin when his mama glanced up at him and said, "I emphasize the 'okay.' Not brilliant. I'm still not entirely pleased with your midterm grades, especially that history test."

"Mama," Kit said, "my history teacher is a date freak. He doesn't care if you understand anything about history except *when* things happened!"

"Aha, the appeal to vague generalities as opposed to

concrete data," Kit's mother said. "Sorry, honey. Not having the dates is like knowing why someone's having a cardiac arrest but not being real sure where their heart is. You're just going to have to work harder at that, even if you can't see the point right now."

"You're gonna tell me that it'll all make sense someday," Kit said.

"It sure will," his mother said, "and on that day you'll suddenly realize that your mom wasn't really as dumb as you secretly thought she was at the very moment you were also trying to wheedle her into letting you go off on a jaunt halfway across the galaxy."

I think this is a real good time not to say anything, Kit thought.

"Okay," Kit's mama said. "I want a commitment from you that you're going to work harder in that history class. Otherwise, the next time you want to go out on a recreational run like this, the answer is going to be no. Even if you work in other worlds, you have to live in this one...and Tom says even wizards need day jobs."

"I promise, Mama," Kit said.

His mother had another drink of coffee, then looked reflectively into the cup. "Of course," she said, "you'd promise to turn into a three-headed gorilla as long as you could go on this trip."

"Mama!"

Her grin broke out at full strength. "I know," she said. "Wizards don't lie. But if I don't get to tease you sometimes, life won't be worth living. When do you leave?"

"Thanks, Mama!" Kit said, and jumped at her and

hugged her harder than necessary, if only to get her back for the teasing.

"It's some time in the next couple of days, Mrs. Rodriguez," Nita said. "I didn't check the exact date—I was looking at the rest of the info package. We can tell you in a few minutes."

"Okay," Kit's mama said. "Get that sorted out and you can fill us in over dinner."

They went up to Kit's room—or, rather, Kit ran up the steps three at a time in his excitement, and Nita came up after him. As Kit passed Carmela's room, she put her head out and looked him up and down as if he were nuts. "What's going on with you?" she said.

"I get to go away for spring break!" Kit said.

"Oh, really? Where to?"

"Sixty-two thousand light-years away," Kit said casually. "The other side of the galaxy."

"Great!" Carmela said. "I'll give you a shopping list."

"You do your own shopping," Kit said as he and Nita went into his room. He glanced over at Nita and saw her grinning. "What's so funny?"

"Your whole family teases you," Nita said. "I've never seen them get so *coordinated* about it before."

"Neither have I," Kit said. "I don't know whether I should be worried or not."

"This is new," Nita said, looking up at a double-hemisphere map of the Moon on the wall at the head of Kit's bed. The map had a lot of different-colored pins stuck in it, in both hemispheres, though there were about twice as many on the "near side" of the Moon as on the "far side." "Are you trying to win a Visited Every Crater competition or something?"

Kit threw her a look. "Go ahead and laugh," he said. "I'm trying to get to know the Moon before it becomes just another tourist destination." But his attention was on his desk by the window.

It was covered with schoolbooks brought home over spring break (the school did locker cleaning then) and notebooks and pens. What it was *not* strewn with were the three objects that had just appeared, between one breath and the next, and were floating a few inches *above* the cluttered surface. They were silvery packages about the size of paperback books, wrapped with "sheet" force fields that sizzled slightly blue at the corners; and they were bobbing slightly in the draft from the nearby window, as its weather stripping had come loose again. "When *are* you going to fix that?" Nita said.

"Later," said Kit. He inspected the little floating packages to see if they had notations on them. One did. A single string of characters in the Speech was attached to it and was waving gently in the draft: READ THIS FIRST.

"Is this what you got?" Kit said.

Nita nodded. "That one's the mission statement," she said.

Kit took hold of the wizardly package, pulled it into the middle of the room, and pulled the string of characters out until the normally curved characters of the Speech went straight with the tension of the pull. As they did, the package unfolded itself in the air, a sheet of semishadow on which many more characters in the Speech swiftly spread themselves in blocks of text and columns, small illustrations and diagrams, and various live and still images.

SPONSORED ELECTIVE/NONINTERVENTIONAL EXCURSUS PROGRAM, said the header. NOMINEE AUTHORIZATIONS AND ANCILLARY DATA. NOTE: WHERE CULTURAL CORRESPONDENCES ARE NOT EXACT, LOCAL ANALOGUES ARE SUBSTITUTED. Beneath the header, divided into various sections, was a tremendous amount of other information about the world where they'd be staying, the family they'd be staying with, the culture, the locality where the family lived, the planet's history, the climate, the flora and fauna, on and on and on....

"It's gonna take me all night to read this!" Kit said.

"Relax," Nita said. "It's not like there's going to be a test or anything! You don't have to inhale it all at once. We've got time for that."

"Yeah," Kit said. It was just beginning to sink in how very far from home they were going. Kit was delighted, and at the same time, all of a sudden it was making him twitch.

He scanned down the data. *Addendum to authorization: You may be accompanied by your adjunct Talent if desired.* "Hey," Kit said, "I can bring Ponch!"

"Great! And there are the dates," Nita said, pointing to one side where the duration of the trip was expressed, as usual on Earth, in Julian-day format—2452747.3333 to 2452761.3333, it said. She had her manual out and was paging through it.

"It sounds close," Kit said.

Nita raised her eyebrows. "No kidding," she said. "That first date is tomorrow at three in the afternoon. I didn't realize it was so soon!"

"You won't hear me complaining," Kit said. "What's the other date?"

"Exactly two weeks later."

"Just before school starts again," Kit said. "Good thing I finished my break work early."

Nita made a face. "I wish I had," she said. "I've got a few reports to do...I'm going to have to bring them with me." Then she grinned again. "Fortunately, that's not a problem. See that one there, the big one?" She pointed at another of the packages floating over the desk.

Kit went to it, brought it into the middle of the room, and pulled its "tag." Instead of unfolding itself, the package rolled itself up tight into a narrow cylindrical shape, losing its "wrapping" in the process. There it hung in the air, a silvery rod about three feet long and half an inch wide.

"What is that?" he said.

"A pup tent," Nita said. "Watch this—"

There was another of those little threads of words in the Speech hanging down from the middle of it. Nita pulled on the thread. As if it were a window shade, a pale sheet of shadow pulled down out of the rod.

"That's really slick," Kit said. "What's it for? Shelter?"

"Storage," Nita said, "for the things you need to bring with you. It's a claudication, but it's a lot bigger than our little pockets." She finished pulling the access interface down to floor level and straightened up again.

"Hey," Kit said, looking through the shadow. He put a hand through the shadow: The hand vanished. Then he put his head in through the access.

Inside was just a gray space about the size of Kit's living room, with a ceiling about ten feet high. The space was softly illuminated by a light that came from nowhere. Through the walls of the "pup tent," he could faintly see his own room. It was a good trick, because from the outside there was nothing to be seen but the rod and the rectangular doorway hanging down from it.

When he pulled his head out, Nita was snickering.

"You should see how you look when just your head vanishes," she said.

Kit thought about that for a moment. "What did my neck look like?"

"A guillotine ad," Nita said.

Kit raised his eyebrows. "My mama would probably be interested."

"We can show her later. Anyway, clothes and books and things can go in there..."

"Some spare food?" Kit said. "In case you wake up in the middle of the night and need potato chips or something?"

Nita gave him a look that was only slightly dirty. Potato chips were a recent weakness of Nita's, one that Kit had started actively teasing her about. "Yeah," she said. "A case or so of those...and see if I give *you* any."

Kit grinned. "Okay," he said. "What's that last one? Did you open yours?"

"Nope," Nita said. "It says not to. In fact, it just about screams not to. Check it out."

Kit picked up the last package. It, too, had a "tag" of characters in the Speech hanging from it, but as Kit started to pull on it, a little half-transparent window appeared in the air, like a floating page of the manual. Nita peered over his shoulder at it.

DANGER!—CUSTOM PORTABLE
WORLDGATING LOCUS—DANGER!
DO NOT IMPLEMENT WITHOUT
READING INSTRUCTIONS!

The display skipped a few lines and then went on, in the Speech:

DEPLOYMENT INSTRUCTIONS:
1. Before departure: Insert coordinates of desired "home" egress points into compacted routine package, including at least two alternate points for each primary point (for use should primary point be occupied).
2. Transport compacted routine package to relocation site. WARNING! DO NOT attempt to deploy routine package before arrival at final relocation site. Note that basic deployments cannot be reversed once exercised.
3. After arriving at relocation site, attach coordinate package to supplied power conduit package, choose an appropriate locus for installation,[1] and activate in the usual manner.[2]

See main documentation for details regarding operation and decommissioning at end of legitimacy period. NOT RATED FOR TRANSITS OF MORE THAN 150,000 l.y.

[1]See attached annotation for cultural and logistical considerations.

²This installation requires a matter substrate. Do not install in areas where matter state is likely to experience unpredictable shifts. Do not deploy in vacuum or microgravity. Retroengineering this wizardry is not recommended unless you are confident that you have sufficient understanding of gate substrates, hyperstring structure and string tension relationships, matter-energy polymorphism. Consult your local Advisory or gating technician for technical assistance.

"They're spatial-only transit gates," Nita said. "*Subsidized* ones. You can use them as many times as you want...come home whenever you want...and you don't have to pay for it. I *love* this!"

"I wonder what happens if you try to deploy them 'before arrival at final relocation site,'" Kit said. He juggled the claudication package in one hand.

"You wouldn't!" Nita said.

"Well..." Kit grinned, finally, and shook his head. "No. But you do have to wonder..."

Kit put the worldgate package aside and looked up again at the cultural exchange mission statement. "So, who are they sticking us with?" he said, looking through the cultural info. "Wait. Here it is—"

"Your host family: The Peliaen family consists of a female-analogue parent (Demair), a male-analogue parent (Kuwilin), and one sublatency Alaalid, your counterpart and fellow wizard Quelt (female analogue). The Peliaens are atypical in that one family member (Kuwilin) has elected to do physical labor as a permanent avocation rather than in rotation, as is common in this society. The family lives in a typical rural dwelling by the shore of the Inner Sea, twenty [kilometers] from the nearest large population aggregate...."

"It's a beach," Kit said. "It *is* a beach! This is gonna be terrific!"

"The last time we had a vacation by the beach," Nita said casually, "I almost got eaten by a shark. Let's hope this goes a little more smoothly, huh?"

"It has to," Kit said. "The Powers wouldn't let anything like that happen to you now! See, it says right there, in big letters, *ELECTIVE/NONINTERVEN-TIONAL!*"

"Yeah," Nita said. "I guess you're right." She let out a breath and looked relieved.

"Kit?" came his mama's voice from downstairs. "Nita?"

"Chicken!" Nita said, and was out of the room before Kit even had time to turn around. He chuckled, folded up the wizardries to bring them down to show his mama and pop, and went down after her.

As he passed through the living room, Carmela was sitting in front of the TV again, looking at a screenful of data. "More chat stuff?" Kit said casually as he passed.

"Oh, no," Carmela said, intent on the screen. "I didn't know there was a *galactic* positioning system! And look, you can put in a planet's name, and it looks in the database, and, see that, here's the address of Earth!"

Kit caught up with Nita as they went into the dining room, where his mama was setting the table. "The sooner we get out of here, the better," he said under his breath. "I just don't know if halfway across the galaxy's gonna be far *enough*."

On the Road

NITA WAS UP LATE that night, reading over the cultural exchange material. A little voice in her head kept nagging her, saying, *You really need your sleep. You're going to be a wreck tomorrow...* But she couldn't help herself: She was too excited. She lay in bed for a long time with her copy of the briefing folder hanging over her head, reading about the planet, the society, the people....

They had never had a war on Alaalu. They didn't seem to have any diseases, and the manual said there wasn't any crime. Their climate was stable, so that natural disasters like floods and hurricanes happened only once or so every few centuries; their planet's tectonics were unbelievably leisurely, so that whole lifetimes might go by without there being even one earthquake or volcanic eruption. *It has to do with the size of the planet, I guess,* Nita thought, sleepily reaching out to touch the folder to get the content she was reading to scroll down a little. *And there's no moon big enough to stress the planet's crust. And the weather stays calm because the axis doesn't tilt, and the sun's the right distance away...*

She lay back after looking at one of the images of a beach—broad, white, and tideless—with that golden sun lying low over an endless blue green sea. *This is going to be just what I need,* Nita thought. *Two weeks at the beach...*

But the beach was full of statues.

Nita stood looking around her in a twilight that, as she considered it, was not the one that came before sunset, but the one that came before dawn. The water ran up and down the beach, strangely quiet. The waves were very small; she thought perhaps she was on a lakeshore somewhere.

At this time of day, everything—sea, sand, sky— seemed to be the same color, a soft bluish gray. The beach ran seemingly to infinity on each side, sloping strangely upward and vanishing in a mist of twilit distance. And in that dimness, dotted here and there along the beach, a hundred thousand tall statues stood.

Every time Nita looked in a different direction, there seemed to be more of them. They were wonderfully made. It seemed to Nita that the statues had been painted to look just like real people: very tall people, of whom even the shortest were six or seven feet high. They wore long, loose, comfortable clothes, tunics and soft trousers and long skirts, and they were all very handsome, with blind, bland faces, all slightly smiling.

Nita went over to the closest of them, admiring the wonderful realism with which the statue had been carved. You could even see the coarse, soft weave in the fabric of the clothes it wore, as if it were real. She reached out to touch the "fabric" of the nearest statue's sleeve—

And found that it *was* fabric, something like loosely woven linen...and the arm underneath it was warm.

They're not statues—

Nita snatched her hand back, shocked. But there was no answering movement from the— *Not a statue. A person. But what's the matter with them? Why don't they move?*

"Why don't you move?" she cried to the night. "What's wrong?"

No voice answered her, at first. But then, slowly, Nita began to hear another sound, one she'd mistaken for the sound of the little waves coming up the beach. It was someone whispering. The whisper said, "We are as we've decided to be. Everything is fine."

"It's not!" Nita said. "There's more to life than just standing around! You should move! You should do things!"

"We are as we've decided to be," said another whisper. And another, and another, until there was a whole chorus of them, all saying, as if in perfect content, "Everything is fine. Everything is fine..."

In the dream, Nita was not convinced. She started to walk down the beach, looking for just one of these people who would say something besides "Everything is fine." Finally, she broke into a run, looking into face after smiling face, and the speed of her running stirred the clothes of the people she ran past...but nothing else. None of them moved. None of them turned to watch her. Finally, after a long dream-time of running, Nita stopped. Because this was dream, she wasn't out of breath. But she could still hear the whispering, endless, like the sound of the sea: "We are as we've decided to be..."

"...and everything is fine..."

She stood there in the twilight, which was slowly growing brighter, and started feeling like she wanted to leave. She didn't want to see the light of full day shine on all these statues and make it plain how stuck they were. Nita started to look for a way to get off the beach. But it was all beach, a beach full of statues, no matter where she turned. She started to despair.

Then, far away, something moved. Nita strained her eyes to see it. Slowly, she began to see that it was shorter than all the other blind, frozen figures, and it was walking right toward her. As it came ever closer, Nita found herself feeling an irrational fear, which grew with every step it took toward her.

She wanted to run. But she couldn't. Now *she* was the frozen one, a statue herself. *No!* Nita thought, and tried and tried to move; but she had stayed here too long, and the statues' immobility had spread to her. And that single moving figure was closer now. Much closer. Only a few hundred feet away—

In terror she stood there, rooted to the sand, and watched him come. He was only as tall as she was, but Nita felt as afraid of him as if he'd been a hundred times taller. He was dark-skinned, wearing pale, long, loose clothes like the statues wore. He had long, dark reddish hair-stuff that hung down his back, and his eyes were dark, too, unreadable. He came to stand right in front of Nita, and nothing she could do made her able to move so much as a muscle, though she desperately wanted to get away.

"I've been waiting for you a long time," the man said. "You know what has to be done."

Nita couldn't speak, couldn't even shake her head.

"It's all right," he said. "It'll be morning soon." And sure enough, dawn was coming on. In fact, it seemed to be coming on with a rush, as if something had held it back, waiting for this man to arrive. Now the whole eastern sky went pale with light, paler, bright, blinding, and the Sun leaped into the sky as if over a wall, and the whole beach went up in a single cry of terror as at last, at last, the statues spoke—

It was the Sun that woke her up, finally, streaming very early into her room through the east-facing blinds that she'd forgotten to close. The briefing folder, programmed not to waste energy, had folded itself up again after Nita fell asleep and was hovering in the air over her head, a neat little dark package. Nita plucked it out of the air, threw off the covers, got up, and stuffed the folder into her backpack, which was hanging over the back of her desk chair. Then she got into her jeans and threw on a baggy T-shirt stolen from her dad.

"Everything is fine..."

Wow, Nita thought. *That's one for the book.* She got her manual, opened it to her "dream log" pages, and added a record of what she could remember of the dream. *Most of it, I think. It was vivid.*

When she finished, she went down for breakfast. Dairine was there ahead of her, which was moderately unusual. She was sitting at the dining room table, half-way through a bowl of cornflakes, with a folder spread out on the table next to the bowl. Spot was crouched off to one side, with no legs in evidence, but he had put up a pair of stalked eyes and was regarding the cornflakes with a dubious expression. "Morning," Nita said.

"Yeah."

Nita put a couple of pieces of bread in the toaster, started them toasting, and went to get a mug from the dish drainer. "What's that you're reading?"

"An orientation pack with information on the incoming guests. Dad's got one, too."

Nita was surprised. "When did that come in?"

"Last night."

"It *is* in English, isn't it?"

"No," Dairine said. "It's got a Speech-to-text converter, though. Very neat. He started in on it last night. I think he's reading the rest of it in bed right now."

"Great. How many guests are we getting?"

"Three, it looks like."

Nita opened the cupboard over the counter and rummaged around a little for the dark tea she liked. "Where from?"

"All over. There's a Demisiv, a Rirhait, and somebody from Wellakh, which I've never heard of."

"Wellakh," Nita said. "Don't think I've heard of it, either." Then it hit her. "*Three?* Where are they all going to stay? We've only got one extra bedroom, and I don't have the bunk beds in mine anymore." She found the tea bags and fished one out of the box. "Assuming they can even use beds, and don't need racks or hooks or something..."

"They'll stay in the pup tents. That's what they're for," Dairine said. "They can put as much of their own stuff in there as they like, if it turns out they need it. Beds, furniture, whatever. In fact"—and Dairine looked up at Nita—"I've been looking over the docs, and they could do a lot more than that if they liked..."

Nita looked around the corner of the kitchen door at Dairine. The expression on her sister's face was one Nita had seen entirely too often—the amused look of someone who's figured out a new way to put something over on the universe. *It's too early in the morning for this,* Nita thought, picking up the kettle and going over to the sink to fill it. "How do you mean?" she said.

"The pup tents have a 'back door,'" Dairine said.

"What, like the main access?"

"No, it's different," Dairine said. There was a pause and some crunching. "If you change the permeability of the pup tent's matter-void interface—"

"Whoa, *wait* a minute!" Nita said. "That's reverse engineering! The custom gate interface said you weren't supposed to do that."

"Oh, to the gate, yeah. But the pup tents—"

"*Dairine!*"

There was a pause for more crunching. "I said you *could* do that," Dairine said. "I didn't say I was *going* to."

This declaration wasn't specific enough to give Nita any relief, but she sighed and put the kettle on the stove, turning the burner on. *And if she does start gimmicking things while I'm not here, well, that's just her problem.* The thought of *not* having to be involved in cleaning up after some trouble of Dairine's made Nita feel oddly cheerful.

Her toast popped up. Nita got a plate and reached into the fridge for the butter. "So how are you guys doing your big transit to this planet?" Dairine said. "What's its name again?"

"Alaalu. We'll use public transport to start with. We'll short-gate it to Grand Central around two, and then go over to the Crossings from there. After that we just pick up a scheduled service for Alaalu. The manual says there are outbound gatings from the Crossings about once every two hours, or on demand. No big deal."

"Leaving early, huh?" Dairine said, reaching out to the cornflake box in front of her to pour another bowl. "Can't bear to see Dad freaking out over the new arrivals?"

"Actually," Nita said, cutting her toast in halves, "I think he'll do just fine...and the sooner I'm out of here, the happier he'll be. One less thing for him to concentrate on."

"*Hnh,*" Dairine said, a noise which suggested both that she was chewing and that she didn't know whether to believe Nita or not.

Nita sat down and started eating her toast. "You packed yet?" Dairine said.

Nita shook her head. "After breakfast," she said, picking up the second piece.

She munched in silence for a little while, and then looked up to find Dairine looking at her with an expression that on anyone else might have been somewhat wistful. "What?"

"This is turning out okay after all, isn't it?" Dairine said.

"I think so," Nita said. "And Dad's calming down a little."

Dairine snickered into her cereal. "I think so. Anyway, it'll be fun to have some other wizards here to hang out with. And Carmela's been wanting to get some more practice with the Speech: This'll be a great way." Dairine poured more milk on her cornflakes. "It'll be good for them to meet a normal Earth person . . ."

Nita smiled slightly as she finished her toast. "Don't let Kit hear you call her that."

"Yeah." Dairine took another spoonful of cornflakes. "Go on, you should start packing. It's gonna take you longer than you think."

It annoyed Nita to have to admit that her sister was right. After her dad went off to work, she spent the rest of the morning and the very beginning of the afternoon putting things into her pup tent and taking them out again. The things that stayed in included Nita's desk, which, she discovered, was too heavy to drag in so that she wound up having to levitate it; a lot of books and CDs and her own little desktop CD player and sound system; a lot of clothes in cardboard boxes, including every swimsuit she owned, and much other junk from her dresser drawers that Nita had gradually realized she couldn't do without. That recurring realization was what stopped her, eventually, as she stood in front of her dresser holding her third stack of underwear. *Am I insane? I can always come back.*

She chucked the underwear back into the open dresser drawer, pushed it shut with her foot, and went into the bathroom for toiletries and a couple of towels. *There's a thought. Beach towels...* She opened the towel cupboard and pulled out a couple of big ones, smiling at the thought of lying around under some alien sun, listening to the ocean, doing nothing....

Sunblock! Nita rummaged around in the medicine cabinet, but all the sunblock in there had sell-by dates in the previous year. *This stuff is useless now. I can always use a wizardry to do the same job...*

She went back into her room, which looked strangely empty without her desk, and glanced around to see if there was anything she'd forgotten. A glance at her watch told her it was one-thirty. *Getting close to time to go,* Nita thought. *Looks like I'm all set—*

"Honey? Good grief, what's going on in here?"

Nita looked over her shoulder. Her dad was standing in the doorway, gazing into her room in some confusion. "Are you going to leave anything in here?" he said. "Are you sure you don't need the posters on the wall, too?"

"Nope, I'm all done," Nita said. As she spoke, she bent down to pull the tag of words in the Speech that controlled the pup tent's access; the gray shadow of the portal slid up into the silvery rod and vanished. Nita took the rod down out of the air, telescoped it down to a foot, and slipped it into her backpack. "You're home for lunch?"

"It's lunchtime, yeah, but I've already had a sandwich. I just thought I'd see if you needed me to drive you and Kit to the station in Freeport."

"Daddy, we're going straight into Grand Central," Nita said, picking up the backpack and slinging it over her shoulder with one last look around her room. "And you should be getting ready for the visitors."

"There's not that much to do," her dad said as they went down the stairs together. "The place is clean— Dairine did a good job of it. I guess I just wanted to see you off."

"I know," Nita said. "Dad, I'll be fine. This isn't any worse than going over to Kit's: I can be home in a minute if you need me. And I see from my manual that Tom's done something to your cell phone so you can call me any time. It'll just come through the manual."

"That's the only thing I'm not sure about," her dad said as they headed toward the kitchen. "My cell phone company has too many different ways it charges me to start with. If phone calls to other star systems show up on my next bill—"

Nita grinned. "If they do, I think you should take them right to the phone company and see what they do. And I want to go with you."

Her dad nodded, smiled, reached out to her. Nita went and gave him a big hug.

"I'll send you postcards," Nita said.

"Just don't confuse the mailman."

Nita grinned. "Bye, Dad," she said, and went out. In the driveway, Dairine was waiting for her, and trying not to look as if she was waiting. "You got everything?" she said.

Nita rolled her eyes. "Yes," she said. "In fact, that's what I'm afraid of. You may see me coming back to return stuff."

"I don't want to see you for at least a couple of days," Dairine said, with such force that Nita was a little surprised.

"Well, just do me a favor and call me if anything starts to happen, okay?"

"If I need you, sure."

This was not the answer Nita had been looking for. "I want progress reports," Nita said. "If Dad—"

"*Dad will be fine!* Don't you trust me with him?"

Nita broke out in a sudden sweat, as any direct answer was likely to get her in trouble either as a wizard or as a sister. "Just set your manual to generate a daily précis, okay? If I don't hear from you, I can check that," she said. "That won't be any trouble." *And it won't find endless, creative ways to cover up whatever's happening, either.*

"Yeah, sure," Dairine said. And, without warning, she hugged Nita. "You take care of yourself," she said. "Don't get in trouble."

"*Me?*" Nita said.

"They say the memory's the first thing to go," Dairine said under her breath. She turned and went back into the house, waving one hand more or less behind her. "Have fun..."

Nita shrugged her backpack into place and turned away.

A few minutes later, at Kit's house, Nita knocked on the back door, then stuck her head in.

In the living room, cacophony from Carmela's chat utility made a background to more urgent voices.

"You should take a heavier jacket, honey!"

"I don't think I need to, Mama. The average temperature there this time of year is eighty degrees. In fact, it's eighty degrees for *most* of the year."

"It might still get cold at night if you're going to be at the beach. You're not going to have to go anywhere nice, are you? Out to dinner or anything? You should take a good shirt."

"Mama, I can come right back here and get one."

"Why waste the time when you can put it in this wonderful magic closet right now?"

"Yeah," said Carmela's voice from the living room. "I want a wonderful magic closet, too! Or I'll take that one when you're done."

There was a silence, which to Nita said more about Kit's state of mind than many words could. "Helloooo!" she said as she walked into the kitchen. "Kit?"

"In the living room."

She went in there and found him standing in front

of his own pup-tent access, looking very resigned and simply throwing through the interface everything his mother handed him. Carmela, sitting cross-legged in front of the TV, as usual, was watching the whole process with intense amusement though not laughing out loud. Nita suspected that 'Mela knew this could be bad for her health at the moment. "Oh, hello, Nita," Kit's mama said. "He'll be ready in a sec. See that, *she's* wearing a heavier jacket—" she said, and hurried past Nita toward the kitchen and the back door.

"What time is it?" Kit said to Nita.

"Almost two," she said. "We should go."

Instantly, if not sooner, Kit said silently. *I'm beginning to feel like a garage sale here.*

You can always smuggle all this stuff back later.

I'm planning on it!

"Here," Kit's mama said, coming in with a jacket that, Nita judged, could probably keep Kit warm in Antarctica. Kit took it from her and flung it through the access to the pup tent, where it vanished. "Mama," he said, "we really have to go, or we're going to be late. Is that it?"

"No," his mother said, and handed him a brown paper bag. "Here's your lunch."

Kit sighed, twisted around, and put the bag into his backpack, which he was wearing fully slung, as if he'd expected to be out of there a good while ago. "That's it," he said.

"I don't know," his mama said. "I keep getting the idea I've forgotten something—"

"Tell me later, Mama," Kit said, pulling up the

"shade" of the pup-tent access interface and stowing its rod in his backpack. "I'll call you. And then I can come back for whatever it is."

Ponch, who had been lying on his back between Carmela and the TV, now got up, shook himself, and stood there with his tongue hanging out. *Is it time?*

"Yes, it is," Kit said. "Mama..."

He went over to her and hugged her hard. Nita was astonished to see Kit's fairly hard-boiled mom actually getting teary, and fighting to manage it.

"Tell Pop I'll call him tonight," Kit said.

"I will, sweetie."

Carmela looked up at Kit and just waved at him. "Bring me stuff," she said.

"If I remember," Kit said, very offhandedly. Nita controlled her smile; she'd already seen the shopping list Carmela had given him.

"Come on," Kit said to her. With Ponch bouncing around them, he and Nita went out the back door and headed into Kit's backyard, making their way to the cover of the sassafras woods out in the back. To anyone who might have been watching, they vanished among the leaves. And then, a few seconds later, with just the slightest *pop!* of displaced air, they vanished much more thoroughly.

Nita and Kit and Ponch arrived in Grand Central Terminal, where they normally went when making a transit at peak times—into a dark and quiet place away from the Main Concourse proper but still inside the terminal, near one of the northernmost of the westward-pointing tracks. The platform between tracks eleven and thirteen was a spot where wheeled wire freight baskets and the occasional locked mail container were left for later pickup. There was rarely anyone there in the middle of the day, and the area was only dimly lit by the red eyes of infrared spots, while hidden security cameras passed pictures of what the spots showed them to the train master's office.

No security camera, of course, can do anything about a wizard who is both invisible and shielded against infrared leakage. Nita and Kit popped out of nowhere into the dark, being careful to minimize the air displacement when they did—there was no point in appearing invisibly while also making a noise like a gunshot.

Carefully, Nita and Kit made their way toward where the train gates opened onto the Main Concourse, and then down to where platform thirty-three joined the main strip of platforms on the upper level. It was still hard to be careful enough, though.

"Ow!"

"Sorry, I didn't see you."

Nita had to snicker softly at that. "It's mutual. There's the door—"

"Yeah. Are we away from the cameras now?"

"Wait a sec . . . Yeah, no new ones since we were here last. Let's lose these."

They both stepped into the shadows, dumped the spells that cloaked them, and flicked back into visibility. Kit slipped out of his backpack, brushed himself down, and put the backpack over one shoulder again.

"Itchy?" Nita said.

"Yeah, being invisible does that to me...It didn't used to." He glanced down at Ponch. "I think I'm catching it from somebody."

It's not my fault, Ponch said, sounding virtuous. *Maybe you're just starting to feel your skin for a change.*

Kit rolled his eyes. "Come on," he said.

They went out through the gate for the platform between tracks fifteen and sixteen and paused just past it, looking up and down the length of the Main Concourse. It was a bright day; the scattered light of the sunbeams striking through the great south windows washed through the dusty early-afternoon air and lit up the turquoise of the painted sky high above them, washing out its stars. As they walked across the Concourse, good smells came from every direction—most obviously from the steak restaurant at one end of the Concourse terrace and the "progressive American" restaurant at the other.

"Whaddaya think," Kit said. "Food hall?"

Nita gave him a pretend-shocked look. "You mean you're not going to just sit down on the stairs here and eat your bag lunch?"

Kit gave Nita a look. "I'm saving it for when I'm feeling homesick. Meanwhile..."

"Aha," said a voice from just below knee level. "I heard you were coming through this morning."

Nita looked down. Standing by them was a big, stocky, silvery gray tabby cat, waving his tail, and Nita knew only she and Kit and Ponch could see him because he was using a form of selective invisibility that left him visible to wizards but invisible to other humans. "Hey, Urruah!" Nita said. *"Dai stihó!"*

Urruah was one of the feline wizards who kept the New York worldgates running properly, cats being much better than other Earthly species at seeing the superstrings on which the gates' structures were hung. "Ponch," Kit said, "would you come sit over here so it doesn't look like we're talking to the floor? Thanks."

Ponch sat down next to Urruah, gazing at him. For a moment or so their gazes locked, then Ponch put down his ears, which had been up, and let his tongue hang out.

Urruah's whiskers went forward. "Nice doggy," he said.

Woof, woof, Ponch said, his eyes glinting. The irony was audible.

"Good to see you," Kit said. "Where's Rhiow today?"

"Our esteemed team leader," Urruah said, "is over in the FF'arhleih Building—that's the old post office over on Eighth Avenue—getting the substrates ready for when we move the worldgates over."

"I didn't think the new Penn Station was going to be ready for months yet," Nita said.

"It's not," Urruah said. "But the more time you give the worldgate substrates to root, the less trouble the gates give you when you put them in place. We're getting ready to install a 'mirror' substrate in the new building. Meanwhile, I see you're going somewhere for pleasure today..."

"A sponsored noninterventional excursus," Nita said.

Urruah grinned. "I did one of those once," he said. "The species was aquatic: I didn't feel dry for weeks afterward. Nice people, though. Where are they sending you?"

"Alaalu."

"Never heard of it," Urruah said. "But why should I? There are a billion homeworlds out there, and no time to see them all. By the way, were you issued subsidized jump-throughs?"

"You mean the custom worldgates? Yeah," Kit said.

"And they're wrapped up tight?" Urruah said. "You haven't tried to commission them?"

"Huh? No," Nita said. "The docs said you absolutely shouldn't do that."

"Okay, good," Urruah said. "That's fine."

"But why shouldn't you?" Kit said.

Urruah gave him a look. "You mean, why shouldn't you take an open worldgate through an open worldgate? Please. Temporal eversions are bad enough. Those you can patch, or revert, if you know how. Even simple spatial ones, if the effect isn't spread over too much area. But a *multidimensional* one—"

"Everything turns inside out?" Nita said, guessing.

Urruah gave her a pitying look. "The reality would be much more complex, much worse, and *very* much less reversible. Since I assume you like this planet as it is, and not as eighth-dimensional origami, let's not do it. When are you two scheduled back?"

"Two weeks."

"Well, have a good time," Urruah said. "Try not to destroy your host civilization or anything. Are you going via the Crossings?"

"Yeah," Kit said.

"I hoped so. Would you mind doing an errand as you pass through?"

"Sure," Nita said, "no problem."

"Great—I appreciate it. Stop by the Stationmaster's office when you get there and tell him we'd appreciate it if they'd route the elective main trunk nontypical traffic around us for the next thirty-six hours. We're doing some maintenance on the local gate substrates."

Kit had his manual open and was making a note. "Thirty-six hours...Got it."

"That should be plenty of time. I'll message him when the maintenance is done, and one of us will drop by in a day or three to discuss some other matters." Urruah got up and stretched. "Meanwhile, your transit gate will be off platform eighteen. We just moved it over there from thirty; the Metro-North staff are doing track welding today. The locus'll be patent for the Crossings in about six minutes, after the two-twenty to Croton-Harmon gets out of your way. If you hurry, you can catch it."

"Thanks," Nita said. "*Dai*, big guy."

"*Dai*," Urruah said to her and Kit, and waved his tail at Ponch as he turned.

"*Auhw heei u'uuw Iau'hwu rrrhh'uiu*," Ponch said to Urruah.

Urruah paused in midturn, and Nita's eyes widened slightly as she caught sight of the look on Urruah's face. It was always dangerous to judge animals' expressions by comparing them with human ones, but wizards' knowledge of the subverbal modes of the Speech lent them some slight latitude in reading nonhuman expressions—at least those of creatures from their own worlds that were not too far removed from them in basic psychology. Whatever Ponch had said, it had been in Ailurin, the cats' language, and it hadn't been something Urruah had been expecting. It had also gone by too quickly for Nita to "listen" in the Speech and hear what it had meant.

"Uh, yes, certainly," Urruah said, recovering himself. He waved his tail at them all once more, then strolled off across the Main Concourse, weaving from side to side to avoid the commuters, who couldn't see him.

They turned away, and Kit looked at Ponch with some surprise. "What was that about?" Kit said. "I didn't know you spoke cat."

Correspondence course, said Ponch, and kept on walking.

Nita threw Kit a glance. *Have I told you recently,* she said silently, *that your dog is getting* strange?

You and the rest of the world...

The three of them made their way to the gate for platform eighteen and, once through it, slipped to the right of it, away from the main part of the platform, where they wouldn't be seen disappearing. *Hurry up,* Ponch said as Kit's invisibility spell came down over him, too. *It itches!*

"So stop complaining and come on," Kit said. They walked down the length of the platform, staying to the left side, where there was no train. People went tearing past them on the right as down at the end of the platform the 2:20's conductor yelled "'Boarrrrrrrrrrrd!" Those last few people made it onto the train, its doors closed, and with a great revving roar of locomotive engines, deafening in that confined space, it slowly began to pull out.

Kit and Nita and Ponch stayed off to the side while a few more people came running down the platform, saw that the train was already on its way out, and slowed to a stop, then turned and went back down toward the Main Concourse to find out when the next train was. "We're clear," Nita said softly. "Come on."

The three of them made their way down to the end of the platform, where steps led down to the track level. The steps were of no interest to them, though: They looked to their left, where no train stood...but where the air just past the platform's edge, to a wizard's eye, rippled gently, as if with uprising heat.

"It's patent," Kit said. "Let's go. Ponch, jump it, the edge is sharp..."

I know that!

Kit grinned, took a deep breath, glanced at Nita. She nodded. They stepped forward together, into the empty air, into the dark, as Ponch jumped past them...

...and the three of them stepped out again a long second later, ditching their invisibility spells in the process, into the white brilliance of the Nontypical Transit area at the Crossings Hypergate Facility on Rirhath B.

The gating was a "hardwired" one, long-established and with a lot of comfort features built in for the convenience of the wizards who used it every day on business. Nita and Kit came out on the other side without feeling the unsettling effects usually associated with moving several light-years between worlds, which were not only spinning in different directions and velocities but being dragged through interstellar space by their home stars along wildly differing vectors. The three of them took a moment to just stand there on the shining white floor and look around. The place was worth looking at.

Nontypical Transit was a wide empty space about the size of a football field, and around it that wide white floor went on and on for so far around on all sides that Nita was fairly sure she ought to have been able to see the curvature of the world, had it not been so completely covered with people of a thousand different species. "Is it rush hour?" she said.

"Probably. Let's get out of here before something materializes on top of us." This wasn't really a concern, Nita knew, as the manual made it plain that the whole NT area was programmed not to allow two different transportees, whether using wizardry or another form of worldgating, to occupy the same space. All the same, she and Kit and Ponch made their way toward the edge of the Nontypical Transit area, looking up at what every tourist passing through the Crossings spent some time admiring: the ceiling. Or rather, the ceilings, for there were thousands of them, real and false, interpenetrating one another or floating under or over one another, in a myriad of airy, randomly shaped structures of glass and metal and other materials that Nita didn't immediately recognize. The effect was like a shattered, miles-wide, horizontal stained glass window, eternally looking for new and interesting ways to assemble itself, and then eternally changing its mind. It was morning at the moment, and the violent silver-gilt light of Rirhath B, only slightly softened by the eternal green-white cloud of daylight hours, burned through the glass high above them and cast bright, sliding shadows on the vast floor in a thousand colors, all changing every moment as ceilings high up in the tremendous structure briefly eclipsed one another and parted company again.

"It's different from last time," Kit said.

Nita nodded as they finally reached the end of the NT area. It had been night the last time they'd been here, and at night the ceilings simply seemed to go away, appearing to leave the whole vast terminal floor open to the view of Rirhath B's astonishing night sky—a crowded vista of short-period variable stars, all swelling and shrinking like living things that breathed light. "This is nice, too," Nita said, and then had to laugh at herself as they headed out into the main terminal floor. *Nice* was a poor word for this tremendous space, for its many cubic miles of stacked-up glass and metal galleries, holding offices, stores, restaurants, and a hundred other kinds of facilities for which English has no words.

Nita and Kit and Ponch made their way down the main drag toward the core of the terminal structure, taking their time. There were three main wings to the Crossings, each several miles long, and there were small intergates strung all down the length of each wing, marked on the floor by ellipses in various visible and invisible colors. There was also a selective-friction slidewalk down one side of each wing, which, while looking no different than the rest of the polished white floor, would scoot you along at high speed if you were in a hurry. But Nita was in no rush, and neither was Kit. Ponch paced along beside them, plainly enjoying himself, looking at all the strange people and smelling the strange smells, and amiably wagging his tail.

Scattered down the length of the mile-wide wing before them, in the middle of the floor, were platforms and daises and kiosks and counters of various shapes and sizes, each with a long, tall, cylindrical black sign on a black metal pole. These were gate indicators, flashing their destinations and patency times in hundreds of languages and hundreds of colors. Kit paused by one of these as they came up to it, a ring-fenced area where a number of people who looked like huge furbearing turtles striped in orange and gray were waiting for their gate to go patent. Kit put his hand on the pole and said in the Speech, "Information for Alaalu?"

On the side facing him and Nita, the jarring red symbols that had previously been showing there blanked out and were replaced by a long string of symbols in blue, in the Speech, which uncurled itself down the length of the sign. "Wing three," Nita said, "gate five-oh-six…"

"In a little more than an hour," Kit said.

"Great," Nita said. "We can sit down somewhere near the gate and have a snack."

Kit got a dubious look. "Uhh…"

Nita laughed at him: Kit had had a major problem with some of the local food their last time through. "*This* time," she said, "just don't eat anything you don't recognize, and you'll be fine."

"Same rule as for the school cafeteria, I guess," Kit said. "Yeah, why not? But let's get that errand done for Urruah first."

"Yeah."

They made their way to the central area for which the whole facility was named: the original Crossings. Once upon a time, two and a half millennia before, it had been just a muddy place by a riverbank—one that became a crossroads over time as its own native species learned to exploit it. Then, much later, it became an interplanetary and interstellar crossroads as well. Soon, now, with the opening of the new extension, it would add intergalactic transport as well, becoming a master hub for worldgating operations among three other galaxies of the Local Group. But the Crossings would remain paramount among the intragalactic hubs, its local space having about it a concentration of those forces that, when entwined with specific planetary characteristics, made gating easier than anywhere else.

All alone in the middle of a great expanse of floor was the spot where a reed hut had stood by the riverbank, not far from the ancient cave that contained a natural worldgate. At the cave's entrance, a sequence of footprints in the mud had suddenly stopped without warning—an image as famous on Rirhath B as the corrugated bootprint of an astronaut in the moondust was famous on Earth. Cave and hut were long gone. In their place stood a cubical structure of tubular bluesteel, no different from many of the other kiosks that stood around the Crossings. This one had nothing in it but a desk, its surface covered with inset, illuminated input patches of many shapes and colors, the shapes and colors shifting every second. Behind the desk was a meter-high rack of thinner bluesteel tubing, shaped somewhat like the kind of kickable step stool to be found in libraries. And inside the rack, more or less—except where its many jointed legs hung out of the structure, or were curled around the racking for support—was the Stationmaster.

Nita and Kit walked up to the desk. Nita was calm enough about it at first: She'd been here before. But then she had a sudden panic attack. *What do we say to it?* she thought, looking at the silvery blue giant centipede, which was busily banging away with its front four or six legs at the input patches on the desk. When you were on wizardly business, the same phrase did the job no matter where you were: "I am on errantry, and I greet you!" But they *weren't* on errantry this time out....

Kit and Nita paused in front of the desk, and the

Rirhait behind it looked at them with several stalky eyes: The others kept their attention on what it was doing. "Oh," the Stationmaster said. "*You* again."

"Nice to see you, too," Kit said.

Ponch sat down beside Kit, looking at the Stationmaster with an expression that suggested he wasn't sure whether to chase it or run away. The Master, in its turn, turned an eye in Ponch's direction, and the eye's oval pupil dilated and contracted a couple of times.

"They're hard on their associates, these two," the Stationmaster said to Ponch. "And on the surroundings. Where they go, things tend to get trashed. Are you insured?"

Ponch yawned. *I'm not too worried about it,* he said.

"It wasn't our fault, the last time," Kit said, sounding just slightly annoyed. "*We* weren't the ones who chased Nita's sister through the terminal with blasters."

"Not to mention the dinosaur," Nita said.

"No, I suppose not," the Stationmaster said, waving a casual claw in the air. "Well, the facility's general fund handled it, and all the damage caused by your broodmate's incursion and departure has been repaired now." It tapped away at the desk a little more. "I assume this isn't a social call..."

"No, actually," Kit said, and pulled out his manual. "The New York gating team asked us to deliver a message, since we were passing this way."

At that, six of the Stationmaster's eight eyes fixed on Kit, all their pupils dilating at once. The effect was disconcerting. "New York," it said. "That would be Earth."

It sounded actively annoyed. "That's right," Kit said, throwing Nita a glance as he flipped open his manual. "Here's what they say—" He read Urruah's message aloud.

The Stationmaster's antennae worked while Kit read, the equivalent of a nod. "Very well," it said. "I'll message them when I have a moment. Let's move on. You have your departure data?"

"Yes," Kit said.

"Excellent. Don't let the gate constrict on your fundament on the way out," the Master said, and it poured itself out of its rack, whisked around and out of the kiosk, and went hastening away across the concourse, on all those legs, without another word.

A few moments' worth of silence passed as Nita and Kit watched him go. "Maybe I'm from a little backwater planet at the outside edge of the Arm," Kit said, "but where I come from, we would call that *rude.*"

"Oh, come on, you can't be judgmental," Nita said.

"It didn't even say thank you!"

"Well..."

"You agree with me," Kit said with some satisfaction.

Nita let out a long breath and turned to start walking in the general direction of their gate. "Yeah," she said. "Even though I'm probably wrong to."

Kit made a face as they turned away. "Okay," he said, "and you're probably right that I shouldn't judge it by human standards. Maybe there was something else on its mind."

"Maybe," Nita said. "Though...it might be possible that Rirhait are just naturally rude."

Kit sighed. "It doesn't matter," he said. "We did the errand. Let's go get some lunch."

He still didn't sound as if he was entirely happy about the idea. "You've still got your bag lunch if you want it," Nita said.

Kit laughed, then. "Nah. What's the point of going to alien worlds if you're not going to at least try to eat their junk food on the way? Let's go down by the gate and see what's there."

An hour later, they made their way over to the pretransit area by their gate. "That wasn't so bad," Kit said. "A lot better than last time..."

"Last time you didn't read the menu," Nita said. She had to grin, though, because this time the problem had been to get Kit to *stop* reading it.

Ponch was wandering along beside them looking as satisfied as Kit. They'd found a little snack bar a hundred yards or so along from gate 506, and once they'd figured out how to convert the seating system to suit bipedal humanoids, they discovered that all the tables had an embedded, programmable menu of a type new to Nita. You told the table, or touched in, the long version of the ten-letter acronym for your species— adding eight letters that concerned themselves only with your body chemistry—and the menu embedded in the tabletop changed itself to show only things that wouldn't disagree with you. Kit, having tested one dish that looked like blue pasta, had been so taken with the flavor that he'd gone on a "blue binge" and eaten six more blue things, sharing them with Ponch.

"I can't believe you pigged out like that," Nita said under her breath as they made their way over to the pretransit lounge for their gate.

"Why not? It was good!"

"It was *free*," Nita said.

"Oh, come on. Nothing's free. You know that."

"Of course I do. I mean, you didn't have to pay for it..."

They had both been prepared to pay for what they ate. Typically, when a wizard was on errantry, the transfer of energy to pay for things was handled by the manual, to be deducted later if deferment was appropriate. But when they'd tried to take care of the bill early, putting their manuals down on the table's deduction patch, the table had simply said CHARGED TO GENERAL FUND — EXCURSUS. Once they'd realized that the cultural exchange program was taking care of their expenses, Kit had gone, to Nita's way of thinking, a little bit nuts.

Now, walking along beside them, Ponch burped happily and wagged his tail. *When can we come back?*

"You've done it now," Nita said. "You've got him spoiled for alien food. Your mom's going to have words with you..."

"Aw, he knows it's a vacation. Don't you, Ponch?"

Yes. But we can come back other times! And Ponch paused. *I can come here by myself, too.*

Nita shook her head as they made their way over to the transit gate. "From now on you'll know where to find him when he's missing," she said. "Shaking down alien tourists for blue stuff."

Their gate was like many others in that part of the terminal: an information kiosk with a big, flat, vertical screen, a tall standard with the gate number, and the outline of a hexagon embedded in the floor, constantly shifting colors and wavelengths of light as it tried to make itself visible to as many species' visual senses as possible. By the kiosk, a gate technician was standing—a tall bipedal humanoid in a green glass jumpsuit cut down the back to allow its rudimentary wings room to move.

Nita went up to her and held out her manual. "We're scheduled for a gating to Alaalu," she said.

"Alaalu?" whistled the gate technician in a cordial tone as she took Nita's manual, waved it in front of the data screen. "Never heard of it. Where is it?"

"Radian one-sixty somewhere," Nita said.

The gate tech's feathered crest went up and down as the display brought up an abbreviated version of Nita's name and identity information in the Speech, along with a little bare-bones schematic of the galaxy. "Oh, I see. Thank you, Emissary," she said, handing Nita back her manual. "How interesting... I've never gated anyone there before. It doesn't seem to get much traffic. But then that's quite a jump; it's nice for you that it's subsidized, isn't it?"

"We sure think so," Kit said. Usually, the energy to pay for such a "fixed" gating also eventually would have been deducted through the manual, either in a lump or as time payment—and even the extended-payment option could leave a wizard fairly wrecked when such distances were involved.

The gate technician put her crest up in a smile. "So do a lot of your colleagues. I've seen quite a few of them through here in the past two hands of days."

Nita stole a look at the technician's claws. *A little more than a week...* "Do these exchanges usually all happen at this time of year, or are they staggered?" she said, curious.

"I've never thought about it," said the gate tech, taking Kit's manual and waving it in front of the display in turn. "I always assumed they were staggered. But there does seem to be an unusual amount of excursus traffic right now." Kit's information came up, and the gate tech examined it for a moment, then handed Kit back his manual and raised her crest to Ponch. "It's probably a coincidence. The time indicator's up there on the standard, Emissary, Interlocutor. Stand clear of the locus until it goes dark, then enter it and hold your position. And go well."

"Thank you." They wandered over to the standard; Nita put her hand on it. "Minutes, please?" she said.

The characters running up and down the standard writhed, gathered itself together into a bright blob, and then resolved itself into the digits 14:03. The last two digits then started counting down in seconds.

"Not long now," Nita said, putting her manual back in her backpack. "I can't wait!"

Ponch sat down, his tongue hanging out, and burped again. *Is there time for a nap?*

"No!" Kit and Nita said in unison.

Ponch let out a big sigh. *Oh, well...*

They waited. Five minutes went by, and then ten, and they were still the only ones waiting there. "This must *really* be a quiet place we're going to," Nita said to Kit.

"That's what the manuals said."

"Terrific!" Nita said. And right at that moment, the hexagon on the floor in front of them went black.

"Let's go!" Kit said. They stepped into the hexagon; Ponch got up, sauntered onto it, and sat down next to Kit. On the standard nearby, the digits changed themselves to read "59," and started counting down again.

Nita became aware that her heart was pounding. She had to smile as the count went down past thirty, and she stole a glance at Kit and saw that he was grinning, too. "20...15...10..."

Nita almost felt like she should be hearing rocket engines igniting, but around them was nothing but the sound of hoots and shrieks and rumbles and roars and laughter, the voices of life. *Here we go!* she thought.

3, said the countdown clock on the standard.

2

1—

—and then Nita found herself under another sky, with the wind in her hair.

She took a first deep breath of another world's air, rich with scents she couldn't identify—and then completely forgot to breathe as she tried to find the horizon and get herself oriented. It wasn't that there was any trouble finding the horizon. In front of her lay endless green fields all starred with blue flowers, until, as she looked much farther away, the blue of the flowers was all she could see. But beyond that, where the horizon should have been, there was more of it; landscape dappled in a hundred shades of green and blue green, sloping upward to gently rolling hill country, sloping further upward still to the beginnings of mountains. They were not so high by themselves, but the horizon was. To Nita, the world around her seemed to climb halfway up that blue, blue sky, three-quarters of the way up it, impossibly high. It felt wrong. But it wasn't. *It's me,* she told herself, working to breathe. *It's just me...*

Nita knew perfectly well that the apparent flatness of her home planet was an illusion. She had seen, on the Moon, the unexpected curvature of a body much smaller than the Earth, so that the horizon seemed cramped and close, and things a mile or so away seemed much too near. What she saw now was the opposite of that. Things that seemed far away would turn out to be farther still. Those mountains towering up against the edge of things were even farther away. And that was the problem. It shouldn't be possible to be under a sky and still see things that were so far away, against a horizon that left you feeling you were at the bottom of a huge, shallow bowl, with all that blue sky pooling on top of you, pouring onto you like water, pressing you down....

It's just big, Nita thought. *Just the size of the planet makes it seem this way.* But it was *too* big. And something else about it seized her by the heart and squeezed, so that she was almost having trouble breathing.

Why do I know this place? Nita thought. *What does this remind me of?*

"Neets?" Kit said to her. "Neets, are you all right?"

She swallowed. "Yeah," she said. "How about you?"

"Uh, yeah."

She glanced over at Kit. He looked a little pale but seemed otherwise all right. "But how can it be this big?" she said. "How can *anything* be this big? And do you feel it—"

"There you are! Sorry I'm late," someone said from behind them. "*Dai stihó,* cousins. Welcome to Alaalu!"

Arrivals

DAIRINE STOOD OUTSIDE the back door, glancing occasionally at her watch and waiting.

Even before she'd been a wizard, waiting had been tough for her. *Nothing happens fast enough*—that had been the most basic motto of her short life. When she'd become a wizard, at first Dairine had thought that that would be the end of waiting, at last—that everything would begin happening at a speed that would suit *her*, and that the world would finally start working. Now, looking back at that early time, she had to laugh at herself. Dairine had discovered the hard way that even becoming a practitioner of the Art that sourced its power from the magic at the heart of the universe was no guarantee of protection against bureaucracy, accident, or failed expectations. Entropy was running, and in an environment conditioned by the never-ending battle against that ancient enemy and its inventor, not even wizardry could necessarily make your wishes come true.

There were other compensations, of course. On her Ordeal and after it, she had seen things that few other human beings have been privileged to see. She had watched the Sun rise through Saturn's rings, heard spring thunder in Jupiter's atmosphere, watched distant galaxies rise over alien landscapes; she had even offici- ated at the birth of a species. But none of these experi- ences had gone very far to make her any more patient. *Maybe when I'm older,* she thought. *By the time I'm twenty I'll probably have it licked.*

It wasn't licked yet, though. Dairine looked at her watch again. *It's ten after three,* she thought. *Where are these people?*

Beside her, on the step, Spot sat and looked at the sunny spring afternoon with a much calmer attitude than Dairine. *Probably gate-traffic congestion,* he said.

Behind the thought came the usual background that Dairine heard when she and Spot were communicating: a sort of stream-of-machine-consciousness, a trinary roar, seething with background thought that sounded like distant surf. The background thought was both Spot's and that of the far-distant wizardly machine in- telligence to which Dairine was a sort of godmother, and with which she had been affiliated since passing her Ordeal. Sometimes that distant activity of mind, half manual, half living thing, looked out through Dairine's eyes and lived with her at what it considered an incred- ibly leisurely pace, thinking thoughts in whole seconds rather than in milliseconds; but mostly it went about its own business at its own speed, a blur of thought of which only the high points emerged in Dairine's consciousness. Now, in that mode, Spot said, *It's not as if they're using a private gating complex. There may be delays at the other end—*

"Yeah," Dairine said. She sat on the step again—this was probably the fourth or fifth time she'd stood and sat down—and picked Spot up. "Let me see that briefing pack again."

Spot obligingly flipped up his screen and went into "wizard's manual" mode. On the screen appeared Dairine's version, in the Speech, of the briefing pack that the Powers That Be, or their administrative assistants, had sent her dad. Dairine had read it through once last night, mostly with an eye to seeing how good the translation was. Even considering the source, she was concerned that a Speech-to-text utility couldn't be perfect. There were words in the Speech that simply didn't go into English, and Dairine had wanted to make sure there wasn't anything in her dad's version of the briefing that he was going to misconstrue. To her relief, though, the material had been translated as perfectly as could have been expected, the translation being more a simplification than anything else.

Each of the visitors had his—or *its*—own page in the package. There were 3-D "live" pictures of them embedded in the briefing pack, though even in manual-based documents there was never any guarantee that the image would be an exact rendition of any being's state or likeness when it actually arrived. But even if the documentation hadn't exactly and accurately portrayed them, they were still, to put it mildly, a mixed bunch. The Rirhait was more like a giant metallic purple centipede than anything else; one of twenty-four of its parents' first brood hatched out, very newly become a wizard—within the past Rirhait year, which was about two Earth years. It was interested enough in other worlds and other scholia of wizardry to have applied for this excursus almost as soon as it hit post-Ordeal status. "It" was probably incorrect: Sker'ret (that being the part of his name that Dairine could most easily pronounce, the rest being all consonants) was more or less a "he."

She keyed ahead to the next page. All of the visitors, in fact, were "he"s, though with the next one, it was hard to say exactly what made him that way. *Maybe it's the berries,* Dairine thought, studying his picture. Filifermanhathrhumneits'elhhessaiffnth was his whole name, a word that to Dairine sounded oddly like wind in branches—and that was probably appropriate because he was a tree. *If there are trees that walk,* Dairine thought. But, plainly, on his world, Demisiv, there were…though *walking* probably wasn't the right word for it. They got around, anyway, and could be surprisingly mobile when they needed to be. As far as Dairine could tell from the manual's description of the Demisiv people, they spent all their lives wading around through the ground, and the whole surface of their sealess planet was one great migratory forest, with mighty bands of trees rooting only briefly and then getting on the move again, hunting other skies to grow under, new ground to grow in. *Maybe the concept of a tree with wanderlust isn't so weird,* Dairine thought as she studied Filif's image, which looked rather like a

Christmas tree with red berries. *His whole people seem to have it, in a way. He's just wandering farther than usual…*

She keyed ahead to the last page in the info packet and looked at it rather speculatively. "Roshaun ke Nelaid (am Seriv am Teliuyve am Meseph am Veliz…) det Wellakhit," said the entry beside the live image of someone who was obviously humanoid. *Good thing Neets isn't here,* Dairine thought, studying that picture one more time, *because he's really hot.*

The manual gave only a head shot unless you requested another view of a subject, and right then Dairine didn't bother. Roshaun-and-all-the-rest-of-the-names was handsome, almost perfectly so—and it was the disbelief in his apparent perfection that kept Dairine looking at him rather longer than she intended. He had a long, fair-skinned face with a very thoughtful expression. This was partially concealed by surprisingly long, blond hair, most of which was tied behind his head, but he also had very long bangs, which he was probably always pushing out of his eyes, and a long lock of hair hanging down in front of each ear. The eyes were a startling green, a shade not normally achieved on Earth without the assistance of contact lenses.

He's definitely a looker, Dairine thought, though the handsomeness was a little less striking now, on her second or third glance, than it had been at the first. *What is it with his name, though? It goes on and on.* She looked at the referral to the planet Wellakh, turned to that page, and tried to find something that explained the name structure. She scanned down the planet's entry, skipping the usual information about size and location and so forth, looking for anything that could give her a hint.

Something's coming, Spot said.

Through him she could feel the faint troubling of local space that meant a worldgating was incoming: a kind of curdling or shivering in the air. Dairine stood up. "Well, finally," she said. "How many? Are they all together, or are they coming separately?"

Separately, I think, Spot said.

"Where's the locus of emergence?"

Out in the backyard, where you and Nita usually vanish.

"Right," Dairine said. She snapped Spot's lid shut and headed through the backyard to the part farthest to its rear, where the sassafras trees had been growing wild for as long as Dairine could remember.

Though her dad was careful about the landscaping, he had purposely left the back of the lot a casual, partial wilderness of trees of all sizes, self-seeding, and blocking the view of the yard from the neighbors' lots. About fifteen feet in among them, well sheltered by growth of all sizes, was an empty patch about six feet in diameter, which Nita had talked into staying that way. There the ground was bare of everything but fallen leaves, and just outside that spot Dairine now stationed herself, putting Spot down.

"How long?" she said.

Any moment—

Her hair blew back in the abrupt breeze of an appearance, which made only a very small *Whumf!* sound as the air displaced. Standing in front of her, low down in that rough circle of brown and gold leaves, was the Rirhait, gleaming softly in the sunlight that was filtering through the new leaves. Likening him to a centipede, Dairine thought, was probably a little simplistic. The body wasn't a series of smooth sections but looked rather as if a number of metallic purple beach balls had been stuck together, flattening a little at the ends. Then someone had attached three pairs of legs to each beach ball—two pointing down, and a third pointing up. *When we get friendly, I've got to ask him what those extra ones are for,* Dairine thought. At one end of the centipede, stalked eyes—Dairine thought there were about eight of them—were fastened to the top of the last "beach ball," and there were some scissory mouth parts underneath.

The Rirhait was doing something Dairine herself had done often enough: shifting a little from foot to foot to check the gravity, to see if he needed to adjust his wizardry to compensate. In the Rirhait's case, this produced an effect something like a spectator wave. All the while he looked around with his own version of an expression Dairine had worn, herself, often enough— that first glance in which you try to get your bearings in an alien environment as quickly as possible, getting the scale of things, while trying not to look as if you're completely freaked out. How she would tell if a Rirhait was freaked out, Dairine wasn't sure. For the moment, the best approach was to keep it from getting that way to start with.

"*Dai stihó!*" she said right away in the Speech, to give her guest something to fix on. "Are you Sker'ret?"

"That's me," the Rirhait said after a moment. "And you'd be Darren?"

"Dairine," she said. "Maybe you want to move over—" But the Rirhait was already pouring himself out of the circle and over toward Dairine. She looked curiously down at him as he came: He reminded her strangely of a favorite pull toy she'd had when she was about four.

"Were you waiting long?" he said.

"No," Dairine said. "How was the trip at your end?"

"The usual," Sker'ret said. "You hurry to get to the gating facility and then you sit around and wait forever."

Dairine had to laugh. Sker'ret looked up at her with all its eyes, in shock.

"Sorry?" he said.

"No," she said, "it's all right. I was laughing. That's a happy sound."

"Thanks, I was wondering," Sker'ret said. "I thought you had something in your throat."

The air in front of them trembled. There was another, even more demure explosion of air and sound, more a *pop!* than anything else. And there stood a tree.

Except he wasn't a tree. "*Dai stihó!*" Dairine said, and was delighted to see the branches of the tree shiver in unison and look at her with all their berries.

"*Dai!*" the tree said.

"I hope you'll forgive me," Dairine said, "but your

name's kind of a mouthful for me. Will Filif be all right?"

"We use that at home," Filif said. His voice was absolutely the rustling of wind in leaves. Dairine wondered how he did it, because all she could see were needles, which wouldn't rustle terribly well.

The tree part of Filif seemed fine; Dairine cast a glance down at his roots and saw that they were shrouded in a kind of portable haze. She recognized this instantly as a decency field, used by some wizards to conceal a part of themselves that they didn't feel it appropriate to show to other people, either of their own species or another one.

"How was your trip?" Dairine said. "Is there anything you need right now?"

"No, I'm fine," Filif said. There was a diffident sound to his voice that made Dairine wonder whether this was strictly the truth—but he was using the Speech, so it couldn't be a lie.

"Good," she said. "We'll go in, in a little while, and get you guys settled in. You have your pup tents all set up?"

"Oh, yes," the two said in unison.

Dairine looked around her. "Speaking of which, where's our third guy?"

Filif and Sker'ret looked at each other. "We weren't early, were we?" Sker'ret said.

"No," Dairine said. "Roshaun of the multiple names seems to be—"

BANG!

The wind blew Dairine's hair back, and a tall figure

imploded into the space in the middle of the circle of leaves. He was nearly as tall as Dairine's dad and was dressed in what even Dairine, the consummate T-shirt and baggy pants fan, was willing to describe as "splendid robes." He was wearing an undertunic and hose and boots in some golden fabric or substance. There was an overtunic or long jacket in scarlet, all embroidered over in gold; and he was wearing gauntlets of gold, and a strange sort of scarf of gold over the outer jacket. And there was a fillet of gold bound around his head, but it was a more reddish gold, which wonderfully set off all that hair, which, it turned out, went right down his back and was long enough for him to sit on. There he stood, looking around imperiously at all of them, his thumbs hooked in the broad golden belt under the overtunic.

Dairine's first thought, which she couldn't control, was, *Noisy arrival. Sloppy technique.*

Her second thought was, *Maybe it's something cultural, dressing up so fancy.* But the back of her mind answered instantly and without reason: *Yeah, sure. He's showing off. And why?*

The new arrival looked around.

"And where is the welcoming committee?" he said.

Dairine didn't know quite what she'd been expecting from the final arrival, but this wasn't it. *"Dai stihó,"* she said after a moment.

That tall, blond figure turned his attention to her, and Dairine abruptly felt so short, so insignificant, so very minor. However, the feeling immediately kicked her into a most profound state of annoyance. "Yes," he said after a moment, "may you also go well. And you would be?"

"You're the newcomer," Dairine said, "and I am your host. It's for you to introduce yourself." Where this made-up rule had come from, she had no idea, but she felt disinclined to make things easy for this guy.

He stood there and continued to look down at Dairine, way down, as if from some inaccessible mountain peak. "I," he said, "am Roshaun ke Nelaid am Seriv am Teliuyve am Meseph am Veliz am Teriaunst am det Wellakhit." And he looked at her as if he expected her to know what it meant.

"Pleased to meet you, cousin," Dairine said, feeling that it was just barely true and desperately hoping that at some point it would be more so. But at the moment she was having all kinds of doubts. "I'm Dairine Callahan. Welcome to Earth."

Roshaun looked around at the scrubby wooded surroundings with those green, green eyes. "This is perhaps a public park?" he said.

"No," Dairine said. "It's part of the property that belongs to our house. We use this area for coming and going on business, because our planet is *sevarfrith.*"

The Rirhait and the Demisiv each nodded or twitched briefly. *Sevarfrith* was a syllabic acronym for several words in the Speech that, taken together, meant "a world where wizardry must be conducted under cover." There were numerous longer forms of the acronym that indicated the general or specific reason for the restriction, but the simple version often was used as shorthand. Dairine knew that this information would have been in the visitors' own orientation packs, but it seemed like a good time to mention it.

"That's a shame for you, isn't it?" the Rirhait said. "I'm sorry about your trouble."

"It's okay," Dairine said. "It's more of a logistical problem than anything else. You get used to it after a while. The best thing to do is treat it as if it's a game. For the first day or so, while you guys are getting used to being here, I've taken the liberty of setting up a wizardry around the perimeter so that the people who live in the immediate vicinity won't see anything, in case somebody's visual overlay slips. If you look around, you can see it—I've left the perimeter visually active for anyone who uses the Speech." She gestured around her, indicating the paired lines of blue green light that ran around the backyard from the left rear corner of the house, down the property line and above the chain-link fence, right around the back of the property, where they were standing, and up the right side toward the garage. "Inside that, you're safe in your own shape. At night, though, there may be some leakage of light from inside the space, and we can't be certain that some of the neighbors might not be able to see you; so it's better to be careful."

The Demisiv looked up through the leaves of the trees at the shifting light of the sky above, where clouds were racing by in a stiff wind. "That's fine," Filif said. "We wouldn't want to frighten anybody."

"Come on this way," Dairine said, and led them out of the woods. "Oh," she said, "and this is my associate, Spot."

Spot put up a selection of stalked eyes and looked around him, fixing on each of the aliens in turn. *"Dai stihó,"* he said.

"Dai," said Filif and Sker'ret. Roshaun peered down at the small laptop in Dairine's arms. "Is it sentient?" he said.

I'm beginning to think he's more sentient than you are, Dairine thought. And immediately after that, she thought, *What is the* matter *with me?*

"We like to think so," Dairine said, as politely as she could. "Though since he and I started working together a couple of years ago, there've been a few discussions over which of us is more sentient."

They made their way up the lawn toward the house. "It's spring here!" Filif said. "I love the colors."

"Yeah," Dairine said. "They haven't really started yet, though. In a few weeks there'll be a lot more flowers here."

"Oh," Roshaun said, "so the look of the place *will* improve, then? I'm glad to hear it. At home, we would have had the groundskeepers reprimanded."

Dairine flushed as hot as if someone had insulted her, or her dad, or Nita, to her face. There was something insufferably superior about Roshaun's delivery. *I have to be imagining this,* Dairine thought. *I've known this guy exactly two minutes. It's much too soon to believe that he's a complete turkey.*

Nonetheless, as Roshaun looked around the Callahan backyard, as he took in the slightly beat-up lawn furniture and the artfully ragged plantings, he radiated a sense that all of this was below him, somehow. *I don't get it,* Dairine thought. *Where is he getting this attitude? All the wizards I've ever known have been nice!*

Well, Spot said in her head, *how many wizards have you* known?

That brought her up short. *Well...,* she said.

Sker'ret, oblivious to what was going on inside Dairine's head, was looking around him in all directions, a job made easier by stalked eyes that went every which way. "Do you have an indoor dwelling place here," it said, "or do you stay outside?"

His tone of Speech was entirely different, suggesting a cheerful interest. "Not this time of year," Dairine said. "It's too cold for us to stay out just yet...though the time's coming. We're heading for the dwelling now—this white structure. Come on inside."

She led the way toward the back door, Spot pacing her. Sker'ret came trundling along behind, followed by Roshaun, with Filif bringing up the rear. "And these other structures built so close to your dwelling," Roshaun said, looking left and right as they approached the house, "more members of your species live in these as well?"

"That's right," Dairine said.

"They are perhaps an extended kinship group?" Roshaun said. "Members of your family?"

"Oh, no," Dairine said. "As I said, they're just our neighbors."

"Neighbors," Roshaun said, as if trying out a completely unfamiliar word. "It's fascinating. At home, it wouldn't be permitted."

Dairine stopped halfway up the stairs to the back door. "Not permitted?" she said. "By whom?"

Roshaun looked at Dairine as if she were insane. "By *us,*" he said. "Our family wouldn't want, you know, *people* looking at them." And the word he used wasn't the plural of the one in the Speech that meant "person, fellow sentient being"; it was one that meant a being markedly less advanced than you in the Great Scheme of Things. Usually the word was used affectionately, or at worst in a neutral mode, for creatures that were aware in some mode but not quite sentient. But Roshaun's tone of voice seemed to put an extra unpleasant spin on it, turning the word into something more like "lowlife."

Dairine stood there wondering if she was suffering from low blood sugar or something of the kind. *It has to be me,* she said. *No one could be so offensive on purpose…and if he's doing it accidentally, then it's not his fault. Why am I finding it so hard to cut him some slack?*

"It must be very lonely for you, then," Dairine said, as politely as she could.

"Oh, no," Roshaun said, "I wouldn't say that…"

The phrasing caught Dairine's attention sharply as she opened the screen door. *You wouldn't say it because it would be true,* she thought.

That insight, if it was one, she filed away for later study. "My father," she said, "isn't here right now. He's still at work. But he'll be along in an hour or so."

"What does he work at?" Sker'ret said.

"He's a florist," Dairine said as they went in the back door into the kitchen.

Filif looked at her with many more berries than previously. "A doctor!" he said.

"Uh—" Dairine paused. She'd translated the English word into the Speech a little loosely, but it struck her as a good idea, on second thought, not to get into the minutiae of floristry any more clearly right now … especially since the image suddenly rose before her mind of what her dad actually *did* with the flowers in his shop. *Yeah, my dad takes the corpses of things that grow in the ground and then arranges them in tasteful designs.* She could just hear herself telling Filif *that.*

"He does landscaping, too," she said hurriedly, having to search around a little for the closest word the Speech had for that. There were several possibilities, but she didn't think the word for terraforming was going to be appropriate here, so she selected a word that implied a smaller scale of operations.

"Oh, an architect," Filif said. "That's a good thing to do for people!"

"Yes…," Dairine said, wishing she'd had a little more time to think about the implications of having a sentient vegetable in the house. *Well, I was the one who couldn't wait to have them here,* she thought. *Now they're here, and I'm just going to have to deal with it.*

"Come on in," Dairine said, "and we'll get you guys settled. Does anyone want some dinner?"

"Dinner?" Filif said.

"Things to eat," Dairine said, as they walked toward the house. "Dinner is the name of the meal we eat, starting around this time of day."

"Definitely!" Sker'ret said. "What have you got?"

"All kinds of things," Dairine said. "We'll see if we can't find you something that will suit your tastes... not to mention your physiologies. This—" she said, indicating the kitchen—is where we do our cooking," Dairine said. Roshaun simply looked around again with that uninterested, down-his-nose expression, but Filif and Sker'ret turned all around, staring at everything in fascination. "Cooking?" Filif said. "What's that?"

"What do you eat that needs to be *cooked*?" Sker'ret said.

"I can see this is going to take some explaining," Dairine said. "It's partly a physiology thing for my people, and partly cultural. But, look, before we get into that, you're going to want to set up your personal worldgates and your pup tents. The pup tents..." She thought about that for a moment. "Sometimes, this time of year, the weather can be unpredictable. Probably it's going to be more convenient for you if you put the pup tents down in the basement."

"Where's that?" Sker'ret said.

"Down the stairs here," Dairine said. "Right by where we came in. See that door? That's the one. Down there—"

Dairine led the way down the stairs. Sker'ret flowed down them past her; Dairine looked over her shoulder to see how Filif was managing. She couldn't see what his roots were doing through the decency field, but he seemed to be having no trouble negotiating the stairs. "Is this okay for you?" Dairine said.

Filif made a little hissing noise that Dairine realized was a chuckle. "I go up and down cliffs all the time at home," he said. "This is a lot less trouble. What's this place for? What's down here?"

"Uh," Dairine said, and then was tempted to laugh. "Nearly everything."

It was true enough. Dairine couldn't remember when the basement had last been cleaned out. The washing machine and clothes dryer were down here, and so was the furnace for the house's central heating. Both of those were off on the left side of the stairs, toward the front of the house. But the rest of the basement... it was a farrago of old lawn furniture, indoor furniture that had been demoted to the basement and never thrown out, a decrepit bicycle or two, cardboard boxes full of old clothes and paperback books that were meant to go to the local thrift store, an old broken chest freezer, in which Dairine's mom had once attempted to raise earthworms....

Dairine found herself wondering whether she should bother being embarrassed about the mess, since at least one of her guests seemed to have no idea what a basement was for. She glanced at Roshaun, who was now looking around with an expression that was more difficult to read.

"A storage area," Roshaun said.

It was the first thing he'd said that hadn't instantly sounded obnoxious. "Sort of," Dairine said. "Though it's gotten a little... cluttered."

"Has it?" Roshaun said. "I wouldn't be an expert in clutter."

Dairine sighed. "I wish I weren't," she said. "Anyway"—she indicated the bare cinder-block wall that was the south wall of the basement—"since you need a matter substrate to deploy your gates on, that should do. And you can leave the pup-tent accesses down here as well."

For a few moments, they were all busy getting out the prepackaged wizardries. Sker'ret appeared to reach into one of the front segments of his body to pull out the two little tangles of light that Dairine knew they would all be carrying. Roshaun reached into an interior pocket of his ornate over-robe for his own pup-tent access, hanging it on the air and turning away from it, unconcerned. Filif, though, didn't do anything that Dairine could see...but a moment later, his pup-tent access was hanging in the air next to Roshaun's, and from a single branch, which he'd pushed out a little past the main bulk of his greenery, there depended a little strip of darkness.

Dairine watched as he flung it at the concrete wall. There the darkness clung and ran down the wall, the black patch widening as it went. After a few seconds there was a roughly triangular-shaped patch of darkness in the concrete wall, the size of Filif's body. Light fell into that darkness and was completely absorbed.

Sker'ret was doing the same with his own customized worldgate. He reared up with it held in his front mandibles and plastered it against the gray cement of the wall. That darkness, too, ran down to create a lower, more archlike shape, black as a cutout piece of night. Standing in front of it, Sker'ret thrust a front claw into it; the claw vanished up to the second joint.

Roshaun turned away, heading back up the steps. "Aren't you going to set up your gate?" Dairine said.

"It can wait awhile," Roshaun said. "I'm in no hurry."

He was halfway up the stairs already, glinting golden in silhouette from the sunlight still coming in through the screen door. Dairine raised her eyebrows, and said to the other two, "Come on, and I'll give you the grand tour of the house."

"There's more?" Filif said, sounding surprised.

"Sure," Dairine said. "I'll show you."

By the time she and the other two were up the stairs, Roshaun had already opened the oven door, and was looking in. "If this is a food preparation area," he said, "it can't be meant to service very many people."

"It's not," Dairine said. "There are only three of us here."

"I know about that," Sker'ret said. "There's you, and your sire, and your sister." He said both the relationship words as if they were strange new alien concepts.

Yes, Dairine thought. *And if you knew it, why doesn't Roshaun know it?* "That's right," Dairine said.

Roshaun closed the oven door and looked around him, still with that faintly fancier-than-thou attitude, but also with a slight air of confusion. "Even so," he said, looking into the dining room as if he expected to see something there and didn't see it, "surely you don't prepare your food yourselves?"

"Uh, sure we do," Dairine said. *Did I miss something about this guy's profile?* she thought. *I should go back and have another look, because he's really behaving strangely...* "My sister's better at it that I am, but I should be able to manage something."

Sker'ret was up on his hind legs, or some of them, carefully inserting a couple of claws into a cupboard door. "I'll be glad to help you," he said. "What's in here? Is this where you keep the food?"

He pulled the cupboard door open—literally. It came off its hinges, and Sker'ret put his head end into the cupboard, holding the door off to one side as he rummaged around. "What are all these bright-colored things?" he said, taking out packages and jars and cans, holding them up, and staring at them with many stalked eyes.

"Uh, yeah, those are all kinds of food. It's just that, you want to watch out for the ones in the glass—"

Crash! went two of the jars that Sker'ret was holding in his claws. It became increasingly apparent that Sker'ret did not know his own strength. The shower of broken glass, various kinds of canning juices, and things like asparagus and peas and peaches in a jar, was shortly joined by more leakage from cans that Sker'ret was holding with his other claws. Roshaun and Filif looked on this, fascinated, but neither saying anything. "Oh, I'm sorry, these are very fragile, aren't they?" Sker'ret said. "Were those supposed to do that?"

"Not exactly," Dairine said, hoping against hope that she could stop this catastrophe before it got much further along, *and* get it cleaned up before her dad got home. "Why don't you let me take care of that, and I'll just—"

Crash! "Oh no," Sker'ret said, "I *am* sorry about

that." Several more jars and bottles fell down and either smashed on the counter or bounced off the floor; a few glass jars bounced and then smashed when they came down the second time. Both Filif and Roshaun crowded carefully back out of the way, and looked at Dairine to see what she would do. Dairine let out a long breath, and started carefully across the wet, glass-crunchy floor toward the basement steps, where a mop and broom were kept.

His claws clutched full of the remains of various cans and bottles, Sker'ret looked after Dairine with a number of its eyes. "Where are you going?" he said.

"Well," Dairine said, "I could do a wizardry, but sometimes a mop makes more sense..."

"What's a mop?" Filif said.

"It's a thing we use to clean up the floor if something wet's gotten on it—"

"To clean it up?" Sker'ret said, sounding shocked. "But we haven't *had* anything yet—"

Dairine opened her mouth to say something, and then completely forgot what, as Sker'ret began to eat.

He ate the glass. He ate the cans. He ate the asparagus, and the peas, and the canned tomatoes, and every other foodstuff that had fallen on the floor. He slurped up every bit of liquid. And when he was done, he looked around him, and with his foreclaws, he picked up the torn-off cupboard door, which he had carefully set aside while dealing with the canned goods.

"Not the door!" Dairine yelled. Sker'ret's head turned in some alarm.

"No?"

"No," Dairine said, trying hard to calm herself. "I'm sorry; that's part of the kitchen."

"Oh," Sker'ret said. "My apologies. I didn't realize." Carefully he set the door aside again, and turned his attention downward.

"No, no, no, no," Dairine said. *"Leave the floor!"*

Somewhat bemused, Sker'ret cocked a few eyes back at Dairine, shrugged some of his legs, and began to levitate.

Roshaun was leaning against the counter by the kitchen sink, his arms folded, watching this spectacle with insufferable amusement. Dairine desperately wanted to punch him in the nose, even though he hadn't said a word. Filif was watching, too, though with a far less superior air. *Maybe it's the berries,* Dairine thought. *It's hard to look supercilious when you have berries hanging off you.*

The back door opened. All four of the occupants of the kitchen looked up, startled.

Dairine's father came in, closed the door behind him, and looked at his daughter, the young man, the centipede, and the tree. "Hello, everybody," Harry Callahan said.

Filif, Roshaun, and the gently floating Sker'ret all looked at Dairine's dad. Then they all looked at Dairine, waiting to take their cue from her.

Dairine had rarely been more embarrassed to have her father turn up without warning...or more relieved. "Daddy!" she said. "Who's in the store?"

"Mike's there for the rest of the day," her dad said. Mike was his new assistant, whom he'd taken on a few weeks back: a young guy just out of high school who had been looking for a job and was good with flowers. "It's been a slow afternoon, anyway. I'm not needed there. Who're your friends?"

Dairine looked at her dad sidewise, admiring his cool, especially since she knew he'd done his reading and knew perfectly well who these people were. There he stood, acting like a man who had aliens in his house every day. And he had looked right at the cupboard door and not even mentioned it. "This is Filif," she said. "Filif, this is my father."

"I am honored to meet the stock from which the shoot proceeds," Filif said. He rustled all over, bending a little bit like a tree in a wind.

Dairine was relieved to see that her dad must have the briefing pack somewhere about his person, as he was plainly understanding the Speech that Filif was using. "Well, you're very welcome," Dairine's father said.

"And this is Sker'ret…"

"Well met on the journey," Sker'ret said.

Dairine's dad reached out to take the claw that Sker'ret offered him. "You don't have to float there like that," he said. "The floor's not so clean in here that you need to be afraid to walk on it." He glanced to one side. "Something wrong with the cupboard?"

"It came off," Sker'ret said.

"That happens," Dairine's dad said. "Just leave it there for the time being; we'll put it back where it belongs later." He turned to Roshaun.

"And this is Roshaun," Dairine said.

"...ke Nelaid am Seriv am Teliuyve am Meseph am Veliz am Teriaunst am det Wellakhit," Roshaun said, and to Dairine's mortification, looked at her dad as if expecting him to bow.

Her dad's response took just a fraction of a second longer this time. "Make yourself right at home," he said to Roshaun. "But then I see you already have." He turned away from Roshaun with exactly the same matter-of-fact motion that Dairine had seen her dad use with customers who were wasting his time at the counter. "So let's all go into the living room and sit down. What's on the agenda, Dairine?"

She recognized the code—her father rarely called her by her whole name unless there was trouble of some kind. At least for once, the cause of the trouble wasn't her... or if it was, she was only the indirect cause. All of them followed her dad into the living room, and Dairine said, "They've spent the day traveling, and I was thinking maybe some food would be nice..."

"Absolutely. I could do with some dinner myself. We can sit and relax and get acquainted. Any thoughts?"

"Well, I thought maybe something neutral." She glanced at Roshaun, who was looking around their living room with an expression of badly concealed confusion, as if he'd found people living in a hole in the ground and liking it. "Some fruit drinks to start with, maybe, and then..." Dairine was grasping at possibilities; this was more Nita's specialty than hers. "I don't know, maybe something vegetarian..."

"That sounds nice," Filif said. "Something to do with my people. What's it mean?"

"Huh? Vegetarian? Oh, around here it means people who eat only vegetables..."

Then Dairine heard what she was saying, and stopped short.

But she hadn't stopped soon enough. Filif stood there frozen in shock, and the decency field around his roots almost went away. "You...eat...*vegetables*?"

Oh, great, Dairine thought, in a complete fury with herself. *Why didn't I just come right out and say, "Hi there, we're cannibals"? Except I just did.* "But they're not, you know, the *people* kind of vegetables," Dairine said, though the look Filif was turning on her made her wonder whether she was going to have any success with this approach. "They don't...They're not alive, I mean, not the way you're alive...I mean, they don't *think*..."

Then Dairine stopped herself again, this time because she was getting onto conceptually shaky ground. When you were a wizard, you quickly discovered that thought and sentience didn't necessarily have anything to do with each other, and sometimes they manifested independently.

Her father leaned over her shoulder and looked down at Filif with an unusually calm expression. "What do you do for nourishment at home, son?" he said.

"Normally," Filif said, having recovered enough to tremble a little, "we root."

"I've got just the place for you," Dairine's dad said. "You come on outside with me. Dairine, you take care of these two for the moment."

Her dad went out the back door, closely followed by Filif. She sagged a little with relief and turned back to the others. Sker'ret was looking out the front window of the living room with great interest, but Roshaun was leaning against the polished wooden breakfront, snickering.

"That was interesting," he said. His tone of voice suggested not that he was trying to restrain his amusement, but that he was intending to let it loose full force as soon as he had an excuse. He found Earth funny, he found Dairine's dad funny, and he found Dairine funny.

Dairine just looked at him. *It would be so very bad,* she thought, *to punch out a guest on his first day in the house. Very, very bad.*

But really satisfying . . .

"Come on and see the rest of the house," Dairine said, rather more to Sker'ret than to Roshaun; and she led them off on the grand tour.

The tour took about fifteen minutes, after which Dairine left Roshaun and Sker'ret in the living room and went into the kitchen again. Her dad was standing there with a screwdriver; he was in the final stages of refastening the cupboard door. "I could have sworn Nita and I brought home canned stuff to replace everything we used last week," he said.

"You did," Dairine said. "I think we're going to need more. Where's Filif? Is he okay?"

"He's fine," her father said, swinging the door back and forth a couple of times.

"He didn't go outside the yard, did he? I put a force

field around the edges of things that'll keep the neigh-bors from seeing anything. But if he went out—"

"He didn't. He may get around, but he didn't feel like going anywhere right now, except under the sky. I get the feeling he doesn't particularly like being in-doors."

"No," Dairine said, "I think maybe you're right."

"And he's enough of a conifer for me to know his tastes, at least a little," her dad said, opening the cutlery drawer where the screwdrivers lived and dropping in the one he'd been using. "Besides that, we chatted enough for me to find out that he likes his soil acidic. I plugged him into that new bed I was getting ready for the rhododendrons and told him to kick back for a while. He should do fine."

"You're certainly taking this well," Dairine said, be-fore she could stop herself.

"I don't know that we have much choice at this point," her dad said, sounding somewhat resigned. "I agreed to this, after all, so I may as well try to enjoy it. Now then—what about dinner?"

"Sounds good." But Dairine immediately started worrying again, as that produced a whole new level of problems. *Filif...*

Her dad was ahead of her. "What have we got in the house that's not recognizably a vegetable?" He thought for a moment. "Pasta?"

"Spaghetti and meatballs," Dairine said.

"How's Filif likely to handle the sight of tomato sauce?" Dairine's dad said.

Dairine thought about that. Tomatoes were vegetables... but a jar of spaghetti sauce might pass if no one actually discussed what went into it. Of course, even pasta had been a vegetable once....

Her father was way ahead of her. "Since Filif isn't going to be eating what we are," Dairine's dad said, "and since I'm not operating under the restrictions you are, I'm prepared to prevaricate if I have to. But let's see if we can't just steer the conversation in other directions if the history of food comes up. Meanwhile, utensils..." Her dad started rummaging through the flatware drawer for a matched set. "I suspect Roshaun can use a fork and a spoon on his spaghetti. If he hasn't had the experience before, we'll teach him. And as for Sker'ret—"

"I think if we can get him to stick to the spaghetti and leave the plates and the table alone," Dairine said, "we'll be doing okay."

Dairine's dad reached up into another cupboard and came down with a couple of odd plates from an old set, which Dairine knew for a fact her dad hated, and had been looking for an excuse to get rid of. "And in case of accidents—" he said.

Dairine grinned, and went looking for a pot for the spaghetti.

As it turned out, the plates survived dinner, though Dairine's temper almost didn't. And the problem, as she'd suspected it would be, had been Roshaun. Filif came in to "sit" at the table in a large bucket of potting soil that Dairine's dad brought in for him, and Sker'ret more or less draped himself over the seat and through the open back of one of the dining room chairs, leaving his front end free to deal with the spaghetti. Dairine's dad only had to warn Sker'ret once that they were only eating things on top of the tablecloth and inside containers. This led to a lively discussion of what humans ate, and Dairine sat there in mostly mute appreciation of how her father somehow confined himself entirely to discussing how things tasted, without ever going near the subject of what they *were*. Dairine spent most of her time ingesting spaghetti—she found that she was ravenous—and forcing herself not to glare at Roshaun.

It took him exactly five seconds to master the fork and spoon, though he let it be known that at his home, his people used several different kinds of tongs to handle slippery foods like this. He let a number of things be known over the course of dinner, dispensing the occasional fact or opinion as if he expected everybody to be eagerly awaiting his every word . . . and paying precious little attention to anyone else's opinions, if they came up. His clothes, his possessions, the size of his house, which apparently would have dwarfed Dairine's, all these came up for brief and tasteful mention. What did not come out was anything personal, anything revealing of the inner nature of the entity who sat there at the table, managing the fork and spoon with the grace of someone who'd been using them for years, and had never gotten spaghetti sauce or any other sauce on him, not once.

Dairine sat there listening to it all, and stewed.

Sker'ret didn't seem to notice Roshaun's attitude, or if he did, he didn't reveal it during his workmanlike and concentrated assault on the food. Filif mostly sat quietly listening to the others, and rustled occasionally whenever anyone said anything with sufficient emphasis to suggest that they wanted a response from the listeners. Dairine and her dad concentrated on keeping the conversation going along in a relatively friendly fashion, but Dairine increasingly felt like she was doing weights, and ones that were getting heavier every minute.

But they made it through the main course without a murder, and through dessert (her dad's chocolate pudding) without trying to keep a medicine ball in the air. And at the end of it all, "Well," Dairine's dad said, looking around the table, "it's been a long day, and I'm sure that it would be a good thing if we all got some rest now."

"But it's not even dark yet," Filif said.

"I know," Dairine's dad said, in a very kindly voice. "But there's the time difference to think of; there has to be at least *some* time difference between your planet and this one. And whatever it is, I'm sure it means that you need some rest now. I know I do." And he stood up.

The others stood up with him. "I think I might withdraw," Roshaun said graciously. "Your local night is how long?"

"Eight hours," Dairine said, while thinking grimly, *It was in your orientation pack, if you had bothered to read it.*

"I'll walk you downstairs," Dairine said. "You all saw where my room is. If you need anything, I'll be awake about an hour and a half after the sun comes up. You all have everything you need in your pup tents?"

"More than enough," Filif said.

"Me, too," Sker'ret said.

"A sufficiency," said Roshaun, and turned away from Dairine with no further acknowledgment. "Your best of rest, then."

Dairine went with their three guests to the stairs, saw them safely down. "Good night, everybody," she said, closing the door to the cellar stairs.

Her dad was standing there by the sink, having just put a stack of dishes down beside it, and presently washing a couple of glasses by hand. As Dairine turned away from the basement door, he glanced over at her.

"A harder day than you were expecting?" he said.

"Uh, yeah," said Dairine. "Did it show?"

"You mean, to the guests? In Filif's and Sker'ret's case, I don't think so. They seem like nice kids." Her father put one glass down on the drainer, picked up the other to rinse it out. "I'd like to know what's going on with Roshaun, though."

"So would I," Dairine muttered. She was sufficiently shell-shocked at the moment, and sufficiently in need of something grindingly ordinary, that she actually found herself picking up a dish towel to help her dad finish up at the sink. "Daddy, it's driving me crazy."

He looked at her with slight concern. Dairine understood why. It wasn't in her nature to make a lot of admissions of that kind, even in the family. Dairine let out a long breath and said, "I've never met a wizard who wasn't..."

"Good?" her father said. "Nice?"

Dairine shook her head. "It's not just that," she said. "All the wizards I know—know at all closely—their wizardry is really important to them. Maybe it's not the main thing their life is about: No one says it has to be. But it's important. This guy, though...it feels like he wants you to think that wizardry's a hobby for him. How can anyone be that way? Wizardry's about talking the universe *right* when it goes wrong...finding out what's going on in people's heads and helping them make the world happen. Finding out how things want to be, and helping them *be* that way. How can anything be more important than that?"

She waved her arms in the air, frustrated. "Sure, it's about having fun, too—you'd have to be incredibly obtuse and clueless not to have fun being a wizard. And there are about a billion ways to do it! But this guy—" She shook her head. Much more quietly Dairine said, "I really don't like him. And I really don't *like* that I really don't like him. The worst part is that I don't have any reasons for it. He's one of my own kind, a wizard, and he rubs me the wrong way."

Her father sighed. "You know," he said, "there've been people I've worked with, occasionally, over the years, that I've had the same problem with. And I've never known what to do about it."

"Wait for them to go away?" Dairine said.

"Sometimes they do," her dad said. "Sometimes you're just stuck with them."

Dairine sighed in turn. "Two weeks..."

"It's only been a few hours," her dad said. "Don't give up yet. Things may improve."

"From your mouth to the Powers' ears," Dairine muttered. But she found it hard to believe that Roshaun was going to shift his behavior in any way that would matter.

Her dad handed her the glass from the drainer. "Before I turn in—anything I should know about the downstairs?" her dad said.

"They've got a pup tent each," Dairine said, "and they're probably sleeping in them. So if you go down there, make sure you turn on the light so you don't stumble into any place you don't want to be. They've also got a worldgate each, fastened to the bare wall, in case they need to get home in a hurry for some emergency. I wouldn't lean any of your tools against those... You might not get them back."

Her dad nodded. "It's strange," he said, "hearing them speak. It sounds like English... but it runs deeper, somehow. You hear undertones."

"That's the Speech," Dairine said. "Everything understands it somewhat. But you're hearing it with better understanding than a nonspeaker usually gets." She finished drying the glass, put it up on the counter. "If it starts to bother you..."

Her father shook his head. "I'll let you know," he said. "But no problems so far." He finished with the last glass, handed it to Dairine, and leaned against the counter.

"So what are we going to do with them for two

weeks?" her dad said. "Regardless of where Nita and Kit might be, it's too cold for *us* to go to the beach... though you might take them out that way once to show them the sea. I get a feeling there aren't many oceans where Filif comes from."

"You're getting to like him already," Dairine said, and smiled.

"I'm not used to having the plants talk back," her dad said. "Or, if they do, being able to understand them. It's an experience."

Dairine nodded. "Well, we can help them get used to suburban life gradually," she said. "Carmela wants to come talk to the visitors, anyway. And once they've got their disguise routines sorted out, we can take them around the neighborhood, to start with. They can even go over to the Rodriguezes' and see Kit's weird TV. For all I know, they may be able to see some program they're missing."

Dairine's dad chuckled at that. "Okay," he said. "Let's try to keep them out of sight until we're sure their disguises are going to stay in place. I really don't want a UFO scandal erupting on my doorstep."

"I'll take care of that," Dairine said.

"Good," her dad said. He had been washing the last couple of dishes; he racked them up in the drainer. "I'm going to turn in, sweetie. It's been a long day."

"Yeah."

Her dad grabbed Dairine and hugged her hard. "A long day for you, too," he said. "No, leave those last two. Throw in the towel and go to bed."

Dairine hung up the dish towel, but not before tossing a last amused glance at the two dishes still in the drainer. "You're just hoping that Sker'ret will wake up with an urge for something in the middle of the night..."

Her dad grinned at her and went to bed.

Dairine took herself to bed after him, first walking through the house and making sure that doors were locked and lights turned off. Once up in her room, the tiredness came down over her as if someone had put a sack over her head. She kept blinking to keep her eyes open. But before she got undressed for bed, before she even thought of doing anything else, she turned to Spot, who was sitting on her desk as usual, and flipped his lid open. "Do me a favor," she said. "Get me Roshaun's profile."

It's right here, Spot said.

Dairine looked at the profile, once again examining that picture of Roshaun. She knew she was imagining it, but on this examination, after meeting the original, that picture seemed to have something that had been missing before: just the slightest sneer.

She glanced down the column of material in the Speech that was the public part of Roshaun's name. There, embedded in the long intertwined tracery of characters, would be information about his personality, his abilities, his power levels and level of accomplishment as a wizard, and much else. But now that she looked at it, there was something strange about that long series of names he flaunted around. *Some family thing,* she'd thought at first. But Dairine had suddenly started having doubts.

Dairine read Roshaun's full name again, slowly, not as a phrase in an alien language this time, worth savoring for the exotic sounds, but this time translating each word. Roshaun ke Nelaid, it began: "Roshaun of the princes' line of Seriv, son of the Sun Lord, beloved of the Sun Lord, son of the great King, descendant of the Inheritors of the Great Land, the Throne-destined—"

Dairine sat there at her desk and was appalled, realizing that Roshaun had actually given her the *short* version of his name. It went on for about six more epithets, which sounded impressive but were difficult to decipher, and ended in the words *am me'stardet Wellakhir,* "royal and kingly Masters, Guardians, and Guarantors of Wellakh."

Oh my god, Dairine thought. The situation was worse than she'd thought it could possibly be. *They've sent me some kind of planetary prince,* she thought. *The Powers That Be really did think I was getting out of hand, and this is my punishment. I'm going to get to spend two weeks' worth of holiday baby-sitting spoiled royalty.*

She tried to read the rest of Roshaun's profile— "Power level 6.0–6.8 ± 0.5; Specialty: stellar dynamics, stellar atmospheres and kinetics, consultant level 3.6..."—but she couldn't concentrate. Very gently she put Spot's lid down. Normally, her next line would have been, *What have I done to deserve this?* But she *knew* what she had done. *Boy,* Dairine thought, *when the Powers That Be get annoyed with you, they don't play around.* She put her face down in her hands and moaned.

Then she opened Spot's lid again and looked one more time at that endless name. That by itself was bad...very bad. It was also full of reasons for Roshaun's self-importance. *Still,* Dairine thought, *it's no excuse for him to be such a snot. Maybe we can do something about that, given enough time.*

But there was something even stranger about the name—not anything specifically *bad*...just odd. Not once in that whole epic string of words was the word *wizard* mentioned, not even as a footnote.

Now what am I supposed to make of that? Dairine thought. Because even if he was the king of a world somewhere, or in line to be one, if he was also a wizard, that fact was more than worthy of being mentioned in the same breath.

Dairine lay there and brooded over it for a while.

You're worried about Roshaun, Spot said.

About him? No, Dairine said. *But he raises questions.*

Like how to avoid killing him, Spot said. And behind the words, Dairine could hear that very characteristic, machine-accented laugh of his. It was something Spot had learned from her. It was one of the *first* things Spot had learned from her.

We shouldn't really even joke about it, she said. *He's our guest. The Powers That Be sent him to us. We have to be nice to him.*

Within reason, Spot said.

I didn't say that! Dairine said.

You were thinking it, Spot said. *I heard you.*

Dairine sighed. *Can't keep much away from you, can I?*

Not for a while now, Spot said. *So what do we do next?*

Hope that nothing gets worse, Dairine said.

She got undressed, and instead of the usual floppy T-shirt, she actually put on pajamas. There was always the chance that something untoward would happen in the middle of the night. Among other possibilities, Dairine had begun dreading any sudden crunching noises that might start coming from the kitchen. *Do Rirhait get the midnight munchies?* she wondered. *If it's just for the dishes, Daddy won't mind. But if Sker'ret forgets himself and gets started on the wood-work... Let's just hope he doesn't.*

The bed creaked under her as she got into it. Dairine sighed, thinking of Nita having a good time far away. *Off getting a suntan on Beach World,* she thought. *I hope she remembered to bring sunblock. She burns so easily...*

Dairine pulled the covers up and tried to snuggle down into the pillow and get comfortable. Her mind, though, was buzzing with the events of the day, and she knew it was going to be a long time before she got to sleep. Especially since there was another issue bothering her, one much larger than the potential impact of a Rirhait on the structure of her kitchen. *This is supposed to be a vacation,* Dairine thought, *a holiday. But at the same time, there are no accidents, and the Powers never do anything without a reason: In a finite universe, energy is too precious to waste. Which means these wizards were sent here for some reason.*

Dairine pulled the covers over her head. *Wizards are always answers,* she thought. *But if these three are the answer to something here, what's the question?*

The image of Roshaun, elegant, completely self-assured, and absolutely infuriating, rose before Dairine's closed eyes. Furious, she squeezed them tighter.

And will I find out what it is before I have to strangle myself to keep from killing him?

Customs and
Other Formalities

NITA AND KIT TURNED TOWARD the source of
the voice that had spoken to them.

"Sorry," its owner said. "Sorry! I was late. I had to
help my *tapi*, my father. Are you all right?"

The first thing that struck Nita was how very tall
Quelt was. Nita was getting tall for her age, everyone
said, though she still felt short to herself. Looking up
at Quelt, her first thought was that she felt shorter than
ever. Her second thought was, *This girl would be a star
at basketball*...

But there was a lot more to Quelt's looks than
just her height. Her whole body was elongated; her
arms and legs were perhaps half again as long as they
would've been on Earth. She looked like a tall, slen-
der, graceful ceramic sculpture, or a sculpture done
in wood—a beautiful, polished brown wood, like teak
or mahogany. Her skin even had that kind of subtle

sheen, halfway between matte and shiny. Her face was long and narrow, with high cheekbones, and she had large, dark, liquid eyes; her head was covered with something that Nita couldn't quite analyze—a silvery blond growth halfway between hair and fur, shaggy at the top and sides, partly covering her small round ears, and reaching into a long, soft ponytail down the back of her neck to about the middle of her back. The effect of the fair hair against the dark, dark skin was striking, and, Nita thought, very stylish. Quelt was wearing a long, loose, sleeveless garment of some kind of woven fabric, and it flowed around her as she came hurriedly to them, her hand stretched out. She was smiling, a great wide smile that went right across her face. There seemed to be no separate teeth inside that smile. Instead, Quelt had two one-piece, dazzlingly white bony plates in the same place where teeth would be in a human.

"We're fine!" Nita said. She was getting over that staggered-by-the-landscape feeling, and now she put her hand out to take Quelt's. Quelt took hers in turn, and pumped it up and down enthusiastically.

"See," Quelt said, "I've been studying your people's customs. *Dai stihó!*"

"Uh, *dai stihó!*" Nita said. And then she laughed. "It's okay," Nita said, "you can stop now. You don't have to keep doing it!" Quelt laughed, too.

"Quelt?" Kit said, offering his hand and getting the same pump-it-up treatment. "Did I pronounce that right?"

"Close enough," Quelt said, and bobbed her head to Kit, producing again that curiously wide smile. "And Kit? And Nita? Is that right?"

Kit turned his head to the left and inclined it forward, an Alaalid nod. "A lot closer than usual," he said. "We hear all kinds of variations."

"I'm so glad," Quelt said. "I'm so new at this—and I've only once met a wizard who wasn't Alaalid. But never mind that. And this is Ponsh?" She softened the sound of the consonant a little bit as she bent down to have a good look at Ponch. He sat down and, without warning, offered her a paw.

Quelt took the paw and shook it nearly as enthusiastically as she had shaken Kit's hand. "This is another of the sentient species on your planet?" Quelt said. "Your associate?"

"That's right," Kit said. "Except Ponch is a little more sentient than most."

"Yes," Quelt said, "it's the contagion principle. I've heard of it." She let Ponch's paw go, straightened up again, and looked carefully at all three of them. "But are you *sure* you're all right? Sometimes when we get visitors here, they have trouble with"—Quelt looked around at that tremendously distant horizon—"just the look of things."

"Well, by our standards, this planet really is huge," Kit said. "In fact, it's almost as big as a planet can be for humanoid life to evolve, isn't it?"

"That's right," Quelt said. "Any bigger and it wouldn't have had enough metal and heavy elements in the crust to keep the atmosphere in place. We were very lucky when our system formed. And we still don't have a lot of metal. But I'm keeping you standing around here talking exogeology, and you haven't had anything to eat or drink yet, or even seen the house! And my *pabi* and *tapi* are waiting to meet you. Come on!"

They started walking downhill from the flowery clearing where the gate from the Crossings had deposited them. Quelt looked up at the sky with a critical expression, and then back at Nita. "Is this weather all right for you?" she said.

"It's just fine!" Nita said. "It feels like summer."

"It's still only spring," Quelt said. "But let me know if anything goes wrong, or if it's cold for you, or anything. If the weather starts to act up, I'll fix it."

"Are you allowed to do that?" Nita said. And then she thought about it for a moment, and added, "Well, I guess you would be, if you're the only wizard here..."

They started to climb a little rise between them and the sea, kicking through the flowers as they went; Ponch romped ahead of them. "Oh, yes," Quelt said. "I listen to what the Telling has to say about the way the weather is at the moment, and if there's a problem, or if I'm not to change it for some other reason, Those Who Are send me word. But beyond that, I've been working with the weather here for long enough now that They seem to trust me with it."

"The Telling," Nita said. "That's your version of the wizard's manual, isn't it?"

"I think so," Quelt said. "Did I understand that correctly? You get the Telling as a physical thing?"

"Sure," Nita said. "Here, take a look."

Nita pulled her manual out of her backpack and handed it to Quelt. Quelt turned it over curiously in her hands as they climbed. "It's so compact," Quelt said. "Isn't it a problem for you, though? Don't you leave it places and then realize you've left it behind?"

"There are ways around that," Kit said. "If we don't feel like physically carrying the manuals, we can always pull the fabric of space apart a little bit and stuff the manual into the pocket."

"That could be a little tricky," Quelt said thoughtfully.

"It can be," Nita said, "but if you—"

She was interrupted by a sudden flurry of crazy barking from Ponch as he came to the top of the rise, saw something that excited him, and dived down over the far side. "Oh no," Kit said, "what's he seen now?"

The barking continued, and Kit ran up to the top of the rise. Nita and Quelt went after him. As Nita made the top of the rise herself, she looked down and saw Quelt's house. "Wow," she said. It was not just one building but an assortment of low, wide buildings clustered together, built in a soft-peach-colored material almost exactly the shade of the pink-and-peach-striped beach that stretched away for miles and miles on either side until it faded from view in the haze before the horizon. The buildings were topped off with conical, pointed roofs made of bunches of the silvery reeds that grew on the seaward side of the rise, as it sloped down toward the beach. Through these long, tall reeds, Ponch was plunging—though he himself was invisible at the moment, the reed-leaves were thrashing with his passage—and heading at top speed for a big pen made of more of the silver reeds interwoven with lengths of darker, silver gray wood, built off to one side of the largest building.

Milling around in the pen were a number of creatures that Nita at first had a great deal of trouble making any sense of. They looked like golden or cream-colored pom-poms, and as Ponch and his barking got closer, the activity in the pen got more frenzied.

"Ponch!" Kit yelled. But it was too late. Ponch came rocketing out of the reeds at the bottom of the rise and shot straight toward the pen. He was within only a few feet of the silvery, wooden fence when there was a sudden chorus of sharp, odd honking noises... and all of the pom-poms leaped into the air...

... and kept on going, as every one of them suddenly sprouted wide, golden or cream white wings, two pairs each, and flew off down the beach in a noisy, honking flock. Ponch danced around on his hind legs, barking at the creatures, and then took off down the beach after them.

"Oh no, I'm so sorry," Kit said, and started running after Ponch.

Quelt started laughing. "No, it's all right," she said. "But this is why I was late! I was helping my *tapi* get the *shesh* off them. It doesn't matter now. We were finished..." But she kept on laughing.

Nita shook her head. "I'm sorry, too," she said. "He really loves to chase things so much. He created a whole universe full of nothing but squirrels once, so he could spend all his time chasing them."

"He created a *universe*?"

"Ponch is unusual," Nita said. "It's a long story."

Quelt nodded a few times, a gesture that Nita was coming to read as the equivalent of an Earth human shaking his head. "I get that sense," she said. "Well, he won't have to create universes to have things to chase here. The *ceiff* are here three times a day, every day—they come back to be groomed and tended—and once we've got the *shesh* off them, Ponsh can chase them as often as he likes."

Quelt and Nita ambled down through the reeds toward the houses. "They're kind of like sheep," Nita said. "And *shesh*—is it the furry stuff they're covered with? Or is it something to do with food?"

"It's a food precursor," Quelt said. "The *ceiff* make a secretion that we process. It's kind of complicated, but it tastes really good when you're done with it. We trade it to other people all over the islands hereabouts: It's very much in demand." She started to laugh again. "And I should warn you, my *tapi* is really passionate about it. Don't get him started—you'll be hearing about *shesh* all night."

"It said in the orientation pack that your *tapi* had 'elected to do manual labor permanently.'" Nita said. "It sounded like most people don't here."

"What, work?" Quelt said. She and Nita paused by the pen, looking down the beach to where Kit was still chasing after Ponch, and Ponch was still chasing after the flying sheep. "No," Quelt said, "no one has to do it all the time. Nonetheless, some people like to, like my *tapi*. Otherwise, our people usually seem to have

enough of everything to go around—food and things
to make clothes and houses. Anything that's unusually
hard for people to get, like metal—either they process
it on a small scale, in local groups, and everybody takes
a turn doing the work, or else I get it for them. It's one
of the main things I use my wizardry for." She looked
at Nita, a little surprised. "Why? Do people on your
world *have* to work?"

"Most people," Nita said. "In fact, pretty much
everybody."

Quelt shook her head in wonder. "You've got to tell
me all about your world," she said, as Kit trotted back
toward them, holding Ponch by the collar. "*Everything!* But we'll have lots of time to talk about it. At
dinner, and for days after. In the meantime, we'd better
get inside! Pabi and Tapi have made great masses of
food for you; they're terrified you'll be hungry after
the trip."

At that, Kit looked slightly embarrassed and Nita
burst out laughing. "I think parents all must go to the
same school," she said. "Though how they get there
and back without us knowing is something we'll never
understand. Ponch," Nita said, "*what* were you doing,
you bad boy?"

Ponch shook himself all over, spraying Nita and
Quelt and Kit with seawater—he had managed to get
in and out of the surf several times while chasing the
flying sheep. *If they didn't want to be chased,* he said,
they shouldn't have flown away.

"Well, Quelt and her dad spent most of the afternoon getting those things together into that pen," Nita

said, "and now look! They're all over the place. Don't chase them anymore! You understand?"

Ponch sat down, looked up at Quelt with big, woe-begone eyes, hung his head, and offered her a paw. *Sorry,* he said.

"It's all right," Quelt said. "Don't go all chopfallen on me. Let's go in; they're waiting for us."

They went down to the house. There on the broad front steps, under the silver thatch of the eaves, they met Quelt's parents, who were dressed like their daughter, in long, loose, pale casual clothing, in two or three layers of cream or gold or beige—a long tunic or a short one with a long, sleeveless overvest flung on top, soft sandals, and, in Quelt's father's case, a soft scarf wrapped around the neck. Nita was astounded to find them even taller and more beautiful than Quelt. Kuwilin Peliaen, Quelt's *tapi,* and Demair Peliaen, Quelt's *pabi,* each towered at least two feet above their daughter.

"Come in, come in," Demair said, laughing like her daughter, easily, and looking at Kit and Nita as if they were neighbors, not people she'd never seen before. Demair had Quelt's hair, perhaps even a fairer version, though hers was shorter, worn in a soft fluffy cap around her head. Kuwilin, on the other hand, was completely bald, and this suited him extremely well— his longer, narrower features gave him an impressive and austere look, but that never lasted long when he started laughing. In fact, all of them laughed at least once every few minutes, at least as far as Nita could tell. And there was nothing artificial about it, nothing nervous. She felt entirely welcomed—entirely at home.

"You were a long time coming!" Kuwilin said. "I thought maybe we wouldn't see you until tomorrow."

"Worldgates," Demair said. "It's the old story: Hurry up and run in all directions, then sit and wait forever. No matter! You're here now. Come in out of the wind and be welcome with us. Come see the house!"

With Quelt and her parents, Nita and Kit walked around the house, looking at everything. Nita was astounded at how technologically advanced this place was, despite its rural look. She immediately recognized a computer and data-retrieval system, disguised as a whole stuccoed wall. There were various appliances for housekeeping and entertainment; at first, Nita couldn't understand how they were powered, but after a few words exchanged in the Speech with Quelt, she understood that these ran on fuel cells of an unusually advanced sort, operating off hydrogen cracked out of seawater.

Yet the whole look of the house was very simple and spare—appliances and storage were mostly hidden away against the walls, or in them, by woven screens or cupboard doors. There was a great deal of artwork, paintings and sculpture done by both of Quelt's parents. Her father's art looked more like what Nita thought of as modern or abstract art: splashes of bright color against the pale, plain stuccoed walls. Quelt's mother's art was mostly portraiture, pictures of her husband and daughter, and very beautiful landscapes—all of these featuring the sea or the hill behind the house. There were also some still-life studies of flowers in the dining room, the work of someone who had sat in front of one of the blue *jijis* flowers up on the hill for a very long time, studying every petal of it, every hair.

"Young cousins," Quelt's mother said when they'd seen everything, "what about latemeal? Did you eat anything on the journey?"

"Uh—" Kit said.

"Everything," Nita said. "But we're ready for more. And so is Ponch. Huh, Pancho?"

Ponch looked at Quelt's mother and wagged his tail. *Food is always nice,* he said.

Quelt's mother smiled. "The perfect houseguest," she said. "Things will be ready in a few moments... Do you change clothes for latemeal?"

"Is it required?" Nita said. She knew places where it was.

Quelt's mother tilted her head sideways. "The careful guest," she said, "perhaps wants to show the other diners honor."

Nita and Kit looked at each other. "Change for dinner," they said in unison.

They unlimbered their pup tents, slipped into them, and changed into clean things. Nita, feeling the heat, got into one of her beach wraps and put a light jacket over it, then went out to see about dinner. Everybody sat down in the great room, on cushions around the long, low table, which groaned with the feast Quelt had threatened. Nita began to understand, with some amusement, that Quelt's mother and father were as much in love with food and its treatment as her own mom had been. It was strange for her, too, to look down the table at the vast array of bowls and plates and platters, filled with dishes hot or cold that sported unfamiliar shapes and colors, greens and blues very much in evidence. She laughed to herself as she saw Kit go straight for the blue foods, so that Quelt's mother laughed and passed him more of them. For her own part, Nita sat there dealing with her first really leisurely contact with alien foods—smells and textures that she'd never encountered before, but that were nonetheless instantly appetizing.

"We're lucky this way," Quelt said, passing Nita a bowl of some bright orange sauce to dribble over a plateful of something that smelled most deliciously of fried chicken but tasted like sweet-and-sour pork. "Our body chemistries are a lot alike; we're both using iron as the heart of the molecule that carries oxygen around in our blood. So that means there'll be certain similarities in—" And then Quelt stopped and laughed. Nita looked up at her with her mouth full, chewing. Quelt said, "As if it matters! Do you want to know what these things are, or would you prefer just to point, and I'll pass them to you?"

"Pointing'll do fine for the moment," Nita said, and she pointed and had many things passed to her. She was grateful that table manners on Alaalu, or at least this part of it, were very similar to those on Earth, right down to the short but elegant grace said before the meal: "Here we are," said Kuwilin, "and here's all this fine food. May it do us good, so we can thank the Powers for it!"

When they were halfway through the meal, the sun was easing down toward the water outside the dining room window—not a window as such, but just an opening with windbreak shutters folded back out of the way of the view. Quelt's mother stretched. "This is a good time to take a rest from the food," she said, "and it won't run away ... or not far." There was some laughter at that, since everyone was feeling a little over-stretched: Dinner had featured at least six different kinds of *shesh*. Nita had started out thinking of this as a sort of alien cheese, but then she realized that such an appraisal fell very far short of the mark. There were too many ways to treat the *shesh*, as she found when she made the mistake of getting Kuwilin talking about it.

Demair rolled her eyes and started talking to Kit about what life on Earth was like, while Kuwilin held forth on *shesh*—the storage, processing, pressing, coloring, and texturization of the foodstuff; the handling of its seasonal variations; and its preparation for dining, using at least a hundred technical terms that Nita hadn't realized even occurred in the Speech. Hearing them now, she found herself wondering whether there were some wizards who practiced their art exclusively in the culinary mode, forsaking all other usages. *Or more likely*, she thought, *it's true what we've always read in the manual ... that wizardry is only another kind of science—just one with its roots sunk deeper into the universe than most.*

For the moment, it didn't matter. After a while, they all got up and left the table, went outside, and strolled down the beach, watching the sun go down in a great blaze of fire—peach and orange and gold against that sky, which, despite a touch of green, or perhaps because of it, seemed more intensely blue than any Nita had ever seen on Earth. That color ran chills down Nita's neck, once or twice, when she looked up at it. *What is it?* she wondered. *What is it about this place that reminds me of something else? Whatever else it reminds me of, it's good...*

Ponch gamboled up and down in the water, running at the slight waves, biting them, chasing them out to sea again. Nita, walking with the others, gazed up and down those miles and miles of empty beach, and was astounded. "Can *anyone* live in a place like this?" she said.

Quelt's mother looked at her in some surprise. "Anyone who likes," she said. "It's a little isolated here, but some of us like that. People in other islands, maybe they don't—but then they have hundreds and thousands of *stad* to sail before they see another human face. This is the biggest island, so we have the Cities here." She shook her head. "I've lived in the Cities— they're nice if you want to see a thousand faces that you don't know every day, and maybe there's a kind of freedom in that. But for my part, perhaps I'm too much of a homebody. Maybe I prefer seeing just two other faces that I know, most days, and hearing the same three flocks of flying sheep come in every day and go again...the water coming up and down, and nothing else." She smiled, a long, lazy, untroubled look.

"For the rest," Kuwilin said, "this is no crowded world. Granted, there's much more sea than land. The sea is openhanded with us, and gives us more than enough food for everyone. People who have more than they need give to those who have less, if they need it, or if they ask for it. Why? How is it in your world?"

Nita started to answer, then stopped herself. She was disinclined to break the perfect spell of quiet that was coming down over her so quickly in this place. She glanced at Kit, who was walking on the far side of Kuwilin, but he was looking out to sea, not paying attention. "It's different," she said. "It's very different. People don't give that readily in my world."

"But what's the matter with them?" Quelt's mother said. "Don't they have enough?"

"Of many things," Nita said, "maybe not. There are so many of us. And while there's a lot more land on my planet than there is on Alaalu, our world is much smaller." She pulled out her manual. "See," she said, paging to the map of Alaalu, which showed Earth beside it for comparison's sake.

"But it's such a little planet," Demair said, looking over Kuwilin's shoulder at the manual. "And small planets like that are usually rich in metal. Metal makes technology so easy: You must all be wealthy. How can you not have enough of everything?"

Nita shook her head. "It would take me a long time to explain," she said.

"You'll be here for days," said Demair. "Maybe you can make us understand. If not, don't worry about it.

This is supposed to be a holiday for you, so Quelt's said."

"Maybe it's strange to us," Kuwilin said, "that people from a rich inner world with so much technology would come here willingly to spend time with..."

"Shepherds," Nita said. "That would be the word you're looking for."

"Shepherds. So you have *ceiff* as well?"

"Ours don't fly," Nita said. "And maybe it's a good thing, bearing in mind what Earth sheep eat, and how much of it they eat, and what they do with it afterwards..."

Kuwilin roared with laughter. "Still," he said, "your planet sounds like a wonder-place! *Ceiff* that don't fly...ground you can just dig the metal out of...cities all over the place, as many of them as grains of sand!"

"We have a lot of cities," Nita said, and shook her head. "But I think maybe this is better." The sun dipped toward that high, distant horizon, went oblate in the thickening atmosphere of the edge of the world—flattened almost to an egg shape—and started to slide down behind the rim of everything. Slowly, high above, stars were coming out.

There was a pause. "About the *shesh,*" Kit said, "can I watch you make it tomorrow?"

"Certainly," Kuwilin said. "I can always use help. Certain people"—he looked at Quelt with amusement—"are always off all over the planet, serving the world and doing Important Things, and can't be bothered to stay home and deal with the beasts."

"Tapi, you're cruel to me," Quelt said. "You know

I'd sooner stay home and do not-Important Things here. But I have to go see about the Great Vein again tomorrow." She turned to Nita and Kit. "We have just two veins of metal in our whole world's crust that are close enough to the surface for me to use wizardry on to pull the metal out directly. Every now and then we need metal in bulk for replacing old machines that have worn out, or building new ones...and I'm the only one here who can get it out in such amounts. All the other metal comes from the plants—"

Kit looked up in surprise. "You get metal from *plants?*"

"Oh, yes," Demair said. "See the reeds up there?" She pointed at the slope far behind them, behind the house.

"The ones we came down through?"

"That's right. That's ironwood. The plants were bred a long time ago to concentrate metal oxides from the soil in their tissues. We harvest the reeds and store them until the mobile smelter comes along, once or twice a year. Then we get the metal's value to trade for other things, if we need them."

"That's such a good idea," Kit said. "Who organizes this? The government?"

Kuwilin and Demair and Quelt all looked at Kit. "What's a government?" Kuwilin said.

Kit opened his mouth, closed it again.

"If people over on, let's say, Dafel Island, find that they need metal, they get together and do something about it," Kuwilin said. "They make arrangements to trade for it; or they find empty islands and plant out ironweed for themselves; or they get in touch with Quelt here, and she helps them. Or they ask other people for it, and other people give it to them. Everybody knows that what you give to the world, the world gives back, eventually. That's its job."

Demair looked at Kit with slight puzzlement. "Do you mean you have some kind of machine that *makes* people give people things?" Demair said.

Nita had never thought of government in quite those terms before. "You could say that," she said. "It's still going to take a lot of explaining..."

"Not right now," said Demair, putting her arms out to turn them all around as a group. "There's the rest of dinner, yet."

Kit groaned slightly. Nita gave him a look. *Just keep quiet and feed Ponch under the table,* she said silently. *I told you you were going to be sorry for pigging out on the blue stuff!*

They went back to the house in the glowing, golden twilight, and Demair moved about lighting little oil lamps in the various rooms and on the dinner table. The rest of dinner was much like the first part, except that the courses that Kuwilin now brought out were sweeter, sharper, the flavors more acute. Nita wondered whether this had something to do with a walk on the beach helping her appetite get its second wind... or whether she was just getting even more relaxed.

"Don't rush yourself," Demair said, leaning toward her. "Everything here will keep. There's time for everything, and you'll be here for a while."

"And tomorrow afternoon," Quelt said, "when I get

back from metal wrestling, you tell me what you want to do. We can go to the Cities, if you like. Or we can can do tourist things." She grinned.

"If you go to the Cities," Demair said, "I have a list for you."

Kit grinned and fed Ponch something under the table. "Not that I'm going to have time for your list if I'm with famous people," Quelt said.

Nita looked up from considering one last piece of *shesh*. "What?"

Quelt laughed. "Of course you're famous," she said. "On a world with just one wizard, if another one turns up all of a sudden—or two—do you think people aren't going to be fascinated? Your pictures are all over the talknets. Everyone thinks you're very elegant. In fact"—and Quelt preened her ponytail—"normally they all take me for granted, but now I'm in danger of becoming famous myself."

Kit and Nita burst out laughing. "It's because you're so small," Quelt said. "Once we weren't as tall as we are now. But in the days of the Ancients, everybody was more your size. Little."

"I don't mind being famous," Nita said, "but what I really, really want to do is lie in the sand, by the water, and do nothing."

Quelt grinned that grin at her and Kit again. To Nita, it seemed to threaten to go right around her face, suggesting that if Quelt did it any harder, the top of her head might fall off. "I like that, too," she said. "It's the only thing I like as much as wizard work."

Then suddenly Quelt jumped up. "I forgot!" she said. "Pabi, it'll be time for the *keks* pretty soon—"

"Yes," Demair said. "You two might like to see that. Our beaches are famous for them."

"*Keks?*" Kit said.

"Come on," Quelt said. "Afterward, I'll show you where we have couches put down for you, in the outbuilding—you can put your pup tents up there. But right now, hurry or we'll miss them—"

Nita and Kit got up to follow her out. Ponch loitered briefly by the table, accepted a couple of final tidbits from Demair and Kuwilin, and then ran after.

Nita and Kit and Quelt started down the beach again together, but this time in the opposite direction from the way they'd gone before. Almost all the sunset glow was gone; stars were thick overhead, and they were bright—the broad band of the back side of the Milky Way was glowing almost as bright as a diffuse full moon in that night unbroken by any streetlight or other artificial light source. Ponch tore past the three of them, racing down the beach, running ahead and romping in and out of the water, a black shape shining in the bright starlight. "I should warn you," Kit said to Quelt, "he's going to do that the whole time we're here. He likes the water."

Quelt smiled. "So do we," she said. "It's no problem." She looked up to their right, where the rise that ran behind the Peliaen house was more of a dune, bare of the ironwood reeds. "We have to go up there, out of the way," she said. "Can you see all right?"

"Sure," Kit said.

"Then come on—"

They climbed the dune. Once at the top, Quelt sat down, facing the water, and Nita and Kit sat down on either side of her, looking out at the starlit sea.

For long minutes, none of them said anything. Nita found herself willing to sit there all night, for no reason at all, just looking at the starlight on that softly moving water. There was no crash of surf here, hardly any noise but the whisper of the little waves sliding in and out, the whisper of the wind, and the starlight glitter. *This is what I came for,* she thought. *All of the craziness to get here would have been worth just this. But we get another two whole weeks of it.*

"Here they come," Quelt said softly. "The *keks.*"

Nita strained her eyes, looking out at the water. Then she saw a motion near the shore: not water, but something else.

Silent, hardly daring to breathe, Nita and Kit watched them come. First one or two, then five, ten, fifty, a hundred, a thousand, ten thousand: a host of tiny creatures, blue green and shining, came flooding up out of the water onto the beach. They had a lot of legs, like crabs, but no pincers. They had eyes like crabs, though; and the general look of them as they scuttled around was very crablike, though Nita couldn't remember ever having seen any crab look quite so busy.

Soon the wet gleam of the sand under the starlight was obscured by them, black with them. All up and down the length of that beach, from right in front of them to (it seemed) the edge of the world, the crabs started to dig, throwing the peach-colored sand up behind them in little showers. The whole beach became obscured by the haze created by sand in the air, sand kicked up by millions of little legs.

"What are they doing?" Nita whispered.

"Watch," said Quelt.

They watched, while some of the tiny satellites that were all Alaalu had by way of moons went sliding by overhead, casting shifting shadows over the shapes on the beach. And slowly, slowly, the beach above the waterline began to be obscured by something that was not flat.

The *keks* were building.

"What are they making?" Kit said, very quietly, as if he was afraid he might frighten them.

"We don't know," Quelt said. "No one knows. They build these things in the sand . . . then they go back into the water by midnight. And the next night, they come and do it again. They've always done it, as far as I know. Since our people began to notice things . . ."

They sat there and watched for maybe another half an hour. There, in the darkness, the crabs sculpted the sand. Shapes reared up—mostly little cones with holes opening out of them. They would collapse, get built again, collapse once more. And, finally, the *keks* got tired of it, and slowly, one by one, they started going into the sea again.

In the darkness, Kit said, "That was so neat . . ." And he let out a tremendous yawn.

Quelt laughed under her breath. "Come on, cousins," she said. "It's late for all of us. No need to get up early tomorrow."

They got up and walked back to the house along the rise, looking down at the strange shapes built on the sand, watching as the sea began to creep up and wash them slowly away. Before too long they were back at the Peliaens' house, where here and there in an open window, a little lamp showed like a star.

"There's your building," Quelt said, leading them to it. It was thatched with ironwood, like the other buildings, and had several open windows that let the warm night breeze in. Screens partitioned it in half. "You have a gender-separability thing at your age, don't you?" Quelt said. "I thought so. Is this all right?"

Kit yawned. "This is fine," Nita said, and started to laugh at Kit, until she yawned herself.

"There's a big couch on each side," Quelt said. "Some coverings and cushions if you need them." And then she bent down to each of them and took them gently by the shoulders. "I'm so glad you came!" Quelt said. "This is going to be fun."

Nita reached up, did the same for Quelt. "You have a good night," she said.

Quelt smiled, slipped out of the building like a shadow. Kit, standing there and looking out the window, smiled, too.

"The coolness of this situation," he said, "cannot *possibly* be overstated." And he yawned.

Nita glanced at him and laughed. "I wouldn't have put it quite that way," she said, "but, yeah, you're right there. These people are really, really nice...and this is going to be a terrific holiday. Now go to bed!"

On either side of the screen, they went to sleep under strange stars—and, for the first time, did it not on errantry, where anything might happen, but in safety, and at leisure. Nothing seemed strange about the stars, here, and that odd, high horizon somehow made the sky seem smaller, a cozier and more protected place. Nita fell asleep with the sound of the sea whispering in her ears. And later on, there were other whispers entirely, but all friendly ones. *This is so great,* she thought once in the middle of the night as she turned over and saw, not her own dark bedroom wall, with the occasional late-night car headlight flickering across it through the venetian blinds, but the nearby low, wide window opening onto the sea, and through it, stars falling like rain, so many of them that she was somehow surprised not to hear them pattering on the roof. *So great. I love being a wizard...*

And she fell asleep again, while all around her, cheerful, unperturbed, like the wind, the whispers went on.

"*Everything's fine...*"

Local Excursions

A VOICE WAS SHOUTING SOMETHING indistinct through a roar of fire. After a while, she could just make it out:

"Dairiiiiiiine!"

She held very still, hoping they would just stop shouting her name and go away. But the roaring just got louder, an indistinct, crackling, rushing sound—

"Dairiiiiiiine." The voice came from downstairs. "Where *arrrrrrre* they?"

Dairine rolled over in her bed and clutched the pillow over her head. Then she jumped, a half-awake version of the falling-out-of-bed awakening. There was a tree next to her bed, rustling in no wind whatever.

"Uh, hi," she said. "Uh, Filif. Yeah. Was there something you needed?"

"You were making a noise," Filif said.

"Snoring," Dairine said. "That's called snoring."

Usually, when Nita accused her of it, she tried to find a way around the accusation, but she and Filif were both using the Speech, so there was no point in trying.

"Also," Filif said, "there is someone who wants you."

Dairine sat up in the bed, rubbing her eyes and trying to become more conscious. Her body was resisting her: She felt wrecked. *If I feel like this at home,* she thought, *what would I have felt like if I'd gone away? Maybe this whole excursus thing wasn't such a great idea...*

"Dairiiiiiine!"

"Coming!" she shouted at the top of her lungs.

"You're loud today," Filif said, sounding amused.

"Yeah, well, I'm about to get louder," Dairine said, getting out of bed and scouting around her room to find a pair of jeans to get into. Then she realized that Filif was standing on them. "Fil," she said, "could I get you to move sideways a little? Thanks."

Filif backed away, looking around her room. "This is interesting," he said.

"How?" Dairine went to her chest of drawers and rummaged in it for another oversize T-shirt.

"It's so...enclosed."

"You've got to show me your home," Dairine said, "when we have a moment. But I have a feeling that's not going to be for a while..."

She went into the bathroom, took care of some things, changed, and then headed downstairs. In the dining room, Carmela was sitting at the table, looking in astonishment at Sker'ret. The Rirhait was mostly coiled up on a chair himself, but had draped the front half of his body over the back of it, and, in turn, was staring at Carmela with most of his eyes. Both he and Carmela glanced up at Dairine as she came in.

"Decide to sleep in this morning?" Carmela said.

Dairine glanced at her watch. It was 9:30. "I don't know if I would describe this as 'sleeping in,'" she said. "Or maybe it would've been, if some people hadn't been shrieking my name at the top of their lungs."

"Oh, come on," Carmela said. "How can you sleep when you've got all these wonderful people in your house?" She leaned across the table toward Sker'ret and grabbed one of his clawed forelegs, wiggling it back and forth. Sker'ret chuckled, a raspy, ratchety little sound. "I mean, look at this guy!"

Dairine stared at Carmela. "I thought you hated bugs!"

"*Bug* bugs, yeah," Carmela said. "But Sker'ret's not a bug! I mean, look at the size of him! Nobody's going to have to worry about him going down their back or getting in their shoes!"

One of Sker'ret's eyes came around to waver almost in front of Carmela's nose. She grabbed the stalk just behind the eye and wiggled it, too, playfully. "And look at all these eyes he's got! He's just terrific!"

"Thank you!" Sker'ret said. "You're an amiable being, and I like you, too."

As she rummaged in the kitchen cupboard for tea, Dairine had to smile: The attitude was so like him generally. *It's a shame he can't stay around a while after this is over,* she thought.

"'Amiable,'" Carmela said. "See that? He's cultured. What a nice vocabulary you have!" she said to Sker'ret.

"You're really going to spoil these guys," Dairine said, filling the kettle and putting it on to boil. "Sker'ret, don't use hard words on her. She's still in the kindergarten level in the Speech."

"I don't think she's doing so badly," Sker'ret said. "It's not like we're going to start talking technical things out of the blue."

The sound of rustling in the doorway brought Carmela's head around. "And what have we here?" she said. "Why, you're just a little shrub! Aren't you cute!" She stood up and went over for a closer look at him.

"You're not bad-looking for a biped yourself," Filif said.

Dairine gave him a look from the kitchen. "You flirt!" she said.

"It's *true,*" Filif said. It was impossible to say how one perceived that a tree was winking at you, but Dairine perceived it. *Maybe it's the berries,* she thought.

What made Dairine have to control herself very carefully for the next couple of minutes was Carmela's response...because she perceived the winking, too. "You tease," she said, and ran an affectionate hand through Filif's needles. "Dairine, is it possible to become an item with a tree?"

"Uh," Dairine said. Many, many possible responses went through her head. "There might be a splinter problem," she said at last.

Carmela burst out laughing. "We'll see. I'm just try-ing to resist the urge to take this kid home and decorate him. You and I," she said to Filif, "we're going to spend lots of time talking, because I want to know all about you."

"That would be good," Filif said. "I want to know about you, too."

"I thought you said that people here didn't know about wizards," Sker'ret said to Dairine.

The teakettle boiled and started whistling: Dairine got it off the stove and poured boiling water on the tea bag in her mug. "Mostly they don't," she said. "Carmela's an exception to the rule. Most rules," she added, smirking slightly.

"I heard that, and I'm taking it as a compliment!" Carmela said.

Dairine heard footsteps on the basement stairs, and winced. The sound was too light to be her father's tread, and he was probably at the shop already, anyway. *Let's give Roshaun another chance,* she thought. *Maybe I just got off on the wrong foot with him yesterday.*

Roshaun came into the kitchen, and at first sight of him, all of Dairine's good intentions evaporated. He was even more splendidly dressed than he had been the day before. Today the long overjacket that he favored was in blue, and it was richly, even thickly, embroidered with jewels, in all shades of blue and green, some of them the size of marbles or quail's eggs. Gauntlets, tunic, boots, all were in metallic blues and greens, and the fillet binding his brows was of some blue metal. The fillet was the only part of the costume that really interested Dairine. *But no way am I going to show it!*

"Good morning," Dairine said to Roshaun.

Roshaun merely nodded at her and swept through the kitchen into the sunny dining room. *It's hopeless,* Dairine thought. *I think all my feet with this guy are going to be the wrong feet. I wonder if the Powers would let me send him back and get another wizard?*

Roshaun paused in the doorway, gazing in at his fellow wizards, and at Carmela. It was a second or so before Carmela turned, most casually, and looked Roshaun up and down.

"A little early for such a big fashion statement," she said, "but maybe some of us *need* to start early. And you would be?"

Roshaun straightened up even straighter and taller than he had been standing, if that was possible, and gazed at Carmela.

"That's Roshaun," Dairine said, doing her best to keep any kind of smile from showing.

"... ke Nelaid am Seriv am Teliuyve am Meseph am Veliz am Teriaunst am det Wellakhit," Roshaun began, and this time went on reciting names for at least twice as long as he originally had with Dairine.

Carmela stood there watching Roshaun go through this performance with the vaguely impatient expression of someone who's arrived at the movies on time and then has to sit through ten minutes of commercials and previews. Finally, Roshaun trailed off and stood gazing imperiously at Carmela, waiting for her response.

"He means he's a prince," Dairine said, not entirely kindly. *I'm sorry, Powers That Be. I haven't had my breakfast yet; it's that pesky blood sugar again...*

Carmela regarded Roshaun in the most leisurely manner possible.

"No methane," she said at last. "*Two* legs." She gave these a last noncommittal glance, which suggested that perhaps he'd put them on backward that morning, but she wasn't going to embarrass him by mentioning it. "Well, one out of four's not bad," Carmela said at last. "Let's go for two. You wouldn't have a battle fleet on you, would you?"

Peering out through the kitchen doorway while pretending to do something concerning toast, Dairine saw that even Roshaun was having trouble looking haughty and completely confused at the same time. "We have not yet been *formally* introduced, in that I . . ." Roshaun finally said, trying hard to sound chilly about it.

Dairine opened her mouth, but had no chance to say anything, for Carmela was once again looking Roshaun up and down, this time with the expression of someone who's been asked a personal question by someone who should have been asking her "Paper or plastic?" "*Formally* introduced? I'll let you know if and when I think we need to be," Carmela said. She turned her back on Roshaun with a grim look and the merest twitch of a wink at Dairine. "Meanwhile," she said to Dairine, "I need to use the bathroom. But make a note for me: When you next hear from my brother, tell him he and I are going to have a talk, because I see that he was pulling my leg, and I'm already planning numerous ways to make him pay." She leaned over and whispered in Dairine's ear—the "whisper" being something that could have been heard at twenty paces— "And whatever you do, *get me a date with that bush!*"

Carmela then walked away toward the back of the house with a demeanor of complete unconcern, leaving Filif and Sker'ret sitting there exuding the pleasure of having met a wonderful being, while Dairine and Roshaun stared after her, both briefly mute with astonishment.

The moment didn't last long for Roshaun. "Her brother was pulling her leg?" Roshaun said to Dairine. "Does this have some cultural significance?"

"I think it's gonna be significant for *him* when he gets back," Dairine said, making a mental note to be there when that happened.

"Who is she?" Roshaun said.

"She's Carmela. Our neighbor," Dairine said. "One of those lesser life-forms you don't want anything to do with."

There was a silence that lasted for several seconds, a noticeable period when dealing with Roshaun. "She's magnificent," he said at last.

Dairine burst out laughing. "Oh, boy," she said, when she got enough breath back to speak, "does her brother ever need to hear that you said that!" *If he does ever hear about it,* she thought. *How do I make best use of a piece of information like this? The alien prince has the hots for Kit's sister. This is too funny—*

"What did she mean," Filif said, "she wanted to decorate me?"

Oh, lord, Dairine thought, as the humor of the moment abruptly evaporated. "Some of us have a tradition here," she said. "We bring trees into our houses"—she was *not* going to tell him that most of those trees had been severed from their roots—"and we put decorations on them. Pretty things…glass balls…lights…"

There was a surprisingly long silence from Filif, at the end of which he said, "*I want to see!!*"

"I'll find you a picture," Dairine said. "It's a pity you weren't here at Christmas." Then she wished she could take the line back. *To see thousands of slowly dying trees standing around in vacant lots waiting to be bought by my people and put on display until their needles drop off?! Do* not *put so much emphasis on this that he wants to come back someday and see this for himself!*

"But if we, uh, if we go to the mall today," Dairine said, desperately trying to cover by manufacturing a plan for his and everybody else's distraction from the dangerous subject, "we can decorate you with *other* stuff."

Carmela reappeared in the dining room as if by magic. "Did someone mention the mall?" she said.

"Let's go!" Filif said. "I want to see the decorations!"

"You all need to put on your disguises first," Dairine said, "because there will be no end of trouble if you go out the way you are. And I want to see the disguises before we go anywhere."

"I'm sure *I* won't need anything to pass unremarked in this culture," Roshaun said.

Carmela started to laugh. "Oh, you are so funny!" she said, and the dry way that she said it brought

Roshaun up short. "No, of *course* you don't need to do anything! You look *just* like everyone around here! Oh, my." She turned away, ostentatiously half covering her face with one hand and throwing a look at Dairine that Roshaun could not possibly have missed.

He didn't miss it. "Perhaps the lady would show me the correct manner of a disguise for this world," Roshaun said, all haughtiness again, "since we have seen so few examples of this world's dress..."

"Dairine," Carmela said, "can we use the TV for a moment? I'll show him a few things and lay a groundwork."

"Be my guest," Dairine said, drinking some tea. "If you think it'll do any good..."

She went in with her mug of tea and sat down at the table with Sker'ret and Filif as Carmela and Roshaun headed into the living room. "So how are you guys this morning?" Dairine said to them.

"Everything's well," Sker'ret said. "Though I'm getting hungry again..."

"We'll find you something," Dairine said.

"And how about you?" Filif said. "Are *you* well?"

From the living room, Dairine heard Carmela's muted chuckle. A moment later, Roshaun said, "Under *no* circumstances will I be seen in anything like *that*—"

Dairine grinned. "Getting better every minute," she said, and drank her tea.

The mall was still fairly quiet when they got there later that morning. It was Sunday morning, and a lot of the most serious shoppers wouldn't be in for some hours yet. There were, however, going to be a lot of kids there who were also on spring break, getting an early start on their malling. It was meeting these that Dairine was secretly most dreading, but she refused to show any sign of her concern to her fellow wizards.

She had been nervous enough, earlier, over the prospect of simply getting them all out of the driveway. But in retrospect, that had worked well enough. Everyone's disguises looked good, and stayed in place, repaying the hour or two of work that Dairine and Carmela had spent on their charges before letting them out.

Filif had needed the most coaching. His disguise was no shape-change, but a visual illusion keyed to a wizardry he built, with some assistance from Dairine, to mimic human limb action, facial affect, and clothing. The illusion would not withstand close examination, such as being touched, but Dairine had no plans to let anyone near enough to touch him, and told him so.

"Your people must be very easily shocked," Filif said, in a pitying tone of voice. It sounded funny coming from the big, stocky, dark-haired guy that he had become, partly with Carmela's coaching.

"They are," Dairine said, "and sometimes so am I. I certainly will be if your disguise falls off in the middle of the street because somebody bumps up against you. So keep your distance from people, and we'll all be fine."

"What about me?" Sker'ret said. "Do I look all right?"

"You look excellent," Dairine said, sizing him up. Carmela had talked him more or less into the shape of a slim, redheaded surfer guy. "In fact, I'm not sure you need any advice from me. You may want to go talk to Carmela about that sweatshirt, though." The sweatshirt was illusionary and looked perfectly orthodox, except for the words "Will Do Magic for Food," which he had added to the front of the illusion, in the Speech.

And then there had been Roshaun. Carmela had worked him over most effectively, and without completely losing her temper—a feat Dairine had to admire. Roshaun was "wearing," over some of his real clothes, a long, floppy shirt and large trousers. "You've got the height to carry them," Carmela had said, just a little admiring. "Not many people do." And Roshaun had fallen for the line. Carmela had also made him reduce his epic ponytail to a more manageable length, at least in illusion. The two long front locks in front of his ears had given Carmela the most trouble; Roshaun adamantly refused to put them behind his ears, where they would show less. "They're supposed to show!" he said.

"What they're going to show here," Carmela said "is that you look too different. All you need is for some wise guy to come along and pull one of those—"

Roshaun looked at her, indignant. "Who would dare?!"

"*I* would," Carmela said, suiting the gesture to the concept. Roshaun winced. "And if it's something I'd do, it's something that will probably occur to other people. This is not your palace you're going into, Your Royal Highness. This is a mall. You are entering a world where anything can happen—mostly having to do with people getting real judgmental about your looks." She raised her eyebrows. "Fortunately," she said, "your looks are okay. But if I were you, I wouldn't push your luck with the hair."

"As you say," Roshaun had muttered, but he agreed with ill grace, if any at all. At the time, Carmela had thrown Dairine a look that said, *This boy is going to take some kicking into shape.* Dairine had kept her face very straight. But Carmela had caught her answering flicker of eyes, and knew that Dairine was in complete agreement.

With everyone's disguises well in place, they had set out for the mall. Originally, Dairine's plan had been to do a private-gating transit there, a variant of Kit's and Nita's "beam-me-up-Scotty" spell. She had long had several sets of prelocated coordinates laid in for each of the major malls nearby. But Dairine was astounded to come up against serious resistance to this concept from all her guests—even Roshaun, who she would've thought would resist so plebeian an option as walking on general principles.

"One cannot truly experience a place by doing fast transits to and from locations," Roshaun said, looking down his nose at Dairine. "Having come all this way, I may as well see what this world looks like from the ground up."

"He's right," Sker'ret said. "I see enough gates as it is. Walking has got to be lots more fun."

Dairine had sighed. "Just so you know that it's not

soft ground we're going to be walking along," she said, looking at Filif. "You can't walk through it. It's all concrete—"

"I can deal with that," Filif said. "I haven't had to walk through any of your floors here; I can manage."

And as a result, they all walked down Dairine's street toward Nassau Road, maybe half a mile away, and the bus stop there. It was beautiful, bright, sunny weather—unusually warm for that time of spring—and people were out washing their cars, mowing their lawns...doing all the things that would make it easier for them to see that there were aliens walking down their street. Dairine found herself praying for rain, gloom, a sudden hailstorm or blizzard—anything that would drive people in out of their front yards and reduce the chances of them seeing some part of her charges' disguises slip.

To her eyes, they were a motley group...but then Dairine was looking for errors. People who lived on the street and chanced to be looking out their windows probably only saw five kids in a ragged group wandering down the sidewalk together. In particular, Dairine was admiring Sker'ret's command of the human gait, which he seemed to have no trouble handling. *Probably*, Dairine thought, *it's all of those legs. If you can manage about forty of them, you shouldn't have that much trouble with two.*

Neither thunder nor rain nor gloom of night answered Dairine's prayer; but somehow, striding, gliding, or just approximating walking the best they could, everybody made it down to Nassau Road in one piece, and without causing peculiar looks from anybody— even the Nassau County police cruiser that went past them at one point. Dairine had sweated as the cops had gone by; she felt as if she had INSTIGATOR OF ALIEN MALL-CRAWLING FIASCO stenciled across her forehead. But the cops barely glanced at them, having better things to do with their time. Nonetheless, Dairine heaved a sigh of relief when they were gone.

On Nassau Road, they had stood for a while at the corner, waiting for the bus. One going to Roosevelt Field, one of the oldest shopping malls in the area, was scheduled to come by every half hour. "It used to be kind of a dump," Carmela said, "but they fixed it up— it's better now."

"And what does one do in a mall?" Roshaun said.

"Walk around," Dairine said. "Look at things."

"What kind of things?" Filif said.

"Decorations," Dairine said. "Like the kind we were talking about before. Not the seasonal stuff—but the kind of decorations you see in Roshaun's and Sker'ret's disguises, the kind that humans wear all the time. Personal ornamentation."

"Clothes," Carmela said with relish. "And there are all kinds of other places to buy things. Electronics and appliances, and there's a food court—"

Sker'ret looked up, instantly fascinated. He was getting the hang of showing his emotions in the human expression. *Probably from watching us,* Dairine thought. *He's a quick study. At the rate he's going, we could pass him off as human in a few days...*

"What kind of food?" said Sker'ret.

Some kinds that we should keep Filif away from, Dairine thought, suddenly remembering the restaurant in the food court that had a huge salad bar. Fortunately, it was at about that point that Carmela began describing one of her favorite places up there—the ice-cream stand. The others, even Roshaun, were enthralled by this.

"You freeze food, and then you eat it?" Roshaun said. "Don't you break your teeth?"

"Not if you're careful," Carmela said. She went on talking about ice cream for some minutes, until the bus came. Dairine was fascinated by how much attention Roshaun was paying Carmela. *He's not all* that *interested in ice cream,* Dairine thought. *Kit is just about going to bust a gut when he hears about this. I can't wait for him to call—in fact, if I have a chance, I should message him myself from the mall.*

The bus pulled up, and Sker'ret and Filif regarded it with wonder. Roshaun eyed it with some suspicion. "There are other people in this vehicle," he said.

"Of course there are," Dairine said behind him. "Wizards are supposed to support public transport. It's ecologically sound. Besides, *you* were the one who wanted to use ground transport and see your local environment. Well, here's the environment for you. So get in, put the money I gave you in the box, and sit down!"

Roshaun did as he was told, though not without throwing a glance at Dairine that suggested he would discuss this impertinence with her later. She snorted and sat down herself.

The ride took about twenty minutes, which ranked among the twenty longest minutes of Dairine's life. She had cautioned her colleagues not to speak in the bus more than they had to. Because they were using the Speech, the other bus riders would hear them exactly as if they were speaking in their own languages—and some of the ethnicities in the area might find that a little strange, in terms of the way the strangers looked. *Especially,* Dairine thought, *considering the* kinds *of things these guys are likely to be saying if they get started.*

But, by and large, the visitors behaved themselves pretty well, at least in terms of not talking. Nothing Dairine could do or say would keep them from plastering their noses up against the window of the bus—at least in Filif's and Sker'ret's cases; Roshaun would not have done anything so déclassé, and sat there looking scornfully unfocused. But even he would steal the occasional glance of wonder out the windows, and the others gawked at everything they saw, exclaiming softly to themselves sometimes when they just couldn't hold it in any longer. Everything was amazing to them. Storefronts, parked cars, parking meters, traffic lights, real estate signs in front of houses, trees and flowers, garbage in the street…and advertising. *Especially* advertising. Dairine spent nearly half the bus ride, from the point where they left her town to the point where they entered Hempstead town and drove through it toward the shopping center, explaining what "milk" was and why it was important that you should "got" some.

Yet at the same time, the bus ride made Dairine nostalgic for the first time she had gone off-planet, when everything had been new and strange. As they piled off the bus in the parking lot of the shopping center, Dairine remembered her first alien parking lot, and how she had nearly been killed by any number of alien vehicles before she got her bearings. *And how I talked to somebody's luggage for the better part of five minutes,* she thought, *before I realized what I was doing.* It seemed like a long time ago now. She had almost forgotten what it was like. But she was quickly being reminded; and the other wizards' attitude toward the strangeness of her world was beginning to affect her. She found herself looking at shopping-cart pens and sliding doors and the displays in the outer shop windows of the shopping center as if she had never seen such things before. It was refreshing.

They went into the mall, and in a matter of seconds, Dairine was being bombarded with questions. "What's that for?" "Why is that colored that way?" "You mean people actually ride on those?" "They should fall off, shouldn't they?" "Isn't that beautiful!" "Why is all this water in here?" "What's that smell?" "Are those 'decorations'?"

That was the question that got asked most frequently. Filif was fixated on the concept. "*Those* decorations," Filif said, "those look especially nice..." He moved over to the window in question and peered in.

Dairine came up behind him, not wanting to touch him—that always ran the risk of breaking the visual illusion—but she leaned over him and whispered, "I don't think these are for you."

"Why not?"

"Well..." Dairine looked up at the sign over the store's door. "Can you read that?"

Filif turned his human face up toward the sign, dutifully. Though he seemed to be looking at it with human eyes, somehow Dairine could still perceive the alert attention of a whole array of berries trained on the letters. "Victoria's—did I pronounce that right? Secret."

"That's right," Dairine said.

"Who's Victoria?" said Filif. "And what's its secret?"

"I've never been clear about that myself," Dairine said. "But if you start wearing those, people are going to talk. Come on." She turned away, having a great deal of difficulty dealing with the image of a Christmas tree in a garter belt.

Filif moved away carefully, but not without a backward look at the bright colors of the lingerie in the window. Then Dairine saw Sker'ret hurrying ahead of them, and she began to fear the worst. "Sker'ret?" she said. "Wait up!"

She went after him as quickly as she could, with a glance at Carmela to suggest that she should keep an eye on the others. But Carmela already had her hands full. She and Roshaun had paused by a window display of clothes and were apparently discussing them. Sker'ret had moved a little farther away and was closely examining a freestanding gift stall stacked high with balloons, cards, gift plaques, and bright-colored candies. *Oh no*, Dairine thought. *What is it with the colors? These guys are like five-year-olds.*

The sound of laughter came to Dairine from down the mall. A group of five older kids—high school juniors, Dairine guessed—came wandering along toward them, much more interested in the shoppers of their own age than in the merchandise. "Hey, sweet things!" one of them called to Carmela. "Who's your skinny friend?"

Carmela didn't respond. "Hey, elf boy!" shouted another of the guys. "Nice hair!" This was followed by a chorus of snickering and laughter.

Dairine saw Roshaun draw himself up to his full height and turned to favor the oncoming group with an expression of truly withering scorn. "'Elf boy'?" he said softly. "What kind of disrespectful, species-ist—" One of his hands moved in a gesture that Dairine recognized as the preliminary to producing some pre-designed wizardry. She gulped and hurried toward him.

But Carmela merely glanced over her shoulder at the approaching group. "Ah, ah, ah," she said under her breath, and reached out sideways to take Roshaun's hand in hers. Roshaun's eyes went wide, and he stopped absolutely still, as if he'd been frozen that way.

Dairine slowed down a little, caught between surprise and admiration. *She may not be a wizard,* she thought, *but she's got some moves.* Just loudly enough to be heard, as the five passed close by, Carmela said to Roshaun, "Don't mind them. They're just wonder-struck by your profound majesty and glory and so forth. We don't get a lot of princes around here, and when they see somebody like you and contrast your elevated station with their tiny antlike lives, it's really hard for them to cope."

Carmela said all this not in English, but in perfect Japanese, the language she'd been studying when she first started to pick up the Speech. As wizards, Dairine and Roshaun had no problem understanding her; they heard the language "through" the Speech and made sense of it that way. But the five guys were completely thrown off. They saw what seemed like a Japanese translator of some kind—who looked at them as coolly as if they were members of an alien species—who was apparently carefully translating what they'd said for someone who looked like a living anime star, someone whose expression was better suited to the last half hour of a samurai movie than anything else...the part where things really break loose.

Dairine saw faint unease ripple through the guys as they found themselves facing something they didn't understand. The guys passed close to Carmela and Roshaun, who watched them with expressions of clinical interest and complete disdain, and didn't stop— just headed on down the mall. It took a few moments for them to get their composure back, and then one of them muttered something under his breath.

Roshaun looked at Carmela in curiosity as Dairine came over to them. "'Duckhead'?" he said. "He called me a duckhead. A...duck? That's some kind of flying creature, isn't it?"

Carmela had let go of Roshaun's hand and was gazing after the five nonplussed guys with barely concealed amusement. Now she glanced over at Dairine, not saying anything.

"Uh," Dairine said. "Yeah, it is. They swim, too."

Roshaun looked thoughtful. "I see. The idiom suggests that a humanoid can share the same attributes of flexibility...the ability to adapt to multiple environments. I like that. Evidently they saw they'd misjudged me, even if it took them a few moments."

Dairine was ever so glad that what Roshaun had said had come out as a statement rather than a question, but then it didn't seem to be Roshaun's style to ask a lot of questions. *Saved by a personal blind spot,* Dairine thought with relief. Normally she hated being saved by anyone or anything, but at the moment, she was all too willing to make an exception.

Then Dairine remembered Sker'ret. She looked around in panic and saw him proceeding quickly up the mall ahead of them, looking in windows, while a shiny, silver, Mylar balloon bobbed and trailed along behind him. *Hey, he's got the hang of money already,* she thought. *Maybe this isn't going all that badly.*

Ahead of her, Carmela was now actually strolling along arm in arm with Roshaun, pointing out things in the store windows to him. *How does she do it?* Dairine wondered. *She's got him eating out of her hand. Maybe I don't want to know...* She hurried off after Sker'ret.

He was going up one of the escalators at some speed. Dairine thought she knew why. The smell of fast food was coming from somewhere up ahead, and Sker'ret had targeted on that with the intensity of a heat-seeking missile looking for the tailpipe of a jet. "Sker'ret," she called after him, "this is really no time for that. We can do this later! In fact we can *all* do it together!"

"Do what?" Sker'ret said.

"Eat," Dairine said. "Again."

Sker'ret was standing in the middle of the food court when Dairine caught up with him. His disguise was firmly in place, but Dairine could still dimly perceive, underneath the illusion, all his eyes writhing in every possible direction, looking around at all the goodies. Sker'ret turned slowly in a circle, looking at the kosher hot dog place, the McDonald's, the Chinese fast food place, the burrito joint.... "This is wonderful!" he said. "Every planet should have places like this!"

"Oh, come on, Sker'ret," Dairine said. "Rirhath B has places like this! Even the Crossings has some."

"Not like this," Sker'ret said, a little sadly. He stopped spinning, training all his available eyes on the kosher hot dog place. "Besides, I'm not allowed to go into the ones in the Crossings."

For the moment, Dairine concealed her surprise. Sker'ret made his way back toward the escalator, stepping sadly onto the downward-running side and riding it back the way he'd come with an expression of deep sorrow. Dairine followed him, wondering what that had been about. *Something else to ask him about later...*

They rejoined the group and then set about systematically wandering through the entire mall, wing by wing, until everyone had seen everything. Even Roshaun was beginning to get a little tired as they got near the end of the "crawl"—a source of irrational pleasure for Dairine. Some of that otherwise indelible arrogance came off him; he looked like he just wanted to sit down for a while.

"Goodness," Carmela said, as Roshaun sat down on the bench at the base of one of the escalators, "we have to do something about your stamina. If you're going to become serious about mall crawling, you can't poop out after an hour like that."

"I have not 'pooped out,'" Roshaun said. "But my feet do pain me somewhat. And keeping up the disguise takes a certain amount of energy. Perhaps a restorative?"

"Food!" Sker'ret said.

Dairine chuckled. "Carmela," she said "could you take these guys upstairs and get them something? Ice cream, probably. Filif..." She looked over at him; he was gazing down the length of the mall with a yearning expression. "I'm going to be your personal shopper for a little while. You and I should go off and see about some of those decorations we were discussing." *That way, I don't have to worry about you stumbling into the salad bar, which is probably going to look to you like the site of a mass murder.*

Filif was delighted. "Yes!" he said. "Let's go!"

"You have enough money on you, Carmela?" Dairine said. "I brought some spare cash—"

"It's okay," Carmela said. "I'm fairly loaded today." She turned to Roshaun and Sker'ret. "Come on, boys," she said. They got up, and she shepherded them through the mall.

"Come on," Dairine said to Filif. Together they

headed down the center of the shopping mall, toward the place that Dairine had spotted Filif looking at with most interest earlier. *Well,* she thought, *the second-most interest.*

The store she had in mind was a chain sportswear shop specializing in bright colors—indeed, colors that were almost too bright for Dairine to look at. But she had noticed several times now that whenever Filif stopped to look in any window for long, it had been one where Day-Glo colors were splashed onto things with abandon. Now, as they headed down the mall together, Dairine became aware of some looks from other kids on spring break who were passing by on the other side of the mall, and looking curiously at Filif. "Hey, kid," one of them shouted at him, "you walk like a dweeb!"

There was a gust of laughter from the other kids. Dairine ostentatiously ignored them, but she stole a glance at Filif and saw that this was slightly true: His mimicked "gait" was already somewhat less polished than it had been when they left home. He, too, was getting tired. "Hey," Dairine said, "never mind this. We'll get you out of here and come back another time. But right now maybe we should get you back home, where you can get that off—"

"Oh, no," Filif said. "Not until we see the decorations!"

She smiled at him. He was so intense about it. "Okay," Dairine said. "Just hang on."

They went into the sportswear store, a tremendous

place full of sneakers and workout clothes and shorts and bathing suits—all in the year's popular colors, any one of which, Dairine thought, should burn her retinas. "Look at the mannequins," Dairine said. "See those models of people, up on top of the racks and in the windows? Those give you an idea how we wear these things. And over there"—she pointed—"are places to try things on, if you see something you like... We can always do that another time, though. There are hats, and T-shirts, and shorts... all kinds of things."

Filif nodded. "I see," he said.

"Okay," Dairine said. "Look around a little, and see what you think of things. We'll go in a little while and catch up with the others."

Filif made his way off among the racks, delighted. Dairine watched him begin unhooking shirts and shorts from the racks, holding them up to the light, admiring the colors. *For all I know,* Dairine thought, *maybe there's not a lot of bright color in his world. And his people seem to go about their lives just walking around in the dirt...* She turned, looked at a T-shirt, and then turned her attention back to the mall outside, listening carefully. There were no sounds of screaming, or of people running. *The disguises must still be holding all right upstairs. I just hope Carmela yells for me if Sker'ret gets out of hand,* she thought. *That boy's appetite...*

She walked idly between the racks of T-shirts, then started looking at some bathing suits. In the background, over the insipid chain-store Muzak, she could

hear one of the staff saying to somebody in the changing room, "Sir, can I give you a hand with that? No?
All right. You, sir, how are you doing in there? You
need that in a twelve? Fine..."

Dairine sighed and turned her attention back to the
T-shirts. *I can't believe how garish the colors are this
year,* she thought. *I can't wait for it to be next year,
when the style changes and things might calm down a
little bit.*

She yawned again. "Sir?" said the cheerful voice in
the background. "How are you in there? Those sizes
all right? Fine. Hello? Sir—"

Dairine stretched, pulled a bathing suit off the rack,
looked in astonishment at the garish print. *Not on your
life,* she thought, and put it back, blinking. Her eyes
still felt grainy; she hadn't had a lot of sleep the previous night. The thought of going upstairs and having an
ice cream herself, a big one, was looking increasingly
attractive. "Sir?" said the voice in the background.
"Would you like some—"

And then she heard the shriek.

Dairine suddenly realized what she had been hearing, or rather, not hearing. She hurried toward the
changing room, flung the outer curtain open. Past it
she saw one of the staff standing half in and half out of
one of the changing rooms, the curtain held in his
hand, frozen. And one after another, other people's
heads popped out of the other changing rooms, staring
at the sales guy.

Oh no, Dairine thought. *Spot!*

She put out her hand, and an instant later Spot was in it. Dairine flipped his lid open as she came up behind the staff guy, pushing the curtain aside. The poor man was staring at something he probably had not seen in a changing room before—a Christmas tree wearing Day-Glo orange Jams and several baseball caps, all brightly colored. The top one was on backwards.

"I like the root covers," Filif said thoughtfully, "but I'm not sure about the hat."

There were about twelve things that Dairine was not sure of at that moment, almost all of them being why she had let Filif out of her sight. *Blood sugar!* But there was no time for that now; there was movement in the other cubicles— *You know which spell I need,* she said silently to Spot. His screen cleared and came up with the general-purpose invisibility spell—a quick one that Dairine had used on herself often enough and had had some practice in throwing over other things in a hurry. Silently she read the words, felt the air in front of her twist itself out of shape and into another refractive configuration entirely, under the influence of the Speech. A moment later, both she and the sales guy, and the three heads peering in from behind them, were all staring at what appeared to be empty space.

"Are you okay?" Dairine said to the sales guy.

He looked at her as if she'd come out of nowhere. "I, uh...," he said. "I, uh, I think maybe I had a little too much of something or other last night..." He stared once again at the mirror in the "empty" cubicle, and then turned and let the curtain fall. The other customers went away, and after that the shop guy wandered back out onto the sales floor, shaking his head.

Dairine rolled her eyes, relieved. Silently, she said to Filif, *I wish you'd asked me for help!*

I didn't need any help, Filif said. *I'm doing fine!*

She said, *You have no idea. I'm leaving that invisibility over you for now. You need to put that stuff down and come out with me. We'll come back for this later, under more controlled circumstances. Let's go!*

She reached through the field of invisibility until she could feel a branch or three, and took hold of them, cautiously, being careful not to squish any of the berries. Trying as hard as she could to look casual about it, trying equally hard not to look as if she was leading something invisible away by the hand or branch, Dairine made her way out of the sportswear store and out into the center of the mall again. There she looked around, took a moment to recollect her wits, and said, *You stay invisible for a few minutes, okay? I'll be back for you. We're going home. Don't let anybody bump into you!*

All right, Filif said. *And then we can come back another time for the decorations?*

Absolutely, Dairine said.

She went up to the food court. There sat Roshaun, Carmela, and Sker'ret, ingesting large ice-cream sundaes. They all looked up at her in surprise.

"Where's Filif?" Carmela said.

"About to be taken home," Dairine said. "The fast way. Meet me back there later, okay?"

"Sure," Carmela said. Dairine turned and headed off again...but not before catching sight of Roshaun's amused smirk.

I am going to get him for that, Dairine thought, heading back to where Filif waited. *And as for the rest of this...I am never applying for anything again. Cultural exchange—!*

She snorted at her own stupidity and went off to find an invisible tree.

Taking in the Sights

"DAD?" NITA SAID.

"I can hear you fine, honey," Nita's dad said. "Whatever Tom did to the phone, you don't have to shout. How are you?"

"I'm fine! *Everything's* fine."

Nita was sitting on the beach with her manual in her lap, while a hundred yards away Kit and Ponch were running along the pink sand, racing. Ponch was winning—this not even the new venue could change. The sun was up, and warm already; the wind was just strong enough to take the sun's heat away, but not so strong as to chill; the waves slipped up and down the beach, whispering.

"What's it like?" said her dad's voice from the manual.

Nita laughed. "Like the Hamptons," she said. "Except they don't have money here."

There was a pause at her dad's end. "*That* takes a stretch of the imagination," he said, sounding somewhat dry, for the resorts and wealthy residential communities of the Hamptons, out at the end of Long Island, were (in the Callahan household, at least) often described by the head of the household as a place where people had "more money than sense." "No money, huh? What do they use instead?"

"It's a barter economy, but with exceptions. For things that are hard to get locally, they have other ways of dealing with getting stuff around. But when the dust settles, everybody here seems to have what they need. And that's good, because the people here are really, really nice."

"How's the family you're with?"

"They're the best," Nita said. "They remind me of us."

Her dad chuckled. "No higher praise, I guess...A barter economy. Are they farmers, then?"

"No. Well, they have sheep," Nita said, looking back toward the grassland. "If sheep fly..." From where she sat, she could see yet another of Kuwilin's small flocks of flying sheep landing, while the first flock he'd been feeding took off. A scatter of feed, a flurry of golden wings, and off they went, and another little flock wheeled down out of that blue, blue sky to take their place. It was like feeding pigeons, except that the effect would have been unfortunate if the sheep had tried to land on you the same way pigeons did.

Nita laughed again as exactly that thing started to happen to Quelt's *tapi*, who waved the sheep off with a weary familiarity. "But you haven't been just sitting there looking at sheep, I hope."

"Oh, no," Nita said. "We've been doing tourist things. The stuff that nobody here does unless they have visitors."

Her father laughed. "They have that there, too?"

"Oh, yeah. We went to the Cities to do an errand for Quelt's mom."

"Which city?"

"The Cities. It's just what they call it...Don't ask me why. As if they were interchangeable."

"They are," Kit said, running past. "Modular. They put them where they need them." Ponch ran past him with a stick of ironwood in his mouth; Kit threw Nita a resigned glance and trotted off after him.

"But they're really pretty," Nita said. "It's as if they did New York, but in pink and peach and cream colors. And there's no garbage."

Her father whistled. "A city with no garbage..."

Nita shrugged. "People here don't seem to litter. I don't know if they even have a word for it. They don't throw a lot of stuff away. Come to think of it, they don't have a lot of stuff, period."

"They don't sound deprived, though..."

"Nope. Did I tell you, we're famous here?"

"No."

"They like us because we're short. And wizards are a big deal here. It's going to be strange to come back and have to keep quiet about it again."

"That would be a sore point around here at the moment," Nita's dad said.

"Oh? How's Dairine doing?"

"I haven't seen her as yet today," Nita's dad said. "She wasn't up when I headed to the store this morning. I think the past couple of days have been a little wearing for her."

"Uh-oh," Nita said. "How are *you* doing, Daddy? Are the guests too weird?"

"Not really," her father said. "One of them's just a tree. That I can cope with. Another one's a giant centipede. That's all right, too. That boy has a healthy appetite and everything interests him. He's a whiz with machinery, too: Yesterday he fixed my lawn mower when it stalled. The third one—" There was a sudden pause. "Oh, good morning to you, too. Yes, right out there. No, not *that* way!"

Nita heard a crash. "They're not making trouble for you, are they, Daddy?"

"It's not the usual kind of trouble," her dad said, "and I don't mind." There was a pause. "Yes, go ahead, just don't tell Dairine I gave it to you."

There were loud crunching noises in the background. "Is that static?" Nita said.

"No, honey, it's fine."

"You didn't say anything about the third guest."

"That may have been on purpose," Nita's dad said.

Nita looked down the beach. "What's he doing?"

"Being himself," Nita's dad said, "for which I suppose I shouldn't blame him. But if he were *my* son—" There was another pause. "Oh," her father said, "there you are."

There was a clunk and rustle as if the phone had been

taken out of Nita's dad's hand. "This was the dumbest idea in the world," Dairine said loudly. "I just want you to know I confess to having been really stupid."

Nita wasn't sure what to make of that. Dairine's confessions could sometimes be extremely heartfelt, but she was also extremely good at retracting them later when circumstances changed. "Well," Nita said, "things are terrific here, so I don't know if I necessarily accept your evaluation of the whole thing."

"It's good where you are?"

"It's super."

"I hate you," Dairine said. And there was another clunk and rustle of the phone as it was passed back to their father.

"I'm not sure what to make of that," he said a moment later.

"I am," Nita said. "When she calms down, tell her I feel sorry for her, and I'll send her a postcard later. We got the portable worldgates plugged in last night, so I can come right home if you need me. And I can send you a postcard, too." Nita had spent a little time that morning designing a wizardry that would "take pictures" of the surroundings and deliver them home through the portable gate.

"I don't know if she'll thank you..."

"I'll take my chances. What about the third one?"

"The third what?"

"Wizard, Daddy. What's his problem?"

"I think he— Oh, good morning, Roshaun. Right over there..." There was another pause. "Not right now, sweetie."

Nita resolved to take a look at Roshaun's profile. *Maybe there's something I can do to help...* Then again, she could imagine Dairine's response to this. It was best to leave matters alone, perhaps.

"Did you get all your homework done?"

"Yeah," Nita said. "Both kinds."

"Do *wizards* get homework assignments?"

"Not as such, Daddy. Just some reading I was doing." Earlier that morning, Nita had been going over the "Bindings and Strictures" material again; it was complex, but fortunately most of the strictures, especially the Binding Oath, could be used only once, anyway.

"Well, as long as the schoolwork's done. Anything you need there?"

Nita sighed. "Sunblock," she said. "I burned yesterday."

"I thought you could do a wizardry for that."

"I got distracted, and I forgot..."

"That's bad for your skin, honey. You be more careful."

"I will," Nita said. "Just leave it in my room, okay? I can pop out later and pick it up."

"Okay, I'll leave it on the bed. Uh-oh... here comes Carmela. I should get off. Things start getting lively when she turns up."

Nita grinned. "Is she getting a lot of practice at the Speech?"

"I think there's more going on than that," Nita's dad said, "but you'd better talk to your sister... She'll fill you in."

"Okay. Talk to you later, Daddy!"

"You have a good time, sweetie. Love you."

"Love you, too, Daddy. Bye!"

The print on the page in the manual in Nita's lap said, "Connection broken, JD 2452749.06806." Nita shut the manual and leaned back, looking around her. Down by the main holding pen, Kuwilin was still scattering feed for the flying sheep. Nita got up, dusted the sand off herself, and went to see if he needed any help.

By the time she got there, he was leaning over the pen's fence, watching the sheep munch up their feed. There were always faint sucking and snorting noises when they did this. Their lips were prehensile, expert at picking up the feed pellets and ironwood seed while avoiding the sand, but every now and then they got greedy and wound up doing a lot of spitting.

Nita leaned on the fence beside Kuwilin, watching the sheep. "It takes such a long time every day to feed them," she said.

"Well, too much at once and they get sick," Kuwilin said. "Was that your 'dad'? How is he?"

"He's okay. But my sister sounds like she's having some problems. I think she wishes she were here. And the exchange wizards...I think she's having problems with one of them." Nita pushed her hair back from where the sea breeze had blown it in her face again. "She'll work it out. Was Kit helping you again?"

"Yes, he was," Kuwilin said, "and if you two didn't have better things to do with yourselves, I'd take you on as migrant volunteer labor. He's getting very good

at relieving them of the *shesh*. They hardly notice."
Kuwilin sighed, a sound that humans and Alaalids had
in common. "Which is good, because this time of year,
it's hard to keep them in one place for long. They want
to wander. And if they run into another big migratory
group, half of them may not come back. Of course,"
Kuwilin added, "they do pass directional information
back and forth . . . so I might lose fifty this autumn and
get a hundred and fifty back next spring. It depends if
they like where they've been better than where they're
going." He smiled.

"They're not birds," Kit said, running up with
Ponch lolloping along behind him.

"What?"

"The things Ponch was chasing last night. They're
not birds: They're bats. Sort of. With fur. And they
have antennae, and flaps."

"Flaps?"

Kit shrugged. "Maybe they're more like webbed feet."

"They sing, too," Quelt's *tapi* said. "Have you heard
them? Well, maybe not yet: We were still eating latemeal when they would have been singing, the other
night and last night, too. You can hear them better if
you go up the hill behind the house. They're mating
this time of year, and the singing can go on for hours.
It can keep you up for hours, too."

Ponch abruptly got between Kuwilin and Kit with
yet another stick in his mouth. "Where is he finding all
these?" Kuwilin said, grabbing it and trying to take it
out of Ponch's mouth. Ponch gripped hard on the stick

and shook his head back and forth, fighting with Kuwilin. "We could be rich, with all the ironwood he brings home. I should hire you all. You do more work around here than Quelt does!"

"I wouldn't let her hear you say that," Nita said under her breath, and laughed.

"Well, it's true!" And Kuwilin laughed as well. "But it's not her fault, I know. She has more important things to be doing for the world, and we try not to bother her about chores."

"When did you find out she was a wizard?" Kit said.

Ponch jumped up and down, growling, with the stick in his mouth. Kit took it and threw it, and Ponch chased off after it. "Why, she just came in at firstmeal one morning and told us," Kuwulin said. "I guess that would be a couple of hundred years ago now—"

"Two hundred and sixty," said Demair, coming out of the house and down to the pen with a jug and a cup of *sepah* for her husband. "You should come in and wash," she said. "You smell of *ceiff.*"

"I always smell of *ceiff,*" said Kuwilin. "So does everything here, even these Earth people. They'll probably go home smelling that way. We should bottle some of the air over the pen and send it home with them, labeled 'A Souvenir of Alaalu.'"

Kit snorted with laughter. Nita jabbed him in the ribs with one elbow. "They'll have to bottle you, too," she said. To Kuwilin, she said, "Was that before her Ordeal, or after?"

"'Ordeal?'" Demair said. "Oh, you mean the Own Choice. After, I suppose." She looked at Nita in slight perplexity. " 'Ordeal'—is that what they call it in your world? Is it normally dangerous for you?"

Nita was taken aback. "Well, yes, in that you usually wind up fighting with the Lone Power, one way or another—"

Both Demair and Kuwilin looked blank. "Who?"

Kit looked surprised. "You know, the Lone Power. You *do* know the Lone One?"

"Invented death?" Nita said. "Got thrown out of Timeheart? Runs around trying to get sentient species to willingly buy into death?"

"Oh, *that* one," Demair said, and laughed. "Certainly, we know about her. But she's no problem."

" 'No problem,' " Nita said softly. Then she looked around at the landscape and thought of the Cities as well, clean, safe, full of smiling people; all in all, it was a world where there seemed to be no such thing as crime or disaster or hatred or anything of the kind. "Yeah," she said, "maybe I see your point."

"But how *come* she's not?" Kit said.

Kuwilin and Demair looked at each other, perplexed again. "I always assumed it had something to do with our species' Choice," Kuwilin said, "but I wouldn't be an expert. Quelt would know more about it, I'd imagine."

Nita looked around. "Where is she now?" she said.

"Up in the meadows. She said she had to talk to the wind about something." Nita nodded. This was an expression that she'd heard a number of times recently and that most often seemed to mean that the person had something she wanted to think about in private.

"But to finish answering your first question," Kuwilin said, "she just came in that morning and said, 'I'm a wizard, and in a few years I have to take over from the one we've got.' She showed us some wizardry; we were very impressed. And then her mentor, the old wizard, Vereich, came along and said, 'I hear my successor is come into her power; we'd better start work.' Of course, he knew he wasn't long for the body at that point—he must have been four thousand or so then. No, five, now that I think of it. A delightful old man; I still hear from him occasionally."

Nita saw Kit start a little at that, but it somehow didn't surprise her at all. "Are you going to eat something now?" Demair said to her husband. "Cousins?"

Nita shook her head. "Not right now," she said, "thank you. I want to ask Quelt about this."

"All right. We'll leave some cold things for you on the sideboard."

Kit and Nita went up the rise together to look over it into the meadowlands. Ponch came bouncing after, with yet another stick in his mouth, or the same one.

"Were they talking about what I think they were?" Kit said. "Do they routinely talk to dead people here?"

Nita was quiet for a moment. "I don't know if *they* think of them as dead," she said. "They do seem to run things differently on Alaalu."

"Tell me about it. Your dad say anything interesting?" Kit asked. "How are things at home?"

"I think Dairine is having a personality conflict..."

"You mean, besides her usual one with the entire planet?" Kit said.

"Ouch," Nita said, amused. They came out on top of the rise, and started scanning the horizon: This being Alaalu, it took a while. Finally, maybe a few miles off, they spotted Quelt, a tiny pale patch moving among the blue flowers.

"There she is," Kit said.

"Yeah. No, I think Dairine's got a personal problem with this third wizard, the humanoid one."

"Oooo, boy," Kit said.

"When she finally has it out with him, the sky'll light up; we'll see it all the way over here."

"Yeah. Meantime, let's go find Quelt."

They walked the distance, because there was no rush. It was hard to feel, here, that there was any rush, anywhere—any need for haste. Maybe it had to do with the Alaalid species being so long-lived, but Nita wasn't entirely convinced. She kept remembering that dream-image of a beach full of statues. *Something else is going on...*

They caught up with her about half an hour later. She had seen them and started walking toward them. Ponch reached her first, having run ahead to greet her. "Did we disturb you?" Nita said, when they got close enough to speak without shouting.

"Oh, no," Quelt said. "I was talking to the wind, to the Telling, actually, about the Great Vein. I think the plates are moving again in that part of the seas. It's going to be harder to get at the metal, and I needed to devise some alternative access points."

"It's at the bottom of the ocean, that vein? Wow," Nita said. Both she and Kit had some grasp of what it was like to function at the great depths. "Tough work…"

"It's not too bad if I can crack the crust, and let the metals come up molten and crystallize out into nodules," Quelt said. "Then we can send mechanical depth-handling machines down to bring it all up. I think that's the way I'll go with this. Are the *ceiff* all fed?"

"Twice," Kit said. "Tapi thinks I'm spoiling them."

"I have news for you. Tapi wants you for a hired hand!" Nita said. Quelt snorted with laughter.

"Trust him to try to get a wizard to do yard work," she said. "Parents!"

There was some group amusement over that. "Still," Kit said, "the yard work has to get done. Quelt, can we ask you a personal question?"

"Cousin! Of course you can."

"I mentioned the Lone Power to your folks," Kit said, "and they barely knew what It was."

"*She,*" Nita said, and shivered.

"I mean, they had to be reminded," Kit said. "Is that usual, here? Your parents—you told them about your—I was going to call it your Ordeal, but our word for it at home seems a lot too rugged, the way they sounded."

"Your 'Own Choice,'" Nita said.

"Normally, we would fight with the Lone Power personally," Kit said. "Very personally. And, normally, most people in our world know the Lone One exists, or have at least heard of It. In our world, Its effects are all over the place, and they have been for a long time, though things are changing. But here—" Kit waved his arms around him. "Your world is so perfect, our people would hardly believe it. How come? Does it have to do with the way you guys made your Choice?"

"And what did you do?" Nita said. "Because believe me, if we could have done the same kind of thing..." She shook her head.

Quelt's expression was somewhat bemused. "Well, it would have something to do with the *ne'whaHüilse't*, the Debate and Decision," Quelt said at last. "But I'm not sure how to explain the differences, assuming they *can* be explained." She mused for a moment. "You should probably come look at the Display."

"Sorry?" Nita said.

"Oh, the Debate and Decision happened right here, on our island," Quelt said. "So we keep an enactment of it. In fact, that's one of my jobs as the world's wizard, to make sure the enactment is kept running. Even though most of us don't think about it a whole lot! I suppose we might as well go have a look at it—"

Then Quelt laughed. "You know, we've done some of the tourist things, but this one is so boring for most people that it never occurred to me to take you there. That's silly of me, on second thought. You are wizards; of course you'd be interested. And I haven't gone through the whole experience myself for a long time, though people come from all the other islands to see it."

Kit looked from Quelt to Nita and back again.

"Let's go," he said.

———

Quelt had a transit spell prepared. "It's in case I need to go do a service call," she said, "but that hasn't happened for a hundred years or so..." The spell looked much like one of Kit's or Nita's "prepackaged" ones; a circle of words in the Speech, which Quelt pulled out of the air and offered to Nita and Kit so that they could insert their personal information—their own names in the Speech and data about their body mass and composition. Both of them routinely carried shorthand versions of these in their manuals, and Kit had a spare one for Ponch. They pulled these out, hooked them onto Quelt's spell, and stepped into it when she cast the line of bright words down among the flowers.

Wizardry dulled the air around them to a blue haze as they read the words in the Speech together. It was interesting for Nita to have a third voice reading with them, a different flavor in the air, as the universe leaned in around them, obeying the spell, and then popped them loose into another place entirely.

Nita and Kit looked around. Here the horizon was no less high, but the immediately surrounding landscape was flatter, a huge plain. As she glanced around, Nita realized that she was in one of the first places she'd seen on Alaalu that wasn't within sight of water.

"It's the heart of the continent," Quelt said, leading them down a very slight slope. "The nearest ocean is three thousand miles away. A pretty distance, for us. And here we are—"

Not far away from them, down another shallow slope, was something Nita at first took for a wide, deep pool of water. But then she realized that there was too much light reflected in that pool; it was radiant by its own virtue. And there was something strange about the surface of the water—it didn't ripple.

"It's air held solid," Quelt said. "You know the spell, I think. A variation of the Mason's Word wizardry, with the spell that produces the forms held down inside it. Come on, you can walk out on it."

She led the way across the surface of the "pool," strolling out as if onto a crystal floor. Nita and Kit followed her, pausing with Quelt at about the middle of the surface to look down into the depths. There they saw eight figures, male and female, plainly Alaalids by their coloration, hair, and dress. Seven stood more or less together; the eighth one stood apart.

Nita started to laugh, then. "They really are short, aren't they?" she said. "No wonder we're such celebrities!"

Quelt laughed, too. "I should have brought you here first to explain it," she said.

They walked above the group standing there under some other sunlight, in another time, in a field full of flowers very like the ones all around them now. When she stood still, Nita found, she could see those figures down below moving, talking, consulting with one another—all but the one who stood apart, an Alaalid taller than the rest of them, dressed all in white, and coolly beautiful, with eyes of a gorgeous burning amber.

"Wow," Kit said. "Who's that?"

"Esemeli," Quelt said.

"She's hot," Kit said, in considerable admiration.

Nita threw a glance at him. Next to Kit, Ponch, too, was gazing down into the depths ... but he was starting to growl softly.

Kit looked at Ponch in shock, and then at Quelt. "Oh no. You mean she's—"

"The Lone Power," Nita said. "The local version."

"That's her," Quelt said. "But we came in in the middle of the story. If you come over here, you can see it from the start."

They walked over to the far side of the Display, and looked deep down into it. The landscape that presented itself was like the one in which they stood, but less groomed-looking, rougher around the edges. There was a field full of the blue *jijis* flowers; it seemed to stretch to the horizon, which was unusual in that world where no landscape seemed to go very far before running into the sea. In the middle of the field stood the seven Alaalid men and women, and in the center, the extremely beautiful one.

"That's her when she first arrives," Quelt said. "And there are our first seven wizards, who're making the Choice."

Nita cocked her ear at something she was coming to recognize since she'd started to study the Speech more closely—the "Enactive mode," one of the most powerful ways in which the Speech could be spoken. Quelt wasn't using the mode itself, but a secondary form called the pre-Enactive voice: a form for talking *about* first-level enactments and other major change, without actually using the words that would bring the change to pass. Its tenses were very weird if translated into any human language, where present and past are usually separate; so Nita didn't bother trying to translate it in her head, and just let it sound like one very large kind of present.

"Come on," Quelt said. "They tell the story better than I can." And she stepped right down into the crystalline surface as if it were water.

Nita and Kit both stared. Quelt looked over her shoulder at them. "It's all right," she said. "It's not an actual portal, just a replay. You can't actually interact with it, but it's as if you were there . . ."

"How do we—" Kit said, and then looked around him in surprise as, very slowly, he started to sink into the crystal where he stood.

"You just let yourself," Quelt said. "There's no problem breathing or anything; the wizardry takes care of that for you."

Do I have to go, too? Ponch said to Kit. *I feel like running now.*

"No, it's fine," Kit said, still sinking. "You go ahead."

Ponch bounded off the Display and into the flowers.

"I think I'd rather do it your way," Nita said, and followed Quelt's lead, just taking a step down as if she were standing on a flight of stairs. The substrate behaved that way, too, letting her foot go down into the crystal.

Nita followed Quelt down into the substrate, while beside the two of them Kit just kept on sinking where he stood, as if he were on some kind of elevator. Within half a minute or so, they were standing in the same field of flowers as the seven figures and the eighth one, standing in the center of the circle.

"Let me get this straight," Kit said. "This isn't actually the past, and that wasn't some kind of timeslide—"

"No, not at all," Quelt said. "I don't think that'd be allowed. You wouldn't want to get involved in time paradoxes where a Decision was involved."

"I don't know," Nita said as they walked toward the circle of Alaalids. "There have been times when I've wished we could do something like that with ours."

Quelt gave Nita a concerned look. "You're going to have to tell me more about that later," she said. "Anyway, this wizardry just makes it seem as if we were there. We can hear what they say, watch what they do."

For the moment, though, none of the figures seemed to be doing much of anything. "The scenario repeats whenever anyone who sees it wants it to," Quelt said. "Most people get taken here once or twice when we're little. I got to see it more often than most people, because Vereich ran me through the Choice a lot while he was training me as his replacement." She looked a little amused by this. "There's not really a lot to it, but it *is* history, and something a wizard here would need to know about…"

They walked around the circle. "So these were our wizards," Quelt said. "That little one there: He's the chief, Seseil. He wrote out the first part of the Telling."

"He *wrote* it?" Kit said, looking at the lean figure, slight for an Alaalid, who stood there among the flowers, barefoot, in breeches and a loose shirt. "Usually, it just seems to arrive somehow. You hear it, or find it, or find that you know the beginnings of it..."

"That's sort of how it went for us," Quelt said. "Seseil wrote the words that he heard the wind Telling the water. All the others did that, too, sooner or later, except they all heard different words. Seseil had to journey all over the settled lands, from island to island, to find other people who'd heard the words and could tell him the ones he didn't know. It took a long time to find them all, but he wouldn't give up."

As they came around the side of the circle, Nita looked into that hard, wise face, frozen for the moment into immobility, and had no trouble believing what Quelt was telling them. "That's the *Imrar*, isn't it?" Nita said. "The poem about the Island Journey. It got mentioned in one of the orientation sources."

"That's right," Quelt said. "It took him three hundred years, and he had all kinds of adventures. But he found all the words at last. And up above us, in physical reality, in that field—that's where they started the argument that ended with Ictanikë arriving."

"Wait a minute," Kit said. "I thought you just said the Lone One's name was Esemeli."

"That's her second name: It comes later. So here you see them with Ictanikë, when she turns up for the first time. They were a little confused about her, because she plainly knew about wizardry, though she wasn't a wizard."

"I've heard many a strange tale on my travels," Seseil said. The sound was fading in slowly, as if somebody was turning it up, and Nita wandered a little closer to hear. "But this is one of the stranger ones. What exactly is it that you're offering us?"

"It doesn't sound like anything new," said another of the wizards. "This is the world, and entropy is running. We have time, and life to live in it."

"But not in power," Ictanikë said. "Not in power that you can depend upon. You sailed the seas from inner to outer and back again, finding a word here and a word there, hoping the wind would bring you what you need to know. Why should you be at the world's mercy this way? With help from someone wise, someone longer in the world, you can find your power much more quickly. I can help you do that."

The Alaalid wizards looked at one another, not quite sure what to make of this. "Help is always welcome," one of them said.

"But you must pay my price," Ictanikë said.

The uncertainty among them grew. Nita saw several of them exchange glances, and, in particular, Seseil began to regard Ictanikë with what looked like the beginnings of suspicion. "Among us," Seseil said, "when one person needs something, another one gladly gives it to them. That way, you know that when the day comes that you need something, another will be ready to give. If you have a gift to give us, we'll accept it gladly ... assuming it's a thing we need. But this talk of price—"

Ictanikë smiled, and there was a sly look to the expression, which Nita didn't care for. "So adult beings conduct their affairs in the worlds beyond your world," Ictanikë said. "Go the way I will show you, and you, too, will do your business among the worlds in such a way as to impress all with your wisdom and power. But you should also know that not all beings even in this world conduct their business in such a kindly way, giving freely and accepting freely. Even here there are places where the creatures of the world take what they please, and give little back, or nothing. You must know how to conduct yourselves in such places, and how to defend yourself from those who would take what is yours by force. I can teach you these things."

"And how is it you know about that in the first place?" Seseil said. "You speak confidently of the worlds beyond our world. You speak of prices to be paid, as if our way of giving and accepting were a trap. Nor do any of us know you, or where you come from. I think any advice you might have to give should be looked at with care."

Nita watched, and saw how most of the wizards drew together toward Seseil. But one or two of them still stood off to one side, regarding Ictanikë with curiosity if not interest. And one of them, an Alaalid with long red hair hanging down below his shoulders, moved a little way toward Ictanikë and said to her, "What exactly would your price be?"

Nita froze... for the redheaded wizard was the small man, just her height, who had come to her in the dream of statues and said, "I've been waiting for you..."

Ictanikë's smile grew somber. "It's as you've said, entropy is indeed running. But with my price, you can buy yourselves... an exemption. Around you, you see what happens to the rest of the world. Even the mountains are worn away in time; all life ends. But for you, for the wise, it doesn't have to be this way. There are ways to go on, to reject the fate of the material things around you. If I help you, you can have life … and then cheat death."

The wizard with the long red hair looked thoughtfully at Ictanikë. "Who is that?" Kit whispered.

Quelt waved a hand, and all the figures froze in place again. "That's Druvah," Quelt said. "He was one of the oldest of the wizards. You can tell by his hair; ours doesn't usually get that red color for a long time."

"Uh-oh," Nita said. "I think I see what's coming …"

Quelt let the Display continue.

"You still haven't said what your price will be," Druvah said.

"It's only a little thing," said Ictanikë. "I know the One who brought entropy into being. For those who're that One's friends, there are privileges and rewards. One of them is to circumvent the waste and pain that come with age. A people who make this bargain have no need of watching the strength and joy of youth slip slowly away. It's theirs forever. They have an eternity to grow from power to power … and if they so desire it, more than an eternity. They can go onward into the time beyond Times, in their own bodies, in the flesh. To do so, of course, they must take entropy's inventor as their master, not some impersonal wind. The relationship is far more rewarding, more personal."

"But is it more free?" said Seseil. "Those who speak in terms of prices, themselves will do nothing for nothing. The wind has spoken the name of one of the Powers that lives in the dead calm, in the sun that beats down and parches the dry isles and dries up everything that would grow. We want nothing to do with that Power, or Its gifts."

And the wizards began to argue. Nita sighed, because she had heard various versions of this argument since she'd become a wizard, and it rarely turned out particularly well for the world in question. The Lone Power had had eons of practice at making Its case, and was extremely good at befuddling the innocent and putting one over on the clever. As she watched, Nita noticed Druvah walking off in an absent sort of way, and Ictanikë went after him.

Kit noticed that, too. "Uh-huh," he said. "Neets is right. I know where this is going." He glanced over at Quelt.

Quelt made a gesture with an upraised hand; Nita read this as a shrug. "It goes on for a while," Quelt said.

Off to the side, Nita could see Druvah and Ictanikë talking animatedly. "I bet *that* one does, too," Nita said.

"Oh, yes," Quelt said. "Do you want to skip ahead?"

"Sure," Kit said.

Quelt made another gesture with her hand, and all the figures blurred about briefly, then came to a stand again. Ictanikë and Druvah were walking back toward the main group now, and the others watched them come, Seseil watching most carefully. To Seseil, Druvah said, "Ictanikë has told me a great many things, and I'm convinced that we should give her suggestions a more careful hearing."

Seseil's face was calm, but in his eyes Nita thought she saw signs of the first anger she had yet seen in an Alaalid. "I feel no such need," Seseil said, "nor I think does anyone else here. We want nothing of her 'exemption.' Through her voice the dead calm speaks, and there's no good in that. We will cast her out. We will wall her out of our world. And, henceforth, we will take our chances with the winds."

The other five wizards in the circle with Seseil held up their hands against Ictanikë in a gesture of rejection. She began to be battered back away from them as if the wind was actually blowing her from the circle, though in the grass around there was no sign of it and only the slightest breeze stirred the flowers. Nita held her breath, waiting for the storm to break. But to her surprise, nothing happened. Druvah stood there and watched Ictanikë forced away and away, and finally turned his back on the Lone Power; but, equally, he turned away from the other wizards and began to walk off through the flowers, a lonely figure.

"You will call me back, before the end of things," Ictanikë said, and looked warningly around her at the circle of wizards. "You think you are acting in virtue, but you are acting in ignorance. And though you are swift in decision now, you will have long to repent it!"

"Never," Seseil said. "We want nothing to do with you. Take yourself away, and do not bother us again."

Ictanikë looked one last time at the other wizards with Seseil. Every one of them was of the same face and the same mind. Her frown became terrible; still in the act of being forced away, she raised her hands.

Nita winced. *Here it comes,* she thought. *I bet now we find out why this planet has what looks like a really big impact crater...*

But, again, nothing happened. Ictanikë let her hands fall, and turned, and walked away from the wizards. She went the way Druvah went, not hurrying. Slowly, she vanished into the dazzle of the day, and was gone from sight a long time before she came anywhere near that impossibly distant horizon.

Seseil and the other wizards lowered their hands, and closed up their circle again. Kit glanced over at Quelt. "That was it?" he said.

"That was it," Quelt said. "Should there have been more?"

"Well," Kit said, "not necessarily. But I've seen Choices that took a little longer."

Nita looked around again at the scenario with some confusion. "This is kind of strange," she said. "The way Druvah was acting—unless I'm misunderstanding it—it's more like the kind of thing the Lone One would do. Are you sure he wasn't—" She paused. It was a word no wizard liked to use about another one. "Overshadowed," Nita said at last, when she realized that Quelt wasn't going to say it.

"You mean actively being influenced by the Lone Power?" Quelt said. "No, not as far as we can tell."

"What happened to Druvah afterward?" Kit said.

"He left," Quelt said. "The reasons given differ. And he did say that he didn't care for the way the Choice had been made...Some versions of the story tell how Druvah said he didn't want anything more to do with his own people. They say he threatened the other wizards and said to them something like what Ictanikë had said—that they couldn't make this Choice without him, or that later they'd wish that they'd listened to him, and that someday they'd need him back and wouldn't be able to find him. But all the stories agree that he went away from the place where he lived and was never seen there again."

"A sore loser," Kit said.

"Maybe not," Nita said. "Maybe he was just sad, or embarrassed when he realized he was wrong."

"You might be right about that," Quelt said. She watched as slowly the various wizards wandered off together across the flowery fields, heading out into the world they'd helped to shape. "There are other stories that say how sometimes people would see him for a day, an hour, on some lonely road, or climbing a mountain, or sailing by himself on the sea, always looking for something, always acting as if something was missing. But it wasn't thought lucky to see him. He was tricky to talk to, they said, and he didn't always make sense. Or you might hear his voice behind first one tree and then another in the forest, always moving in front of you when you got close, never staying where you thought it was."

Quelt turned and started walking up through the crystalline air again. Kit and Nita walked up the air behind her. "Sort of a trickster," Nita said.

"That's right," Quelt said. She shrugged. "There's even one story that says he went wandering right out of the world, among other worlds, looking for whatever he was missing. It doesn't really matter in terms of the Choice. It's made now. And pretty well made, I think."

They broke the surface of the crystalline Display and walked out across it, back to the sward that surrounded it. Kit looked all around him at the bright day, as if wondering whether he should say something, and then, finally, he said, "So people here do die..."

"I don't know that we would've ever had any choice about that," Quelt said. "It's always going to happen eventually, isn't it? But it's not so bad. We live a pretty long time. And it's not as if the dead people go away."

Nita looked up at that and nodded. "I've been meaning to ask you about that," she said. "There've been times I woke up in the middle of the night here and thought I heard people whispering..."

Quelt looked at Nita and purposely nodded, using the human gesture. "That's right," she said, "I thought you'd probably be able to hear them. When we die, we don't die dead. We don't die out of the world. We die *into* it. The people who were here are always around." And Quelt looked at Nita with a little less certainty than usual, an expression a little less serene. "It's not like that for you, in your world, is it?" she said.

Nita shook her head. "No," she said, and couldn't keep the sadness out of her voice. "Definitely not."

Kit looked up. "Here comes Ponch," he said.

Nita glanced up. She couldn't see anything but a vague troubling of the flowers across the field. "What has he got?" she said, and began to trot off toward him.

Behind her, she could just hear Quelt saying, in a slightly lowered voice, "I've been meaning to ask you, since you seem interested in the subject. How *do* you die?"

Nita said nothing.

"Uh...let's save that for a little later, okay?" Kit said.

They went back to the house by the sea.

Disruption of Services

DAIRINE WANDERED THROUGH the house early
that morning, looking into every room except the one
she was trying to avoid looking into: the basement.
Filif was in the kitchen, watching her dad get ready for
work. Nobody was in the dining room. Sker'ret was in
the living room, watching TV and playing around with
the remote. Nobody was in the bathroom or any of the
bedrooms.

She let out a long breath and wandered back the way
she had come, glancing at the TV as she passed through
the living room. "That really looks a lot better," she
said to Sker'ret.

"Something was wrong with the green color matrix," Sker'ret said. "I talked to the irradiation module
and got it to tweak its voltage a little. Everything seems
to be behaving now."

"You could have a word with my stereo upstairs if
you felt like it," Dairine said. "But not right now."

"Are we ready to go?"

"A few minutes."

She wandered back into the kitchen. "Did you see what Sker'ret did to the TV, Daddy?" Dairine said.

"I sure did. That boy's a whiz with the machinery, isn't he?"

"He's kind of a structures specialist," Dairine said. "A taking-things-apart-and-putting-things-back-together fan. I'd say everything would be fine with him around until you ran out of broken things to fix." She smiled. "Then would be the time to hide..."

"When he has a free moment, he can come down to the shop," Dairine's dad said, finishing his coffee and going to the sink with the mug. "My copy machine..." He shook his head.

"I'll put it on the list." To Filif, she said, "Have you seen Roshaun this morning?"

"Not today," Filif said. "He went into his pup tent when we all did last night, and I haven't seen him since."

He raised a branch and pushed his baseball cap into what was intended to be a jaunty angle. It flopped back down again, because it's hard to keep a baseball cap in a given position when your head is a single conifer-like branch, similar to the top of a Christmas tree.

"*Hmf,*" Filif said, and started weaving a few outer limbs around in a gesture that Dairine recognized as the beginning of a wizardry, Filif's invocation of a shorthand or "macro" version of something he'd set up before. He had a lot of these for physical manipulation, which made sense for a tree. Dairine's neck hairs rose a little at the feel of the Speech being used in a nonverbal mode.

Dairine's dad, drinking his coffee, eyed this procedure with some interest, watching the baseball cap come up to level and settle itself as if there were a head underneath it.

"Slick," Dairine said.

"I don't know," her dad said, looking with dry humor at the baseball cap, and turning away again. "I'm not sure what you're doing bringing something like that into a house full of Mets fans..."

The cap was a Yankees cap, and Dairine hadn't had either the inclination or the heart to start explaining to Filif why such a cap could possibly be an issue. He'd really wanted it, and Dairine had gone back to the shopping center and gotten it for him. But she felt fortunate in having been able to talk him out of the Jams, convincing him that they were "very last year."

Dairine headed past the two of them, sighing. *There's no way to avoid it. I'm just going to have to go on down there,* she thought. "You about ready to go?" she said.

"Yes," her dad and Filif said in unison, and then both burst out laughing, since they were each talking about going to a different place.

"Great," Dairine said. "Back in a minute."

She went down the stairs into the basement and looked around. There were the three pup-tent accesses, each hanging from its silvery rod. One of them was active.

Dairine let out a long, annoyed breath, went over to it, and most reluctantly put her head in.

The inside was illuminated, not with the standard directionless lighting of a basic pup-tent installation, but by a number of ornate lamps positioned here and there across the carpeted floor. *Carpets?* Dairine thought. But there they were, beautifully woven in alien patterns of many colors, some of them embroidered as well. They were scattered all over the inside of a space that was significantly larger than the others' pup tents, which she'd seen when they'd invited her in.

And the place was decorated as if it were a palace. There was elaborate artwork hanging against the walls or, in some cases, unsupported in the air; there was a great couch in the middle of everything, with rich coverings and ornate cushions scattered over it; there was enough furniture—sofas and wardrobes and chests— to supply a good-sized furniture store, except that no furniture store Dairine knew would be likely to carry *this* kind of stuff, everything glittering with gold or inlaid with green or blue metals that Dairine didn't immediately recognize. *Just* look *at all this junk,* she thought. It was dazzling but, to her eye, overdone.

Then again...if I grew up in a place that looked like this, maybe I'd think it was normal, too.

She tried very hard to believe that but had trouble. *Why are you bothering with him?* part of her brain kept shouting. *He's a waste of your time!*

Dairine looked around. *Anyway, he's not here,* she thought. *Well, maybe he had something to take care of at home, and used his custom worldgate this morning, before anybody noticed.* She shrugged and was about to turn away and go back upstairs when something in the back of the pup tent caught her eye: a subtle shimmer in an empty patch on the back wall. Dairine walked over to it, looked at it, curious; reached out a hand... then stopped herself.

Should I put on a 'glove'? she wondered. As a rule, it wasn't terribly safe to stick your hand through an interface without being sure of what was on the other side. *Then again... there's air in here, and the pup-tent interface isn't one of the impermeable types. So there has to be air on the other side of that...*

She pushed her hand into the interface, saw it vanish to the wrist. Her hand didn't feel unusually hot or cold, and there wasn't the strange dry tautness of the skin that exposure to vacuum produced. *No, it's okay,* she thought. Dairine stuck her head through, looked around.

And froze.

She was looking into not another artificial space, not an extension of the pup tent, but an area that was almost the outdoors; daylight wasn't too far away. She stepped through. A translucent terrace roof arched over Dairine's head, and she slowly walked out from under it onto the terrace proper—a huge spread of golden-colored stone, reaching hundreds of yards to her left and right, with a carved stone railing standing about a meter high in front of her and running all down the terrace's length. At the railing she stopped, looking out in wonder at an immense landscape all covered in a massive garden of red and golden plant life. Everything was manicured, managed, perfect, the strangely shaped trees not seeming to have so much as a leaf out of place, the amber-colored grass seemingly mown with micrometric precision. There wasn't a molehill or a hump or a hill anywhere in sight. It was as if a myriad of gardeners had worked the place over with rollers from right where Dairine stood to the distant horizon, where the sun was setting in a glowing blaze of cloud.

Dairine let out a breath. This was beautiful, but she couldn't spend all day admiring the scenery. She turned around to go back the way she'd come—

—and froze yet again. There was the terrace, and the terrace roof, but above it reared up a huge, graceful, imposing mass of a building, all built in the same golden stone as the terrace, and spreading away far in both directions. It was at least a New York City block square—*And a long block, not a short one!* she thought—and reared up before her in stack upon stack of towers and spires and turrets and battlements, spearing defiantly upward as if to make up for the flat countryside all around.

This is a palace, Dairine thought. *His palace.*

She immediately looked around her guiltily, as if somebody might catch her being somewhere she shouldn't and dump her in a dungeon. Then Dairine straightened, held her head up. *He shouldn't be here, either. Not like this!*

She marched back under the terrace roof, toward the long line of glass-paned doors she saw at the back of the roofed-in area. One of them stood open, near where the illicit pup-tent access still hung down. Dairine headed on past it and through that door.

If she'd thought the furnishings of the pup tent were opulent, she'd been seriously mistaken. She now found herself in a high-ceilinged, elliptical space that was nearly the size of the auditorium at her school. This, too, was filled with massive and ornate furniture, rich carpeting scattered across the goldstone floor, figured hangings on the walls. The gold and gems were everywhere, inlaid or appliquéd or just stuck onto things with wild abandon. Dairine shook her head, gazing around—

And someone laughed at her. Her head snapped around. There he was, in more of his trademark glittering robes, leaning back in a gaudy chair that was halfway to being a throne, and with his feet up on a footstool.

"I wondered how long it would take you to sneak in here," Roshaun said, stretching and lapsing back into a comfortable slouch again. "I admit, you kept me waiting longer than I thought I'd have to."

I wish I'd kept you waiting a lot longer, Dairine thought. "What are you doing here?" she said. "The pup tents are what you're supposed to be sleeping in, on an excursus, if you're not using the actual host family space for it. And you're not supposed to sleep away every night, either!"

"The guidelines are just that," Roshaun said, "guidelines. You'll have noticed that there's not a lot of heavy enforcement. The Aethyrs have better things to do."

His word for the Powers That Be, I guess, Dairine thought. "And that's another thing! You're not supposed to retroengineer the wizardries They gave us, either—"

"That restriction is only on the custom worldgates," Roshaun said, "not the pup tents." He smiled slightly.

Dairine stared at Roshaun, remembering how obvious and casual this rationale had sounded when she was considering it, and wondering why it now sounded so outrageous and annoying.

"And why are *you* so stuck on every little rule all of a sudden?" Roshaun said, obviously amused at Dairine's expense. "You've broken a fair number of them in your time."

She looked at him in shock. "Oh, yes," Roshaun said, "I've seen your précis. Something of an early star, weren't you? But suffering something of a decline at the moment. Ah, that tough time when you have to redefine yourself as something less than you dreamed..."

Dairine opened her mouth, but managed to stop what she was about to say on its way out. The best she could find to replace it was, "Why are you such a pain in the ass?"

"Probably for the same kinds of reasons you are," Roshaun said, and turned away. "But I don't propose to discuss my developmental history with the likes of you."

The likes of—!! "That's not *good* enough!" she shouted. "Why did you even bother *applying* for this excursus if you didn't want to be with other—"

Suddenly doors burst open all around. Dairine looked

around her in shock as a sudden inrush of people arrived from what seemed every possible direction. Most of them were dressed like Roshaun, in long overtunics over shorter tunics and breeches and boots, though all of these people wore the style in plainer, more sober-colored fabrics. Some of them were actually carrying spears, and Dairine's wizardly senses detected a number of energy signatures hidden about those servants' persons that had nothing to do with spears. *Pulse weapons,* she thought, *and a few other niceties...*

Dairine stood there with her head up, but inside her head, she said eighteen words of a nineteen-word spell that would bounce back at them anything they threw at her. *And if Roshaun gets a little singed, well, tough—*

Roshaun, though, just laughed and waved his servitors away. "No, it's all right. You're not needed," Roshaun said. "You may all go."

"Lord prince," said one of the spear carriers, looking at Dairine. "This is an alien! You shouldn't be alone with—"

Roshaun laughed. "Nonsense! She's no possible danger to me," he said. "Go on."

All of the servants bowed and departed, though the armed ones gave Dairine a number of hard looks as they left.

She had to smile grimly at that, though she was trying to contain her annoyance at the assessment that she was "no danger." *Never mind. People a lot more important in the big scheme of things have thought otherwise...*

The room emptied and the doors closed. Roshaun

dusted his hands off as if he'd actually done something, and sat back down on his "throne," stretching his legs out lazily. "So what's on your little agenda today?"

Dairine collapsed the almost-built shield-spell, deciding she didn't need it anymore. *And as for him, listen to him! Every word out of Roshaun is a needle,* Dairine thought. *Well, I'm just going to stop jumping when he sticks the needle in, no matter what he says.* "We're going up Mount Everest and K2," she said. "Those are two of the highest mountains on Earth. A lot of people climb them—some just for the challenge, some almost as a tourist thing. But they leave a lot of garbage behind...so every now and then some wizards go up there and clean it up a little. It's kind of an art form, taking away enough of the oxygen bottles and so forth to keep the place from turning into a dump, without taking so many that people notice they're vanishing. That's all we need, to turn into a yeti myth or something."

She stopped, because he had actually yawned at her. "I don't think so," Roshaun said.

"I don't think so *what?*"

"Housecleaning," Roshaun said, "wouldn't normally be a part of my job description."

Despite all her good intentions, Dairine instantly got steamed again. "Neither would doing wizardry, most times, from the look of things around here," she said. "Why lift a finger when all these people will jump out and do everything for you?" And once again she stopped herself. "Well, never mind," she said. "The whole point of the excursus is to see what other people's wizardly practice is like. This would have been good for that. And besides it being a kind of fun service-thing to do, I'd have thought you'd enjoy the view. You don't seem to have a lot of high ground around here."

"We have a fair amount of it elsewhere," Roshaun said, "on the other side of the planet—"

He was still trying to sound bored, but somehow it wasn't working. Dairine glanced over at him quickly, but if anything had shown in his face while she was looking away, it was too late to catch a hint of it now. He had sealed right over again. "Look," Dairine said, "I really don't know what your problem is. But let's just drop it, okay? Why not come on back with me and we'll—"

"At the moment, I'd rather not," Roshaun said.

There was still something ever so slightly different about his tone of voice. Some of that snide quality had come off it, if only a few percent's worth.

"If it's just a personality thing…," Dairine said, after some hesitation.

"It's nothing so simple," Roshaun said, turning away from her and reaching out to some kind of data pad by his chair. "I don't much like your little world, and your Sun pains me."

Dairine wasn't terribly sure what to make of the second remark, but the first was easy enough to understand. "Well, you have a nice time here by yourself," she said. "Lie around and take it easy…Have someone peel you a grape or three. And don't feel rushed into hurrying back."

She headed back toward the access to the pup tent and made her way back through its overdecorated interior, growing gradually more annoyed. Halfway through, though, Dairine stopped, turned, and looked over her shoulder at the extra access Roshaun had added.

Somebody could get him in trouble for that...

Dairine stood there absently biting her lower lip for a few moments, considering possibilities. Then she grimaced at her own ill temper. *This guy is really messing me up... and I hate it.*

Never mind.

She slipped through the main pup-tent access into her basement and trotted up the stairs. "Roshaun's not going to be with us this morning," she said to Filif. "Something's going on at home that he had to take care of. Let's just get ourselves up Everest and do some tidying."

Her dad was still standing by the counter, keying numbers into his cell phone. He held it to his ear, shook his head, and glanced at the phone.

"Honey, before you go," her dad said, "what's going on with the cell phones today? I was trying to call one of my suppliers. Is it the usual network-busy problem, or is the magic possibly interfering with it?"

"I really doubt that," Dairine said. "Tom's too good at this kind of wizardry. But you know what, I heard something on the news this morning. Let me check—" She turned to Spot, who was sitting on the counter. "Get me a weather report? The SOHO satellite'll do."

Spot flipped up his lid and showed Dairine the manual's version of the live feed from the SOHO solar-orbiter satellite, with a selection of pictures of the Sun taken in various wavelengths of light—red, green, blue. "There you are," Dairine said, pointing to the blue version, where one particular detail was clearest. "We're having a little bad weather."

Dairine's dad peered over her shoulder at the image of something like a big bump or bulge of light on the side of the Sun. "That happened last night," Dairine said. "It's a CME, a coronal mass ejection."

"In English, please?" her dad said.

Dairine grinned. "Think of it as a solar zit."

Her dad made a face. "Honey, do you think you could possibly have put that *more* indelicately?"

"Gives you the right impression of what's happening, though," Dairine said. "Every now and then the Sun shoots out a big splat of plasma into space. No one really knows why. But if the splat's aimed toward Earth, when the front of the plasma wave gets here, there's all kinds of trouble with satellites because of the ionized radiation. Radio gets messed up for a day or so, phone connections get screwed up until the wave front passes." She shrugged. "It's no big deal. These guys make sure everybody gets enough warning to turn their satellites' sensors away from the wave front before it hits." She put Spot's lid down. "Probably the phones'll come back up later today or tomorrow."

Her father sighed, turning to the wall phone and picking it up. "It's a nuisance," he said as he started to dial.

"Yeah," Dairine said.

Sker'ret came in from the living room. "So where are you three off to?" Dairine's dad said.

"Mount Everest," Dairine said.

Her father looked at her. She was wearing a T-shirt and shorts: It was more like summer than spring outside, at the moment. "I don't suppose there's any point in telling you to dress warm?"

"We all have force fields," Dairine said. "We'll be fine."

Her dad watched her and hit a key on the phone's dialing pad. "Voice mail," he muttered. "I hate this. Mount Everest, though? Why?"

"We're taking Sker'ret out to lunch," Dairine said, grinning a wicked grin. "Nepalese food...sort of. See you later."

They vanished.

It was much later that evening, after latemeal, when lamps were lit and Nita had gone down to the beach again for one last swim, when Kit finally had time to sit down in private on his bed-couch, with his manual, and page through it for some more detail.

Much of what Quelt had shown them and told them was there, and more information about the way of death on Alaalu. Entropy might have its way with the bodies of the people who lived there, but not with their spirits. Those lingered on. Kit saw from the manual that this Choice had, in fact, not taken place as quickly as it had seemed at first glance. In particular, the wizards making this Choice had understood that without entropy, there was no passage of time, no way to live or be. They'd seen that any bargain they might have struck with the Lone Power in an attempt to eliminate entropy completely would've been a cheat. Naturally, the Power that had invented entropy had some control over it; the exemption It had been offering the Alaalids would have been real enough, a kind of eternal life. But Kit knew enough about the Lone Power's intentions to understand that whatever advantage over death they purchased by accepting the bargain It offered them, they would eventually have paid dearly in some other coin.

Still, he thought, *the way they've got it here...* *they're lucky.* There was a passing, but it was nothing to be afraid of. And afterward, the one who died became simply one more part of a world full of whispers, all friendly...the relatives and cousins of an elder time, passed along but not passed away, at peace after life as their people were at peace in life. *She's been hearing them,* he thought, remembering what Nita had said earlier.

He looked down at the manual again. "And as for the Lone One, now the Relegate, and defeated, the new way of the world meant she was part of the world, though made new. So they gave her a new name," the manual said, translating the local version of the Choice story, "which was Esemeli, the Daughter of the Daughter of Light; and she did them no more harm, nor can do again. She went into the place prepared for her, the Relegate's Naos, and there she dwells still, in peace, as all things are at peace. And the world goes its way, and its wind speaks the One's name, and all things are well, forever..."

Kit closed the manual and looked out through the window on his side of the room, out to the twilit sea.

The Lone One defeated, he thought. *I'm not sure I like the sound of that.* It wasn't that such defeats were impossible: They weren't. But they were difficult to maintain, and to defend. Death might be thrown out of a scenario, but It had ways of sneaking back in if you weren't very, very careful....

He tucked his manual away under his pillow, pulled the light covers up over himself, and lay there looking out the window. *She'll be back soon,* he thought. *It's almost crab time. Nita won't be swimming then.*

At the end of Kit's couch, Ponch lay with his chin on the covers, his eyes shifting occasionally out to the twilight, as Kit fell asleep, considering....

Nita was walking far down the beach, well above the waterline, watching the *keks* and trying to distract herself from the stinging of her neck and shoulders.

This always happens when I get distracted, she thought, feeling her neck and then stopping; the stinging just got worse. *First I forget the sunblock, then I forget the wizardry that's supposed to do what the sunblock would have done if I'd remembered it.*

She sighed, watching the hurly-burly down on the sand as the *keks* bustled around and climbed over and under each other, building their strange little sand castles. Besides her sunburn, the main problem for Nita at the moment was Alaalu's thirty-two-hour day, which was making her experience something like jet lag without the jets. Kit, for some reason, seemed to have snapped very quickly into the local rhythm and had no trouble sleeping for sixteen hours and waking for sixteen, as the Peliaens did. But Nita's body stubbornly insisted on hanging on to its own ideas about when morning was, and when 7:30 A.M. rolled around back home, it woke Nita up with a snap and wouldn't let her go back to sleep. She could have done a wizardry on herself to force the issue, but she found herself resisting that option. *This place is so super, why do I want to waste hours sleeping? And no one here minds if I'm up in the middle of the night, anyway.*

Nita looked over the whispering water as a small flock of moons started to come sailing up over the eastern horizon. Because of the size of the planet, there were a lot of them—even the smallest of them the size of Earth's moon, but all out at a distance that made them look a third or a quarter the size. The planet's gravitation held all these little moons in a very large and vaguely defined "ring" pattern, like a skinny doughnut stretched around the world. Inside that doughnut, or torus, the individual moons' gravities caused them to speed each other up and slow each other down and generally behave in ways that were impossible to predict. *Like more flying sheep,* Nita thought, as the present "flock" rose and sailed across the night sky, throwing shifting silvery lights down on the water. In the light, the *keks* seemed to be working faster, though this was probably an illusion.

Nita wandered down to the waterline and stood just out of the *keks'* way, peering down at the little structures they were building in the sand. None of the structures lasted long: The *keks* would clamber over them, knock them down, start over again. Or else a chance wave would come up higher than normal and wash everything away. The *keks'* response was always the same: Start building again.

"What are you guys doing?" Nita said in the Speech.

What we must, one of them, or all of them, said, and kept right on building.

Nita shook her head, amused. It was exactly the kind of purposeful but unilluminating answer you tended to get from ants when you asked them where they were going, or from a mosquito when you asked it why it had bitten you. Bugs had very limited agendas and had trouble talking about anything else.

"Why?" Nita said.

Because.

She shook her head and smiled... then winced as the motion of the headshake made her neck sting. "It's nice to have a purpose in life," she said to the *keks*.

Yes, it is, they said, and started working faster, as if trying to make up time for having been distracted by her.

Nita smiled and let them be. She walked off up the beach again, thinking, *I really should just go back and get the sunblock.* Her dad would be annoyed with her when he saw the burn, but all the same, she wanted to see him. The précis that her manual had been passing on to her, via Dairine, were too dry to give her any sense of what was really going on at home.

Slowly she walked back to the Peliaens' place. The absolute peace of it, as she came within sight of the house and its outbuildings in the moons' light and starlight, impressed itself on Nita once again. Yet, also, at the same time, up came that strange something-wrong, something-missing feeling that she'd started to experience more and more often as she and Kit settled in.

I think I'm just not used to things being so peaceful, she thought. *I've got to let myself get used to it.* She smiled ruefully as she made her way quietly to the outbuilding that was her and Kit's bedroom. *With my luck, I'll get used to it just around the time we have to go home.*

From the other side of the big room's dividing screen, as she went in, she could just hear Ponch snoring softly. *I wonder if the dogs have started acting normally back home,* Nita thought. *Or if they're behaving worse. Well, I'll let Kit find out about that.*

Very quietly, she went over to the darkness against the far wall of her side of the room, the worldgate that led back to her house. Being careful of the edges, she stepped through.

Without any fuss, she was in her mostly empty bedroom. *Maybe I should put the desk back in here,* she thought, *because I don't think it's going to get a lot of use where we are.* With her schoolwork done, she was determined not to think another thought about school for at least a week, if she could help it.

Nita glanced out the window. It was midafternoon. The bedroom's wall clock said 3:30. *I thought it would be earlier,* she thought. *My time sense is so screwed up.* She looked at her bed, saw no sunblock there. Either her dad had fogotten to put it out for her, or he just hadn't gotten around to it yet.

She went out of her room and paused by Dairine's door and looked in: No one was there. *Out with her new buddies,* Nita thought. *Or visiting them in their pup tents, possibly.*

She went on down to the bathroom and rummaged among the various sun creams, sunblocks, and tanning oils in the cupboard under the sink. Finally, she came up with a bottle of high-factor stuff only a few months past its use-by date. *This should be okay,* Nita thought, and went quietly down the stairs.

The living room was empty, but from the dining room she heard a voice, Tom's voice. Nita froze only a few steps from the stairs.

"It's something we just have to deal with," Tom was saying. "Sometimes you hit— When we speak of them in English, we call them 'cardinal events,' which is a vague equivalent to a word in the Speech that's derived from the Speech's root word for 'hinge.' There are moments in the lives of people, of nations, of cultures, of worlds, on which everything to come afterward hangs, or turns—like the hinge of a door. If intervention comes at one moment, the door swings one way. If it comes a moment early, a moment late, the hinge swings another. And sometimes no intervention, regardless of its size, is enough to change the way the door swings. There are some changes that simply have so much impetus behind them, driven by the force of earlier events—the way in which other 'hinges' have swung—that there's no stopping them, no matter what you do. As a result, a life changes, or ends...or a thousand lives do, or three thousand...and whole avalanches of change come tumbling down through the opening left by the way that door swung. All a wizard can do, in the face of one of these avalanches of chance and change, is pick a spot to intervene in the consequences and try to clean up afterward." And Tom sighed. "No matter what we do," he said, "entropy is still running."

There was a long silence. "I'm so sorry," Nita heard her dad say.

"Not half as sorry as we were," Tom said, "that we couldn't stop it." Another painful breath. "But day by day, in the aftermath, we do what we can, and try to be ready for the next 'hinge'...try to recognize it when it comes. It's all we can do. And we have to keep reminding ourselves, because we know it's true, that what comes of what we do will eventually make a difference; and the Powers That Be will find a way through even our species' worst cruelties to something better, if we just don't give up."

There was a silence. "The way you look," her dad said, "you haven't been getting a lot of rest lately."

"No," Tom said. For a moment or so there was silence. "There's trouble coming."

"Worse than what we've got now?"

"Unless we can stop it," Tom said, "much, much worse. But we've got a head start: a fighting chance. Actually, a lot better than just a chance. We can't do anything now but see how it goes."

A chill ran down Nita's back. "Let me know if I can help," her dad said.

"This is help," Tom said after a moment. "And I appreciate it."

Nita breathed in, breathed out, unnerved, then turned softly and went back upstairs. *I'll come see Daddy tomorrow. This isn't the time.*

Once upstairs, she put her head into Dairine's door again, on the off chance that she might have come back from wherever she was.

"She's out," said a scratchy little voice from Dairine's desk.

Spot was sitting there, looking strangely forlorn under Dairine's desk lamp. Nita went quietly in, thought about sitting on the bed, then decided against it; it would creak.

"You okay, big guy?" Nita said.

"Okay," Spot said.

Nita shook her head and stroked his case a little. He was such a one-person machine. "Tell Dairine I was here, all right?" she said. "I didn't talk to Dad...He was busy. But there's some stuff I want her to check into for me. I'll talk to her about it tomorrow."

"All right," Spot said.

"Thanks."

Nita went back to her room. As she came in, the

worldgate came alive enough to display a faint shadow of itself, a circle hanging in midair, through which the rest of her room appeared grayed out. Nita ducked a little, stepped through it again.

On the far side of the bedroom, Ponch was still snoring. Nita sat down on the edge of her bed-couch, suddenly feeling very tired, even though she'd spent no energy whatever on the worldgating. It was strange to hear Tom, someone on whose strength and expertise Nita depended, sounding like he needed to lean on someone else in turn. *But why wouldn't he, sometimes?* she thought. *He's just a wizard like the rest of us...*

And, "Trouble coming," he'd said. Nita was going to get Dairine to look into that and report back to her. *In the meantime...maybe I could sleep a little.*

She got undressed and crawled in under the light covers. It was not one of those nights when it "rained stars" in a periodic fall of dust and small fragments from the moonbelt. The darkness remained quiet except for the whisper of the sea, and the softer whispers of the voices in the air, untroubled by anything Nita might have seen or heard in some other world far away. Here everything was fine; here the world was going the way it was supposed to go.

That soft insistence itself troubled her for a while. But, eventually, Nita did sleep....

At dawn, Nita woke up from a completely irrational dream of ice and icebergs and snow.

She sat up on her long couch and felt the back of

her neck, rather gingerly. *At least I won't burn any worse now,* she thought, *but this still bothers me...*

There were things she could do now, of course. She could talk the nerves in her skin out of feeling the pain...though that would cost her some energy and, afterward, the pain would come back. Or she could use a different kind of wizardry to speak to the nerve endings and trim back their connection to the damaged skin. That would cost her, too—rather more than the first wizardry—but it would heal the burn.

She stretched, and winced. *Or, alternately,* she thought, *I could just get up and go in the water, which is nice and cool and won't cost me anything...and put off dealing with the problem until later.*

Nita found her bathing suit and pulled it on—she wasn't quite yet as comfortable as Quelt was with skinny-dipping—then shrugged into a linen sun smock, hissing once or twice in irritation as the rough texture dragged across her sunburn.

But the memory of cold came back to her. She sat back down on the couch for a moment, grasping at the memory before she should be awake too long and it should fade.

Ice, she thought. There had been a lot of it. She had seen her share of cold planets, both "solid" ones, where the ice was made from water, and gas giants, where the ice was made from methane or helium, and the snow was that strange metallic, pale blue color. What she'd seen in her dream had been water ice, though. Her memory came up with a pattern suddenly—parallel lines and striations that ran curving down like a river between jagged stone walls all slicked with newer, clearer ice. But the oldest stuff, colder, deeper, discolored with the powdery, dark scrapings of ancient stone, ran like a fissured twelve-lane highway through the pass between old mountains rearing up on either side. *A glacier.* Nothing had happened in that dream, unless the slow, cold progress of the glacier down its valley, a tenth of an inch a day, would count as something happening.

Nita shivered, and then laughed to herself. *Typical body reaction: get burned, dream of cold.* Yet when she thought of that glacier again, another image from the dream surfaced. The ice spreading from the glacier, spreading up the mountain walls as more snow fell, as the cold grew. *An ice age,* Nita thought. Glaciers sheeting up and over everything, the contours of landscape being swallowed by them and the incessant snow that fell on them and fed them—everything happening slowly in real time, but with an ugly relentless speed in her dream, where the progression of events was compressed. "The heart of the world is frozen," something had said to her. The voice was slow, cold, as if buried in snow itself. And it was not entirely sorry about the ice.

Nita sat in the dawn stillness and thought about that a little. On the other side of the screen, Kit was still asleep, but one sound she couldn't hear was Ponch snoring. Nita slipped out the reed-screened door into the dimness of early morning.

She made her way out of the cluster of the Peliaens' household buildings and down onto the beach. There Nita stood just breathing for a while in the immense stillness, a silence broken only by the tideless sea slipping softly up and down the sand. All around her, the world sloped up to the sky at an impossible distance, to an impossible height, but Nita was getting used to it now. Its largeness now seemed to enlarge her in turn, rather than crushing her down into insignificance.

Away down the curve of the beach, she saw, two small, dark shapes were also looking out at the water, at the dawn, neither of them moving.

She walked toward them, not hurrying, for that dawn was worth looking at. In fact, every one Nita had seen so far had been worth looking at, and no two of them were the same. This one featured vast stretches of crimson and gold and peach, streaked and speckled with smaller clouds in dark gray and pale gray, edged with burning orange, and with blue showing in the spaces in between them until the sky looked like one huge fire opal. In that light, fierce but still cool, Quelt and Ponch sat on the dune-rise, looking out over the water. Nita sat down next to Quelt. "Were you up early seeing your *tapi* off?" she said. "He was going to follow the *ceiff* when they flew today..."

"No, he was gone before I got up. I came out to talk to Ponsh."

Nita glanced over at Ponch, who was lying there with his chin on his forefeet, gazing out at the sea. "About what?"

"All kinds of things. He's good to talk to," Quelt said. "He knows a lot."

Nita had to smile at that. This was a dog whose vocabulary, not so long ago, had consisted almost entirely of words for food. "Not when he's got a stick in his mouth," she said, to tease him.

Ponch rolled over, gave her a look, and then, as if not deigning to respond, rolled onto his belly again.

They sat there like that for a while. "Do you ever have times," Quelt said eventually, "when you think there's something important you should know that you *don't* know?"

Nita let out a long breath, leaned back against the sand dune. "The question's more like, are there ever any times when I *don't* think that?" she said. "And when I think I know all the stuff I need to, I'm almost always wrong."

They sat quiet for a few moments more, looking at the water. "Why?" Nita said.

"I don't know," Quelt said. "It's only the last, oh, hundred years or so. I'll be in the middle of something, fixing the weather or something like that, and—" She stopped, looked at Nita. "What?" Quelt said. "What's so funny?"

Nita was having trouble restraining her laughter. Finally, she managed to get some control over herself. "Sorry," she said. "It's just cultural. 'The last hundred years or so.' That's a whole lifetime where I come from."

Quelt shook her head in wonder. "It sounds strange

thinking of a life that short," she said. "It doesn't really seem that short for your people, though, does it?"

Nita looked out at the water as it lapped at the shore, turning slowly peach-colored under the growing glow of the dawn. "Not really," she said, "if you get the whole thing, or close to it. Seventy, eighty years..." She trailed off. "A human life span's getting longer these days, I guess. We're better at curing sick people than we used to be, and we eat better, and all that kind of thing. But for Earth humans, yeah, around eighty or ninety, a lot of people start getting tired. Their bodies don't work terribly well. Things start breaking down. Sometimes their memory starts going."

"It seems so soon."

"I don't know," Nita said. She idly grabbed the end of Ponch's tail and started playing with it; Ponch looked over his shoulder at her, made a grumbly *growmf* noise, pretended to snap at Nita, and then rolled over on his back and started to squirm around in the sand. "It's as if a time comes when even if your body does stay pretty healthy, the rest of you is ready for something else." She looked at the white tip of Ponch's tail, considering it, and then let it go again.

"My nana," Nita said, "that was my dad's grand-mother—she got that way when I was small. I can just remember it. At the time, I didn't know what was the matter with her. She wasn't sick, and she could get around all right. But she slept most of the time, and when she wasn't sleeping, she just sat in a chair and watched television, and smiled. Everybody was always trying to get her up and get her to go out, be more active. I tried to do it, too. And once I remember trying to get her to play ball with me . . . something like that . . . and she said, 'Juanita, dear, I'm ninety-three, and I'm tired of running around and doing things. The time's come for me to just sit here and see what it's like to *be* ninety-three. It's part of getting ready for what comes after.'"

Nita smiled. The memory had no pain about it; it seemed a long, long time ago. "Then, I thought it was kind of funny. Now, though, I wonder sometimes whether it's such a bad thing that after a while you should *want* to go on to the next thing. Even though there's a lot of argument on my world about what the 'next thing' is . . ."

She trailed off again. "Hey, I interrupted you," Nita said. "Sorry about that. You were talking about fixing the weather." She grinned. "That's funny, too, but for different reasons. We have a saying, 'Everybody talks about the weather, but nobody does anything about it.' Except that whoever made up the saying didn't know there were wizards."

"Do you do weather, too?"

"Kit and I did a hurricane last year," Nita said. "With a consortium of other wizards. It looked like it was going to cause a lot of trouble if it came ashore, so the North American Regional Wizards did a risk assessment on it with the Western Europe group, and when it turned out it wouldn't go anywhere else if we were careful, we pushed it out to sea—"

They discussed storms for a while, the wizardries of

wind management and heat exchange, of what to do with the leftover kinetic energy after you've pushed ten million tons of relentlessly cycling wind and water off its intended course. Alaalu was sedate enough in terms of weather—its star was quiet and predictable, its orbit very nearly exactly circular, and its seasonal tilt very small. But there were still biggish tropical storms in the equatorial belt, twice each year, and dealing with those made up a surprising amount of Quelt's steady work.

"It seems so strange that that's all there is for you to do," Nita said. "Or mostly that."

"It didn't always seem strange to me," Quelt said. "When I was younger, anyway. But now I keep getting this feeling, like I said, that there's something else that's supposed to be happening, something I haven't noticed. I'd notice it if I stopped and looked around ... that's the feeling I get. And I do stop and look. But so far ..." She shrugged.

"I know another wizard," Nita said, "a cat—that's another of the sentient species on our planet—who told me once that sometimes the Powers have a message for you, but it's like a spell that you're building: You have to put it together piece by piece over time, and the rest of the time you just leave the bits and pieces scattered around in your head and give them a chance to come together."

"That's what I'm doing, I suppose," Quelt said. And then she flashed Nita one of those grins. "But I'm impatient, I think! Something our people aren't, usually ..." She stretched her legs out on the sand. "Still, it

269

nibbles at me. Like the *keks* if you stay around after they start work..."

"It'll come together eventually," Nita said. She yawned and stretched. "I'm surprised to see you out here," she said to Ponch, "when the boss isn't up yet."

Ponch, upside down, looked at Nita with one eye. *He's lazy.*

"*He's* lazy? *You* should talk. You sleep all day!"

I've been doing my job, Ponch said. *I don't have to hunt. I don't have any puppies to guard. So I sleep, and the rest of the time I have fun.*

Nita chuckled. "Sensible," she said. "Okay, I take it back." She stretched again, ran her hands through her hair. "You know what I love about this place? No bugs."

"Bugs?"

"Insects. Little life-forms that come and bite you."

"The *keks* would do that."

"Yeah, but the *keks* you can get up and walk away from. These things fly after you in the air and sit on you and bite you. Some of them are so small you can hardly see them. They're a real pain."

"But you can talk them out of biting you, surely..."

"I've tried. It's an uphill battle, believe me. You get better reactions out of walls and rocks than you do out of most bugs."

Quelt laughed, and got up, and stretched. "I should go put the laundry in to run," she said. "I told my 'mom' I would."

Nita laughed. "We're corrupting you with all these strange foreign words," she said.

"Oh, I don't think so. I hear what you call my *tapi*…"

Nita and Quelt smiled at each other. "Go on," Nita said. "Ponch, go on and kick the boss out of bed. It's a sin for him to miss this."

Quelt and Ponch went back toward the house, and Nita watched them go with a slight smile. Chores on this world didn't seem as onerous as chores did at home, somehow. *And even less so when I don't have to do them*, she thought. But Quelt didn't seem to mind doing them, either.

Nita sat there a while longer, looking out at the sea and watching the tiny waves slide lazily up the sand, so unlike the energetic surf of the South Shore. *But then the Great South Bay has tides, because Earth has a Moon. That's the only thing I miss here: a really big moon.*

Still, this is gorgeous…

Very slowly, the east started to turn a fiercer orange red than before. Nita sat in that fiery light and soaked it up with endless appreciation.

But the dream would not quite go away.

The heart of the world is frozen, and so there is *no heart.*

Nita blinked, and then she shivered, her sunburn briefly forgotten.

Dairine and Filif and Sker'ret got back from Mount Everest late that afternoon to find that Roshaun had arrived while they were gone. Carmela was sitting in front of the TV with him, discussing clothes once more. Annoyed as Dairine was with the prince, she had to be

amused—at least Carmela had found someone as interested in personal adornment as she was. *I didn't
think it was possible,* Dairine thought. And at least
Roshaun had come back. *Though not because of anything I said* ...

Filif, wanting some relaxation, joined Roshaun and
Carmela in the living room. Dairine's dad was sitting at
the dining room table, making some notes about sup-
plies for the store on a pad. As Dairine and Sker'ret
came in, his head jerked up, a little guiltily, Dairine
thought, to make sure Filif wasn't in sight.

"You okay, Daddy?" she said, bending over to hug
him and give him a kiss.

"Huh? Oh, fine," he said. "How was your day? You
guys have a nice lunch?"

Sker'ret looked most satisfied. "Very filling," he
said.

"Oxygen bottles, mostly," Dairine said.

Her dad glanced up at that, amused. "Nothing
wrong with a little roughage in the diet. Where are you
off to?"

"Just down to Sker'ret's pup tent. He's going to
lend me some music. Stick your head in and yell if you
need me."

"Okay."

They went down the basement stairs more or less
together—it always being a question, when Sker'ret
was on forty legs and she was on two, who was ahead
and who was behind at any one time, if not both at
once. On the mountain, Dairine and Sker'ret had started

discussing popular music while Sker'ret ingested carefully chosen chunks of garbage—including some climbing expedition's very broken tape recorder—and Sker'ret had suggested that when they got back, they could use one of the manual's data transfer options to pass some favorite selections back and forth. Dairine promptly had Spot grab a wide and peculiar assortment from the big computer at home—everything from boy bands to Beethoven—and was curious to see what Sker'ret was going to pass to her in return.

They slipped in through his pup-tent access. Dairine looked around and saw several of the sitting/ lying racks Sker'ret's people preferred, sort of a cross between a giant step stool and monkey bars. Dairine looked around at the stacks and racks of storage. "Very organized," she said.

"Not what my parent says," Sker'ret said.

Dairine snickered. "None of us is ever neat enough for our parents. One of those universal traits." Sker'ret laughed and started rummaging around for his own version of the manual, a little flat data pad.

Dairine sat partly down on one of the racks—it was impossible for a human to get really comfortable on one of them, no matter how she tried—and perched there, swinging her leg, while Spot spidered around, peering into everything. "You told me before that they wouldn't let you into the restaurants in the Crossings," Dairine said. "Why not? Did you misbehave in there or something?"

Sker'ret's laugh acquired something of an edge. Dairine heard a hint of bitterness about it. "Oh, no," he said. "It's just that families of employees aren't expected to use the same facilities as the patrons."

Dairine stared at him a moment. Abruptly, the data slipped into place. "Oh no," she said. "You're not just some Rirhait, are you? You're related to the Stationmaster..."

"I'm the youngest of his first brood," Sker'ret said.

Dairine breathed out. "That means you inherit management of the whole place when he retires, doesn't it?"

"It would mean that if I were normal," Sker'ret said. "But I'm not, am I? I'm a wizard." Now there was no mistaking the bitterness. "I'm supposed to run the Crossings, and become one of the most powerful beings for light-years around. It's as much a political position as anything else: Control worldgates and you control so much else. No one argues with the Stationmasters."

"But you can do that and be a wizard," Dairine said. "Can't you?"

Sker'ret looked at her with several eyes. "I want to," he said. "But *they* don't want me to. As far as my parent is concerned, to be a wizard is a distraction from what I'm supposed to be doing, from the business of life, and the 'real world.'" He snorted, a most peculiar, rather metallic sound. "Not precisely a waste of time— we know as well as anybody else how useful wizards are. But my parent is furious with me. He wants me to reject the wizardry, to give it up. And I can't!"

Dairine drew a deep breath. *Wizardry does not live in the unwilling heart.* That was one of the first laws of the Art. You could give it up, if you were unwilling or unable to hold by the strictures embodied in the Wizard's Oath. It could leave you of its own volition, if pain or illness or changes in your life made it impossible for you to keep the Oath any longer. But the prospect was horrible to imagine, at least for Dairine. To actually have the people around you trying to force you to give up wizardry, to give up that most intimate connection with the universe and What had made it—

She shuddered. "You go your own way," she said to Sker'ret. "You do what your heart tells you."

"Hearts," Sker'ret said.

"Whatever. You *do* that! That's how They talk to you. Don't let anyone push you around."

"That's easy to say," Sker'ret said, "when your 'father's' not the Stationmaster of the Crossings."

Dairine gave Sker'ret a look. "I have news for you," she said. "I think you're tougher than he thinks you are. I think there's room in the universe for you to be exactly what you want to be. Your father—sorry, your parent—may be the most powerful entity for lightyears around, but if he were *sure* of that, he wouldn't be pressuring you so hard. So I think you still may have some bargaining room left."

He looked at her, all those stalked eyes weaving in a gesture of uncertainty. "There's no harm in *trying,*" Dairine said. "Dig your feet in. There are enough of *those* to make anybody think twice. Anyway, what's the worst the family can do?"

"Disown me," Sker'ret said.

Dairine swallowed. "So what?" she said. "You'll always be a wizard. You have a bigger family than just your *family*. And you'll always have a place to stay: You can sleep in my basement anytime."

They locked eyes for a few moments. Shortly Dairine said, "You really need to stop moving them around like that. You're making me seasick."

Sker'ret laughed. So did Dairine.

They spent half an hour or so swapping music between Spot and Sker'ret's manual, and after checking the sound quality, they headed upstairs again, where Sker'ret wandered into the living room to see what the others were doing. Dairine got the urge for some milk and opened the fridge, pouring herself a glass. Then, hearing laughter coming from the living room, she leaned in through the door to the dining room to see what was happening in there.

The aliens were watching cartoons. Carmela was still sitting cross-legged on the floor, rocking back and forth in amusement, while Roshaun sat in Dairine's dad's easy chair—*That's probably the closest he can get to a throne,* she thought—and was laughing, too. Not as hard as the others, perhaps, but he was plainly enjoying himself. "Someone needs to tell me what mice are," he was saying to Carmela. "And why do they bang the cats over the head with these hammers so often? Is it class warfare of some kind?"

"I don't think so," Carmela said. "It's one of those cross-species things."

The cartoons and the laughter went on for a while, and Dairine sat down at the table, scrolling through

Spot's manual functions while listening to the Rirhait music. It was surprisingly symphonic, though written in the key of M, and only occasionally did it become so weird that she had to skip ahead. The music combined strangely but amusingly with the bonks, hoots, and shrieks of the cartoons in the living room, and the metallic, hissing, or humanoid laughter of the room's living inhabitants. Finally, a little peace came with a station break.

"Enough of that," Carmela said. "Let's look at some of the news." She changed the channels.

"—the Suffolk County Pine Barrens," said an announcer's voice suddenly, "recent dry conditions have combined with a passing driver's carelessness to produce the season's first brushfire. Some fifty acres south and east of Pilgrim State Hospital, at the edges of Brentwood and Deer Park, were blackened after a—"

There was a sudden terrible rustling in the living room.

"What the—" Dairine's dad said. He got up, and collided halfway through the living room door with Filif. The effect was much like that of a man trying to catch a falling Christmas tree, except that the tree was still trying to fall after he had caught it.

"No," Filif said, and the word was mixed with a high, keening whine, entirely like the sound that Dairine had heard green pinewood make in the outdoor fireplace, sometimes, when her dad was burning brush.

"Oh no," Filif said. And he hastened into the kitchen and leaned against one of the counters there, rustling uncontrollably.

"What's the matter, son?" Dairine's dad said, alarmed.

"It's here," Filif said, broken voiced. "Death—"

Her father went a little pale. "Death in Its own self," Filif said. "The Ravager, the Kindler of Wildfires. I thought..." Filif sounded stricken. "I was beginning to think perhaps this was one of the places where the Lone Power hadn't come. Here and there you do find places like that, worlds or planets or continua It forgot or hasn't been to yet...places where the Bargain was done differently." Filif looked around him with all his berries. "It's so terrible," he said. "I never knew— I didn't know It was here, too. I thought this was paradise!"

Her dad looked at Dairine rather helplessly, then did all he could do in such circumstances: He hugged a tree, not to draw strength from it, but the other way around.

"It's not going to get you here, son," Dairine's dad said. "Nothing like *that* is going to get you here. And as for the powers of darkness, yeah, they're here, too. But we know they're here. And we fight as we can."

There was a long silence. Finally, Filif pulled himself away. "That's all we can do," he said. "Isn't it?"

"That's all," Dairine's dad said.

Slowly he went back into the living room, leaving Dairine and her dad gazing after him.

"There are really places like that?" Dairine's dad said after a few moments. "Places where they just haven't taken delivery on Death?"

Dairine nodded. "Here and there," she said, and she

turned away. For her, too, the subject was too close for comfort.

She went to rinse out the empty milk glass and put it in the sink. After a little while she wandered outside and looked up at the sky. The Moon was coming up in the east, and as it slid slowly up through the twilight, her dad put his head out the back door and looked at her. "You all right?" he said.

Dairine breathed in, breathed out. "Yeah," she said. "Are *you*?"

Her dad let out a long breath. "How do other places get to operate like that," he said, "when we don't?"

Dairine shook her head. "It's a long story," she said. "But right now I really wish we were one of them..."

Her dad nodded and vanished back inside.

She came back in, thought about another glass of milk, fetched Spot into the kitchen from the dining room, got another glass, and went back into the fridge for more milk. While she was pouring, Sker'ret came back in.

"Ah," Sker'ret said, "the 'got' stuff."

"Yup," Dairine said. "Don't tell me you're hungry again!"

"Not again," Sker'ret said. "Still."

Dairine glanced at her dad. "Daddy," she said, "have we got any scrap metal...or wood?"

"Or matter of any kind," Sker'ret said, with the air of someone trying to be helpful.

"Let me see what I can find," Dairine's dad said. "Now that you mention it, I've been thinking of replacing the old woodshed, but I keep putting it off. If I *had* to replace it because somebody, uh, *ate* it..."

Dairine snickered. Her dad got up and came into the kitchen, putting the kettle on to boil. Then he picked up his cell phone and dialed. After a moment he snorted. "It's still not working." He looked over at Sker'ret. "I'm tempted to give this to you as an hors d'oeuvre."

"No, Daddy," Dairine said. "It's probably still just the Sun. The effect can last a day or so, sometimes."

Roshaun wandered in while Dairine and her dad were looking again at Spot's display from the SOHO satellite. "Do these people know they're feeding their data to wizards?" her dad said, as he took the kettle off the stove, put decaf instant coffee into a mug, and made himself one last cup of coffee before bed.

"I don't think they'd mind," Dairine said. "It's more or less a public service."

"That smells wonderful," Roshaun said. "What is it?" And then his eye fell on Spot's display.

Roshaun froze.

"It's coffee," Dairine's father said. "Well, it's sort of coffee. How much you can really consider something to be coffee when there's no caffeine in it is a moot point."

He wandered out of the kitchen, and so entirely missed seeing Roshaun's ashen expression.

"Is that your star?" Roshaun said, very softly.

"Huh?" Dairine looked over her shoulder. "Yeah. It's just a CME. You don't have to look all worried about it."

But he did look worried about it. "Dairine, how many of these have you had lately?"

Dairine stopped dead. She couldn't remember Roshaun having ever spoken her name directly to her before, not once. "I don't know," she said, after taking a moment to get over the initial shock. "We're in a sunspot maximum now, and we expect a lot of them. One or two a week, we've been having, but—"

Roshaun looked stricken. "Dear Aethyrs, that's the first sign," he said. "I've seen this before. Don't you know what this means?"

"No," Dairine said. "Should I?"

"Are you insane!" he shouted at her. "Your star is about to start having a crisis! And if you want to *have* a star for much longer, or you want your planet to be in any state to notice that it has a star, you'll *shut up and listen!!"*

Completely astounded, Dairine shut up.

"I wondered why the thing pained me to look at it," Roshaun said. "It's going to bubblestorm. Your Sun's got to be fixed before it goes into a catastrophic flare cycle—"

"Are you crazy? You can't just run off and fix the Sun! We don't even know if it's really broken or not!"

"I do," Roshaun said. "It's broken. And if somebody doesn't fix it right away—"

"This kind of thing happens all the time here. This is normal!"

"This is not normal," Roshaun said angrily. "You don't know what you're talking about. This kind of behavior is very, very abnormal in a star of this class, and

it has to be dealt with before it starts to accelerate toward a crisis process that can no longer be stopped!"

Her father appeared in the kitchen again. "I assume," he said softly, "that someone is going to get a grip on himself or herself and explain all this shouting to me?"

"Roshaun is completely out of his mind," Dairine said, "and thinks the Sun is broken. And he wants to go fix it. Which he is not going to do, because you've got to get permission from at least a regional-level wizard if you're going to screw around with a system's primary!"

"I don't care. Unless something is done—"

Dairine had awful visions of Roshaun going off and doing something on the sly, and messing up Sol past all repair. "Look," she said, "we really need to at least talk to Tom and Carl about this before you go off and start playing around with my star. *My* star, not yours, right? Thank you." She went over to the phone, picked it up, dialed.

"Hi there," said Tom's voice.

"Tom? It's Dairine. Listen, I—"

"—know the drill. Leave a name and number and we'll get back to you as soon as we can. Thanks." *Beep!*

Dairine swallowed. "Tom, it's Dairine. I need to talk to you right away. I'll get you via Spot. Bye."

She hung up. *Where* are *they?* she thought. She'd never called Tom and Carl's house before and failed to get one or the other of them, except when they were on vacation, and they always warned everybody about that first. "Spot?"

Yes?

"Message both Tom and Carl right away. Flag it emergency and high-urgent. I need to talk to them right now."

Spot sat silent for a moment. Then he said, *The message has been bounced.*

"What??"

The bounce message says, "Subjects are on assignment, unavailable."

Oh no, Dairine thought. *Oh no. What does* that *mean?* She sat there and stared into space for a moment. *It may be nothing,* she thought. *There may be all kinds of times they go off on assignment together and I don't know anything about it. It's not like Nita or Kit or I call them every five minutes to see where they are.*

But the cold feeling at the bottom of Dairine's gut told her that this was *not* just nothing. She remembered something Tom had said once, when Dairine's dad had asked him why he wasn't off the planet more: "Harry, would you normally open the door and get out of a car you were driving?"

"They're not there, are they?" her dad said.

"No."

Roshaun was looking at her in increasing anger. "We're just going to have to do something, then."

"No we are *not,*" Dairine said. "We are going up to at least planetary level on this one."

She turned back to Spot and began firing off messages in all directions.

But there was no response. It wasn't as if the Planetary Wizard for Earth wouldn't talk to her; wizards at even that level were remarkably accessible to their colleagues. But again and again Spot simply said, *Subjects are on assignment, unavailable.*

"What can I do to help?" her dad said.

"Daddy..." Dairine shook her head. "Nothing right now. Go on...I'll let you know what happens."

Silently, her dad kissed her, and went. An hour later, Dairine was still sitting in the dining room, in shock, realizing that no one in the upper wizardly structure was available at all. *Good lord,* she thought, *where is everybody? Who's minding the planet?!*

And, horrified, she knew the answer, at least for the moment. *We are...*

Travel-Related Stress

DAIRINE'S FIRST URGE WAS to go off and physically look for somebody in the echelons above the
planetary level. But she couldn't. The limitations that
Tom had put on her ability to use wizardry for transit
were still in place, whether he was here or not. She was
limited to Sol System, and couldn't even get around the
prohibition by going elsewhere on the planet and using
a fixed gate. All of the worldgates had monitoring wizardries built into them that would recognize Dairine's
banned status and refuse her access.

Roshaun was looking at her from where he'd sat
down across the table. All the time Dairine had been
trying to find someone higher up the wizardly command structure, he had simply sat there, not saying a
word, watching her. It was perhaps the longest time
she'd ever seen him be quiet. Now he said, "You're
wasting time."

She looked at him with profound misgivings. There was no arguing that he was an expert of sorts in this business; it was his specialty as a wizard. Even Spot's manual functions confirmed that. But—

"You don't trust me," Roshaun said.

"Not as far as I could throw you," Dairine said.

"And why not?" Roshaun said. "Because I'm not like you? Maybe not. But I am still a wizard. The Powers That Be trust me, if you don't."

"And why?" Dairine said. "That's what I want to know! You are the least wizardlike wizard I've ever met! You don't even *use* wizardry if you can help it! You're a whole lot more interested in being a prince than in being a wizard, the way it looks to me! The rules say that wizardry can't live long in the unwilling heart. How long do you think you're likely to *be* one of us if you keep acting the way you do? How long is it going to be before the act becomes the reality?"

He stared at her, and it took Dairine several breaths to realize how stricken, and then furious, the look in his eyes was becoming.

"That's it," he said, and stood up. "That's it. I'm off home. I'm weary of your arrogance, and your bad manners, and your mistrust, and your—"

Dairine jumped up, too. "You're weary of *my* arrogance? Why, you stuck-up, self-centered, self-important—"

"—don't have to explain myself to the likes of *you*, you parochial, controlling little—"

"—always so sure you're right, then go ahead, go

home and be right there, where all your people are so busy bowing and scraping to you that none of them has the nerve to confront you when you're—"

Suddenly Dairine's face was full of greenery, and a number of berries were looking at her from very, very close, in a chilly, annoyed sort of way.

You should stop this now, Filif said.

Filif's silent speech was forceful. It was like running suddenly into a tree. Across from her, beyond the greenery, she could tell that Roshaun was feeling the same impact.

You are frightened, Filif said to Dairine. *It's clouding your thinking. Sit down and be quiet until you've managed the fear.*

Dairine sat down, hard, as if she'd been pushed. *Maybe I was,* she thought, somewhat dazed. She wasn't quite sure if Filif hadn't given her muscles a hint.

And you're frightened, too, Filif said to Roshaun. *And it's making you angry because you feel powerless. Sit down and be quiet until you find your power again.*

Roshaun sat down as hard as Dairine had. She watched this with both confusion and satisfaction, but at the bottom of it was a kind of scared awe. She had been fooled by Filif's diffident manner, and had been treating him as a bush in a baseball cap, someone faintly funny. She'd had no idea there was such power underneath.

For some few moments there wasn't any sound but both Dairine and Roshaun breathing hard. Eventually this sound, too, started to slow. When it did, Filif said, *So. What does one do about a problem like this?*

"There are a number of possible solutions that would cure this problem permanently," Roshaun said. "Most of them need a lot of time for assessments, though, to tailor the wizardry to the star. And I don't think we have enough time for that right now. There are some faster interventions, though. Effective at least in the short term. They buy you time to enact the more complex solutions."

What is the best intervention for this problem, then?

Roshaun took a long breath. "Bleeding the star."

"What?" Dairine said.

"Bleeding the star. You remove a small percentage of its mass."

"*Remove* it? To where?"

"Anywhere you like, but out of the star's corpus. Yes, it's dangerous! Bleed off too much mass, and fusion in the star fails. Bleed off too little, and the intervention merely makes the star's core go critical sooner."

"Its core—" Dairine broke out in a sweat. "It's not going to go nova, is it?"

"No. Nothing like that. But there are worse things."

"Worse than the Sun going nova?!"

Roshaun gave her a bleak look. For a moment he didn't speak.

"How would you like it," he said at last, "if your star flared up just enough to roast one side of your world? That happened to our planet once. I would have thought you'd noticed. Or maybe you didn't read the orientation package. It's right there on the first page of the historical material—"

Dairine flushed hot. She was a fast reader, sometimes too fast. She had missed it, and now felt profoundly stupid. "My great-great-ancestors were a family of wizards, back then," Roshaun said. "In their time, our star flared without warning. The land on that side of Wellakh was blasted to slag and lava; the seas on that side boiled off. The air on that side all burned away. The wizards of the world had just enough time between the flare and its wave front's arrival to isolate the spaceward side of Wellakh from the worst effects of the flare, and to keep the planet's ecology from being completely destroyed in the terrible winds and floods and fires that followed. But only *just* enough. It was very close, and almost all of the wizards died from giving all of their power to keep the world and its people alive. Then, after that, it took centuries of suffering and rebuilding for our world to recover. The quick obliteration that a nova would have brought would have seemed merciful by comparison."

Dairine swallowed. "But afterward," Roshaun said, "my ancestors, wizards and nonwizards both, spent generations learning how the sun behaved, finding out how to cure it. And they *did* cure it, finally, though again, almost all of my line's wizards died in the cure. Why do you think my family are kings now? They gave their lives to save the world, to make sure it would never need to be saved again from death by fire. So that in any generation where a wizard is born into the royal family again, everyone looks at them and says, 'See, there's the son of the Sun Lord, the Guarantor, there's the one who'll give his life to protect us...'"

Without particularly asking what you had in mind to do with your life besides that, Dairine thought, hearing Roshaun's voice go rough with abrupt pain. And she found herself thinking of the view from the balcony of Roshaun's family's palace, right across that very flat, strangely featureless landscape... right in the middle of the sealess, mountainless, melted-down side of the world. *Who built that there to make sure that the "Sun Kings" never forgot what they were there for?* Dairine thought. *As if to say, "We'll give them everything they want... but when the bad day comes again, they'd better deliver!"*

She sat there in silence, feeling shock and shame in nearly equal parts. Roshaun's bleak look was turned more inward now, and he seemed not to register Dairine looking at him. Finally, he did glance over at her once more, and something of the old cool distance was back in his eyes. But now Dairine knew it was a mask, and she also knew what lay under it.

"I'm an idiot," Dairine said.

Roshaun simply looked at her. So did Spot.

She looked down at him. "Yes, I am," Dairine said. "This is no time for misguided loyalty. We've got to do something." She looked back over at Roshaun. "But we still have to get permission," Dairine said. She looked down at Spot. "Any luck finding the planetary supervisor yet?"

No.

Dairine covered her face with her hands. "Great. We can't do this, we *can't,* without making sure that no one else is—"

I do have an authorization, though, Spot said.

Dairine looked up, surprised. "What? From where?"

Spot popped his lid up and showed her.

In the Speech, very small, Dairine saw the characters that spelled out the words "Approved. Go." Following those was a shorthand version of a wizardly name, but even the shorthand version was very long, and the power rating appended to it was so high that Dairine looked at it several times to make sure she wasn't just misplacing a decimal point.

"This is a Galactic Arm coordinator's ID," Dairine said softly.

It made her feel no better in terms of an answer to the question of where Earth's wizardly command structure had gone all of a sudden. But at least she knew now that she wouldn't be interfering with anyone else's intervention.

"All right," she said. "Let's go fix the Sun."

Kit woke up with Ponch's wet nose in his face.

Nita says you should get up.

"Nita is a nuisance," Kit muttered.

And Quelt is here.

Kit blinked. "That's another story," he said. "I want to catch her before she goes out on business or something…"

Kit rolled off his couch, grabbed the bathrobe he'd brought with him, wrapped it around himself and headed out the door at such speed that he nearly knocked Quelt flat. She was carrying a basket of laundry, and she staggered, and then laughed.

Kit grabbed her and steadied her, and then rocked back himself, off balance. "Are you all right?" Quelt said.

"Yeah, I'm fine," Kit said, "and I have one question for you. What's the 'Relegate's Naos'?"

Quelt looked at him in some surprise. "Uh, it's where the Lone Power lives," she said.

Kit stared.

"It lives here??"

"Of course she does," Quelt said, putting the laundry basket down and looking at Kit very peculiarly.

"Since when?"

"Well, since after the Choice. When she lost out, they built her a place of her own."

Kit stood there with his mouth open and didn't care who saw him. "Why in the One's Name did they do that?" he said.

Quelt looked at him with some confusion. "Well, she had bound herself into the world, and when she lost, she couldn't dissolve that relationship. She was stuck here. So they made her a place to stay. It's very nice; it's a few thousand miles from here. That's where you go for an Own Choice, when you're a wizard here. We go see her, and have a good talk with her, and tell her she should have behaved herself."

Kit looked at Quelt in astonishment.

"And you just walked away from that little conversation without having any further trouble?" Kit said.

"Well, yes," Quelt said. "Why not?"

Kit was utterly dumbfounded. He looked at Ponch, who was eyeing him with some moderate confusion himself.

"Come on!" Kit said, and headed off. Ponch ran after him, leaving Quelt gazing after them.

"Well," she said to no one in particular, "no help with the laundry this morning, I see..."

Kit made his way straight back to the great Display, via his "beam-me-up-Scotty" spell, into which he had laid the Display's coordinates. "There's something I'm looking for," he said to Ponch as they popped out in the early morning over the crystalline "pool."

Tell me about it.

"What we're seeing here, down below..."

Ponch's answer was a few minutes in coming. *They decided, here, what the rest of this world's life would look like,* Ponch said. *Is that right?*

"That's part of it," Kit said.

Ponch looked up at him with an expression that was both quizzical and somehow sad. *But not all.*

"No," Kit said. Standing there on the brink of the interface, he hesitated, and then sat down in the grass and flowers.

Ponch sat down beside him, his tongue hanging out, still giving Kit that uncertain look. *You understand it,* Ponch said. *Make me understand it, too. I think it's important.*

Kit pulled his knees up, wrapped his arms around them. "The universe is running down," he said. "It's the Lone Power's doing. It invented entropy, the Great Death that's the shadow over all the smaller ones. Whether the results of that invention are *all* bad—" Kit shrugged. "It gets too complicated to just say yes or no. But wizards do what they can to slow down the speed of energy running out of the world, that's all."

Ponch had looked away and was gazing down into the Display. *I think I understand that.*

"Okay. When enough members of a species get to the point where they know they're alive, and they know they can think—when they start to understand the world around them, and they realize they can do something *about* it one way or another—then they're offered the Choice. As a species, they can elect to slow down the Great Death, or at least *try* to slow it down. Or else they can just give in and decide to do nothing about it. They can even go over to Its side, the Lone Power's side, and help make the worlds die faster..."

Ponch shuddered. *How can they do that?!*

"I've never been real clear about that myself," Kit said. *How* can *they do it? How can someone be angry enough, or crazy enough, to say, "Sure, if things are going to hell anyway, let's have them go there faster'?* "Sometimes it looks like a species can get tricked into it," Kit said. "When a Choice happens, there are always representatives from Life's side and Death's side to argue the case. And there are always wizards there: sometimes a lot, sometimes just a few, or even just one. But finally it comes down to what the species itself decides, through its representatives at the Choice. If the Lone One offers them something they like the sound of—better than they like the sound of what Life's offering—and they go for it, then..." Kit shook his head.

Then bad things happen to that species, Ponch said.

He was still looking down into the Display. Kit glanced over at him, wondering what was going on. Ponch was usually more voluble than this, even when he was upset.

"That's right," Kit said. "And usually bad stuff happens to the other species around them, too, if the one making the Choice has the biggest population of sentient beings on that planet. If they already had death to begin with, then it tends to get a lot worse than just their bodies stopping, or whatever. If they didn't have death...they get it."

It was some seconds before Ponch said anything else. Finally, he lifted his head and looked Kit in the eyes again. *That's awful.*

Kit nodded. "So all the people in that world have to deal with the results of that Choice until their species ends," he said. "And wizards get born to try to make it better, if it went badly. You could say that a wizard's Ordeal is his own version of that Choice." Kit smiled, a small smile and not a happy one. "Whether we like it or not, it looks like it's Choices all the way down..."

Ponch flicked an ear at the Display. *Including down there.*

"Definitely down there," Kit said. "Most species only have old stories about their Choices, and it's hard to tell whether everything in the stories is true. These guys—" He shook his head. "It's pretty unusual to have such a clear telling. It's nice for the Alaalids. But I can't get over the idea that there's something missing."

Something they've left out?

"Maybe. Yeah. Or else something they didn't think was important. What I wish I could see...is that left-out part."

Ponch looked stumped. *Let me think about that for a moment,* he said.

That, Kit thought. *The part with the Lone One. In all other Choices that I've seen, It's been the major player. In world after world, It haunts even the species that came close to* winning *their Choices. But* this one... He sat down. *This species has death. They accepted that part of the Lone Power's "gift" even before the Choice process began. So the heart of their own Choice, and something they accepted—or threw out—has to be even more important than death.*

Kit stood there in the bright day, turning that over and over in his mind. Something more important for this species than life and death. More important than what comes after it.

What could that be?

Ponch looked up at him. *The thing you want to see,* he said, *I can take you there.*

"Do it!"

Together they walked down into the crystal. Once again they found the eight characters of the Choice waiting for them. But this time the air of the past, or the past-made-present, wasn't quite so pellucid. There was uncertainty in it, a kind of haze.

"Where is that haze coming from?" Kit said.

Me, possibly, Ponch said. *But pay attention. I don't know if I can do this more than once.*

The Lone Power and Druvah had stepped aside, and

Kit and Ponch stood nearby, watching, listening. "You are the wise one," the Lone Power was saying. "You know what day your people are coming to, in the far future. You know to what place they will come: the place from which they will not be able to move without help. My help."

"I'm not so sure about that," Druvah said. "I think our Choice will still remain our own. Now tell me what you want."

"The destruction of hopes," It said. "The devaluation of life. The end of things, early or late. The dissolution of the created. What else?"

"No," Druvah said. "I mean, what do you want of *me*? You wouldn't have called me aside unless I had the ability to do something you want."

"I want you to let me into the heart of things," It said.

"You want me to betray my people," Druvah said.

"Nothing of the kind! But I can give you the power to make sure they won't destroy themselves. They will, eventually. You know it. They're very happy with the way they are. But to every species comes a time when the way they are is not enough . . . when if they're going to go on living, they have to become something more, something different from what they've always been. If your fellow wizards enact the wizardry they're building at the moment, they'll also find that they've built themselves a trap from which there's no escape. And you know that's what they're doing, too. You're trying to save them. But they're not listening to you."

"They're likely to listen to me even less," Druvah said, "if I talk to you much longer."

"Why should you care about that?" Ictanikë said. "You're the oldest of the wizards on this world, the wisest and the strongest. And you're the power source for this spell, the one without whom a wizardry of this scope and importance simply can't happen. If they become offended, why, you just walk away from the spell—"

"And leave the future of my world unprotected from disasters and pain and sudden death, and alienated from the One?" Druvah said. "I don't think so."

"Whatever the One may do for you," Ictanikë said, "without me included in your world, your species will never be able to change, or grow."

"I suspect that to be true," Druvah said, and for the first time, he looked troubled. "But I don't trust you."

"There I can help you," Ictanikë said. "I will gladly give you enough power so that, for the rest of your life, if indeed you don't trust me, you can step in to right whatever wrongs you think have been done."

Druvah was silent for a while, gazing off into the distance. Then he looked up again. "You're very cunning," he said. "But what's one lifetime against the lifetime of a world? I'm not so irresponsible as to cast away responsibility for what happens in Alaalu after I leave it. If you're going to give me power in return for changes I make in the wizardry we're about to work, then it will be this way—that by your gift, I'll be able to live here in the state of being I please, in the shape and way I please, until the last of the Alaalids passes from the world."

Uh-oh, Kit thought. He recognized the veiled cruelty in the smile on the Lone One's face, having seen it before. Whatever Druvah was asking for, it was something that the Lone Power thought suited Its own desires perfectly.

"After the Choice is done," the Lone One said, "what you've asked for will be yours."

"*Before,*" Druvah said. "I know perfectly well who you are. And I know that the gifts of the Powers can't be recalled once bestowed."

The Lone One looked somewhat taken aback.

"My way, or not at all," Druvah said.

Ictanikë looked at him, narrow-eyed, furious. Finally, she said, "Very well."

"And when you give me this power," Druvah said, "what am I supposed to do for you?"

"Just a small thing," the Lone One said. "Simply leave me a foothold in your world... a place where my essence can lie dormant until the day comes when you do need it for the Change that is to come. With you as the eternal guardian of your world, I won't be able to do any harm."

Kit knew that innocent look, and he went cold at the sight of it. *The Lone One's going to make sure something happens to Druvah, sooner or later,* Kit thought. *Probably sooner. It'll find a loophole in the promise It's made, and It'll kill him somehow. And then the Alaalids will be stuck with It in their world forever.* He had the urge to go over to Druvah and shake him and say, *Don't do it!*

But Druvah was hundreds of thousands of years away from Kit. He said to the Lone One, "I agree. Pay me my price now, or I do nothing for you."

The Lone Power looked at him for a long moment, then closed Its eyes.

The ferocity of the released power staggered Kit where he stood, even at this remove in time and space. Druvah, though, did not stagger. He went rigid as iron-wood, and then, as the rigor passed, he looked at Ic-tanikë with the slightest smile.

"Now," he said, "to work."

Druvah went back to the other six wizards, who looked at him dubiously. "Well," he said, "I've listened to Its words. Now you'll listen to mine in turn. I am the power source for this Choice, this work we do to protect our world for all the generations that will come after. The spell we've built so far has many good things about it. Lives will be long in our world, and there will be peace and prosperity and joy for an endless-seeming time. The Lone One will have no more part in our world than entropy, Its child, makes absolutely neces-sary. Our world's center, its kernel, It will never be able to reach, and this world will be a good one, a glad one, for a very long time. But not forever. I see the doings of the day after forever, when our people realize they must change and cannot, and there won't be any release from the trap our present wizardry will have built for them."

"You only say this because the Lone One has said it to you," Seseil cried. "Power passed between you, just then. She has bought you!"

"Many will say that," Druvah said. "Only the day after forever will reveal the truth. So for now, if you want to enact the Choice we've made here, the wizardry that will protect our world, let's do so. But I will only power the wizardry if we add to it this stricture: that, come the day after forever, when the children of the children of a thousand millennia from now finally realize they need to change their world and themselves, our descendants in power will be able to repeal this Choice, this protection, and make another that suits them better."

"Never! We know what's best for them—"

"So parents always say of their children," Druvah said. "Sometimes they're even right. Nonetheless, if we make a Choice-wizardry today, or ever, this is how it's going to have to be. However, so that no such change of our whole world will be made lightly, let us add this to the stricture: The decision must be unanimous."

Kit saw Seseil smile then. Under his breath, the Alaalid said to one of the other wizards near him, "That will never happen. So let us do as he asks."

So the wizardry went forward. Kit watched it through to the end, watched the actual implementation of the massive working that was meant to keep this world safe from the Lone Power's malice forever. It shook the earth when it was done, and thundered against the sky, and rooted itself into Alaalu's star and into the fabric of all the space in Alaalu's system, right out to the heliopause. When it was over, all the wizards went away to their homes, well satisfied that they had made their world safe from the evils of the universe until their star should come naturally to the end of its life span and go cold. Only Druvah was left. He stood and watched his colleagues go, and finally turned his own back and walked off the way Ictanikë had gone.

Kit watched him go with a strange feeling. The silence that fell after that mighty working was deafening. In it, only the wind blew. Everything seemed finished, and Kit almost expected to look up into that piercingly blue sky and see hanging there the words THE END. But the way he felt, if there were going to be words written in the heavens, they could only be TO BE CONTINUED.

We need to get up out of this, Ponch said from beside Kit, panting. *It's over.*

They stepped up out of the pool. Kit had to struggle, gasping, up the last six or ten feet of the climb; and when they came out onto the surface, he looked down and found everything beneath them empty—just water. No wizards, no past.

I think maybe I broke it, Ponch said, apologetic.

"Oh, great," Kit muttered. "Well…never mind. We found out what we needed to. Let's get back and tell Nita. And then we have to talk to Quelt. We've got to do something. They've made a terrible mistake, and we have to help them somehow."

If they'll let us, Ponch said.

In Dairine Callahan's kitchen, hectic planning was in progress.

"This data source is useful," Prince Roshaun said, looking over Dairine's shoulder at Spot's rendition of the SOHO satellite's data feed. "But does it have history? If we're going to avoid collapsing your star, I need data for at least the past fifty years."

Dairine laughed weakly. "We've barely been in space that long," she said. "The satellite's only a few years old. For earlier data, you're going to need the manual."

"We'll use both," Roshaun said, running a finger down Spot's screen and bringing up an array of solar views and a great many complicated-looking charts and graphs. "We don't have a lot of time. Here, they have ultrasound data. And magnetographs. Good." He went quiet for a moment, studying the images. "The star's active side is pointing away from us right now. That buys us time..."

"But it won't stay that way forever," Filif said, looking over Roshaun's shoulder. "The star rotates..."

"What's the period?" Roshaun said to Dairine.

"Six hundred hours," Dairine said. "Just a little less, actually."

"And the spot that's starting to bubblestorm has gone around more than three quarters of the way already—" Roshaun was silent for a moment. Then he said, "We have perhaps nineteen hours before that particular crisis point rotates toward us again. And maybe twenty-six or twenty-eight hours before it boils over—"

He shook his head, looking at the data. "It's going to take nearly that long to design the wizardry," he said. "And then we have to go implant it."

"We have to *go* to the *Sun*??" Filif said.

The excitement in his voice was astonishing—and Dairine found it difficult to reconcile with the creature who had only hours earlier been emotionally shattered by the fact of a forest fire.

"We don't have much choice," Roshaun said. "We're just four wizards against a star that weighs, oh, nine hundred octillion tons or so. We'd need a lot more power than we've got to just sit here and throw the wizardry at it from a distance. It makes more sense to do the serious work up close."

Filif was trembling, and not with fear.

"Can you?" Roshaun said to him.

"Watch me!" Filif said.

Dairine shook her head. "Better show me where to get started, then," she said to Roshaun.

He looked at her with an expression she'd never seen on his face before: just the faintest glimmer of respect. At another time, this might have either annoyed her or pleased her, but right now Dairine found that she hardly cared one way or another.

They spent the next twelve hours and more constructing the wizardry—first the "rough" version, then the real one. Dairine had never been involved in such a detailed, exacting, exhausting piece of work in her life, not even when Nita had called her in to assist with a big group wizardry in Ireland. This time, there were many fewer wizards involved, and the work the four of them were doing was, in its way, far more complex.

Conceptually, it wasn't that much of a problem. "We have to go into the Sun," Roshaun said, "stick a conduit into it just underneath the tachocline—that's the layer just above the radiactive zone and just under the convective zone—pull out some mass, and then pull the shunt out and leave without burning ourselves to cinders."

"Oh, well," Sker'ret said, "nothing to it."

Roshaun and Dairine had found themselves giving Sker'ret the same somewhat skeptical look. Then each of them had registered the other one giving him that look...and things had, from Dairine's point of view, somehow, irrationally, gotten a lot better between them.

"Nothing to it" was more an expression of Sker'ret's natural ebullience than anything else. Simply having stated the problem itself produced a number of further problems. Dump the extracted solar material *where*, exactly? What was going to come out would emerge at a temperature of at least a couple of million degrees centigrade and would expand like mad before cooling down to ambient-space temperatures. "Expand like mad," Dairine thought, would be a mild description of the result. The associated explosive expansion would closely mimic that of any number of H-bombs, with only the pesky radiation left out. Additionally, the wizardry itself had to be capable of conducting the material and not failing under the forces to which it was exposed, which meant pushing a tremendous amount of energy into it to produce the result. That was Dairine's main concern, as she studied the problem with Roshaun and Sker'ret and Filif, and started building the response. *Where are we going to get that kind of power?* she thought. *Where in the worlds?*

And then, assuming they successfully built a wizardry that could handle these forces without withering away like straw in a fire, the *real* excitement would start... because not even a relatively small and tame star like the Sun, a G0 and nothing particularly exciting, was just going to lie there and let you suction out this much mass without complaining bitterly about it. The star would throw more CMEs—several of them at least—but this time the effect wouldn't be to breed further ones. It would be to leak off energy, the way small earthquakes prevent big ones. And after that, there would be quiet....

If everything worked.

Toward the end of the first part of their work session, Roshaun, who had been helping rough out the major spell diagram in the air above the spot where they would inscribe it for real, suddenly sat back on his heels, wiping his brow with the back of one hand and looking completely horrified.

"What's the matter?" Sker'ret said to him.

Roshaun sat looking at the rough spell diagram. "This is all for nothing," he said. "There's no way we can make this work."

He's seen it, Dairine thought. *I didn't want to say anything. I was hoping he was going to pull some kind of rabbit out of the hat. Oh, god, what are we going to do now?!*

"What do you mean?" Filif said.

"The problem is—" Roshaun looked around at the others. "The problem is power," he said. "It's one thing to design the conduit that's going to take the mass out of the heart of this star. But it's another thing to power it. There are just four of us. There's only so big a conduit we can drive to dump the mass at a safe enough distance. Unless we get a lot more wizards—"

"There's no time for that," Sker'ret said. "You said yourself, it's only a matter of hours now—!"

Dairine sat there, frowning silently at the diagram hanging in the air, as the others started to debate other ways of handling the problem, but the argument started to get desperate, for there were no other ways around the power problem. Wizardry was not a forgiving art: You got what you paid for, and you paid for results in effort, in power subtracted from your personal ecosystem . . . sometimes in terms of a deduction from your life span. When she had gone on her Ordeal, and for a little while after she passed it, Dairine's power levels had been such that she'd hardly ever bothered wondering whether she could "afford" a spell or not. *There was a time,* Dairine thought, *when I could've driven this spell entirely by myself. In fact, I did do a smaller version of this, once.* It infuriated her to think how easily, almost carelessly, she had once expended the kind of power that would be needed for a work like this. *It's true, what Roshaun said,* Dairine thought. *I was a star once, but I'm now having to deal with the limitations of not being a star anymore.*

The other three sat arguing while Dairine sat just staring at the rough spell diagram. *I guess there just comes a time,* she thought, *where you can't bully the universe anymore. You think you can. You assume that you'll be able to power your way through any problem that comes along. But sooner or later, the world asserts itself. That's when you have to start substituting cleverness for raw power. And it's really annoying, because raw power is more fun.*

Still...

Dairine stood up, smiling slightly. "Would you guys excuse me for a moment?" she said, and went down into the basement.

A few moments later, she came up with something in her hand. They all looked at her, confused. Dangling there from Dairine's fingers was one of the custom worldgates, a loose "hole" of blackness in the air.

"Er—aren't you supposed to leave that deployed onto a matter aggregate?" Sker'ret said, looking uneasy.

"You can remove it for short periods," Dairine said. "But this has other uses." She looked rather pointedly at Roshaun. "*Someone* here has some talent for reverse engineering when it suits him. And this, unlike any of us here, has no limit on how much matter it can move. It's subsidized!"

The look of embarrassment and annoyance that had started forming on Roshaun's face abruptly evaporated.

"So it is," he said. And, very slowly, Roshaun began to smile.

"The problem," Dairine said, "is going to be control, isn't it? You say that the amount of mass we have to remove from Sol is very specific. Whereas once you stick *this* into the middle of a star and open it up, it's going to throw matter out the far end like a fire hose... and what we need is the kind of control you get with a garden hose. Or an eyedropper..."

Roshaun looked at the wizardry. "Calibrating it," he said, "is going to be the exciting part."

"Taking it apart so that it *can* be calibrated, without sucking the whole area into deep space, or another dimension," Sker'ret said, "*that's* going to be the exciting part." He flexed his front fourteen or so legs. "Let me at it!"

"Just drop it there," Filif said, indicating the ground with a spare frond, "so that we can all get a good look at it. I can root it in one place and keep it from jumping around while you mobile types work on it."

Dairine dropped the worldgate to the ground off to one side of their spell diagram. Immediately a black hole opened there, one into which light fell and vanished. The other three wizards bent over the hole, intent. But Roshaun looked up at Dairine first, and the expression was hard to read. *Forgiving?* she thought. *Possibly apologetic? Maybe even a little more mellow than usual?*

I'll settle for the last, she thought. She got down on her knees along with the others and got to work.

The work that followed was complex beyond anything Dairine had ever done by herself. In fact, part of the complexity lay exactly in that she *wasn't* doing it herself, that she couldn't do it herself because she no longer had the power for that kind of thing. They all had to do it together, and without wasting time on disagreements. The Earth and the Sun were both rotating into a configuration that was going to be deadly enough without letting personalities get in the way.

As darkness fell, Roshaun laid out the outlines of

the full spell diagram—a glowing circle with four big lobes inscribed inside, like a four-leaf clover. *Be nice if it was lucky for us,* Dairine thought as she bent over the lobe that was her responsibility. For nearly half an hour now she had been referring back to Spot again and again as she laid in detailed information about the Sun's interior characteristics, tracing out the numbers and constants and technical terms in pale long curves of the cursive form of the Speech, lacing them into the spell structure. Spot had been quiet and had let her get on with it, hearing Dairine's tone of mind as she worked. It was not a time for cheery conversation.

Her back hurt; her eyes hurt from squinting at the more delicate parts of the spell. She wondered if she was possibly getting astigmatism, as Nita had had years back. *She grew out of that, though, and she doesn't need the glasses anymore. But if we live past tonight, I won't care if I need glasses...*

She swallowed, or tried to: Her throat was dry. *If we live past tonight.* Dairine didn't seem able to get past the thought, to her shame, while the others seemed a long way from worrying about it at all. The three of them were crouched over the spell diagram, all their concentration bent on it—Roshaun tracing glowing-spiderweb curve after curve of the wizardry's interface between the portable worldgate and the conduit that would suck the plasma into it, out of the Sun; Filif's branches all hung with faint delicate statements and syllogisms in the Speech, like luminous angel hair, as he shed them with precise control onto the "probe" part of the wizardry, which would slide into the Sun and find the right place to bleed it; Sker'ret knitting glittering cat's cradles of fire between his claws and weaving them into the spell's basic control structures, the shields that would keep them alive in that terribly hostile environment. *He's the real star here,* Dairine thought. *He's good at everything. Look at how good he is at troubleshooting—he can find a weak link in a spell just by the smell of it. If we live through this, it's going to be because of him—*

Dairine breathed out in annoyance at herself and shook the thought aside for the twentieth time. *What's the matter with me that I can't stop thinking about it? It wasn't like this on my Ordeal.*

Much . . .

But that seemed like such a long time ago now. And during a lot of her Ordeal, she had been running for her life. She hadn't had a lot of time for heavy thinking when she was on the run. It was when she stopped and tried to do something else, like a wizardry, that the thoughts caught up with her and came tumbling all over whatever she was trying to do. *Like now . . .*

She ground her teeth, a bad habit the dentist had warned her about, and then just got on with it. For quite some time, Dairine didn't look up, but kept her mind on the structure of the Sun, the pressures and stresses and temperatures. The numbers were so insane that here, kneeling on the damp ground on a cool spring night, it was almost impossible to believe in them. Temperatures in the millions or even billions of degrees, fluid gases denser than molten metal— *I should borrow Nita's sunblock. No, she took it to Alaalu, didn't she? Never mind...*

Dairine straightened up, her back immediately rewarding her with a spasm of pain. She rubbed it, looking around. Roshaun and Sker'ret were kneeling on opposite sides of the spell diagram, fine-tuning the wizardry's power equations. Filif was nowhere to be seen.

Took a rest break, probably, Dairine thought. *I could use one of those myself.* She stood up and stretched, turned her back on the spell diagram for the moment, and walked a little way toward the house.

—ashamed of myself—

She paused. "I don't see why," she heard her father say.

Dairine stood where she was in the shadow of the sassafras saplings just before the main part of the lawn. Maybe twenty feet away, over by the lilac hedge on the left side of the property, she could just see a shadow standing in the darkness, and another shadow, no longer hung with wizardly angel hair but faintly starred with lights. Dairine hadn't noticed before that Filif's berries actually glowed a little in the dark.

"After all," Dairine's dad was saying, "the fire you jump into isn't anything like the one you run away from."

It may burn you as badly...

"Maybe," her dad said. "But...I don't know. The quality of the pain's different when you're not running."

You do *know,* Filif said.

Her dad was silent. "Maybe I do," he said at last.

Yet that's how my people became sentient, they think, Filif said, and there was a desperate laughter about his thought. *They learned to run from the fire. They evolved mobility and, later, the beginnings of intelligence. And then the darkness at the Fire's heart spoke to us and said, "You can be safe from Me, if you pay the price. Instead of burning terribly, and dying in it, without warning and in awful pain... you'll burn just a little. But all the time, all your lives. At least you'll know what's coming, instead of having to always live with the unexpected..."*

"And you decided," Dairine's dad said, "that it was better to take your chances with the wildfires."

There was a rustle of branches, the sound Filif made when producing his people's equivalent of a nod. *Even though some of us said that we wouldn't be what we are without the Fire,* he said. *That without it, all growth chokes together, and chokes out the Light.* Dairine could just make out an uplift of branches toward the sky, all the berries going dim, from her angle, as they looked upward.

"Well, I think your people were smart," Dairine's dad said. "Light's better, in the long run... even though you may not always like what it shows you."

A few moments passed in silence. *You were kind to me when I was frightened,* Filif said.

"At a time like that, what else could I do?" Dairine's dad said. "You're my daughter's colleagues. And her friends. I may not be a wizard, but I've been scared in my time: I know how it feels. Any time you're feeling scared, you're welcome here."

Then I'm welcome now, Filif said, *because though where we're going is the source of the Light as well as the heart of the Fire, and it'd be all kinds of glory to die there, I'd really rather not.*

"I'd rather none of you did," Dairine's dad said. "And you're not going to. My daughter's a pretty hot property as a wizard, and she's not going to lose anybody on her watch."

The absolute certainty in his voice was somehow worse than anything Dairine could have imagined, and it made her eyes sting. Hastily, she stepped back into the shadows and turned her attention back where it belonged, to the spell.

I will make Dad right, she thought, *if it kills me...*

Subversive Factions

NITA STOOD ON THE BEACH, a few miles down from the house by the sea, and watched Alaalu's sun come up. It always seemed to take a long time, and today it seemed to be taking even longer than usual.

Something's missing, she thought.

When she'd first started to get this feeling, she'd discounted it. *That's how stressed out I've been,* she'd thought at the time. *They take me to an island paradise for a week, and already I'm dissatisfied with it, looking for some way to find fault. The problem's probably in my own head. I should kick back and relax, let everything be all right for a change. I've just gotten out of the habit of trusting the world.*

For a day or so, she'd talked herself into believing it. But this morning she knew that that was exactly what she had done. She had talked herself into believing, however temporarily, something that wasn't true. She had mistakenly, but purposely, deactivated one of a wizard's most useful tools: the hunch.

What her hunch told her—contradicting the whispering voices that spoke to her while she slept, the voices of the joyous but complacent—was that not everything was right here. That there was trouble in paradise. Not with the people. Not with the creatures living here. But something else, something much more basic.

Something's missing.

And in at least one case, she thought she knew what it was....

Worlds had hearts. This was information she had started to work with when her mother got sick. People, planets, even universes—all the places inhabited by mind, either on the small scale or the grand—had "kernels": hidden, bundled constructs of wizardry, of the fluid interface between science and magic, where matter and spirit and natural law got tangled together. The rules for a universe were written in its kernel, and the matter in a universe or a world ran by those rules, the way a computer runs by its software. The rules could be altered, but usually it wasn't smart to do so unless you really knew what you were doing.

Nita was still far too new at kernel studies to fall into this category. But she had a fairly good grasp of the basics, after working hard at the subject over recent months, and she'd learned a lot of the places and ways in which a world's kernel might routinely be hidden. When she'd first started to get the "something is missing" feeling, the state of Alaalu's kernel was one of the first things to occur to her. A lot of planets' kernels were hidden for good reasons—mostly so that they wouldn't be altered by those who had no right to do so. But that didn't normally keep a properly trained wizard from at least detecting that a kernel was indeed present. And Nita hadn't been able to confirm that by casual sensing... which was unusual.

Now she pulled out her manual and sat down in the sand with her back against a dune, twitching a little, and not from sand getting into her clothes. She felt slightly guilty about what she was doing. It wasn't as if Quelt wasn't taking really good care of her world, as far as Nita could tell. And normally you didn't start investigating another wizard's environment or practice of the Art unless you'd been asked to; "no intervention without a contract" was the usual order of business. *But we're here to see how this world works, among other things,* Nita thought, *and when I notice something as weird as this, what am I supposed to do? Ignore it? A world's kernel shouldn't be separated from it without good reason. There are too many things that could go wrong.*

Maybe even things that have gone wrong already—

Nita let out a long breath and paged through the manual, bringing up the custom kernel-detection routines she had started designing over the past few months. She'd come to be able to sense a kernel directly, if it was anywhere at all nearby—usually within some thousands of miles; and if she did a wizardry to augment her internal sensing abilities, her range increased greatly. To save time, Nita had started to file away the spells she used for this purpose, hooking them into a matrix that kept them ready to fuel and turn loose. Now all she had to do for routine kernel-finding was plug in the details about a planet's or space's physical characteristics, and turn the spell loose.

Nita came to the pages in her manual where she kept the routines stored, and once again she looked guiltily up and down the beach. But there was no sign of Quelt, nor did Nita really expect there to be—the whole family was extremely thoughtful about one another's privacy, and their guests'. *But if you're so concerned that something's wrong here,* Nita's uneasy conscience said to her, *why don't you just take the problem straight to Quelt?*

Nita sat thinking about that for some moments, and finally shook her head. *Because I really think something's wrong here. Because I'm not sure she'll see it the same way I do... or maybe even see it at all. Because—*

Just because. I don't really know why. But I have to look into this. It was, finally, just a hunch. Tom and Carl had told her often enough to trust them....

She laid the manual open next to her on the golden sand and started to read. The wizardry wasn't a showy one, and wouldn't manifest its results outside of her manual, but it was complex, taking several minutes to read straight through. It seemed to take forever for the listening silence to give way to the normal sounds of day with the spell's completion, and when it finally did, Nita had to slump back against the dune and just gasp for breath for some minutes more. The wizardry was not a cheap one to enact.

It was maybe fifteen or twenty minutes more before she felt up to actually starting to use the running spell to look for Alaalu's kernel. After that she lost track of time, something she found herself doing with great ease here where the day was thirty percent longer than at home. When she finally closed the spell down and shut the manual, it had to be at least a few hours later, to judge by the sun's position.

Nita sat there a while more just listening to the water slide in and out, to the occasional songbird twitter of the bat-creatures that soared and swooped over the sea. *It's just nowhere here,* she thought. *Nowhere in the ground or in the sea, not even anywhere inside the planet's orbit. Not even for a hundred million miles outside.*

Where have they put it? And why isn't it closer? What's going on?

Above her Nita heard the faint scratching sound of someone coming down the dune toward her. She looked up over her shoulder and saw the twin silhouettes of Kit and Ponch sliding down the dune, cutouts against the bright sky.

"I was looking for you back at the house," Kit said. "Demair was there, but she said no one had seen you all day."

"I skipped breakfast," Nita said.

"Did you sleep okay last night?" Kit said to her.

Nita shook her head. "No."

"Dreams again?"

"Partly. But I was thinking," she said. Kit sat down beside her with his back against the dune, and Nita told him what she'd been thinking about.

At the end of it, she looked at Kit and said, "Does that make any sense to you?"

Kit nodded. "More than you'd think. I was doing a little exploring this morning..."

He told her where he'd been. Nita's eyes widened as Kit told her about the conversation he'd overheard, with Ponch's help, between Druvah and the Lone Power. When he finished, Nita looked down at the sand and started digging in it idly with one hand.

"What I don't like," Nita said, "is that what for us is the most interesting part of the Choice, and the weirdest part, almost didn't seem to matter to Quelt at all. She just skipped past it..."

"And we took her at her word that it was just a boring part."

"A cultural blind spot maybe?" Nita said.

Kit shook his head. "I don't know. But I think that now we're going to have to go see the Relegate's Naos."

Kit stood up. As he did, Ponch came running up the dune behind him.

Are we going somewhere?

Kit reached down and roughed up Ponch's ears a little. "Yeah," he said. "To see the Lone Power. Come on..."

They stood there on the edge of the valley and looked down into it. The valley itself was huge. Looking across it, Nita wondered if this spot had indeed been one of the impact craters she'd been expecting to see, for it was like a gigantic bowl, and it had its own mini-horizon inside the greater one, where the snowy mountains of the Tamins range could be seen off to the north and east. Away down in the middle of the great round valley, Nita could just see something small and pale: a little building. There was nothing else to be seen, for what looked like miles and miles, except flowery meadows, some scattered patches of woodland, and occasional flocks of *ceiff*, ambling from place to place or taking flight without warning.

"That's it?" Kit said.

Nita nodded. "It's probably a lot bigger than it looks from here," she said. "The distances keep fooling me."

"We can do a quick transit spell over to it," Kit said.

Nita nodded, and Kit constructed the spell and spoke it. The hush of the universe listening to the words leaned in around them; they vanished, and the soft *bang!* of the air rushing away from them as they reappeared reached them before the more distant *bang!* of their disappearance.

The Naos was a simple structure done mostly in the peach-colored sandstone that the Alaalids favored. Nine tall columns upheld a round dome that glittered in the sunlight as if polished slick; inside the dome was another, smaller structure, constructed of screens of the same stone, intricately carved and pierced. Pointing toward each of the directions of the Alaalid compass were six broad sets of steps, running down to the surrounding greensward from the main pedestal-level on which the columns stood. The whole structure gave an impression of elegant and airy lightness, at least as far as architecture was concerned. To Nita, it suggested an extremely beautiful trap.

They walked slowly toward one of the flights of steps and paused there. Ponch looked at it, wandered over to the side of the steps, lifted a back leg, and made a liquid comment.

Are you ready for this? Kit said silently.

Nita nodded. She had ready a set of wizardries that had been effective enough against the Lone Power in other times, and she had some newer defenses, not yet tried, that might work even better if it turned out she needed them. *Let's go,* she said.

They walked up the stairs slowly, in step, in the hot sunlight—she and Kit, with Ponch between them. Nita felt a little grim amusement: The only thing missing from the present scenario was the jingling of spurs, and someone whistling menacingly off in the distance. At the top of the stairs they stopped, looking through the columns toward the curved, pierced stonework shell inside. That was the *naos* proper, the center of the structure. It wasn't precisely dark in there, but by comparison with the bright day outside, it seemed shadowy enough. Right in front of them, the stonework was interrupted by a wide doorway that led into the interior.

Kit and Nita glanced at each other, walked toward that opening. Inside, it wasn't as dark as it had seemed on first glance. For one thing, the dome that topped off the building wasn't solid stone, or if it was, it wasn't any thicker than half an inch or so—like the thickness of an eggshell compared to its size. Sunlight filtered through it in a soft, vague shimmer of pink, gold, cream, and white, all mingled together. That light fell on something inside, a structure all by itself in the center of the *naos,* which was circular like the pedestal and columns that contained it. It was another pedestal, of only three great, broad, shallow, concentric steps, with six long, curved, stone benches arranged around it. On the pedestal sat a huge blocky chair, exceedingly simple, made of blocks of squared-off and polished creamy stone—a back slab, two side slabs, and a horizontal slab between them. *It's kind of like the one in the Lincoln Memorial,* Nita thought. *Except—*

—except that sitting with her legs curled up under her in that great chair, and leaning on one arm of it, with her chin in her hand, looking at them with an expression of ineffable boredom, was an Alaalid woman of staggering beauty. Mahogany-skinned, she wore a loose white sleeveless tunic over a long, loose white skirt. She had a long and perfect face, striking red-and-gold-streaked hair that tumbled down around her on all sides, and eyes that shone like orange amber with the sun behind it.

Kit and Nita came to a standstill and simply looked at her for a moment. Ponch, between them, regarded the woman sitting in the chair, and let out one long, low growl. Then, rather to Nita's surprise, he fell silent and sat down.

Nita looked at Ponch hurriedly to see what was the matter... if the Lone One was doing anything to him. But Ponch was simply looking at It, with his head tilted slightly to one side and a thoughtful expression on his face.

"Fairest and Fallen...," Kit said.

"Yes, yes, greeting and defiance, thank you very

much. I really wish you people would come up with something *else* to say," the Lone Power said. Her voice was as beautiful as her face, but it had an edge to it.

Nita stood there, wondering what in the world to say next. "So nice of you to drop by," the Lone One said. "You're a nice change from the school groups and the mothers with bored toddlers. But don't just stand there glaring at me," Esemeli said, and she waved a languid hand at the bench nearest to where they were standing. "Go on, sit down. That's what they're there for. I'm a tourist attraction."

Nita glanced at Kit and then sat down.

"Do a lot of people come and visit you here?" Kit said, sitting down beside Nita.

"Not that many," the Lone Power said, leaning on one elbow. "Of those who do, most think I'm some kind of live entertainment meant to follow that little multimedia show they've got in the valley. A few of them...a very few...realize what I really am, and have the sense to be scared. But most of them never make it past vague interest. It's been too long since they've had any *real* trouble in this world."

"I can see how that would bother you," Kit said.

The Lone Power's smile was slow and grim. Nita had to shiver at it, for she had never seen a look of such malice on any Alaalid face. "Well, I do try to keep my sense of proportion about me," It said. "Earth, for example; there've been some changes there."

"Tell us about it," Kit said. "But I wouldn't call them changes for the better."

"There speaks a typical, shortsighted human

being," the Lone Power said. "Things always get a lot worse before they get better. You'd know that if you took the long view of the worlds. But you can't help yourselves; you're stuck in time. Those of us who just visit Time but live in Eternity see things a lot differently." It sighed and sat back in Its chair. "Look, can we put that aside for the moment?"

"Sure," Nita said, "as long as it's to tell us exactly what you're doing here."

"I'm doing what I don't have any choice but to do!" It said. "Which is to sit around in the Relegate's Naos. I'm the Relegate! I've been relegated. Left over, dumped, thrown out of the running. Into *this*." It waved a hand around at the beautiful warm stone, the polished floor, the exquisite, shell-like dome.

Nita looked over at Kit. Ponch yawned and lay down on the floor.

The Lone One gave him an exquisitely dirty look. "See that?" It said. "That's the kind of respect I command these days. Nine-tenths of the people here don't even begin to understand the import of the events that left me sitting here. They've even given me a sweet little name: Esemeli, the Daughter of the Daughter of Light." She made a face.

"Well, you *were*, once," Nita said.

"Don't patronize me. I was the Star of the Morning!" the Lone Power shouted. "I was a Power among Powers. I was what quasars are a watered-down version of; the light of me denatured *space* when I had cause to turn it loose! 'Daughter of the daughter of...'" She made an annoyed gesture and muttered off into silence.

"And now it comes to this," Esemeli said after a moment, "that you two come along and I have to ask you to—" She rubbed her face with one hand.

Nita and Kit waited, but nothing further seemed to be forthcoming. Finally, Nita said, "You have to ask us to what?"

"You know what's wrong here," It said. "Something's missing. They made it impossible for themselves to achieve it. But they're not a whole species without it... not really." She smiled. "And the funny thing is, I even warned them of what they were doing. But none of them believed me. Well, maybe one." Esemeli's expression darkened. Then the look passed. "But they froze their species' nature in place when they made their Choice; they walled it away from any possible assault. Either from me or from other sources."

Meaning good ones, Nita thought.

"And you can't do anything to them, either."

"I couldn't do anything to them a hundred thousand years ago," It said, just barely annoyed. "You saw it! They made their Choice and rejected me in about fifteen minutes. It happens... but I don't often get invited to stick around afterward. I saw what they did to themselves... or failed to do. Afterward, I couldn't do anything but sit here and wait for help to arrive. And you're finally here. You took long enough, by the way. Can we get on with this?"

They looked at each other. "Before we ask you what we should get on with," Kit said, "tell us why we should believe anything you say! After everything we've been through with you—"

"Atomic explosions," Nita said. "Stars going nova or snuffed out. Being chased all over two different Manhattans by you and your homemade monsters!"

"Nearly being eaten by sharks," Kit said. "Losing Nita's *mom.*"

The Lone Power actually looked bored, and waved one hand in a *Spare-me* gesture. "You've been through all that," It said. "I admit it. But not with *me.* Listen." It sounded more annoyed as It saw the glance Kit threw Nita. "Why are you going to give me trouble about this? It's not just in your world that there have been changes. *I've* had my share of them. Huge ones... which you were deeply involved in, you and your sister. How is she, by the way?"

"Grounded," Nita said. "You should count yourself lucky. Otherwise, she'd be here instead of us, and she'd have fried you to a crisp already, just on general principles."

"No, I doubt that," the Lone One said. "For one thing, she's well off her peak power by now, and dealing with all kinds of trouble secondary to that. For another thing, she wouldn't have been sent *here.* She wouldn't have been the beginning of the answer to the Alaalids' problem. Whereas you two are... unfortunately for me. They *would* send me someone with whom I have so much history." It looked disgusted. "Just common pettiness, that's all it is with Them..."

Nita threw Kit a glance.

The Lone One sat there for a moment, drumming Its fingers on the arm of Its severely plain throne. "*You* know how the shift in me happened, a while ago," the

Lone One said. "You two and Dairine were simply party to a change of nature that the Powers That Be and just about all of creation had been pushing on me for aeons...slowly wearing me down until the last big push came. You just happened to be part of the breakthrough, part of the point of the spear. Because you live in Time, it looks to you like that was a thing that happened *then* and was over with, whereas *outside* of Time, the event both happened aeons ago and is still happening."

It gave them a look, seeing their expressions. "Sorry, even the Speech doesn't have some of the syntax needed to talk about this kind of thing. Or it does, but since you're still stuck inside Time, you can't parse it...Anyway, I *did* tell you at the time that there would be shadows of me around for a long, long while, doing what they've always done. That's part of the nature of time in physical universes; it helps things persist." The Lone One looked resigned. "We shadows all partake of the nature of the Power that casts us, but in different degrees, according to the local 'lighting.' Some are 'darker,' more aggressive than others...fighting the final realization of the shift, trying to make it take as long as possible." It smiled slightly. "The one that went after your mother, for example: That one was pretty proactive, or maybe I should say abreactive. Others have been less effective."

"Like the one of you who came after our buddy Darryl a few months ago," Kit said.

The Lone One waved Its hand again, looking annoyed this time. "When it comes right down to it, there's not a lot you can do to someone like that, a creature the One's using as a direct power conduit," It said. "They tend to be too contaminated with innocence, anyway. Assaulting them is like beating your head against the wall. I'd have thought that fragment of myself would have been smarter to cut its losses and go after an easier target." It laughed a little breath of laughter. "Small loss. That's not my problem."

"No," Kit said. "Your problem is that you're stuck here."

The Lone One looked more annoyed than before. "Yes," It said, "you would notice that. And doubtless it's going to amuse you all out of proportion that I'm going to ask for your help in getting out of here."

Nita's eyes widened. "Oh, sure," she said, "we turn you loose and you go manifest on some *other* planet and make their lives miserable..."

Esemeli gave Nita a look that suggested she needed her brain augmented. "I'm already everywhere," the Lone One said. "I don't have to 'go' anyplace. What you need to get through your heads is that *this* particular manifestation has had its turn to do its job, and has failed. I offered the Alaalids their Choice, and they turned me down. And that was that."

There's a little more to it than that, Neets! Kit said silently.

I believe you. But don't interrupt It! It's on a roll; It might drop something useful...

"I mean, look around you!" the Lone One said. "Does this look like a place where I've been particularly successful?"

It actually sounded aggrieved, which could have

made Nita burst out laughing had she not had the creeps about this whole situation. "And then," the Lone Power said, "to add insult to injury, when they realized I was stuck here, they built me this place so I'd have somewhere to stay! They felt *sorry* for me."

For just a moment Its eyes held a hint of the kind of balked fury that Nita was used to seeing in the Lone Power. This faded, but what it faded into was a glint of nasty amusement that, though much less intense than the first expression, still looked natural on Its face. "The joke, though, is that the Alaalids missed something when they made their Choice," It said. "What's even funnier is that they brought it on themselves. And you noticed it, didn't you?"

It looked at Nita. "Yeah," she said after a moment. "I spent some time feeling around for this world's kernel, its heart. And I can't find it. It's been hidden a lot more securely than they usually are...and besides, there's something else that's not right about it. Something's missing."

"You *are* smart for a mortal sometimes," the Lone One said. "It's a real pity you won't see things my way: We could do well together." Nita bristled. "Well, it doesn't matter. I offered the Alaalids eternal life, as usual. Unfortunately, they were smart enough not to buy into that one." Esemeli glanced briefly upward in annoyance. "And they realized that since they were physical beings, they were going to need time to move through, as well. So they also didn't make the mistake of trying to shut entropy out of their world-system entirely. A shame...I've had endless fun with the species that've tried that approach. Literally endless." The Lone One smiled. Nita shivered. "But then they tried to do an end run around me, instead. They worked a wizardry on their world's kernel, the purpose being to freeze or lock down the other, lesser side effects of entropy, besides mere timeflow, everywhere in this whole pocket of space-time. And you can't do that."

"Why not?"

"Because one of those lesser side effects, on the macrocosmic level, is *change*," the Lone One said. "They didn't foresee the consequences to themselves. Did I say, 'You *can't* do that'? I meant, you *can*, but it's stupid. And after they set that wizardry into their kernel, it was too late for them to do anything about it. There's some room for small, personal change...just. But as for the big changes that every species needs to go through every now and then, to avoid stagnating and just dying away—those are all shut away from them. They can't *evolve*. And you've seen what their world's become as a result! It hardly even counts as a world anymore. It's a theme park. They've turned it into 'Nice Land.'"

Kit gave the Lone One a dry look. "You wouldn't have a lot of time for 'nice,' of course. So forgive me if I think your opinion's a little biased."

It gave Kit an annoyed look. "All right, so I'm ambivalent," the Lone One said. "But isn't ambivalence preferable to pure evil?"

Kit considered that one for a moment. "See? You're buying it already," the Lone One said. "I was getting bored with absolute evil, anyway. I find that you can do a lot more damage with ambivalence…and it's not as easily detectable from a distance, not anywhere near as memorable. Pure evil sticks out the way pure *anything* sticks out in a world full of mixtures and mélanges and shades of gray. Ambivalence can be discounted, or explained away, or mistaken for confusion or a mind not completely made up yet."

"Sometimes it really is…," Kit said.

"Oh, sure. But how often? The rest of the time, in humans, it's usually more about the *refusal* to make a choice. People are eager to excuse it, though. Ambivalence is seen as a sign of maturity, whereas actually taking a stance on one side or another is easy to describe as simplistic…or juvenile." It smiled that nasty, sarcastic smile again.

Nita looked at It and asked herself, as she had been doing about once every ten seconds during this conversation, how likely the Lone One was to be telling the truth at any given moment. *Yet it really did go through some kind of transformation at the end of Dairine's Ordeal,* she thought. *Other Powers told us It has the chance to be otherwise now. "I'm getting bored with absolute evil"—could that be the beginning of a change?*

Whether it is or not, it's still important to be careful!

"Let me get this straight," Nita said, "You're telling us that in some ways, entropy would have been at the root of that big species-wide change. And when they froze it, or locked it down, they locked you *in.*"

Esemeli looked at Nita with those ironic golden eyes and smiled. Nita shivered again. "The point is," It said after a moment, "these people don't need to be physical anymore. They've passed all the tests and dealt with all the issues that rise out of the life that spirit lives when trapped inside matter." The Lone Power made little whoop-de-do circles in the air with one shapely finger. "In fact, they passed them quite a long time ago. So they've long been ready for the next thing... whatever that turns out to mean for *them*. But they're as locked in now as I am. Alaalu needs to be made unsafe again. Once that happens, they can move on."

"To what?"

"How should I know?" the Lone One said, Its tone suddenly shifting enough so that she sounded grumpy. "With what they did to local space-time, I can't look far enough ahead to see any more."

"You did see *once*, though," Kit said.

"That was before they set their Choice in stone," It said. "They would have evolved, and become glorious and wise and powerful and all the rest of it, blah, blah, blah." It waved one hand in annoyance. "And now, who knows what'll happen, after they've kept themselves from their destiny for so long? But *nothing's* going to happen if they don't take the kiddie gate off this part of space-time and give themselves a chance to fall down stairs like any other species."

"They're not going to do that," Kit said.

"You're a veritable fount of observation," the Lone Power said.

Its tone is really starting to annoy me, Kit said silently to Nita. *You know what's weird? It bothers me less when It's a guy.*

Hah. At least It's just sitting there. Would you rather have It insulting you or trying to blow you up?

Ask me again when we leave. Assuming that we do...

"So what are we supposed to do about all this?" Nita said.

"Unlock the kiddie gate," said the Lone One. "Find a way to break the wizardry on the kernel. Let them out."

"Which will also let *you* out."

It looked demure. "An unavoidable side effect."

Nita sighed and got up. As she passed him, Ponch rolled over and lay looking at the Lone Power upside down, further increasing the surreal quality of the entire encounter, from Nita's point of view. "Look," she said. "before we agree to help *you*, of all beings, with anything, we need to have some questions answered, even if it upsets you. We're still not entirely clear about what happened with you a while back, at the end of Dairine's Ordeal. We know what it looked like, and felt like..."

It *tsk*ed at her. "And a wizard is supposed to trust her feelings..."

"Not without taking a look at them occasionally to see how they measure up against reality," Kit said.

"It looked like you," Nita said, "were thinking about turning over a new leaf. Giving up being the force behind evil in the worlds."

The Lone One said nothing, just nodded slightly. Its expression was unreadable.

"It also looked like the other Powers That Be...and the One...were actually willing to take you back," Kit said.

"You were there," It said.

Nita and Kit looked thoughtfully at It for a few moments. "Even though we were," Nita said, "sometimes it's hard to believe what seemed to have happened... especially when we keep running into other versions of you who don't seem to have heard the word yet."

"We've been over that."

"And it would be easy to believe that it was all an illusion of some kind," Kit said. "I mean, lots of people might never believe that you could ever be forgiven for what you've been... what you've done."

"That could be so," the Lone One said softly. "As there might also be those who've become a little smug, over time, about their own redemptions... enough so that they'd feel comfortable dictating to the One their own minuscule ideas about who else ought to qualify for forgiveness." It laughed, a suddenly bitter sound. "And it's a fool's game, because there is *no* sounding the One, no grasping It." It looked, and sounded, angry, and scornful, and a little haunted... even disturbed. "All we can be sure of is that, whether we like it or not, the One means us all well, more so than we can ever comprehend. And the details of that meaning are sometimes going to be impossible for any created being to fathom... even the Powers That Be." It leaned back in Its throne and scowled. "It has no taste, no discrimination... that's what's so infuriating," the Lone Power muttered under Its breath. "It'll redeem just *anybody*..."

"Even you? Well, whatever," Nita said. "But you can still understand why we'd have trouble trusting you. Me, in particular."

Esemeli sighed and looked at Nita with those lazy, thoughtful eyes. The uncomfortable moment had sealed itself right over again, leaving Nita feeling both sorry for this particular version of the Lone One and still rather cautious. "Yes, well," It said. "If you're so enlightened, being a wizard and all, you'll get past it, and get on with the work at hand, won't you?"

The mockery was almost a relief after Its unsettled tone of a few moments before. "Well, I'm not sure exactly what we're supposed to do," Kit said.

"I have an idea," Nita said. "But I'm not sure I like it. We're going to need to investigate the species' Choice more closely."

"The only way you're going to do that now," the Lone One said, smiling slightly, "is to find Druvah."

"As if he's around here somewhere," Kit said, annoyed.

"Oh, he is," Esemeli said. "Somewhere..."

Nita thought again of the incessant good-natured whispering in the air: the whispers of the "dead."

"So we have to find him, is that it?" Nita said. "And then we have to find the planet's kernel? And after that, since this is Quelt's world, not ours, we're going to have to tell her what's wrong here, and get her in on fixing it. Thereby turning *you* loose..." Nita looked over at Esemeli.

"Once this world is set free to pursue its proper course," the Lone One said, "there won't be any need for me to hang around here anymore, I assure you."

Nita didn't quite glance at Kit, but she knew what he was thinking: The Lone One's assurances weren't necessarily something they were going to feel comfortable depending on. "And what exactly is going to happen when the world *is* set free?"

"Well, there are a lot of different ways that can go…"

Nita gave It a stern look. "Really? Then you'd better start listing them."

It laughed at her then, and there again was that old, malicious humor that was almost a relief to hear. "Why should I do your work for you?" the Lone Power said. "You should be grateful that I've consented to give you even this little interview. It's more than the other Powers would do. They leave you with hints and riddles, and make you work everything out for yourselves."

Which, considering who we're dealing with, may be the best way to proceed, Nita thought, grimacing slightly to herself. "Kit," she said then, "I don't know about you, but I'm enjoying this vacation. I think this planet is just fine the way it is, and I don't see why we should waste any more of our time playing Twenty Questions in a deserted bandstand with a Power That Has Been! I'm gonna go lie on the beach for a while, and after that I'm gonna go back home and get on with my life."

She turned to go, but not before catching just a glimpse of the expression on Esemeli's face as It became suddenly alarmed. "Yeah," Kit said, sounding infinitely bored. "Let's go. C'mon, Ponch. Bye," he said to the Lone Power, waving, and turned to follow Nita toward the entry.

The silence stretched and stretched as they went across the polished white floor. Nita didn't turn her head, just looked at Kit out of the corner of her eye. She could just see him looking back at her, sidelong.

They'd actually made it to the third step down from the top of the plinth when the Lone One shouted after them, *"Wait!"*

Both of them paused, turned.

Esemeli was off Its throne and hurrying toward them. "You can*not* leave me here like this!" It said.

"Watch us," Kit said. He turned again.

"No, *wait*!!"

They both stood there and watched the Lone One come out into the sunlight. It winced at it a little, but then it *was* bright after the shadows of the Naos. "Forget everything else," It said. "Do you have any idea what it's been *like* for me, being trapped here?" And It actually waved Its arms around in the air in frustration. "The eternal boredom of it, here in the land of flying sheep and sweet-tempered people? I may exist mostly outside of Time, in the depths of eternity, but what happens here echoes there, and do you think I don't *experience* what this is like? *Tedium!* The whole planet's a playpen! There are no storms, there are no floods, no earthquakes, no disasters— Even eavesdropping on the dark sides of these people's hearts isn't any fun. They hardly *have* any dark sides! The most they manage is the spiritual equivalent of sitting in the shade! They don't know how to hate each other. They're not greedy, they're not envious, they don't get sick, they don't die in pain! They're not even *accident-prone*—there's not so much as even a stubbed *toe* to enjoy some days!

Damn eternally graceful, temperate, loving, goody-goody—"

For the first time, Nita saw an old idiom come true, as the Lone Power began to curse and around It the shocked air literally turned blue with a haze of locally annihilated water atoms and oxygen broken down to ozone. Nita waved a hand in front of her face, rolling her eyes at the stink. When It ran out of curses, which took a while, It glared at Nita and Kit and got ready to turn some of that anger on them—until It noticed their frowns and the slight in-unison body movement that suggested they were getting ready to turn their backs on it again. Then It dropped the anger and just got desperate. "Just help me get out of here!" It said. "I'll tell you whatever you want to know about what to do—"

"Yeah, sure," Kit said.

"I'll do anything you like—"

"Hah! We're supposed to take your word for that?"

"—promise you anything you like—"

"Promises!" Nita said, and sniffed. "I've heard it all before."

"There's no promise you wouldn't break," Kit said, bored and scornful. "No oath you could take—"

"Well," Nita said softly, "actually, there's *one*..."

The Lone One suddenly looked even more alarmed than It had before.

Kit threw Nita a concerned glance. "What? Are you sure?"

"We've heard It get wizards to swear this particular oath before, in shorter versions," Nita said. "It's at the very center of wizardry, embodied in all the Enactive modes of the Speech. Not even one of the Powers That Be would dare break it: They're held by the stricture, whether They're renegade or not. It's at the root of creation. Even the Wizard's Oath is derived from it."

The Lone Power's expression was becoming more than merely alarmed: It looked suspicious. "Where have you been getting information like that?" Esemeli said.

Nita's smile was grim. "You made me do a lot of research when my mother got sick," Nita said. "A *whole* lot of reading in the manual. Do you think that after she was gone, I just gave that up? And since I started really working on it, I've been getting access to all kinds of information I didn't know was there before. You have no *idea* what trouble you've made for yourself."

There was a brief silence.

"So swear," Nita said. "Come on, it's not so hard. And I can only do this once: It's not like you're ever going to have to repeat yourself on my account. 'I swear by the One to perform what I promise—'"

The Lone Power looked at her, stony-faced, silent. "You know," It said after a few moments, "what you're likely to be bringing down on yourself, at some later date, by *making* me do something—"

Nita folded her arms and looked at the Lone One. "Threats are a bad start for what's going to happen now…"

Esemeli glared at her.

"Won't swear, huh?" Nita said. "No, I didn't think so. You've just been yanking our chain this whole time." She looked over at Kit. "I guess it's true," she said, with a sigh. "Evil can't change. Or else," she said, looking back at Esemeli, "you're even more stuck than you say you are, you poor thing. Never mind. You just have a nice time sitting here in the shade for another aeon or three!"

She turned her back and started down the stairs again. Kit shrugged helplessly at the Lone Power, and turned to go after Nita.

"Wait!"

Nita didn't stop.

"I'll swear!"

Nita went down a couple more steps, a little more slowly, and then stopped and looked over her shoulder.

"Let's hear it, then," she said. "And don't leave anything out."

"I swear by the One," Esemeli said, standing there in the sun and casting a longer and blacker shadow every moment, "to perform what I promise—"

"Fully and without any reservation," Nita said, "nor with any mechanism or execution founded in the intention to deceive; to fully inform the wizards of all manner of things of which they inquire; to carry out this information at a speed and in a way best suited to these wizards' desires and the achievement of their ends; and at the end of said achievement, to depart without doing any harm to them or any thing or person affiliated with them in whatever degree, and when the conditions of this swearing are discharged and acknowledged to have been discharged, to go peaceably again into my own place. And all this, by the Power of that One in Which all oaths and all intentions rest,

inviting It on my abroachment of this Oath to withdraw the gifts It allows me to enjoy, I swear—"

Phrase by phrase, scowling more and more blackly
with every word, the Lone One recited the Binding
Oath. It got as far as "any thing or person affiliated
with them in whatever degree," and then stopped, glaring at them, while its shadow boiled with half-seen
nightmare shapes of fury. "Oh, come on, that could be
construed as meaning your whole *universe!*" It said.

Nita ignored Its shadow, kept her eyes on Esemeli's
face. "So it could," Nita said. "And if you cooperate
with us, there won't be any need to take you to arbitra-
tion over it."

"Assuming you survive that long," the Lone One
said, grinding Its teeth.

"Anything can happen," Nita said. "And if you start
trying to sabotage us after you've sworn this Oath, I
wouldn't make any bets on *your* longevity, either. You
know what that last clause means. The only reason
you're here is because the One hasn't yet seen fit to
abolish you by withdrawing the energy It gave you at
the very beginning of things. If you break this Oath—"
Then she grinned. "Nah. You're infinitely destructive
but you're not actively *dumb.* Come on, just get it over
with! Stalling isn't going to help you."

Esemeli grimaced, and then started reciting again.
When the Oath was finished, Nita nodded and said,
"All right. That wasn't so bad, was it?"

The Lone One said nothing.

"Never mind," Nita said. "Kit?"

"Right," Kit said. "First question: Where is Druvah?"

"I don't know."

Kit gave Esemeli a skeptical look.

"I mean it," Esemeli said. "He used the energy I gave him to change his way of being. After the Choice, he bound himself into the world physically. Finding him is going to require making some preparations."

"Then make them," Nita said. "I want to hear all about them, of course, when they've been made, before we actually go looking. But don't take too long. We're only here for another week or so, and after we get this sorted out, I want lots of time on the beach to relax with Quelt."

The Lone One nodded in a surly way. "You'll hear from me tomorrow dawn," It said, then turned and slowly went back up the steps into the Naos, vanishing into the shadows.

Kit and Nita went down the stairs again, with Ponch following after, wagging his tail. At the bottom of the stairs, they paused briefly as Ponch hurled himself off into the flowery fields, jumping at the occasional furbat that flapped up, startled, out of the *jijis* flowers.

"Weren't you a little mean to It?" Kit said under his breath as they went after Ponch.

"After a whole week on the Planet of Nice," Nita said, equally softly, "and come to think of it, a week without Dairine, I kind of wanted an excuse to get cranky about something." She smiled slightly.

"Do you trust It?"

"Now? After It swore the Binding Oath? Sure." She glanced at Kit out of the corner of her eye. "About ninety percent. I wouldn't put it past Esemeli to keep trying to find a way out of what I made It swear. But at least the odds are on our side. And we've got to find out the truth about what's going on around here. Druvah is definitely still here ... and he'll be able to tell us."

They walked on a little ways.

"So this turns out to be errantry after all," Kit said.

Nita nodded. "Just not formally declared, nothing that the Powers officially sent us on."

Kit shook his head. "But why not?" he said. "Why didn't they just send us here and say, 'There's something wrong with this planet and we need you to fix it'?"

"Or," Nita said, "why didn't They just get in touch with Quelt and tell *her* what the problem was?" She picked up a small rock and threw it off into the flowers. One flower moved slightly in a sea of them as the rock came down, and then everything was still once more.

She and Kit sighed more or less in unison. No answers were going to be forthcoming. They were just going to have to get on with it.

"It's like Rhiow said, a while ago," Nita muttered. The little black cat who was head of the New York gating team had been describing a pleasure trip when she'd routed outward through the Crossings and had wound up spending days there, helping them repair a recalcitrant worldgate. "Wizard's holiday ..."

Kit grinned. The phrase meant a vacation or pleasure trip that rapidly turned into something else, usually involving errantry, but was still pleasant in a strange way, simply because of the change. "I don't know why the Powers let us think we're ever going to get a real vacation," Kit said.

"Maybe They don't get any, either," Nita said, "and They think the situation's normal."

"If you're right," Kit said, "I feel sorry for Them."

"So do I," Nita said, "if I'm right. Meanwhile…"

"Back to the house by the sea."

"It'll work," Roshaun said.

In the darkness, they all knelt (or in Filif's case, rooted) above the wizardry together. It lay glowing on the ground under the sassafras trees, now almost completely interwritten with the long, delicately curling characters of the Speech.

"You're sure?" Sker'ret said.

Roshaun nodded. "The final layout confirms it. Suck the matter out from underneath the tachocline, and you get a brief but big shift in the way the Sun handles its magnetic fields—for the tachocline is the dynamo for the star's whole field. When you pull the matter out, the tachocline collapses back just a little and cools. The magnetic field drops off, and you get an artificial 'quiet star' period. All the other 'inflamed' areas have a chance to quiet down as a result. If you're very careful with the calculations, you can get as much as a month of quiet time and derail the cycle entirely."

He looked down at the wizardry and sighed.

"The big problem remains, though. We must *put* the far end of the conduit in place, by hand, as it were, underneath the tachocline. We can't just sink it in from above and pray. The height of the tachocline changes from hour to hour, even minute to minute. Put the conduit in too high, and take out too much material of too low a density, and nothing happens. Put it in too low, take out too much higher-density material, and then the star's core, and the nuclear burning process, are affected."

Everybody did their own version of shaking their heads emphatically.

"We've got to get it right the first time," Roshaun said. "Once the sunward side of the conduit is in place, the rest is easy. The far end will dump the matter out well beyond this solar system's heliopause, out past—" He looked at Dairine. "What's that last planet called?"

"Pluto."

"But we can't let the Sun end jump around," Roshaun said. "Otherwise..."

He trailed off.

The others looked at one another, nodding or rustling or waving their eyes around.

"We need rest now," Sker'ret said then. "No point in trying to do a wizardry when you're tired. It's a recipe for failure."

"I'll be in my pup tent," Filif said. Then he looked up and around him at the night, with his berries. "No, I won't," he said. "If this might be my last night on a planet, I'm going to go root." And he wandered off toward the rhododendron bed.

"I wish he wouldn't put it quite that way," Dairine muttered.

"Let him," Sker'ret said. "I'm for my own pup tent. When do we start, Roshaun?"

He looked at Dairine.

"Three A.M. local time," she said.

"You'll call me?" Sker'ret said.

"No," Dairine said, "you big dumb bug. Of course we'll let you sleep through it and do it all ourselves, and then let you go home to a promising clerical career."

Sker'ret snickered at her, a sound that did Dairine's heart good. He went trundling off on all those legs.

She sighed, stood up, and after a few moments followed him, though she didn't go into the house but rather paused outside, by the steps to the back door. Over the lilac hedge that separated the Callahan property from that of the next-door neighbors, she could see the Moon through the leaves.

She more or less ignored the tall dark shape, glittering slightly from the usual jeweled clothes, as he came to stand in front of her. *But I can't* really *ignore him,* she thought. *What if something goes wrong tonight?*

Dairine looked up at Roshaun.

"I owe you an apology," she said.

"You owe me nothing."

"Yeah, well," Dairine said, "in that case I have a word or two for you, Mr. I'm Prince of Everything I Survey. 'We wouldn't want people looking at us?' 'It wouldn't be permitted?' You don't have a neighbor within a thousand miles! The only reason your palace is there on the Burnt Side is so that no one *has* to live by you. Your people are scared to death of being without you. And scared to death *of* you. Aren't they?"

Roshaun turned to look up at the Moon, and didn't say anything.

"You're all that stands between them and destruction," Dairine said, "at least in the version of history

that most of your people know. They're terrified of
what would happen without you. And you've let them
get that way, haven't you? It's easier than going out the
front door every now and then and explaining that
you're just like other people, just with a few extra tal-
ents that were given you for *their* good, too, not just
yours. Wizardry is service! But your family seems to
have it a little backward. And the people all over
Wellakh bring you everything you want, you live nice
comfortable lives, all that. But someday, when wizards
are a little commoner on your planet—"

Roshaun looked at Dairine with some discomfort.

"I don't set family policy," he said.

"You will someday," Dairine said. "Someday *you'll*
be Beloved of the Sun Lord and all the other stuff that
translates into *king* on Wellakh. And I hope you start
letting your people look at you then, because otherwise, I think that as soon as they find a way to do without you, they will. It's only a matter of time until
technology catches up to what only wizardry can do
now, in terms of protecting your planet. And then
where are you?"

Roshaun looked up at the Moon, and then, without
much warning, sat down on the back step, half leaning
on the scraggly climbing rosebush that went up the
chimney.

"Are you always so reticent?" he said.

Dairine blinked.

"I didn't want to go on this excursus at first,"
Roshaun said. "My mother said she thought I should.
She wouldn't say why. She discouraged me from coming

back, even from using the pup tent. I was angry about that. And then, a couple of days ago, a message came. My father has stepped down as Sun Lord. When I come back, I *am* king. For me, it starts now."

He looked up at the Moon. "And it's just as you say," Roshaun said. "We're— I found the Earth word, the...English word? Anyway, I looked it up. We're *pariahs*. In people's minds, we've become associated with the Burning. We're its cure, but some people believe that maybe we were also its cause. They don't dare live without us. They hate living with us. So they kill us when they can." Roshaun shrugged. "It's not easy, especially when the person they're trying to assassinate is a wizard. But even wizards have to sleep. My father got tired of being the target; he's been one for forty years. He resigned and it's my turn now."

Dairine's knees felt weak under her. She had often enough had the Lone Power trying to kill her. She'd learned to cope with it. But having just *people* trying to kill you...that was something else entirely, and, strangely, it felt more awful. She sat down by Roshaun on the step and stared at the Moon so that she wouldn't have to look at him.

"*That's* why we have to fix your star," Roshaun said.

"You're not involved," Dairine said. "Nobody's expectations are looking over your shoulder, saying, 'He *had* to do that. He didn't do it just because it was the right thing.' "

There was a long silence.

"It would be nice if we had one of those," Roshaun said.

Dairine looked up, confused. "What?"

"That." He gestured with his chin at the Moon.

"Yeah," Dairine said. "We like it."

"We had one once," Roshaun said, "a little one. But it was destroyed in the Burning."

"We almost didn't have this one," Dairine said. "It was an accident. Something hit the Earth when it was still molten, and *that* splashed out."

Roshaun looked at her in amazement. "*Really?*"

"Really." Dairine looked up at the first-quarter Moon. "It took a long time to round up and get solid. But there it is."

"But if whatever hit your world had been just a little bigger—maybe neither piece of matter would have been big enough to coalesce, and there would never have been an Earth at all." Roshaun sat there shaking his head.

"Yeah. It's kind of a symbol," Dairine said, "of how sometimes, even against the odds, you can get lucky."

In the silence that followed, resolve formed. She stood up. "Come on," she said. "It's a nice view of the world from there. I'll show you."

Roshaun stood up, too, but for once he looked uncertain. "I don't know," he said. "It'll be time soon—"

"We have time for this," Dairine said. "Come on." She looked over her shoulder. "Spot?"

He was nowhere nearby, which was unusual for him. "I can handle it," Roshaun said, and opened his hand to look into the little sphere of light that was his manual, and showed what the Aethyrs told him. "Give me the coordinates," he said to Dairine.

She recited them, and as Roshaun spoke the words after her, the circle of the wizardry formed up on the ground around them. Dairine bent over to add the bright scrawl of her name in the Speech, across the circle from Roshaun's. *His name is much shorter than I would have thought,* Dairine thought, as she straightened up and began to recite, in unison with Roshaun, the words of the translocation.

It was probably completely unnecessary for her to reach out and take Roshaun's hand as the wizardry closed in around them and the view of her house and driveway dulled through the glowing curtain of Speech expressed and space bent slightly awry. *It's just a precaution,* Dairine thought. *I wouldn't want to lose him at this crucial moment—*

They vanished.

Areas to Avoid

AFTER THEIR VISIT TO THE Lone Power, Nita and Kit had little to do but sit around on the beach for the rest of that afternoon, because Quelt was away dealing with the issue of the Great Vein again and wouldn't be back until later, so Kuwilin told them. Ponch spent the afternoon running up and down the beach, mostly in the water; Kit and Nita, in no mood to play with him, sat trying to work out how to tell Quelt what they'd learned.

"Why should she believe any of this?" Kit said under his breath. He'd amassed a small pile of stones and was throwing them into the water one by one.

"Because we're wizards," Nita said, "and we wouldn't lie to her. We can't, in the Speech! And she knows that."

"She should," Kit said, throwing another rock in the water. "But even if she knows we're telling the truth, I'm not sure she's going to like what we have to tell her."

"No," Nita said. "She might even think it was just some weird misperception of ours, because we're aliens..."

Kit nodded, looking morose. "Where's Ponch gone?" he said, looking up and down the beach.

Nita shook her head. Trying to keep track of a dog who could make his own universes, and walk at will through ones he hadn't made, was always a challenge. "No idea," she said. "Weren't you working on a thing to do with his special leash, so that you can track him down?"

"I was working on that, yeah," Kit said. "It's not perfect yet." He reached into the little local space-pocket that followed him around, rummaged around in it, and came up with Ponch's leash. Kit had made it of the Speech, with some added ingredients. The whole wizardry was wound together into a soft, infinitely extensible cord that nothing could break and that would allow the wizard who held on to it to safely follow Ponch wherever he might walk.

"Let's see," Kit said. He ran the leash through his hands, closed his eyes for a moment. Nita could feel the direction-finding part of the wizardry come awake, but that was all—the wizardry was tuned to Kit specifically, and couldn't otherwise be overheard.

He opened his eyes a moment later. "It's all right," he said. "He's ten miles away, down the beach. He loves that he can just run and run and never run out of sand." He stood up. "I don't know how he's got any pads left on his paws with all the running he's been doing the past few days."

Kit got up. "I'll be back in a few minutes," he said, and vanished with a soft *pop* of imploding air.

Nita sat back against the dune and looked out at the glitter and roil of the sunlit water. *This was working so well,* she thought, *until I started to feel that something was wrong. Have I ruined myself somehow? Am I always going to go looking for what's wrong, forever, so that even when things are perfectly all right, I can't let them just be the way they are?*

She sighed and picked up one of Kit's stones, turning it over and over in her hand. *We could have spent a lovely couple of weeks here and left these happy people living their happy lives. And, all right, so there's something else going on at the bottom of it all. So what? Is it my business to go out of my way to make the Alaalids unhappy, just so that they'll possibly evolve into something better? Is there—*

A shadow fell over her, and Nita looked up, startled.

"Quelt!" she said.

"Nita..."

Quelt had just come over the top of the dune. She stood there looking at Nita for a moment, and then sighed and came down, step by step, rather slowly.

"Are you all right? You look tired."

"I am," Quelt said, and sat down by Nita, looking at the water. "I am tired."

She looked troubled, too, but Nita wasn't going to say anything about that; she had too many troubles on her mind to be accusing anyone else of having difficulty dealing with theirs.

"There's going to be more trouble with the Great

Vein than I'd thought," Quelt said. "The crust really is shifting down there: The layering's become more complex than it used to be. It's going to take days yet to sort it out."

She sighed, leaning back on her elbows.

"And on top of everything else, there seems to be something wrong with the Display," Quelt said. "It seems to have stopped functioning, and I have no idea why...or what to do about it. It's puzzling. The wizardry laid into that was always very resilient: Vereich told me that Druvah himself put it in place." She shook her head.

Uh-oh, Nita thought. *I wish I could put this off, but there's not going to be a better time, and we can't just sit around and hope that this issue goes away.* "Quelt," Nita said, "I think I know how that happened."

Quelt looked surprised. "You do?"

"Kit and Ponch were down in there, and it stopped working while Kit was viewing something to do with Druvah," Nita said. *There. That's the truth...*

At that, Quelt turned a very strange look on Nita. *Anywhere else,* she thought, *in anyone else, it would look like suspicion,* Nita thought.

"Something to do with Druvah," Quelt said. "What about him?"

"Uh, well..."

Nita suddenly saw Kit coming down the beach. Trotting along beside him was Ponch; the wizardly leash was around his neck, and Ponch was carrying the other end of it in his mouth, like any more ordinary dog out for a walk. "Here he comes," Nita said, feeling awful to push this off onto Kit. *But he was there. He can tell her better than I can.*

"Hey, Quelt," he said, as he came up to them, "*dai.*" Ponch, with the leash in his mouth, went straight to Quelt and started nuzzling her. She took his head under her arm and started rubbing his ears.

"He's got you trained already," Kit said. Nita caught his eye. *Here it comes...*

After a moment Quelt looked up at him. "Nita says you were down in the Display when it failed," she said.

"Yes," Kit said.

Ponch looked up into Quelt's eyes. *I think it was my fault,* he said. *Please don't be angry at Kit.*

Quelt produced a strange, unhappy smile and roughed up Ponch's ears some more. "I can't let him try to take the blame for this," Kit said. "I asked him to alter the way the Display was working. I wanted to hear what Druvah actually said to Esemeli."

Quelt didn't look up. "And what did you hear?"

Kit told her.

It took a long while. Kit's memory was excellent, Nita thought; the phrasing he was using was that of an older time, and she could almost hear the ancient wizard speaking through him. All the time, though, Quelt's expression never changed. She sat looking down at the sand until Kit finished.

"So then," she said, "having heard that, you went to see Esemeli."

"Yes," Nita said. Now, she figured, it was her turn. She told Quelt everything the Lone One had said to them, leaving out not a word. It was surprisingly easy for her, for she had been turning all those words over again and again in her mind, looking for anything dangerous hidden under them that she might have missed the first time around.

Once again, Quelt held very still, kept very silent, while Nita told her what the Lone Power had said about the Alaalids' need to evolve. And then Nita fell silent herself, waiting to see what Quelt would do.

The silence lasted a long while, and Nita forced herself to listen to the water slipping up and down the beach, and the little hissing noises that happened when air got trapped in the sand and bubbled out. When she looked at Quelt again, she found the Alaalid gazing at her with an indrawn expression very unlike anything Nita had seen on her before.

"And you believe this?" Quelt said at last. "You believe these things It told you?"

Nita took a deep breath. "Yes," she said.

"Because of the Oath you made It swear?"

"Not just that," Nita said. "After I started hearing the whispering, it seemed to me that there was something"—she paused—"not *wrong* about it, not as such. But there was something missing about the world. I went looking for your world's kernel. It's not here, Quelt. It's been separated from your world—and it shouldn't be."

"Or it wouldn't be in your own world," Quelt said, her voice very strange. "Is that it? That you think my world should be more like yours?"

Nita gulped. "Not at all," she said. "But your world's kernel—"

"Enough of that for a moment," Quelt said. "I must come back to this. You believe what the Lone One told you?"

"Yes, because this once, It had no choice but to tell the truth," Kit said. "Not after Nita was finished with It, anyway."

"And we ought to make the best of it," Nita muttered, "because this is the last time I'm going to be able to manage that stunt. One per customer . . ."

Quelt was silent. Finally, she looked up again, but not at either of them: out to sea. "I want to say this without being rude," she said. "You're our guests, and Those Who Are sent you here. But—"

She shook herself all over, like someone under intolerable pressure, and leaped up. "What makes you so sure you're right?" Quelt said, standing very stiffly, with her back turned to them. "How dare you think you can interfere with something like this, with our Choice? What gives you the right to tell me that my people should repeal it—just throw away everything we have here and start over? What makes you think you know better than *we* do how we should be growing as a species, what we should be doing with ourselves?"

Nita couldn't think of anything to say right away. "Quelt," Kit said, "it might just be that we have more experience with this kind of thing, with the Lone One, than you do."

"I think perhaps you do!" Quelt said as she turned back toward them. She was shaking all over as she stood there. "I asked the wind to tell me about your world! I had to, because every time I asked you, you'd always stop and say that it was going to take a long time to explain. Well, it did! It seemed like it took forever for the wind to tell me everything I wanted to know. And there was always more. I thought it would never stop." She was nearly in tears, but she was hanging on to her control...just. "I didn't know what a war was, until it told me about one. I'd never heard of murder. Or plague. Or a hundred other awful things."

Nita wanted to say something...and couldn't for the life of her think where to begin. And it was questionable, she thought, whether she could have stopped Quelt anyway. "I wasn't going to say anything," Quelt said. "I thought, Those Who Are wouldn't send us wizards who would hurt us, who were dangerous. It's not *their* fault their world is so horrible. But now I have to ask. What's the *matter* with you people? What happened in your Choice that you got it so wrong, that you kill each other all the time?"

"We're not sure," Nita said. "We spend a lot of time wondering about that ourselves."

"Is that true?"

Kit looked at her in shock. "Why would we lie?"

"Because when you're not using the Speech, you *can*?" Quelt said.

Nita and Kit were stunned silent.

"Your world seems to be full of that kind of thing," Quelt said. "I was terrified when I found out about it! It's got to be one of the worst things that's wrong there. How awful it has to be for people in your world when

you can never know for sure whether something someone tells you is *true!*"

"That's one reason we use the Speech," Nita said.
"It's one less question to ask—"

"But then you have to go on to the next one," Quelt
said. "Yes, people can't lie in the Speech. Fine. But if
they're confused, they can say what they believe to
be the truth, conversationally, and what they say will
still be wrong. How do I know It hasn't somehow
tricked you into believing all the things It told you are
true?"

Nita looked helplessly up at Kit. She couldn't think
of an answer to that.

"Or worse yet," Quelt said, "how do I know you're
not *working* for that one?"

Kit went ashen. "Wizards *can't,*" he said. "Or not
willingly!"

"Not here, no," Quelt said. "But in other worlds,
they can be 'overshadowed'—unwilling accomplices.
And what about in *your* world? What are things really
like *there?* The Lone One practically runs that place, it
seems! I never *knew* It could do things like that to a
world. And here It sits on our planet, and we made It
welcome here—" She was pacing back and forth on the
beach, her fists clenched, like someone afraid she'd ex-
plode into some terrible action that she'd regret.

Finally Quelt laughed, and the bitterness in the
laughter pained Nita terribly. It was so alien for an
Alaalid, and it echoed, in an awful way, Esemeli's laughter. "Well, at least this excursus has done something

good for me," Quelt said. "It's taught me what a monster Esemeli can be, once people start really believing in her!" She was actually angry, and it frightened Nita a little: She'd never seen any Alaalid angry before. "But for my own part, I'm my people's only wizard. We beat Ictanikë once: I will not give her another chance at my people, just on a stranger's say-so. Repeal our Choice? Why ever would we do that? Just because the Lone One says we might possibly turn into something better? It's madness. And you're mad, or deluded, to believe It, no matter what wizardry you worked on It. The Lone One tried to sell us our own destruction once, and we warded It off. Now it sends you to try to get us to throw away what we have and buy our destruction from a different source, instead?"

Nita stood up. "Quelt!" she said, and reached out two hands to take her by the shoulders.

Quelt backed away a step, and then another. "No," she said. "I think perhaps you should both stay away from me for a while. I don't know what to think, and looking at you makes me more uncertain every moment. I thought you were my cousins," she said, and now the tears genuinely were starting. "I thought you were *good*!"

She stood there, trembling, for just a moment more, and then she fled down the beach toward her home.

In silence Kit and Nita watched her go.

"Now what do we do?" Kit said.

Nita shook her head. Her heart was heavy; she felt like crying herself, except that it wouldn't have helped anything. "I have no idea," she said.

Kit was silent for a long time. "I think I know," he said at last. "For one thing, we sleep in the pup tents tonight."

"I'd almost rather go home," Nita said.

"I know," Kit said. "So would I. Which is why I think we should stay here."

Nita thought about that for a long moment. Finally, she nodded. "Yeah," she said. "Going home would feel too much like running away."

"And if Quelt decided she wanted to talk to us again between now and then," Kit said, "wouldn't we look guilty if we couldn't be found?"

That was something that had occurred to Nita only seconds after wishing she could go home. "But if we're in the pup tents," she said, "she'll know we wanted to give her a little privacy, a little room."

"Yeah." Kit got up, dusted himself off. "Then, as soon as Esemeli's ready tomorrow, we get It to help us find Druvah, if he can be found. If he can, we get the truth from him and we can bring it to Quelt. And then we get our butts out of here before we do any more damage."

Nita rubbed her eyes. "Yeah," she said. "Yeah. Let's get it over with."

They got up together to go down to their building and put what they needed for one more trip to the Relegate's Naos into their pup tents. Behind them Ponch came trotting along, the leash around his neck, holding the loose end of it in his mouth, and with a thoughtful look in his eyes. . . .

At about quarter of three in the morning, Dairine stood at the garage end of the driveway, once more gazing up at the Moon and waiting for the rest of the group to join her.

"Dairine," a voice said out of the darkness.

It was her dad.

"Yeah," she said.

"Where are they, honey?"

"They'll be here soon."

He came down the back steps and stood beside her, looking up at the Moon. For a few moments neither of them said anything.

"Remember when Nita went away," Dairine said at last, "and we thought she might not come back again, because of the wizardry she was doing out in the ocean, with the whales?"

"And the shark," her dad said. "Yes, I remember that."

"This is like that," Dairine said. "This is my shark." She looked at her dad.

In the darkness it was hard to see expressions. Her dad laughed, and the laugh sounded strange and strained. "And here I was concerned about Nita because she might wind up being sent off somewhere else by the Powers That Be to do something dangerous," he said. "Now it turns out the problem was going to be a little closer to home, right under my nose—"

"They didn't send her," Dairine said. "Not as such. But if when you're away you find a mess, or a problem to fix, you don't just walk away from it: You fix it.

Now I have to go do the dangerous thing...and the stakes are bigger this time."

"Are you *sure* you have to do this?" her dad said.

"It's my star," Dairine said. "I can't just send my houseguests off to deal with it! I have to go with them. Especially—" She fell silent.

Dairine's dad said, "I meant, are you sure what you're planning to do to the Sun really has to be done?"

"Oh." Dairine gulped, dry-mouthed, and nodded. "It was sanctioned," she said, "at a very high level. We'd never have gotten the sanction in the first place if the job didn't really need doing."

She was finding it hard to speak. "I have to go pretty soon," she said. "We have to. We're who gets this job."

Her dad was silent for a moment. "I don't have to tell you not to do anything stupid," he said then. "That's the last thing you'll do."

"How can you be so sure?" Dairine said. "After the dumb thing I did that started all this—"

Her dad shook his head, plainly feeling around for the right words. "Maybe it wasn't so dumb after all, what you did," he said. "It brought these particular wizards here just in time to do a job that at least one of them is a specialist in. Prince Unlikely."

Dairine nodded and said nothing. Her feelings about Prince Unlikely were far too complex for her to discuss. For the moment, she was scared to death, and upset, and didn't dare say how she felt for fear that it should overwhelm her and make her useless for what had to be done in a very little while. All she could do was go to her dad and hug him.

"Dairine, you may be thoughtless sometimes," her dad said, "but never stupid. If there's anything you've got, it's a brain...and I'd say your heart's in the right shape, too. Go do what you have to do. And be careful."

He didn't let her go for a long time...then finally released her and went inside.

At 3:00 A.M., Filif, Sker'ret, and Roshaun joined Dairine out at the far end of the backyard. The circle of the wizardry lay glowing on the ground, ready to be implemented, the elaborate interlace of sigils and symbols pulsing gently in the night.

With Spot in her arms, Dairine was doing as the others were doing: moving slowly around the periphery of the wizardry, checking its terms, making sure that everything added up, that nothing was misspelled or misplaced, and—most important—that each of their names was correctly included, and that each name was tied into the wizardry correctly for the role that wizard would be playing.

The roles divided fairly neatly for this piece of work. Roshaun, as main designer of the work and the one most familiar with the theory behind it, would be watching the timing of the wizardry and directing the others in when each stage should implement. Sker'ret, the fixer, would be the one to actually "flip the switches," speaking the words in the Speech that would take them in, help them locate where they needed to be, and manipulate the Sun's mass once they got to the right spot. Filif would be the main power source for the wizardry, the one whose job it was to "get out and push," leaving the others free to do fine adjustments and to react to situations as they developed. "Our people's life comes from that of our star," he'd said to Dairine while they were still in the design stages, "a little more directly than usual. This is a chance to give the power back. The universe appreciates such resonances..."

And as for me, Dairine thought, *I go along for the ride.*

Roshaun glanced over at her and said nothing. Dairine paid no attention, being in the process of checking her name for the third time. Sker'ret finished his check and came along beside her, peering at her name.

She waved the darkness she was holding in her hand in front of Sker'ret's various eyes. "You sure you can spare this?" she said.

He spared a few eyes to peer at it. "It's not like I'm going to have much trouble getting home even if we blow this one up," he said cheerfully. "I'll just go through Grand Central."

"You'll love it," Dairine said absently. "The food's great there. Just please don't eat the trains."

She looked at her name one last time and sighed. It was no shorter than it had been when she first started her wizardry, but some of its terms had changed to shapes not strictly human, and a number of the characters were truncated, or indicated power levels much reduced. "You guys hardly even need me for this," she said, "it's so perfectly tied up."

Filif rustled at her. "You're here," he said, "because this is your Sun. You're its child, native to the space inside its heliopause. It knows you. It will listen to you where it might not listen to us."

"Yeah," Dairine said, allowing herself a breath of laughter. "Sure." She knew she was no longer quite the power at wizardry that she had been, but she was good enough to hold up her part of a group working and make sure that if anyone else needed help, they would get it in a hurry.

She glanced at her watch. "We'd better move," she said. "The bubblestorm area's going to be coming around toward the Sun's limb soon."

Roshaun nodded, and took his position near the part of the wizardry that held a précis of its blueprint and the coordinates they were heading for, along with the latest data that the manual had for them on the depth of the tachocline. There would be no more precise data until they got closer to the Sun and could correct for relativistic errors and other problems.

The others arranged themselves around the rim of the wizardry, and then each took one step into it, into the locus prepared for them—the area that held optimum life support for each and that also contained a last-ditch "lifepod" wizardry intended to at least get them out with their lives if anything went wrong. *But if anything goes that wrong,* Dairine thought, *we're not likely to have time enough to implement the lifepods, anyway...*

It was a thought she kept to herself as she looked past the circle and saw the tall shadow standing there in the dark, watching her, saying nothing. She raised a hand to him. He didn't move for a few breaths... then raised his own.

"Ready?" Roshaun said.

"Ready," each of the others said, and "Ready," Dairine said, though she was starting to shake. This wasn't like the wizardries she did by herself, where if anything went wrong, she was the one to blame, and the only one who would suffer.

"Then let's speak," Roshaun said, "and the Aethyrs be with us, because we really need Them tonight."

The four wizards looked down at the wizardry that surrounded them. In unison, they started to speak its basic propositions in the Speech. The fire of it came up around them, blue green to start with, rapidly tinged with the gold of the star on which they were about to operate. The silence of a listening universe leaned in around them as they spoke the words; the power built—

They vanished into a suburban silence only slightly troubled by the echo of the hiss of solar wind....

Flashpoints

NITA AND KIT LEFT the Peliaens' homestead early the next morning, partly with the intention of seeing no one. And they did see no one, which hurt Nita, but there was nothing she or Kit could do about it right now. *They've got to feel we've violated their trust,* she thought. *Quelt, especially. And we so very much didn't mean to, but—* She let out a long breath of discomfort. Explanations would have to wait.

"You ready?" Kit said to her.

"Yeah."

Doing a short transit to the Naos was the matter of a few moments; there, in the morning mist, Nita and Kit stood at the bottom of one of the flights of steps and looked around them uncertainly.

"She's late," Kit said.

"I very much doubt that," Nita said. "The big question on my mind right now is, where's Ponch? I thought you said he would meet us here."

"I thought he would," Kit said. "After he's been out all night, he usually meets us first thing in the morning."

Nita sighed. "Where's the leash?"

"That's the problem. I left it on him last night." Kit shrugged. "I do that sometimes. He usually comes back at night so that I can take it off him. Last night he didn't come back." Kit shrugged. "He'll turn up."

Nita sighed and sat down on the bottom step. "I feel so rotten," she said.

"I know."

"But I didn't think she was going to react so badly. I mean, this isn't as if it was something that was going to happen overnight. Or even terribly soon. Think about it! The stricture said that if the Alaalids wanted to reject it, and remake their Choice, they had to do that unanimously. They're never going to—"

Kit shook his head. "Yes, they could. Or, specifically, not them. The wording Druvah used was, 'Our descendants in power.'" Kit shook his head. "When you were reading the orientation pack, did you look up the Alaalid word for 'wizard'?"

Nita shook her head.

"*Tilidi't,*" Kit said. "'One who walks in power.'"

Nita gulped. "Oh no," she said.

"And it's easy for a decision among wizards to be unanimous," Kit said, "when in a whole world there's only one..."

"Oh no," Nita said again. Suddenly it all made sense. She could just see herself if someone offered her such a piece of information. *Know what? Your whole species is in danger of never achieving its potential. But you can do something about it...you, all by yourself. And what happens to all of them hinges entirely and only on you...*

Nita shivered. "Shouldn't Ponch have turned up by now?" she said.

"Yeah..."

But they waited, and waited, and he didn't turn up. The one who did turn up was Esemeli, still impeccably clad in white and looking wearily amused. "So," It said, "you've decided to trust me after all."

Kit didn't say anything. Nita said, "Let's get on with it. Where are we headed?"

"Down," the Lone One said. "Do you want to handle the transit yourself, or shall I do it?"

Kit made an ironic after-you gesture.

The three of them vanished.

"This is where it begins," the Lone One said.

They were standing somewhere else, in the mist at the bottom of a huge cliff. The cliff was some dark stone, towering up into the mist, lost in it; and in the stone of its base was a huge vertical cleft that ran down from the cliff, across the ground, nearly to their feet.

Nita and Kit looked dubiously at the great opening in the Earth. Nita had started taking Latin in school, and the sight of the crevasse suddenly made her re-member something she'd translated from the *Aeneid* last semester: *It's easy to get into the Underworld. The door stands open night and day. But retracing your steps, getting back up to the light—there's the real work, the tough part....*

She took a deep breath. *It doesn't matter,* Nita thought. *We're as prepared as we can be. Except for one thing—*

She glanced over at Kit and saw that Esemeli was regarding him with an expression of concern. "Where's your doggy this morning?" It said.

Kit looked at the Lone Power. "I can't believe, somehow, that you don't know."

"I told you," Esemeli said, "that my ability to perceive what's going on is severely limited here. So I have no idea where your dog is. And, anyway, after what she made me promise"—and It glanced in annoyance at Nita—"if I knew, I would *have* to tell you if she asked."

"Where's Ponch?" Nita said immediately.

"I don't know," the Lone One said.

Kit stood still and closed his eyes for just one last try. Nita heard him calling Ponch silently.

But there was no response.

"You can wait, if you want," the Lone One said.

"No," Nita said. The state in which they had left Quelt was very much on her mind. "The sooner we get the proof we need for Quelt, the better. Let's get going."

They turned and entered the mouth of darkness, vanishing.

At first the path downward seemed nothing spectacular: a winding passage between stone walls, the walls growing closer together, the rough ceiling growing lower and lower as they went. Nita, looking around her, began to get nervous as they went downward and the walls began to close in. She had never been wild about tight, constricting spaces; and in this one, her general cast of mind was not helped by the strangely organic feeling to the stone. It had that same warm color, a muted gold with pink overtones, that was seen in many of the buildings on the continent. As the path twisted and turned and descended, it was very hard to keep from thinking that they were descending not into the bowels of the planet but—

Nita pushed that thought aside vigorously, and concentrated on keeping an eye on their guide. Esemeli walked casually and confidently ahead of them, seeming untroubled by the way they went. "How can you be sure Druvah came this way?" Kit said, pulling out his manual and producing a small light to bob along ahead of him.

"He's left traces," Esemeli said, "even after all this time. He was, after all, the greatest of the wizards who met to enforce the Alaalid Choice." It chuckled a little. "There's a joke there, actually; if he hadn't been so scrupulous about bowing to the wishes of the majority, none of us would need to be here now. The Alaalids would've moved on to the next stage in evolution, oh, thousands of years ago...if he'd made them. But like so many wizards who are too wholeheartedly on the side of the Powers That Be, he insisted on making his work difficult for himself. And for the people he was supposed to be serving..."

They made their way around a tightly curving corner in the stone, a place where all of them had to put their backs against the wider side of the curve and inch around it, little by little. Nita breathed in, trying to make herself as thin as possible, and kept herself moving; but she had to keep her eyes closed. The downward-pressing closeness of the stone was beginning to affect her.

Ahead of her, Esemeli moved slowly but with no sign of distress. Nita could hear Kit's breathing becoming labored. He was no fonder of these tight quarters than she was. "We could just go through the stone," he said at one point, when he was finding it difficult to follow the Lone Power.

"No," Esemeli said, "we can't. All this road into the heart of the Earth is permeated by Druvah's power." She smiled a secret, rather uncomfortable smile, which Nita could just make out by the faint gleam of Kit's wizard-light. "He made sure that anybody who was going to follow him on this road would have to go through exactly what he did when he first found his way to the world's kernel. Even if it was going to be the wizards who would repeal the Choice he oversaw— they would have no easier time of it. He wanted to give them plenty of time to have second thoughts."

I'm having plenty of them right now, Nita heard Kit thinking.

Not just you, Nita thought. "How do you know where he hid the kernel?" she said.

"I watched him do it," the Lone One said. "He was using the power that I gave him at the time. And at the time, that made it impossible for him to hide his whereabouts from me." She was smiling, amused again.

They came out of the tight, close tunnel into a slightly more open area. Kit had to stop and get his breath, and for a moment he stood bowed down with his hands on his knees, gasping. Nita wiped her forehead. It was definitely getting warmer. She tried to work out how far underground they might have come, but she wasn't sure exactly how to tell. *I could look in the manual,* she thought. But at the same time, she found herself thinking that even that wasn't likely to do her any good. There was a strange sense coming down over her as if this journey was not exactly a physical one, or not *merely* a physical one....

She looked up to find the Lone One gazing at her with that amused expression. "Yes," It said, "you do feel it. I was wondering if you would."

"We're not exactly inside Time," Nita said. "Or outside it. This is one of those 'complex states.'"

"Yes," Esemeli said. "I'm afraid that, as wizards go, Druvah was fairly expert."

"Which has to be bad for you," Kit said, straightening up, "and good for us..."

The Lone One threw him an annoyed look. "Let's get moving," It said. "We've got a ways to go yet..."

They moved on, downward again. Kit dropped back toward Nita a little. "Neets, this is weird," Kit said under his breath. "It isn't like the real inside of a planet...any planet. This is more like another dimension."

"It could be a little of both," Nita said. "There are

ways to make a place's mythical reality coincide with the physical one...or make one temporarily a lot more powerful than the other." She shook her head. "But normally you need a kernel to mediate that kind of overlap or substitution."

"That, at least, means we're on the right track," Kit said. "You've been doing a lot of reading. Are you thinking about changing specialties? Maybe turning into a research specialist, like Tom?"

"I don't know," Nita said. "Things are changing, all right...but into what, I'm not entirely sure."

Kit nodded, moved ahead again. For her own part, Nita was relieved to find that the path they took widened out a great deal. But the passage was always downward, and the weight of millions and billions of tons of rock continued to weigh on her. At least she was able to partially distract herself with the splendor of their surroundings: for the chain of complexes of caverns through which Esemeli led them in the next hours—or what felt like hours—would have been a first-class tourist attraction on Earth. One after another they passed through gigantic multicolored arenas and caves of stone, festooned with stalactites, or growing great crops of stalagmites like petrified forests. There were some caverns in which the stone itself glowed, and there was no need for wizard-light at all; they wove their way among pillars and chandeliers of down-hanging, luminous rock, their shadows stretching in ten different directions, or abolished entirely by the glow. But always the way led down, and down, and further down.

It was getting warmer all the time as they went. But this didn't reassure Nita; it wasn't nearly as warm as it should have been underground, and she knew that they were, indeed, not entirely in the physical world anymore. She had done some reading in the manual about these so-called "complex states," in which normal space was blended or "affiliated" with constructed spaces that could be based in myth, or one mind's delusion, or some commonly held belief. Such complex-state spaces could have physical realities that mirrored some old fairy tale or ancient legend...or a physical reality that had once existed but was now long gone. As they passed out of one deep cavern and into another, always with Esemeli leading the way and Kit following It, Nita's misgivings grew, despite the Binding Oath she had made the Lone One swear. It was very old, and very wise...and entirely too clever. But it was hard to know where she might have gone wrong. *We're just going to have to rely on the manual for the moment, and try to keep our eyes open,* Nita thought, as they went down, and down, and down...

The walk through the caves began to seem more and more like a dream that had always been happening, and always would. In front of her was Kit, with his wizard-light; in front of him, Esemeli, a white shadow that never paused, never got tired. *Not like me,* Nita thought. She was beginning to regret not having eaten at least something for breakfast that morning. *And when* was *this morning?* she thought. *How many hours ago? How many years?* It was becoming increasingly difficult even to believe in "this morning," except as something that had happened in a dream a long time ago.

The way before them opened out again, the sound of their footsteps echoing against distant walls as it hadn't done for some time. Esemeli stopped for a moment, and Kit behind It, and the three of them stood still on the shores of a vast cavern lake under a huge, high-domed ceiling dripping with more stalactites, which glowed. The water was a strange, milky blue color in Kit's and Nita's wizard-lights; and everything was absolutely still, not the slightest ripple of air touching that water. It was like blue glass, as solid-seeming as the crystalline surface of the Display had been.

"It looks too deep to wade," Kit said.

"Indeed, I don't know that it has a bottom," Esemeli said. There was something strange about Its tone of voice. Nita glanced over at It and was surprised to see the uncertainty in Esemeli's face and stance, normally so self-assured and lazily mocking. *Maybe even It's a little out of Its depth here,* she thought.

But the next moment, Nita reminded herself once more that this was the Lone Power, or a fragment of It—immensely old, immensely powerful, and absolutely not to be trusted, no matter how secure you thought your hold over It might be. *And just how sure am I about that?* Nita thought.

There was another issue, too, one that she hadn't mentioned to Kit, but that she suspected was going to come up in the near future and probably make him yell at her. Such strictures as the Binding Oath could not be one-sided; there was also a price to pay by the one doing the binding. What is bound eventually breaks loose, the manual said; the power of the binding is directly proportional to the power of the backlash. *Sooner or later,* Nita thought, *this is going to come back to haunt me. Later, I hope…*

And down they went through the darkness, and further down. Slowly, though, Nita noticed something strange beginning to happen. She had been starting to slow down, so that every now and then she would have to force herself to hurry to catch up with Kit and Esemeli, who had moved ahead. But now she was having less trouble keeping up, and this confused her. *It's not like I'm any less tired. I'm not!* But walking was less trouble. And the further downward they continued, the less of a problem it became. Stranger still, she was starting to become aware of light filtering up from below them, as they continued downward through the caverns and passageways in the depths of the world. The caverns seemed brighter, somehow, though there was none of the glowing stone they'd seen earlier—

Nita followed Kit through one more exit from a vast cavern into one more new one, and put her foot down wrong on a place where the stone was uneven. She tripped, and thought she would fall.

She didn't. She bounced, and came up on her feet again, and bounced once more before she settled.

Hearing the scuffle of Nita losing her footing, Kit turned and saw her bounce. Behind him, Esemeli stopped, too, watching them.

G is less, Nita thought. "Kit," she said. "Gravity's decreasing!"

He stared at her. "How can it?" But then he jumped, and Nita saw him hang there briefly in the air before he came down.

"Maybe half a g," Kit said. "How can this be happening?"

Nita shook her head. "Come on," she said.

Esemeli turned to lead the way again. Kit and Nita went after, bouncing a little in an adaptation of the astronauts' walk that everyone who went to the Moon learned, because until you did, you spent a lot of time lying face first in moondust. Esemeli, for Its own part, did not bounce; possibly It considered that beneath Its dignity.

They continued downward, and as they went, the gravity kept lessening, and the caverns all around them seemed progressively brighter, as if the stone of them was going translucent. *This is beyond weird,* Nita thought. It was nothing like the smothering heat and pressure that they should have been experiencing even fairly high up in a planet's crust, let alone down into its mantle. *This is definitely a complex-state environment, someone's myth about the middle of the world coming true around us. Well, I don't mind the lessened gravity, anyway...*

That was fortunate, for it got less the deeper they went. Nita was grateful that she was used to it; she'd spent enough time on the Moon that she wasn't troubled anymore by the human body's usual reaction to microgravity, which was to complain bitterly that it wanted to throw up anything that had been eaten recently. *Just as well, maybe, that I didn't eat any breakfast this morning,* Nita thought. *Not that I felt like it.* The pain and betrayal on Quelt's face was still very much with her, and the anguished cry, "I thought you were *good!*"

They were becoming light enough now that it was becoming something of a difficulty to stay on the ground. Nita had to grab on to handholds in the stone of passages and tunnels they went through. But ahead of them, she could see a huge portal into another cavern, and there would be nothing to hold on to there. *We're going to fall up,* Nita thought wearily. *We're going to fall into the sky.* She had walked on air often enough in her work as a wizard, but falling was never entirely pleasant, whether you did it up or down. She swallowed, trying to keep her stomach under control; it was already trying to do backflips at the thought of what was coming—

They passed through that gigantic archway, and everything happened at once. Nita saw Kit's shadow leap out behind him, and Esemeli's as well—but Its was longer and far blacker than it should have been in that light. Before them lay a great broad plain with a high horizon... but the plain was above them, and the horizon was upside down.

Nita's stomach flipped in earnest now. It was as if, for all the descending they'd been doing for all these weary hours, they had somehow come right around through the heart of things and out back on Alaalu's surface again. Yet they hadn't. They were still in the middle of the world: Nita knew this for sure as she looked at that horizon and realized that it didn't stop—there was never any sky at the top of it, just more and more land. And suspended in space before them, like a pillar buttressing the center of the world, was one great needle of stone, reaching down, or up, an incredible distance into that silvery-glowing, blinding sky. The confusion assailed Nita completely; she no longer could tell which way up or down was. And as if that confusion wasn't all that was needed to complete the effect, it was then that the earth seemed to let go of them, and all three of them fell into the sky....

Fortunately, the fall itself partook to a certain extent of that dreamlike quality, so that what might otherwise have left Nita screaming in terror now left her in a muted state of astonishment and mild annoyance, like Alice falling down the rabbit hole. Up and up the three of them fell, and closer and closer to that peak of stone. "Toward that!" Esemeli cried; and Kit and Nita, having learned in passing a little about handling themselves when free-falling in atmosphere, spread out their arms and legs and did their best to maneuver themselves toward the top of the peak. They were falling up at enough speed for Nita to erect a personal-shield wizardry around herself; she was concerned about the possibility of slamming into the rocks. But she was pleased to find that the velocity of their fall seemed to be lessening as they got close to the top of that peak. By the time the haze of distance disappeared, they had slowed to a leisurely plummet; by the time they were within perhaps a mile of it, they had slowed to a glide. And as they came to the top, or the bottom of it—

Who knows what it is anymore? Nita thought, as she concentrated on somehow putting her feet flat down on stone instead of air. *Let it be up or down just as it pleases. I only want to stand still!*

And she was standing still, on the stone, and Kit and Esemeli were standing there on it with her. Nita breathed out and looked around.

The plateau on which they stood was the pale plain peach-colored sandstone of the Inner Sea lands. Nita made herself hold still and breathe and try to get used to some kind of normality again...if you could call *this* normal. *We're on a pillar of rock maybe a thousand miles high, inside a planet,* Nita thought, *at a level where there should be nothing but magma, or maybe even molten iron under millions of tons of pressure. There's a sky here where there can't be one, and air here where there can't be any. If I were a pseudoscience freak, this would be terrific, and I'd be expecting flying saucers next. As it is, I think maybe normality needs an overhaul...*

Next to her, "Wow," Kit said softly.

"What?" Nita said, looking around.

Then she saw Kit turning slowly, looking all around him. And Nita saw that he had good reason. The perspectives of things had shifted again, or rather their topologies, so that what had been the truncated top of a cone was now the flat top of a shallow rise, and all around them, from perhaps thirty feet away to the horizon, and seemingly right up into the impossibly glowing sky, there were people.

Nita's mouth went dry with sudden irrational fear at the sight of them. All around her she heard, more strongly than ever, the sound that had been trembling at the edge of her hearing since they came to Alaalu... an incessant, friendly whispering. Now she knew where it came from. It was from these people, a myriad of Alaalids, all standing around with their amiable, interested faces, looking at her, and Kit, and Esemeli, and the Alaalid man who stood nearby the place where they had come to rest.

Nita found herself experiencing a case of the shivers. The people were the dead: everybody who had ever lived on Alaalu, in their many billions, filling all this vast space out to the edge of the sky.

And as for the man—

He had a shock of red hair that was rather untidy and casually kept, by Alaalid standards, but a face that was composed and good-humored, even for an Alaalid, with those dark and liquid eyes suggesting a profound wisdom underneath the good humor. He was very casually dressed, in the long kilt that some Alaalids wore, and a long loose jacket thrown over it. He looked like someone who'd just been out for a swim. But he carried in his hands something that not many beachgoers would have brought with them. It was a tangle of near-blinding brilliance, lines of fire in many colors and many thousands or tens of thousands of words in the

Speech, all knotted together in one complex structure. It was Alaalu's world-kernel, the "software" in which was contained the laws—natural, physical, and spiritual—that governed Alaalu and its homespace.

The man holding that kernel nodded, first of all, to Esemeli. "I thought you'd turn up here eventually," he said.

It smiled and bowed to him. "You and I," Esemeli said, "have unfinished business to transact."

"So we do," the man said. Then he looked over at Nita and Kit.

"Druvah," Kit said.

The Alaalid bowed a little to Kit, and then to Nita.

"Cousins, well met on the journey," he said. "You're very welcome to the heart of things."

"Thank you," Kit said.

"Yes," Nita said, "thank you. But I have a question…"

"Ask," Druvah said.

"When we're finished talking to you…how do we get out of here?"

"No one does that," Druvah said, "until we change the world."

And Esemeli smiled.…

Dairine, Roshaun, Sker'ret, and Filif were standing in position in blazing light, perhaps two thousand miles above the Sun's photosphere, while the invisible corona lashed space with superheated plasma above their heads.

The wizardry was protecting them from the heat and more than ninety-nine percent of the visible light that boiled out of the Sun's nuclear furnace to express itself in the photosphere's glare. That outermost layer of the Sun's actual body was no more than an eggshell's thickness compared to the vast bulk of the star beneath it, but it boiled and roiled with golden fire. It was beautiful, but instantly deadly to anyone not protected as they all were. Even so, none of them intended to linger a moment longer than necessary. But the beauty was compelling.

"Look at it," Filif said, gazing into that furious brilliance with all his berries, which caught it and glinted red as blood. "So magnificent, so dangerous—"

Dairine had to smile just slightly at the poet living inside the bush who liked baseball caps. Her own impression was more prosaic. "It looks like oatmeal," she said. And so it did, if oatmeal boiled at seven thousand degrees Celsius and every grain of it was a capsule full of burning liquid helium eight hundred miles across. The motion was the same, though—new grains bubbled up every second, persisting in the violent roiling pressure for maybe twenty minutes, and then were pushed away to be swallowed into the depths. They rumbled, and the sound was real; sonic booms from them rippled incessantly across the surface of the Sun.

"Where's the tachocline?" Roshaun said.

"Two-hundred-eighteen thousand five hundred kilometers through two-hundred-twenty-one thousand six hundred," Sker'ret said. "It's fluctuating, though."

"Which way?"

"Up."

Roshaun looked uncertain. "We could wait for it to stabilize," he said. Then he shook his head. "No point in that. I'm going to adjust the wizardry to take us in, and hold steady at two-twenty-two. Everyone, check my numbers."

They all watched as Roshaun brought out his version of the manual, a little tangle of light like a miniature sun itself, and read from it a precise string of words and numbers in the Speech. Inside the wizardry, the "depth" constant changed to reflect the shift. Everyone looked at the numbers.

"Did you all check me?"

Dairine read the numbers three times. "You've got it," she said.

"Check," Sker'ret said.

"And I check you, too," said Filif, trembling.

"Then let's go—"

They vanished again—this time into the inferno.

In the heart of hearts of Alaalu, Nita and Kit stood looking at the planet's oldest surviving wizard—if his present state—half myth, half spirit—could be described as "surviving"—as he said, "We've been waiting for you here for a while."

"Not too long, I hope," Kit said.

Druvah's smile was reassuringly ironic.

"Long enough," he said. "But I don't mind." He bowed to Esemeli, and It looked at him and eyed him with an expression of reserved disdain.

"You did a good job hiding your kernel," Nita said.

"It seemed necessary," Druvah said. "Under the circumstances, it seemed wise to keep it in an ambivalent state: not quite in the real world, in Time; not all the way into the deeper world, out of Time; but oscillating between them, a million times every moment, so that its location was always more a possibility than a definite thing."

"Uncertainty," Nita said to Kit. "The way you get it in atomic structure, with the electrons more or less certain to be in a given area, but never really just in one spot…"

"That quality of matter I borrowed for this wizardry, yes," Druvah said. "And for myself as well, so that I could keep an eye on what our destiny was bound to." He looked at Nita and Kit. "But where is the last wizard?"

They looked at each other.

"Well," Nita said.

"Unfortunately," Esemeli said, "she will not be coming."

Druvah looked at her in a shock so stately, it resembled composure.

"The strangers on whom you pinned all your hopes," Esemeli said, "unfortunately have given your wizard the fright of her life, by telling her the truth. A choice irony. She's seen what the Telling showed her of their world and wants nothing to do with it, or them. Or, by extension, *you*, Druvah. She even made herself unavailable enough to them this morning that they couldn't be warned in time about what they were so eager to do."

Esemeli turned Its attention to Nita and Kit and smiled at them sweetly... a little too sweetly. "You, at least," the Lone Power said to Nita, "will recognize the source of the Whispering you've heard in the nights. This is the Whispering's core, the place into which the souls of the Alaalid die, when they die into the world. Here, by virtue of the Choice the Alaalids made, everything is preserved forever as it was when it arrived. Think of it as a sketchy little version of Timeheart." The furious, hating twist It put on the word gave Nita an abrupt shiver. "Too sketchy, though. And also by virtue of that Choice, nothing that comes here ever leaves here, whether it comes of its own free will or not."

Esemeli directed the full force of that infuriating smile on Nita. "You should have asked fewer questions about how soon you could get where you were going," the Lone One said, "and more about whether you could get out afterward. But most to the point, you forgot the line in the Binding Oath about not allowing *you* to err by inaction."

Nita felt all the blood run straight down out of her face, leaving her staggered and shivering.

She and Kit looked over at Druvah.

The most powerful of the ancient Alaalid wizards nodded regretfully. "What It says is true," Druvah said. "I have no power to change it. And the one who *has* that power has not come with you, as I had hoped she would." His voice was filled with regret, and Nita looked over at Kit, her mouth suddenly going dry with fear. "Indeed, that was my only hope. But the future has not turned out the way I thought it would. It seems my people must remain as they are. And here we must all stay, until the day after forever..."

The Lone One's laughter began to echo in that bright place, filling it, and drowning out all other sound, even the sound of the Whispering....

The wizardry brought Dairine, Roshaun, Filif, and Sker'ret out in the midst of a hurricane of fire.

Not exactly in the middle of it, Dairine thought, trying desperately to keep hold of her nerves, for the status readouts hanging in front of her own part of the wizardry told her exactly what was going on out there, and it terrified her. It was one thing, as she'd once done, to sink a skinny little spatial slide into this nuclear fury and pull out a pencil-sized stream of molten mass. When she'd done that, she'd been dealing with a star's core, and the core was a placid pool on a windless night compared to the place where they now found themselves. By definition, the tachocline was turbulent. Its name meant "the place where the speed changes," and it was where the more placid motion but more terrible temperatures of the radiative zone below met the boiling madness of the convective zone above. The tachocline slid between the two zones like ball bearings rubbed between two hands, in wide belts and roiling spots like the atmosphere of Jupiter, but at wind speeds that made Jupiter's seem tame. "Wind," though, seemed a pitiful word for the insensate power that was raging around them in wildly varying directions. The solar medium was no denser than water here—but even water becomes a deadly weapon when it's blasting past you at twenty times the speed of sound, and at two million degrees.

Filif was pouring power into the wizardry at a prodigious rate, but even so, the wizardry itself was suffering under these atrocious conditions. It would not hold forever. And it was being buffeted around like a Ping-Pong ball in the terrible, constantly shifting pressure.

Roshaun was trying to get a reading on the lowest levels of the tachocline, but Dairine saw that every second the readings changed more violently. The layer was like a blanket being wildly shaken up and down by people holding it at the edges. Until it calmed, there was no chance that they were going to be able to do what they needed to do. And it was not going to calm—

Come on, Roshaun said to the Sun in the Speech. He spoke silently to be heard over the roar. *Come on, cousin! What are you waiting for? Why all this trouble? You know what you need to do. Otherwise, life on all your planets is going to be problematic. Give us some help, here. Let us help you sort yourself out!*

The Sun raged around him; the tachocline bucked and heaved like a live thing, stung by the approaching magnetic anomalies swinging around from the far side of the Sun, the skin of the border layer twitching and shuddering. Dairine started to hear something she never would have imagined it was possible to hear: the

Sun itself speaking, like a sentient thing. It was using the Speech, but she couldn't understand the words. It wanted something; it was trying to tell her, but she couldn't understand—

That's impossible. I have to be able to understand; it's the Speech. What's the matter?

There's something wrong here, she heard Sker'ret saying in her mind. *Something's interfering with the magnetic flow at this level.*

The bubblestorm area? Dairine asked.

No. Something else. A darkness . . .

Sunspots? Dairine said.

No! Something else. But dark—

Under them, the tachocline heaved ever more violently. *It won't stay still!* Dairine cried. *How are you going to get the worldgate down in there long enough to bleed the mass off if it keeps heaving around like this?*

There was a long silence from Roshaun. *There are ways,* he said conversationally.

Something about the tone of that thought brought Dairine's head up, made her look him in the eye. But he wouldn't meet her eye.

Roshaun?

You know what I am, he said to the Sun, ignoring her.

A blast of reply.

Yes, Roshaun said. *A Guarantor.*

Another blast.

He could understand it and she couldn't. It wasn't fair—

Sker'ret, Roshaun said, *detach the worldgate for me.*

"*What?*" Dairine shouted.

If Roshaun heard the thought behind the shout, he didn't betray it. At any rate, the way the roar of the Sun was coming through even the wizardry now, there was no point in using normal speech. Sker'ret said three words, very quickly, and the black shadow that was the worldgate, reduced to a thin scrap of grayish fog in this terrible light, leaped straight into Roshaun's hands as if he'd called it.

What are you thinking of? Dairine demanded. *Let me help you—*

You need to stay here and let me do this, Roshaun said.

But if I can just—

You can't, Roshaun said, looking at her with that infuriating, amused expression. *But then that's what "Guarantor" means. If the world can't pay the price... if the people around you can't pay the price...* you *do.*

The price? No! Dairine said. *No! You don't even like my little planet—you said so—*

No, Roshaun said. *Which is possibly the best of all possible reasons to do this.*

He stepped out of the wizardry.

"No," Dairine whispered. "No! *Roshaun!*"

Roshaun vanished in the fire.

Interim Destinations

IN THE HEART OF ALAALU, Kit looked at Nita in complete horror. "You mean *that's it*?"

She looked over at him, shivering, and nodded. "I think It's right," she said. "We're stuck here..."

"You were so earnest," the Lone One said. "And so careless. And so *patronizing*. You have deserved this so profoundly, I can barely express it. A failed fragment of the Lone Power, am I? Oh, very failed. But not so failed that this species will have any further chance to go on into whatever lovely bodiless stage of evolution might potentially await them. Their only wizard will remember her betrayal until the day she dies, and will warn all her successors never to be tempted to consider Repeal. Generation after generation of them will live out their happy little lives and die into the world. They'll keep on doing that until their star goes cold and their species oh-so-gracefully surrenders as a whole to what they will wrongly consider Fate. So much for *their* intended glory; the One is just going to have to do without them ... And as for me, not only do I have all these poor frozen fools to amuse me the few idle aeons until Time's end, but now I also have *you* two to laugh at for the rest of this universe's eternity ... your faces to entertain me as your souls writhe endlessly for the mistakes you made, the loved ones who'll never see you again. Priceless," Esemeli said, "priceless!"

Kit and Nita looked at each other helplessly as the Lone Power's laughter once again drowned out the Whispering, echoing all through that place—

—and then Esemeli suddenly cried out, *"Ow!!"*—

—because something had dropped a stick of ironwood right onto the Lone Power's head.

Everyone looked up in shock, most particularly Esemeli. Her face went in a second from an expression of pain to one of terrible fury. Standing there in the air above them all, looking down, was Ponch ... and holding the other end of his wizardly leash, also looking down at that immeasurable assembly with an expression of relief and wonder, was Quelt.

They walked down the air together, and everyone looked at them, most specifically Esemeli. There was a curse in Its eyes, but It said nothing.

The two of them came down onto the mountaintop, and walked into the heart of that great gathering. *She was wondering where you were,* Ponch said to Nita and Kit. *So was I. So we came looking.*

And Kit started to smile. *We're not the only one who made some mistakes,* he said privately to Nita. Aloud, he said to Esemeli, "You know, you're to blame for this."

It turned to glare at him. "If you hadn't hurried us along and had waited for Ponch to catch up with me," Kit said, "he'd be stuck in here with the rest of us. But, no, you had to get going and get us nice and trapped." Kit glanced over at Nita. "That Binding Oath is really something," he said, "if it makes the Lone Power help us even when It's trying to screw us up."

"Or else," Nita said, looking over at the Lone One with an expression that was difficult to read, "someone's found a really good way to do the right things without looking like they were." And she smiled just the slightest smile. "Didn't somebody say they were getting a lot more mileage out of ambivalence these days?"

The Lone One turned away. "This will only work this once," It said. "Make the most of it. When she releases me, you may later come to regret all this. In fact, I guarantee that you will."

Kit and Nita turned their attention back to Ponch and Quelt. Everyone else in that place was staring at them in astonishment, and the one looking hardest at them, though with the least look of being surprised, was Druvah. "Yes," he said at last. "I foresaw this happening... but, I have to admit, not quite *this* way..."

Quelt, for her own part, hardly gave Druvah more than a glance at first. She went straight over to Kit and Nita and took first Kit, then Nita, by the shoulders in her species' greeting. "I am so sorry," she said. "I treated you so badly when you were only telling me the truth. I feel terrible about it. And I felt terrible before, as well! *I* got you started on all this!"

Nita stared at Quelt, confused. "I thought *I* got *you* started on it!"

"No," Quelt said. "You just said things idly that made me think more about things I'd been thinking already. Remember how I said that there was something missing? I hadn't been really serious about it before, but after you said you had the same thoughts, they started to matter much more. When the thoughts were inside, I was discounting them. They didn't seem important or real. Yet you were so different, and the place you come from is so different...and you still had those feelings. That was the key."

Ponch ran over to Kit with the leash in his mouth, dropped it, and then began jumping around him, whining and trying to lick his face. *You went farther away than usual without me,* Ponch said. *I was worried about you. Don't do that again!*

Kit hugged Ponch's head to him. *Okay,* he said. *Just remember this the next time you go running off across the universe without telling me!*

Ponch sat down and looked up at Kit with big soulful eyes. *I'll be good...*

Quelt looked over at Druvah and smiled suddenly. "You're taller than you looked in the Display," she said.

He smiled. "Too great a distance in time does alter the perspective somewhat," Druvah said.

Quelt turned to Esemeli. "And as for you," she said. "Now you'll tell me that all the things you said just now were a lie."

"Why, of course they were."

"Say it in the Speech," Quelt said.

The Lone Power glared at her.

Quelt turned away from It and looked around at all that gathering of people, all the dead of Alaalu, ranged away around the mountain and up the slopes of the world, to the high horizon and beyond, it seemed.

"For now, though," she said, "before we can go forward, something is missing."

Nita and Kit looked at each other as the air around them shimmered and rumbled with power. Wizardry was being done here but not in a mode they recognized, and Quelt was at the heart of it. She simply seemed to be standing with her arms by her sides, murmuring in the Speech—

—and a moment later, the crowd surrounding them seemed, impossibly, much larger than it had.

"*Everyone* needs to be here for this," Quelt said softly, but her voice traveled effortlessly right across that mighty assemblage. Nita looked at the people standing nearest her and Kit and realized that it wasn't just the dead of Alaalu who were surrounding them now. The living had arrived as well, in spirit if not in body, and were looking around in astonishment at the heart of the world.

"Now that we are all here," Quelt said, "now comes the time to make another Choice—whether to choose again—"

The Whispering, massive already, started to turn to a mutter, the mutter to a roar, at first distant, like surf crash on Earth, then closer and closer. All around, the Alaalids closest to Nita and Kit in that great crowd were turning to one another, murmuring, distressed.

"Oh no," Kit said suddenly.

Nita turned to see what he was looking at. There was a stir of motion in the crowd, and through it came Kuwilin and Demair.

They went to Quelt, who looked at them with tears suddenly standing in her eyes.

"Daughter," Kuwilin said, "what are you doing? Do you know what you're saying?"

"Very well," Quelt said.

Her mother reached out to Quelt, took her by the shoulders. "Quelt, sweeting, you can't! Don't you hear yourself? If you do what you're planning, you're going to kill everyone alive on the planet!"

"Their old lives will end," Quelt said, "yes." The tears began to fall.

"We're happy!" Kuwilin said, desperate. "Our lives are good! How can you want to end them?"

It pained Nita to see that proud, good-natured face suddenly so frightened, to see Demair's easy grace gone tense with terror. She saw that it pained Quelt, too. And all around, other voices began to cry out as well.

"Everything is fine just the way it is!"

"Why should you destroy the way a whole planet lives just because you have the power?"

"How dare you decide for us what's right for us all to do!"

"Someone *has* to decide!" Quelt cried at them all. "Because *you* can't do it anymore! Listen to you! You should hear yourselves! You're like a bunch of little children who don't want to take a nap in the afternoon because you're afraid you'll miss something! But you *have* missed something. Didn't you hear the Lone One now, speaking truly for a change? It's told you everything you need to know. But you never needed It to tell you that, not really. You weren't listening to the world. None of us has been! We were too *happy* to listen!"

The Whispering started to die away a little. "Can't you hear what we've been trembling on the brink of?" Quelt said. "Can't you hear the darkness, the potential that's been chasing around our world forever like the night, just waiting for someone to look up and see it? Our own Whispering's drowned out that deeper silence. We talk to ourselves all the time so we won't hear what the silence holds—the risk, the chance—"

"The danger!"

"Yes, the danger!" Quelt said, turning toward whoever it was who'd spoken. "How long has it been since there was danger in our world—any *real* danger? Oh, occasionally there's an accident, or some passing pain or personal sorrow—but why doesn't it last? We've outgrown passion! These bodies are too used to this world, where all the edges and sharp corners have been rubbed off and everything made safe for us. We live and we die and everything is perfect and fine. What do we have to do with the rest of the universe anymore?"

"What, then?" someone's voice cried, desperate. "Do you want our world to go back to the way it was in the very first times, before we awoke as a sentient species, where death is dreadful, and whole nations die in horror and pain, and the Lone Power has Its way with Life?" And here Kit covered his face, for he remembered the look on Quelt's face when he'd told her about his world. "Do you want to—"

"I don't want to go back to anything," Quelt said. "I want to go *forward*. To the thing that waits."

The stir and hush that went through that vast emptiness was awful.

"I'm afraid," said one voice, trembling.

"I'm afraid!" said another, and "I'm afraid, too!" said another voice yet, and another yet, and whole crowds of voices together, and choruses of them, cities of them, nations of them. *Afraid, afraid, we're afraid!*

The roar rose to a shout, the shout to a rumble like an earthquake all around them. Finally, in a great voice, Quelt cried, *"SO AM I!"*

Slowly silence fell again.

"But I'm going to do it anyway," Quelt said. "So that we can all make the leap together. Think about it! One way or another, we've all got to die eventually. That part of the Choice was never in doubt if we were going to live in Time. Now we can go forward and find another way to do it. If we fail, what's the worst that can happen? We all go down into the darkness at once. But we'll still be together. And even in the darkness, there's still the One!"

At that, the Lone One turned Its face away, and Nita thought she heard teeth grinding.

"And if this succeeds," Quelt said, "we'll all be together, and go on into—" She shook her head. "There aren't words. I don't think there can be. But every one of you has looked up, or out, sometime, and thought, 'There's something else that's supposed to happen. What is it?' *This* is it! *This* is the something else! Let's go!"

The roar died back, slowly, to a murmur again. There was no great cry of acclamation, no uproar of acceptance. Her people were, indeed, too afraid. But Nita could feel the change in the air, and glancing over at Kit, she knew that he could, too.

It's happening, Nita thought in silent wonder. *And, holidays aside, this is why the Powers That Be sent us here. Because even if they'd told Quelt Themselves, face-to-face, what needed to happen, she wouldn't have believed Them. The proof had to come through someone she knew personally, someone she liked. Strangers just passing through, people with no agenda. Somebody she sat on the beach with and talked to about nothing important, at dawn.*

Us . . .

Quelt waited until the silence fell. More and more strongly through it, strongly enough for even Ponch to feel it, so that he sat there wagging his tail, the silent acquiescence grew. It was another of those out-of-time moments that might have lasted an hour, or a day, or a month: In this otherworldly worldheart, there was no telling. But there came a time when the acceptance was complete, and when that happened, Quelt moved slowly to the center of it all, where Druvah stood, and held out her hands.

He gave her Alaalu's kernel. She turned it over in her hands a few times, regarding it, and then looked up and around.

"We made a Choice once, as wizards, for our people," Quelt said.

Druvah said, "We did."

"And the Choice can be unmade," Quelt said, "by all the living wizards of Alaalu, unanimously."

Druvah said, "So the original structure of the Choice was built."

"Then it's time to unbuild it," Quelt said. "I am all the living wizards of Alaalu. I say now to the Choice that was made, be unmade in this regard: that our people may go, not merely our own way, but the *whole* way, the way that lay in the One's mind before we could perceive it clearly!"

The silence became complete.

Kit and Nita stood there waiting for whatever would happen. The Lone Power turned Its back on the proceedings, though It moved no farther.

It started to get brighter, in the world inside the world. The radiance from that dazzling and impossible sky began to build, thickening in the air around them the way a low cloud thickens into mist near the ground, but here that mist was radiance that washed out colors in light, starting to dissolve away the outlines and details of things as it grew. Nita glanced down at her hands, wondering if she should be nervous about the way they were beginning to refine themselves away into something that was more light than shape—

Ponch nosed Kit, and put the leash in his hand. *We'd better get out of here!*

"Seems like a real good idea to me!" Kit said. He grabbed Nita's arm. Just before they took a step forward together, she glanced over and caught just a flash of eyes in her direction, as Quelt's arms went around her mother and father, and she buried her face against her mother's shoulder. But she was smiling. And that smile spread to Kuwilin's face, slowly, and then to Demair's, as the two of them looked up and the light indwelling in the world-kernel of Alaalu spread and spread outward from them, flowering into something long awaited, something long denied, blinding—

Nita stepped quickly forward with Kit and Ponch.

Ponch brought them out far above the planet, looking down from space. The shield-spell that Kit had inlaid into Ponch's leash for times like this instantly took hold, protecting the three of them from the cold and the vacuum. There was air, too, which was important, but for the moment, Nita had forgotten to breathe.

Below them, the whole surface of the planet was coming alive with lightning strikes. From cloud to cloud, from cloud to earth, they crackled across the day side, the massive discharges clearly visible, and on the night side, the clouds flickered with them like electrified milk. Auroras whipped and crackled at the poles, even lashing up and out along the lines of the planet's magnetic field, and all over the planet, Alaalu's horizon burst out in spiky spurts of blue-jet and red-sprite lightning, and curving prominences of ion-fire.

"A little leftover Alaalid anger?" Kit said under his breath.

Nita nodded. "But I think not for long…"

Slowly, the atmospheric fury died away. The night sky went quiet first; on the day side, a few genuine lightning bolts, startled out of several great storm systems by the less natural discharges, let themselves loose for several minutes. Things went still.

Then, slowly, light began to grow here and there on the world's surface. It was most obvious in the Cities, from which it seemed at first that white fireworks were rocketing upward. But the lights came from scattered islands, even from far out in Alaalu's immense seas… and they were not fireworks. They leaped and curved through the lower atmosphere, yes, but then the lights found their way up and out, and once into space, shot free, like meteors in reverse—growing brighter and brighter as they pierced up and out of the atmosphere, shooting up and out of the planet's gravity well, burning brighter still as they fired themselves up and outward into the eternal night.

Nita swallowed as the upward-streaking fires increased in number. It was the starfall she had awakened to, late their first night, but in reverse, the stars falling back up into the sky now; and like that other starfall, they fell upward more and more thickly every second, a shower of fire bursting off the planet in every possible direction, out into the unending starlight of space, getting lost in the blinding radiance of Alaalu's sun, or persisting for an amazing time as they streaked out toward the system's heliopause. For what might have been a very long time, or a very short one, Alaalu rained a new kind of life into the night. *A billion and a half of them,* Nita thought. She knew that for the moment they all had to be at least a little ways outside of Time; otherwise, seeing a billion and a half of anything go by would have taken forever. *But this is the day after forever...*

Slowly, the rain of fire began to taper off. Kit and Nita and Ponch stood there, watching the world go quiet again. "Well," Nita said at last, "I guess that's it."

"Wait," Kit said.

They waited. That stillness persisted for a little while longer—

And the planet erupted all over in one last blast of brilliance, with uncounted and uncountable streaks of soulfire piercing upward and out of the heart of the heart of the world, as those who had gone before and had been in the Whispering now erupted into a freedom that only one of them had ever anticipated. Nita and Kit both threw up a hand to shield their eyes as all the rest of the souls who had ever lived on Alaalu departed, in a storm of outward-streaking fire, for a far wider ambit. But at last all the new light died away, leaving them able to look down again at a blue world turning underneath them, a place both very old, and suddenly new.

Nita and Kit glanced at each other.

"Now what?" Kit said.

"I guess we go home early," said Nita.

Ponch looked at them both reproachfully. *Not without my stick!*

Kit gave Ponch an amused look. "We did leave some of our stuff down there," he said. "The worldgates and so on. We'd better go pack them up and bring them back with us."

"Yeah," Nita said. "Come on, Ponch."

They vanished, making their way back to an empty world.

Dairine stared into the roiling fire, and at the empty spot in the wizardry across from her. *We've got to get him out of there!* she shouted at the others.

Filif and Sker'ret looked at her, stricken.

How? Sker'ret said anxiously. *Filif's nearly out of energy. I can't retool the whole wizardry while we're in here. We'll never last! We've got to get out, or we'll all—*

No! Dairine gulped. *There's still one thing we can try. Spot!*

Spot popped his lid up. *We're not going to lose anybody in* my *solar system,* she said. *Not on* my *watch!*

Dhhairihn, Filif said, his needles all trembling, *what are you—*

I'm going to get him *out of there,* she said. And turned—

What in the Powers' names are you doing? said a casual voice, infernally calm, intensely annoying.

He came walking up out of the Sun, the way someone would come walking up out of the water—occasionally slipping a little to one side or another, blown off kilter by the furious wind inside the Sun, but otherwise unhurt. And slowly the tachocline was beginning to calm.

Dairine looked at Roshaun as he ascended calmly and regally back into the wizardry and locked himself once more into the matrix.

We should get out of here as quickly as possible, he said, *because there are about to be three or four CMEs in rapid succession, and anything in the solar atmosphere that's not Sun is likely to be smashed like an egg within seconds.* He looked over at the Rirhait. *Sker'ret?*

Sker'ret said one word. The second after that, they were standing in the incredible darkness of a backyard in suburban Nassau County, and the wizardry that had surrounded them flickered and went out.

Dairine staggered out of her place, snapping Spot shut and holding on to him, because if she didn't she would do something else. She was ready to weep with terror and relief, and was intent on not doing so. She lurched toward Roshaun, who stood several paces away from her, and stopped.

"*Why did you do that?*" she shouted at him. Or at least it was meant to be a shout: Her throat seized up on her and it came out as more of a squeak.

Roshaun paused for several breaths. "Because I didn't have to," he said at last. And he said it in the Speech, so it was true.

But his eyes, which would not meet hers, told her that there was more to the matter than that.

Still breathing hard from what she'd been through, Dairine turned away and walked back to the house, slowly, and went into her room and shut the door. And only then did she allow herself, somewhat later, the very smallest smile.

Eventually, Dairine heard the others make their way down into the basement, seeking out their pup tents. She let them do it undisturbed. The morning would be soon enough for debriefings. *We've had enough stress for one night,* she thought to herself, as she got undressed and got into bed.

But she lay awake in the dark for a long time, considering the annoying economy of the Powers That Be, Who hate wasting anything. *And none of this was an accident,* she thought. *They saw the trouble coming. And we were sent exactly what we needed to prevent a catastrophe... exactly the right tools for the job. An expert in solar dynamics. A tree who's afraid of any fire but* that *one. And a fixer par excellence... All crazy people, all with nothing to lose because it's not their world, not their star. And all personally committed beyond even their commitment to the Powers...*

... because of knowing somebody here.

Dairine had no idea when she finally fell asleep. In the morning, the sunlight streaming in her window woke her up...and it was just normal sunlight, not something much more terrible. Spot sat on her desk with his lid open, showing her the SOHO satellite feed, which was showing three of the most spectacular CMEs anyone had ever seen, bubbling off the inward-rotating limb of the Sun in great splendor and fury. But they were decreasing in energy rather than increasing, and the speculation among the satellite people was that the Sun was in for some quiet times ahead.

She got up and dressed. *And as for me,* she thought, *maybe some less quiet times.*

Dairine grinned and went down to say good morning to the houseguests ... to one of them in particular.

Epilogue

Nita and Kit waited there a long while, in the darkness beyond atmosphere, to make sure everything was safe. But, finally, the lights in the sky died down, and there were no more of those fading cries of joy to be "heard," no matter how they listened. Space's own silence, briefly jarred out of its ancient composure, reasserted itself.

Come on, Nita said silently to Kit.

They transited back down to the planet's surface and stood above the house by the sea, looking down at the thatched buildings, the warm lights still in the windows, the flying sheep in the pens, all gathered together; everything looked utterly normal, peaceful. Nita let out a long breath. Peaceful the place might be. But normal?

They heard nothing but a great silence. It was not merely a matter of sound, but of the effect of many minds that had been in that world but now were gone, gone off to do other business, to live other lives. They left behind them a world that was empty, and strangely innocent and clean: an old world made new.

Quietly, the two of them went down to the house and moved through it, looking around one last time. Kit blew out the lamps. Nita went out to the little outbuilding that had been their bedroom and undid the worldgates from the wall, collapsing them. Then, she didn't know why, she folded up the coverlets they had been given and left each of them carefully at the foot of its bed.

Afterward Nita went outside, having packed up the pup tents and worldgates, and found Kit over by the pen, letting the *ceiff* go free. Ponch charged joyously into the pen one last time. The *ceiff* flew up in a storm of wings, honking, and Ponch chased them down the beach, well into the distance.

"They'll be okay," Kit said. "They were wild a long time before there were any more sentient species here to take care of them."

"I know," Nita said.

They stood there, watching night fall on Alaalu. From Nita's point of view, this was a world she would not be coming back to for a while. It was too full of memories, and too empty now by comparison. *And some of the stuff I heard here,* she thought, *I'm going to be digesting for a while...*

"I wouldn't have missed it," Kit said. "Not for anything."

Nita nodded. "*They're* okay, anyway," she said.

Kit laughed softly. "Considerably more than okay," he said. "Imagine it. Not needing bodies anymore. They've got a whole world of new worlds to get used to."

The silence fell again, and in it there were no whispers, no voices except the most ancient one—the immemorial whisper of the tideless Alaalid sea, saying the single word it knew how to say, over and over again. "Come on," Kit said. "We should get back and see how things are at home."

"Yeah," Nita said.

There was a pause while Kit yelled for Ponch, and Ponch came bouncing back along the beach. *Is it time to go home?*

"Yeah."

Oh, boy, Ponch barked, *dog food again!*

Kit threw Nita another of those looks that suggested he thought his dog was making fun of him. She rolled her eyes. If there was anything she knew about Ponch today, it was that she understood him even less than she thought she had the day before, but this wasn't necessarily a bad thing. "So how do we route this," she said, "now that we've decommissioned the custom gates?"

Kit shrugged. "We still have return tickets for the Crossings in our manuals," he said. "I guess we just go back to the drop-off point and call for pickup. After that, we route back home through Grand Central."

And then he started to laugh.

Nita stared at him. Kit was laughing so hard that he had to lean against the rails of the fence. "What?" she said. "What is it?"

"Oh, jeez," he said, and tried to speak, and then had to stop and give himself over to the laughing again. Nita rolled her eyes and leaned against the fence until he should get over it.

"*Well?*" she said.

"What Urruah said to us before we left," Kit said, and started snickering.

"Which was?"

"You don't remember?"

"He said a lot of stuff," Nita said, shouldering her backpack and starting to walk back up to the slope to where the worldgate from the Crossings had originally dropped them off.

Kit walked with her. "I'm not going to tell you," he said. "Strain your brain a little."

Nita did her best to replay, in her head, their conversation with Urruah. As she and Kit got up to the top of the dune, where Quelt had met them that first day, and he got out his manual to call the Crossings for their pickup, all Nita could hear was Urruah's voice saying, "Nice doggy."

She got out her own manual, paged it open to where the worldgating pickup information would be...and as the page showed her the words "Outbound/return transit approved, pickup imminent, please hold position," *that* was when she remembered.

"Try not to destroy your host civilization or anything..."

A pang went through Nita, but then she smiled. If there was anything they hadn't done for their host civilization, it was destroy it. It had become something greater than it had ever been before, something it had been destined for millennia to become. That they'd been there at the time to help it along was...not luck. Nita knew better than to describe the Powers that sent wizards on errantry by such a name. *It was lucky for us, though,* she thought, and smiled one last time, not entirely sadly, at the thought of Quelt's face.

A moment later, she and Kit vanished. Night came down on the Inner Sea of Alaalu.

And not very much later, the *keks* came out of the water, up onto the dry land, and began at last to build, not models, not the plans for their new civilization, but the real thing, the civilization itself, in a world that at last had been vacated by its old tenants and was ready for the new ones.

It took them some hours to get home. The Crossings was as busy as always, and Grand Central, too, was congested when they passed through. For Nita, getting into her backyard at last was a tremendous satisfaction, if a little strange. She came out of the sassafras trees into the backyard proper and stood there for a moment in the twilight. Softly she said to Kit, "Look how close the horizon is."

He nodded. "Weird..."

Together they went through the yard, with Ponch bouncing along behind them. Down the driveway they went, and up to the back door of Nita's house. Nita pulled the screen door open, and they went in.

"Hey, I'm home!" she said.

There was no answer at first. Then her dad came out

of the living room, went over to Nita, and hugged her hard.

"I missed you!" he said. "And you!" he said to Kit, and hugged him as well.

Nita looked around her. The house seemed smaller than it had when she'd left: cozier, somehow. But this wasn't necessarily a bad thing. "How are things going?" she said.

Her father laughed weakly. "Uh, not too badly," he said. "The past few days have been a little hectic... but let's not get right into it. Want some tea?"

"Wow, yes," Nita said.

"Kit?"

"You could convince me," Kit said, and sat down at the dining room table with a look of great pleasure.

Nita went to put the kettle on. "Where is everybody?" she said. "Where's Dairine?"

"The boys are over at the mall," Nita's dad said. "Dairine's having a shower. She'll be down in a little while."

On the counter, her dad's cell phone rang. "Hey," he said, "*that's* the way it's supposed to work. And about time..."

"What's the matter? Was the network busy again?" Nita said.

Her dad picked up the phone and answered it, shaking his head. "Hello?"

He listened for a moment, then shook his head again. "Just a moment, please." He handed her the phone. "It's for you."

"Uh-oh," Nita said. Her father was firm about not

having Nita's friends call her on his phone. "I'm sorry, Daddy! Who is it?"

He looked resigned. "Someone on Mars."

She took the phone and threw Kit a bemused look. "Holiday's over," she said. Kit shrugged and went to get some tea.

...And in the living room, none of them saw Spot crouching down in the middle of the floor, and whispering in a voice dry with dread and hardly to be heard:

"Uh-oh. Uh-oh. *Uh-oh...!*"

15

15